Doom Bar Days and Nights

For Pete

Martyn Benford

Published by New Generation Publishing in 2021

Copyright © Martyn Benford 2021

First Edition

The author asserts the moral right under the Copyright, Designs and Patents Act 1988 to be identified as the author of this work.

All Rights reserved. No part of this publication may be reproduced, stored in a retrieval system or transmitted, in any form or by any means without the prior consent of the author, nor be otherwise circulated in any form of binding or cover other than that which it is published and without a similar condition being imposed on the subsequent purchaser.

ISBN   978-1-80369-030-8

www.newgeneration-publishing.com

New Generation Publishing

A dedication.

This book is my third in a series of stories set in North Cornwall in the latter part of the last century and the early part of this. It is dedicated to the one person who believed in me, when even I did not. Thank you Mum!

Lillian Beryl Benford - Martyn

1922 – 2015

Three new novels set in North Cornwall by Martyn Benford. Martyn settled in Cornwall in 1970, both living and working in Padstow for many years and eventually marrying a local girl. He currently resides in Lanivet – the geographical Centre of Cornwall!

*****

The Mermaid and Bow by Martyn Benford. Published 2019. First in a series of stories of the Tamryns, a slightly dysfunctional, perhaps multi-functional North Cornish family.

*****

Little Petrock by Martyn Benford Published July 2020. Second in the series featuring Maccy Tamryn, his family and his friends.

*****

Doom Bar Days & Nights by Martyn Benford. Published 2021. Third in the series featuring Maccy Tamryn, his family and his friends.

*****

Book four: In preparation. Tamryn goes West. Fourth in the series featuring Henry Tamryn.

*****

Book Five: In preparation.

These books are available locally at 'dydh da', Padstow, as well as various other retail outlets throughout Cornwall. A full list of local retailers is available by request, direct from Martyn Benford, either by telephone, email or facebook.

They can also be purchased direct from Martyn Benford. Martyn will sign and even write a personal message on request. Martyn can take orders by phone or email and can be contacted on social media as stated below.

Facebook Martyn Benford

Pablo18812000@yahoo.com

Mob: 07434803382

Alternatively, order from Amazon, Waterstones and W H Smith, etc

Padsta!

Whatever there is to know, whatever there is to see

Padstow, that for a while, once belonged to me.

Nowhere I could not go, no place I did not know by sight

Watching, staring out over all, on a darkened moonless night.

Swaying masts bob together as a new dawn breaks free

I stand sentinel, alone, where not one other can see.

Waves crash inshore, boats dance wildly in the dim, early light

Ropes heave, stretch, as small craft ride out the very last of night

Early morning, long after dawn has woken the old town,

as the first coach arrives, doors open and they all climb down

Pensioners, pacemakers and mobiles all charged, ready to go

In this harbourside town known, as Old Padstow.

There is no other place else like it quite

Padsta Town is a one off you see,

No longer is it mine, no longer will it be!

Copyright Pablo

Introduction

The Doom Bar

The Doom Bar, The Bar of Doom, call it what you will. For a thousand years and more it has been said the stretch of water just outside the harbour entrance at Padstow is cursed. Hundreds of ships of all shapes and sizes have crashed and broken onto the Doom Bar, thousands of travellers have perished on there. Let us hope the last were indeed the last. Whatever the figure, it has been far too many.

A little known legend outside of Padstow but known to many of the local populace may explain. It has been said that long ago an archer fired an arrow from his longbow that would fatally wound a Mermaid. As the poor mermaid lay dying, legend suggests she scooped up a handful of sand and tossed it into the estuary. The handful of sand grew as it hit the water and so the Doom Bar was formed. Maybe a curse was uttered from the dying mermaid. The legend would grow. There are folks who believe this, there are folks who do not. I know what I think! All legends have a grain of truth. At a very low tide children will dig with their spades where so many lives have been lost. A playground? Beware the Doom Bar when it isn't.

Anyway, if it weren't for the legend, The Mermaid and Bow Public House would not exist at all. It would just be called The Red Lion or The Bristol Inn, The Boat Hotel, The Shipbuilders, or The Quayside Inn. My problem is this: should I give thanks to the archer or the mermaid? I am in two minds. The biggest problem for me is they are both rather tiny or so I am regularly informed! I have no defence. Such is life!

The good news is over the last ten years or so we have lost no-one, not the slightest hint of a funeral. Obviously, wishful thinking does not work in the slightest, we are all still here. Of course, some to a lesser degree! The new crew is beginning to become the not so new - I include myself here. Lenny, Alice, Lavinia, Jill and Jack all still hang around in the hope something better might come along. Peter, Lyndsey and Michael still exist near enough, so too Ronnie and Reggie, who are still preaching in their own way. Dusty? No, there is still nothing important to add about my brother. Ma and Padraig just watch from afar with no good opinions concerning any of us.

I was once advised to never employ family and friends. I took little notice and did just that. As it happens, my own 'doom' is hopefully still some way off as both pubs are somewhat mysteriously doing well. It's a mystery to me anyway. As for the above entourage of strange misfits – some are female, some are not – I have many times doubted my sanity by employing them in the first place. They are here, they are different.

Chapter One

Shaggy Dog Story

"Wosson, mucker?"

"Lenny, have you any idea where Stan is?"

"I do sort of mate; I was just about to call you buddy. Thing is if you go looking for the old dog, you idn't gonna find 'im. Not unless you come here at any rate. It would be better if that did 'appen."

"Where are you then?"

"We are 'ere Maccy, but Stan can't be disturbed."

"The bleddy dog 'ave always been bleddy disturbed, Lenny. He wouldn't have chased the bleddy speed boat if he wadn't a smidgen disturbed and that was fifteen bleddy years ago. He 'aven't been right for a while if you think about it. So, you're, here, where?"

"I am in the Mermaid. Stan idn't chasing anything now, not ever. He is lying down Maccy, his bleddy chasing days are proper done."

"Well, kick his arse and put him outside, he can find his own way home. I feel sorry for the Mermaid!"

"Maccy, it idn't right, I can't do that, t'wouldn't be proper, I idn't bleddy doin' it."

"What do you mean, just send him home."

"I would mate, I can't. I believe it is impossible."

"Don't bugger about, Lenny."

"Maccy, his legs idn't working."

"What are you talking about?"

"He's gone mate."

"Gone where?"

"Didn't Billy let you know? I sent him to tell you what 'ave 'appened."

"He's here now, he hasn't told me anything so far."

"He can't tell you. He does have a note under his collar, mate."

Lenny is exasperating me now. I search and find nothing. There can only be one reason the note isn't there.

"There is nothing Lenny, no note."

"Sorry Maccy, he must have eaten it. Smack his bleddy arse for me, he is damned unreliable, it was bleddy important."

"Why, why was it important? Billy wouldn't have known it was important, he's a bleddy goat!"

"It was a note about Stan, he can't go out, he idn't very well, Maccy. I believe he have cleaned himself for the last time. He is sleeping now under the pool table. I am so sorry my friend. Anyway, it's not the sort of thing you can tell somebody easily. The Mermaid is so bleddy quiet now, she is saddened to 'ell."

"He's sleeping? Wake the bleddy dog up, kick his arse and send him back home."

"I cannot do what you ask of me Maccy, tidn't right. I'm not bleddy doing it, you wouldn't."

"Lenny, do as I say, I might kick his and then I might kick yours!"

"Maccy, he 'ave passed on. Stan idn't gonna wake up. Billy would 'ave told you if 'e hadn't eaten the note. They do say we eat more at a time of sadness, tis only natural."

So, mystery solved. My dog has suddenly expired. I guess it was sudden. When I think after all the long years, I had never called the Alsatian 'my dog'. Not once, that I remember. Stan adopted me years ago. He has been with me through thick, thin and maybe worse. He was never before mine, we were just company for each other. I have just never realised it. The dog needed me; I needed the dog. My regret will be I wasn't with him when he might have needed me most. Lenny's goat-like dog has let me down badly.

Lenny bought the animal as a pup. The 'pup' is growing into a full-sized billy goat. The goat ate Lenny's note.

"Okay Lenny, thank you mate. I won't tell Billy off; he couldn't have known."

"Fair enough, Maccy. What shall I do with Stan now? You do know Billy is a goat, Maccy."

"Yes, I was beginning to work it out, just leave Stan where he is mate, 'til I have thought what to do."

"We do have people eating, bleddy emmets they are."

"That's okay, just ask them politely not to disturb him. Tell 'em to look away. Make the buggers eat in the bleddy garden, everyone will be doing it one of these days!"

"I will do as you say, mucker. They idn't gonna be best pleased mind, it's raining cats and dogs."

"Bleddy animals get everywhere. Give them the table with the umbrella, Lenny."

"I idn't doing that, they will only bleddy steal it."

"Fair enough, though we did steal it ourselves in the first place."

"Keep your bleddy voice down mate."

"Yeah, sorry Lenny, I wadn't thinking."

"The buggers have been feeding him chips. He haven't eaten them, he couldn't. They are all over the floor now. I 'ope he didn't die of starvation!"

"Just tell them not to give him anymore. Give the tossers a dustpan and brush. Don't let their kids bleddy play with him. He most likely didn't eat them as he did like salt and vinegar on his chips but no ketchup."

"Why not? I didn't get a chance to ask him if he wanted anything on them. He was already off his food, like I said."

"The poor little sod might catch something. We don't want them emmet mums and dads to worry, do we! So, try not to let on what have happened."

"You're right, Maccy, I didn't think of that. Leave the bleddy dead dog alone, you little bastards. Piss off back to your bleddy tent. Go and annoy the bleddy lifeguards and take your bleddy parents with you. Better still, take your tent and go to Rock, they will be pleased to see you. Fred Flintstone lives there; you might get his autograph if you're lucky."

"We ain't got a tent, we're dossing in the toilets. Not going to Rock, they are too bleedin' snobby. Fred who?"

"Perfect, you're right, you idn't as stupid as you look. What's the matter, are all the laybys full up? Anyway, just piss off and don't come back drekly or you'll get my boot up your arse! Tell your dad the same."

"Good work buddy, don't let them get the better of you, Lenny." My oldest friend, Lenny does have a way with words. He doesn't know many, just the right ones for the right occasions, when he does, he uses them well! We two had sat in the classroom as tackers and heard many, we just didn't take them home with us. What was the point, we'd be back to school the next day for more? We had us a good teacher sort of, he was only interested in parting another teacher's hair which allowed us to do what we liked pretty much. The two are married now with a couple of sprogs. I know all of this to be true as they did come into the Mermaid once and I told them to bugger off. The bloke was nagging me about my use of the English language while I was pouring their drinks. I wasn't having that.

That teacher's parting shot was 'Tamryn, you are a waste of space boy!'

I said to him, 'so are you and mine is mine to waste, get out and don't come back you nasty little shit!' It was fair comment, he had said the same to me when I was thirteen. Karma! I don't know what it means, don't know what it looks like, it's there and it does seem to work.

"Lenny, are you sure?"

"What about, mucker?"

"About the bleddy dog?"

"I think so, he does 'ave his leg in the air and it is mighty stiff, his mouth idn't moving. I think he has demised. Come and 'ave yourself a look."

"Okay sounds about right. I don't want to look, Lenny."

Lenny would never make a veterinary surgeon; he wouldn't know how to drive a Chelsea Tractor for one thing. You have to have a large motor to be a vet I believe, not forgetting posh wellies!

Stan has been a great and true friend, good company for easily more than ten years. He just appeared in the Mermaid and Bow one day and stayed for the remainder of his lifetime. I didn't buy him, I wasn't given him, I didn't find him. He found me, we rubbed along. I will miss his ugly mug. I was told years ago the dog had had a disagreement with a power boat engine, the result had been the dog was not completely there after that. Some of his face had detached; an ear, an eyelid, you know the sort of thing. It could happen to anyone. Luckily, Stan had kept all his bits. If he hadn't, his life would not have been worth living. The dog had possessed the cleanest reproduction organs known to man and canine. He ate, washed, slept under the pool table, washed, shat, washed, chased a few bitches, washed. What more could he have wanted? He was never 'man's best friend' though he did become mine; I hope I was his. Rest in Peace Stan, put your best foot forward old son. When you get where you're going, don't try to shag anyone's leg. I would have taken him to Spec Savers but with half an ear missing he would never be able to keep glasses on.

I have a good mind to call Michael in to say a few words for the mutt. Michael is and always has been one third of Lenny and I. Mike is a minister now. It doesn't seem that long ago when the three of us had stared down the weathervane on the church roof. Michael, Lenny and I must have been five or six back in the day. We three had been pulling faces behind ma's back and she caught us. 'Your faces will stay like that if the wind bleddy changes,' she had warned us. We spent the next few hours doing the very same in front of the weathervane on top of the church across the road. Nothing happened at all. Mind you, old Lil the Tart must have done similar when she was a kid, difference was it worked for her!

Michael did the training and followed in his father's footsteps. Not literally obviously, as they would have been bumping into each other all the time on the stairs. Michael and I do play snooker occasionally and at times I let him win. If I didn't, he would curse something awful. He hates to stretch for a shot as his cassock will get caught in a pocket or he would commit a foul. I remember the last time we played, he was stretching too far and allowed his cue to be on show. I told him to put it away or wear jockey shorts, he told me to go away. That isn't quite the truth he did use two different words. When Michael is preaching, he is a man of many words, when he is playing snooker, he is a man of very few! They are usually all the same ones. The snooker table is in the loft at the Methodist chapel. I don't think he should talk that way in the holy building. I have told him so many times. Mike won't change, he hadn't better!

My Yank appears again suddenly, she's good at it. She aids my exit from the memory bank I've made enough withdrawals from for one day.

"What's happened my bird?"

She is truly a yank, but she has been here in Padstow for a little while now. She is getting the hang of using my most favourite greeting, 'my bird'. It just makes me melt when sent in my direction. There is nothing I like better than to be addressed in this way. A softy? Yes, I must confess I am.

"The old dog is shagged out my lover! He have gone to the great boneyard in the sky." I can say that without fear of being accused of uttering something offensive. He was always given a beef bone after the Sunday Roast servings had been completed in the Mermaid and Bow or here in the Maltsters Arms.

"Oh, Maccy, I'm so sorry, I know how much you loved him."

"It's okay love, he passed on whilst he was doing what he did best. 'Loved him', I'm not so sure about that maid. I'm sure I didn't."

"Have it your own damn way, I know better. Under the darned pool table, I bet?"

"Exactly."

"That's good, he was amongst friends then."

"Naw, a bunch of bleddy emmets more's the pity. Stan must 'ave already gone on when they sat down, he wouldn't 'ave let 'em sit otherwise. He could be a tad fussy where furriners were concerned, present company accepted. Still my 'ansome, it's better than being alone, just! I will admit I did like him a tad."

"What will you do?"

"I will take his ashes to the Bridge of Tears and sprinkle them in the Creek. It's only proper I do. The poor little dead kiddies that were dropped in there just after being born will have some company that way, something to play with. They wouldn't ever have seen an Alsatian before. They wouldn't have seen a dog before. They won't even know he is a dog, They'll be like Lenny in that respect, it won't matter."

"You're right Brit', good idea. We will do it together."

"Thank you, darlin'."

"We should shut the pub for the day out of respect, the same as you did when my dear Grandpa passed on to his happy hunting grounds out the back."

"No dear, we will let it fill up and then lock the doors. No one will use the pool table today mind, I won't allow it to happen. We will have us a lock-in. I'll ring Sergeant Twotrees and let him know to keep his officers away for the day as we don't want any trouble. On thinking about it, they might want to pop in and show their respects while downing a pint or two in their crib break after we are closed."

"Whatever you think best, my lover."

It is strange to hear the Texan talking as she does, using our favourite local endearments and such. She is typical of her compatriots; her words seem to go on forever. She now has a mixture of American and Cornish dialect and it makes me laugh when they both are used in the same sentences. It makes her curse while I find constant amusement in it all. Don't feel sorry for her, it was her choice to come here and become my wife. I don't think I could have done it.

Dona Marina and I had met some years ago beside a creek in Kansas. She was just a kid and it was a fleeting moment; we never even spoke. We didn't meet again until almost ten years later when we had a difference of opinion about fishing. Again, it was a creekside meeting. I caught a fish, she shot it. Okay, she caught the fish and shot it but it was my creek and a borrowed rod. Once again it didn't last long although a tad longer than our first glimpses of each other. One day she arrived in Little Petrock, I wasn't even there, I was out in the sticks at Tredinnit near Golden Mill. No one bothered to call me and let me know she was here. The strangest part of all this is, I didn't even find out her name until we stood in front of Michael at the altar. It never seemed that important. As for anyone letting me know of her arrival, almost everyone has a phone in a pocket, it won't be long before they have one in each. I had been ignorant of her being here. I returned from Tredinnit a few days after and she had been sleeping in my bed. Everything just fell into place. I only ever went back to Kansas the one time since then. We must go back again one of these days; it will most likely be for the final time. The ancient ghost town, Hickok might stand a while longer, a few years maybe, but it is slowly turning into dust. There is no need for us to go right away.

It's last real inhabitant, Dona's Grandfather, had come here for the wedding and stayed even after our big day. He passed on peacefully a little while ago and is buried beside the lake at the back of the pub. It was his wish, we had to get special permission and it was granted. If it hadn't been, we would have done it anyway. We don't always do as we're told but we do always ask first. What's the point of the 'no' word if you can't use it occasionally? The authorities had said yes after some bickering. The old man was a bona fide Comanche Native American. The old geezer called himself a 'redskin'. We're not supposed to use the term, it is politically incorrect apparently. I don't understand why we can call a dark-hued man 'black' and we can't call a native American chappy 'red', it makes no sense. Ours is not to reason why! The old feller was a good friend to me when Jen' passed away. He gave me something to think about and something to laugh about when I journeyed to Kansas. A good man, he'll be spittin' tobacco juice past St Peter's earhole now. The old feller was expert at his chosen subject. His granddaughter is no slouch either. To be fair, spitting watermelon seeds is harmless enough though I didn't think so at the time. I thought she was a rattlesnake. It's an easy mistake to make.

The old chap was born of earth, wind and fire, he has and will experience more of the same, plus water obviously. The Indian was the last surviving member of her family. Her parents were killed in a road accident just before she came to the Duchy. She is not alone as she has the Tamryn clan as her family now. It's not much, it will do.

In the beginning, I thought she would need looking after, a steadying hand, guidance. I had to quickly think again. She did want to be cherished and still does. She does not need a steadying hand. She is of a tough breed, being part Comanche, part Texan. God help any children we might have; they won't have a clue what they are! Dona is not to be taken lightly. She must suffer fools gladly or we wouldn't be where we are today!

"So, yank, is it true your people go out into the wilderness to have their babies?"

"You watch too many movies, husband."

"I don't watch movies, I read. I idn't sure it happens here either, but they may go up Style Field to begin the process."

"Comanche women are taken into a well-prepared tepee and must stay there until it is all over, however long it takes. The men are not invited in either, so you best remember that and keep away."

"Oh, I won't forget, maid."

"You sure won't, white man!"

See what I mean? She can call me a 'white man'!

"I could get Dusty to move out, so you can have the yurt."

"I could, gee thanks Maccy, that's so darn thoughtful of you. I ain't no squaw, I don't bleddy think so."

"Why not, it's okay, isn't it?"

"No, god willing, I'll use a damn hospital. I'm only part Comanche ya damn fool!"

"Well, I don't know which bleddy parts do I!"

"Let's just get Stan sorted out, shall we?"

"Yes maid, whatever you say."

She passed the driving test between Little Petrock and Padstow easily. She swore ten times, might have been eleven, when only ten were essential. I can't wait until the season starts; she will break all cursing records for certain. I thought I was pretty good myself; she beats me hands down! I should bow to her superior knowledge. There were some words I hadn't heard before, I thought I knew them all. There are some I know and never use in her hearing. I have no idea where she learned hers from, my brother Dusty most likely.

"So, where is he, Lenny?"

"Under the pool table, like I said."

"No, he idn't, there's nothing under there. Are you sure he's thingy, dead?"

"Deffo, 'e has passed on, Maccy."

"Then he's passed on somewhere else now mate. For Christ's sake, you 'ave lost my bleddy dead dog, Lenny!"

"I didn't see 'im go anywhere. One minute 'e was 'ere, the next 'e idn't. Maybe the bleddy emmets did steal him and have took him to a taxi place."

"A taxidermist, could be, why didn't I think of that. Have you asked Alice?"

"Alice idn't a bleddy emmet, she's my sister."

"I knaw that, have you asked her if she knows where the bleddy dead dog is?"

"Do you think she might have taken him for a walk, Maccy?"

"It wasn't my first thought to be honest mate, no."

"Lenny!"

"Yes maid?"

"Ask Alice where the bleddy dog is, please."

"Okay Dona."

"She said she 'ave put him in the cellar because it's warmer in there."

"But the dog is already cold, he's bleddy deceased. He doesn't need warming."

"She says she didn't like him being too cold, so she put him in the cellar. It's warmer there than in the pub."

"It's supposed to be cold in the cellar, Lenny."

"I knaw that but you knaw Alice, Maccy."

"Let me speak to her Lenny, give me the phone."

"No way Maccy, buy your bleddy own, you scrounger!"

"I want to ring the vets to see if they will do a cremation. You can have it back when I've finished."

"Who for. I might not want it back."

"For the bleddy dog!"

"Thank god for that, I thought you weren't feeling well mucker. Alice have said for me to put a blanket on Stan to keep him warmer."

"Stan won't bleddy know he's cold, Lenny. It doesn't really matter."

"I think she might be right Maccy, we need some better heating installed. It's like a damn * 'Texas Blue Norther' in here darn it!"

"If you say so darlin'."

"What a shame Maccy, he was your dog, my bird."

"It is a shame, as you say, he was my dog, my luvver." She is right as much as I try to deny it. I will miss the beast.

"My lover?"

"It is 'my luvver', not 'my lover' my 'ansome. It does 'ave 'a 'u' not an 'o'! Now you bleddy say it back to me. Where are you going? That idn't very nice! Come back 'ere. You can't just walk off mumbling maid!" It is true you just can't help some people however hard you try and I'm trying!

"You can say that again, Brit!"

"It's not fair!"

"What ain't fair?"

"You reading my bleddy mind, yank."

"You're damn right but I will while I still can."

A few days later we took Stan's ashes and scattered them from the little humpback bridge in the centre of our village, Little Petrock. It was a sad moment but most fitting. I was told sometime later ashes shouldn't be put into running water. How the hell was I supposed to stop it from moving? I'm not related to King Canute. In any case, he failed miserably. I guess he was miserable with cold, wet feet and seaweed in his boots!

Author's notes:

* A **Blue Norther**, also known as a **Texas Norther**, is a fast moving cold front marked by a rapid drop in temperature, strong winds, and dark blue or "black" skies. The cold front originates from the north, hence the 'Norther,', and can send temperatures plummeting by 20 or 30 degrees in merely minutes. Blue Northers occur multiple times per year. They are usually recorded between the months of November and March, although they have been recorded less frequently in October and April as well. The Blue Norther phenomenon is especially common in November, when the last vestiges of autumn are still clinging to life. One of the most famous Blue Northers was the Great Blue Norther of November 11, 1911, which spawned multiple tornadoes and dropped temperatures by 40 degrees in only 15 minutes and 67 degrees in 10 hours.

Chapter Two

A Shagged-Out Dog Story

My village – it belongs to dozens of us - *Little Petrock, a huddle of new and ancient cottages interspersed with the odd farmhouse and a handful of modern bungalows. The narrow thoroughfare - somewhere to drive through almost unnoticed. There is no need for yellow lines at the side of the road, no one wants to stop anyway. Let me tell you, the village time seems almost to have forgotten is worth so much more.

A pub, an ancient blacksmith shop, even a watch and clock repairer, across the road a little homemade stall presided over by a local couple trying to make some extra housekeeping, their juvenile son scrawling little sketches in the slate which tops the parapet of the humpback bridge known locally as the 'Bridge of Tears'. The boy waiting impatiently for the time when he is able to walk up the hill and get home, parents hoping to make much needed revenue on the little homemade stall where one could buy locally grown vegetables. A tumbledown farm building where milk, eggs and a newspaper could be bought. Lastly, less than a handful of holiday homes. Sometime deep in the past, the village may well have been noticed by pilots of the German Luftwaffe, as a pair of Messerschmitt's had screamed low overhead on their journey of the Seventh August Nineteen Forty-Two. The planes would fly on to Golden Manor to shoot and kill a brace of cows before flying low over Truro and destroying a large part of the local infirmary. Two days earlier, German fighter bombers had attacked, causing havoc to the very centre of Bodmin Town. It's a damn site worse now and without any airborne violence.

The Maltsters Arms: Little Petrock's village pub, a meeting establishment where locals could once watch silent movies on an ancient projector whilst supping pints, maybe playing euchre, darts or dominoes. A previously run-down inn which is now on the up again, thanks to Macdonald Tamryn – yours truly – Lavinia, a yank, Jill, Jack, Peter, Lenny and others, too many to mention. I had better mention my brother Dusty here or I'll never hear the last of it. The Maltsters is slowly relocating into the twentieth century. Of course, it is the twenty-first now, but it will catch up eventually, another hundred years to go. The age-old problem for Little Petrock is the road. It cuts right through the village and is halfway between Wadebridge and Padstow. It is just a means to an end. Either you're going to Padstow from Wadebridge or from Wadebridge to Padstow to marvel at the notorious, unforgiving sandbank known locally and even far and wide, as the Doom Bar.

There is no need to stop here. Simply, there are no yellow lines in Little Petrock as no-one wants to park here. The tiny car park is only used for courting couples or walking a dog, or even a goat – I'll explain later. There is an ancient machine to purchase a ticket from when you enter. When you leave, if you leave, a bloke would come up to you and give you your parking money back. Watch out for the tiny hillside church all done out in French style splendour. The graveyard must be one of the steepest anywhere.

The previous incumbent of the Maltsters has recently retired due to ill health; not hers, her late husband's. Anyway, she moved away after he became deceased. They had been popular, but it seems it all got too much for her and she called time. Some might think differently but I don't. Our village has character, it has history. The Maltsters is or was a cider pub most recently. It hadn't always been a cider pub; it was just a pub that sold some. In recent years it has declined to just selling cloudy, yellowy liquid in a misty sided glass. There are still a few of the old timers who won't change their tipple from the fruit to the hop; gradually the gap is slowly decreasing. It's a good job cider doesn't go off easily!

The Maltsters building is four hundred years old, possibly older. It has seen or heard it all and when you are alone, if you listen carefully, you can hear it whisper its historic tales. They say walls have ears; the Maltsters has much more than that, it has a voice. I have it on good authority the old pub was used for many things. One that is a complete surprise is that seventy or more years ago the villagers could come inside, buy a pint and watch a film. No, not that kind of film, not as far as I know anyway! The pub was once a tiny impromptu cinema. It's amazing what some people can remember and what would have been passed down to them from older members of their families. Even today there is a peephole in the wall between one room and another where the projector could shine through to entertain all those present, those who might still be awake anyway. Little Petrock might have had a cinema even before Padstow acquired theirs.

Lost Souls Creek. What can I say about this sad piece of Cornwall's landscape? The course of the Creek cuts through the centre and beneath it's little humpback bridge, continues to echo the sounds of agony and misery and will do so for millennia. The creek sweeps round in a horseshoe journey from behind Padstow, passing the Maltsters and onwards towards Sea Mills where it will enter the Camel estuary. We can only hope it will no more carry tiny lifeless bodies with it. One could be forgiven for thinking Little Petrock is a meeting place for the supernatural. I know personally of at least three places where the supernatural has been heard or sighted in the village. One other place in Little Petrock has more than just its inhabitants; a friendly spirit, I know, I have seen with my owns eyes what it can do. At the Mermaid and Bow a gentle seamstress of a different century will make herself known and show how proud she was of her intricate and necessary work washing and mending bandages for those returning from the trenches at the end of the Great War. There are others; Frank and George frequent the place also, at least when they are not haunting the fish and chip establishment in the town square. A square it is not but that's what we locals do call it.

The Maltsters Arms is also said to be four hundred years old and may have begun as a haunt for smugglers. To this modern day, smuggled goods or the evidence of such have been found along the creekside. Occasionally, tiny bones have been discovered further along the outreach, possibly the bones of children who may have only lived for just an hour or even less, maybe only a minute or two before being put into the old well by Mother Ivy and washed seaward. Even today the ancient well hides its shame behind the old building. It is sealed up now, but I still give the spot a wide berth when I cross the yard. We all do.

Many have told of hearing the mournful cries late at night whilst crossing over the Bridge of Tears. The sounds might emanate from bats that live under the bridge, they might not. When we were tackers, we were always warned by our elders to cover our ears so as not to hear the shiver-inducing sounds that travel on the salty breeze. Lenny Copestick is one who still does. Lenny is in his thirties now, we both are! The two of us had spent every school year in the same classes. We're pretty much inseparable now unless we are in bed, should I rephrase that and add, our own separate beds. My mate will still cup his ears to cross The Bridge of tears!

Lenny and I have two pubs in our care. They are both legally mine. Lenny and his brilliant sister Alice, manage the Mermaid and Bow in Padstow and I manage the other, The Maltsters Arms, here in Little Petrock.

My one and only sibling, Dusty, has a sea taxi, or the Sea Bus as he likes to call it. It only has two stops, the Mermaid and Bow and the Fly Cellars, a part of Newquay's ancient harbour. Newquay holds no allure for me. It never has, it never will.

Travelling folks only go to Newquay so that they may tell their friends when they get back to home in West London, 'we went to Newquay, we had a brilliant time!'

I've never had a brilliant time in Newquay. Dusty most certainly has.

I reside at the Maltsters. I haven't always. A few hundred yards down the road are two old railway carriages, my grand name for cattle-cars which would have carried cattle on the now long-gone Padstow to Wadebridge line. We bought them sold as seen – I use the term loosely – for a few quid and now they, plus a few extra bits and extensions are a real home. I lived in them for a handful of years, nowadays they are used by my staff. I could not possibly say what they use them for! The same things I did I don't doubt. I would say my staff and the Mermaid's are all local, but it would constitute a lie. We gave those that needed it a crash course in Cornish dialect. Now you can hardly tell us apart. Bullshit, they sound like they should all be living in London or some other area where the locals talk strange, Newcastle, Manchester and even India, the strangest of all in my opinion!

When I did eventually get my hands on the Mermaid and Bow at the grand old age of eighteen and a bit, we had us the crew, a fabulous bunch of misfits pretty much. There are very few left. Most are now our loved and lost. We had One Armed Frank, a loner in many ways but he and Lil the Tart got on well enough, probably more than they should have. Frank got on more than most if you get my meaning. Obviously, Frank did the getting off bit too, Lil would have helped. You couldn't have one without the other where Lil was concerned. I will call her a 'night-lady', it sounds much more salubrious. Maybe I won't. It still points to the proper title for someone who works the narrow streets of Old Padstow Town.

Now dear Lil has finally walked the plank, I will award her a shred of decency. Lil has passed on. No more will I shiver with fear whenever the lady got close. My friend, a fellow crew member has pulled up anchor and is even now sailing into the sunset. I miss Lil, the Mermaid misses her, we all miss Lil. It seems like she had been around all my life. I am only in my mid-thirties but that doesn't matter. She has departed, the old girl will never be forgotten.

If it had not been for the lady, I would never had become the incumbent of the Mermaid and Bow. I took her throwaway suggestion seriously and threw my hat in the ring. One armed Frank had gone on some years before Lil. She used to role Frank's ciggies for him, as you might imagine, Frank had a bit of trouble trying to do it himself. So, I have much to thank Lil for. Not as much as some I could mention but plenty. I guess her clients did thank her. I seriously believe they broke the mould; I hope they did and there will never be a replacement. I'm pretty sure Lil won't mind me telling you, she was unique in a way, she was an ace lady and might well have been employed to the last. Maybe not to the last. Lil was always in the Mermaid and Bow for last orders; that's last drinking orders, I wouldn't agree to her taking any other kind whilst in my establishment. We had an agreement, we both kept to it. She left me alone and I left her alone. Lil mostly only came in for a liquid lunch break four or five time a day.

Once the old girl had decided for me my direction for future self-employment, ma took on the license. I was unable to legally use the term Landlord and so Ma bought the pub and handed it over to me lock, stock and barrels, as agreed. Twotrees, the local bobby even supported what we were doing in the end. He wasn't too happy originally, but Twotrees knew he wouldn't have to worry. I would keep the Mermaids' clientele in line. I used the title 'manager' just for the required legal reasons. It was no hard task as all the pub's clientele had known me since I was a kid with a shitty nappy drooping down to the back of my knees. At just seventeen, I worked for Bligh at the Mermaid and Bow as a Saturday boy. That's how it started. By the second week I was a weekday boy, the Blighs hardly ever came into the bar. It was all just for a few months until I headed to London to learn the culinary arts. I learned them and returned home as quickly as possible. I still shiver at the thought of this college period in my life.

Frank was retired when he drifted away, he never could do much apart from ironing and drinking beer. Still, he didn't have to iron shirts with two sleeves; every cloud has a silver lining. Frank only needed one good hand to sup his beer and to, well you know to get it out, have a pee and put it back again. The old feller never had the opportunity to be ambidextrous after he lost his arm. Dear old Lil the Tart used to help him out by rolling the ciggies. No no, see, dirty minds! The pair hardly ever spoke to each other, they just needed to be close together. When Frank passed away one evening in the Mermaid, Lil took up his baccy tin, his papers and what have you. I wonder where they are now. Lil had never smoked as far as I know, though she did just the once, the night Frank passed. It was a personal tribute I believe.

Now we have lost Lil. The old girl was a tad scary especially if you can't remember what you did last night. Think about it, she wasn't called Lil the Tart for nothing. Lil never really did have any redeeming features. She tended to look like she had just eaten a raspberry jelly without a spoon. After she put her lipstick on, it would be all over the place. At Halloween she never wore a mask, she didn't need to, the kids would scream anyway. You could be forgiven for thinking Lil had gone ten rounds with a large bull from Pamplona. I would feel sorry for the bull personally. The lady's face looked like it had been crayoned on by a couple of three-year-old tackers.

Once again, Lenny and I had taken the responsibility of organising a funeral, as we did for Frank's departure. It was only right. As far as we knew he had no other family member to do it for him. I even paid the undertaker for Frank, as I did for Lil. I doubt she had much folding money shoved inside her bra, probably just the normal things. Lil never did carry a purse, she was always grappling around inside there for the means to pay for her gin and tonic, when I wasn't paying for it. I had saved her the worry on the odd occasion, so have many other members of the crew. Even Bligh used to dip into his pocket. In fact, he did more than any of the others. Bligh had an ulterior motive of course; he and Lil were a tad more than just good friends. Their non-secret assignations will stay just that. Blen' knew, Bligh knew, and Frank and I knew, Lenny knew. Pretty much the whole town knew. It was a mass secret! Now Lil is the last of the oldies. I suppose now I am the oldie.

On thinking about it, I realise the one living, breathing item I already miss the most is Stan. I haven't got used to not being followed everywhere I go. Sometimes the Alsatian got there before I did. They do say when an animal loses a sense, the others gets stronger. It is nothing but the truth!

"Lenny, is that you mate?"

"Ang on bud, just a minute ..... yes, it is me, Lenny Copestick, how can I help, Maccy? Wosson pard'?"

You'd think Lenny was on Mastermind the way he goes about things.

"Stranges', mate, I'll meet you there in half an hour."

"Half an hour, bleddy hell, Maccy."

"Okay, thirty minutes then!"

"That's better. You knaw I don't like to bleddy rush things."

"That's what Lavinia told me!"

"That idn't bleddy on!"

"She said it to me once or twice. I wadn't really that interested. I'll see you soon."

"How soon might that be mucker?"

"Twenty minutes."

"You said half an hour, Maccy."

"That was ten minutes ago. I'm just leaving, see you in a minute."

"Stop it you bleddy tosser, Maccy, you have changed it again, I can't bleddy keep up with you."

"Just wait there, Lenny."

"If I do what you say, you won't know where I am. You told me to meet you at Stranges'! Now I do 'ave to wait 'ere. I can't be doing with any of it."

"Where are you mate?"

"I'm in the bog!"

"When you get bored of it, meet me at the undertakers in town."

"I gotcha, Maccy. When?"

"Fifteen minutes."

"Why do you keep doing it?"

"It idn't me, it's you, you dopey git!"

"I better go, some folks wants to use the bog."

"I'm not bleddy surprised, must be a coachload of oldies turned up in town."

What can I do, Lenny is Lenny? It's too late to change him now. He is what he is, always has been, always will be. I envy him I suppose. He is never stuck for words. They aren't always in the right place, hardly ever. They do come out thick and fast at times. Keeping up is not easy.

"Who was that woman in the undertakers, Maccy?"

"I don't have a clue mate. Bit odd."

"Me?"

"No Lenny, the woman."

"Thank god for that. I thought you meant me. Why do you think she was crying?"

"She must have lost someone."

"She'll probably find him or her somewhere mate, can't be far away."

"I mean lost someone. That's why she was in the undertakers crying."

"You mean like Lil?"

"Yeah, like Lil. Lenny, did you notice anything else about her?"

"Naw, not really. Like what?"

"The woman, she did look a tad like someone we used to know."

"I didn't look at her. 'Tis rude to stare."

"Bleddy strange."

"Who, Strange? He's always like that, he's an undertaker mate."

"Can't be helped bud."

"There we are then!"

"Got to get back to Little Petrock, Len. Speak to you later bud."

"Will do, it'd be best. Can't talk while you're driving mate."

"Yes, we can."

"How's that then."

"Mobile phones, they can go anywhere, even under water."

"Not on their own Maccy, that idn't bleddy possible."

"No, they can't go on their own mate, they have to be accompanied by a deep-sea diver or a friend, if you don't have one it won't work. There are plenty of mobiles in the quay. It's what happens if you're leaning over to see if there are any bodies floating around on a Saturday night. Everything falls out of the top pocket of your sports shirt and plops into the water."

"I don't know a deep-sea diver, I don't have many friends, who would I ask?"

"Anybody else I suppose, somebody."

"A body? There were loads of them at Stranges'."

Dear Lenny, like a bull at a gate sometimes, when he isn't eating or sleeping. Talking of bulls, I think here I should mention Blencathra and Cap'n Bligh again. For one thing when dear Blen' passed away, she didn't need a coffin, she looked like a Redwood Oak anyway. Bligh resembled a flagpole. They were chalk and cheese; Blen' was hewn out of granite and flags could be flown off the Cap'n. It was from these two I bought the Mermaid. I was trying to do the pub a favour. It took about three years to complete it.

The ancient pair could not have existed without each other. One followed the other in quick time. Half the town turned out when they made their last journey. The other half were mostly emmets who never knew them. They don't make them like Bligh and Blen' anymore. Dear Blen' was both two and twenty stone dripping wet. She was a profuse sweater, her skin used to leak permanently. Blencathra was a human waterfall. The twenty stones were her torso and the other two were her head. I believe she had relatives on Easter Island at one time. They are still there I guess.

Now to another special member of the crew. Actually, they were all special. Bert was the cleaner in the big café on the quayside. Bert knew everyone in the town in his heyday. If he didn't know something he would go and find out, just so he could tell anyone else who didn't know. Bert was a confidante for me. He would come up with answers to all my problems, after he had asked the questions first – I had plenty at times and he would remind me of them. Then it would be, I idn't sure, what do ya know, 'ow the 'ell did that bleddy 'appen? What was 'er name Maccy? Where 'ave 'e bin boy? What did I bleddy tell 'e? All good questions mostly, but I can't remember everything. I never told him if I did. He would find out somehow and call me a dirty bugger! When Bert would turn up for work, I would many times be there before him. I would make him tea and a breakfast while he washed the floors and pocketed any cash he found while doing it. It was as if Bert had stolen all the pensioners hearing aids without them noticing. The oldens would drop cash and never hear it hit the ground. Bert was paid for his cleaning and self-employed in picking up 'droppings', as he called them, whilst mentally counting the cash and giving me a bollocking because he had to start again.

The Birdseyes, aka the Birdsalls, lived in the quay when we first made acquaintance. They had themselves a boat, they never did spend twenty-four hours a day swimming! They were retired accountants and like to 'roll with it'. The little sloop had a double bed and a bar. Many a time I hopped aboard for five minutes and got off three hours later. They knew how to party. The Admiral was first to go. Alma put a flag up at half-mast, the aptly known Jolly Roger. Alma was a tad on the fruity side if you get my drift. She tried to get hold of my pair more than once. Stop it, I mean she was always grabbing my buttocks! One day a few years ago they were evicted. We went into town with a tractor, turned their tub around and took it to the Maltsters. It's still here on my oversized pond, which is a small lake after heavy rain. Nowadays we let the old tug out as a holiday let!

Whether I like it or not and I do, all these folks I have mentioned have had some part to play in my upbringing. Everyone has had some kind of effect on my life. All but one have helped to direct it. The last, my eldest son, has not. He, unlike the others, has forced upon me to behave myself. The others just preferred me not to. I could be wrong but doubt it. Regrets? None at all. Maybe just one, Danny Boy. The one son who can affect my life or not affect it. His mum, Alice and I, did a bit of overzealous toe-dipping many years ago. Trouble was we went a tad further and ended up in deeper water than we had expected, and Alice became expectant. I'm still not certain Danny knows how he came about, whereas Alice and I do. I forget, although it doesn't much matter now, Bert knew, he always knew. Bert was one of those you couldn't teach new tricks, the old dog taught himself plenty years ago.

For myself and my escapades, it was like becoming a Knight minus the gong and the bit of ribbon!

As for the Alsatian? Stan was a dog who didn't actually know his name. The old Alsatian used to dutifully stand up whenever I called it. It's a shame old Bert wouldn't let it have a couple of hearing aids. Anyway, I digress. The Alsatian was the ugliest mutt known to man. The story goes he was swimming in the quay one day and got his snout caught up in an outboard motor. Yes, it does sound a bit iffy, I agree. But that's what I was told when I asked Bligh one day. Bligh told me the dog was swimming too fast as the boat with the outboard motor was putting to sea. The mutt and I took to each other and we became firm friends. Wherever I was going, he almost always got there before me, wherever I'd been, he would have been. I don't think I will follow him just yet though; lampposts aren't really my thing. Dear Stan, is not so much a Shaggy dog story as a Shagged out dog story.

As for myself, I have much to do stopping a baby boom between my staff in Little Petrock. They're at it like rabbits but instead of being caught in headlights, they would be caught trespassing into someone else's accommodation. I'm not sure it ever happened to me. I mean I don't think I ever got caught. Not for the want of trying, unintentionally obviously. For those who wonder why they only ever find one trainer along a street somewhere, it's probably because I dropped it whilst trying to do my trousers up at ten miles an hour. Yes, I know, a slight exaggeration but I'm sure you know what I mean. Those days are behind me now thank god. My eldest, Maccy J, has taken up the running so to speak. Most of his running is done on the campsite he now oversees. He is either running after a female or he is running away from one whose goose hasn't been fully cooked. Of course, he might just be out jogging early every morning. Nobody jogs with an irate father or boyfriend running behind, I certainly didn't. I was gone like liquid shit off a tin miners shovel, or for the more refined, gone like the clappers! The father son comparison scares me a tad occasionally!

Authors note:

* Little Petrock. Aka Little Petherick is a village and civil parish in North Cornwall, England, It is situated two miles (3 kilometres) South of Padstow and 6 miles (9 kilometres) West of Wadebridge. As of the 2011 census, its population is included in the civil parish of St Issey. Little Petherick, sometimes known as Little Petrock, lies in the valley of Little Petherick Creek, a tidal tributary of the River Camel. However, upstream of Little Petherick the creek ceases to be tidal. The village straddles the Wadebridge – Padstow road which crosses the creek at the East end of the village.

Chapter Three

A Comanche Moon

The old Indian, the grandfather of my Texan wife, passed onto the Happy Hunting Grounds around this time. He had belonged solely to the earth, which is where he lies now, out the back of the pub beside the lake.

We two had been acquainted, though unrelated for quite some time – can someone have a grandfather in-law? The old geezer only had the two bad habits that I know of; he was a tobacco spitting champion and had the completely useless habit of doing the 'rain dance' every other day. This is Cornwall, why would we need the rain dance? If the sun isn't shining in the Duchy it's either precipitating or just about too! There are days we locals would keep our sunglasses in one pocket of our waterproof jackets and our flip flops in another. Not me obviously, my show-off brother, Dusty, is definitely one of the aforementioned.

The old Indian – I never did find out the name of the old chap – had departed just as unexpectedly as the Alsatian. It was what you might call a sudden passing. Early one morning I found Sitting Bull perched on the circular bench. I thought he was asleep. He was in a way; he never awoke again. He was just staring out as if at something I could not see. It was definitely a time of peace. I had the feeling he had been there since last evening. When I go, I want to go the same way although I doubt I am as religious as he was. He had been a good friend from the time I first met him, he eventually became part of the family. I think he must have known time was being called. Why else would he have had been all dressed up in fancy clothes? I've only ever seen him do that once before and that was at our wedding; not mine and his, mine and his granddaughter's obviously. He had some smart gear. The old man didn't spit once during that great day, not even feathers, although he was sporting a dozen or two!

The old feller was a tribal medicine man apparently, not a good one as he might have kept himself in better health. He might still be breathing if he was any good. So a doctor and an Indian chief. There was me thinking he was just a petrol pump attendant when we first met. I never really saw him do much at all apart from spit liquid tar. The old Comanche could have been employed as a one man pothole filler, or as we prefer to call them around here 'pottle' repairer!

The cemetery at Hickok City will need someone to tend it now he has passed on. The yank is right now attempting to find a 'curator' as they call cemetery attendants in their neck of the woods. The phone bill is taking a beating but neither of us can abide to see that old ruin disappear completely. The old Indian might or might not have had a pension, He probably had a couple of oil wells stashed away somewhere. I'm sure he would be happy for us to find someone to look after the tiny cemetery. It makes me wonder what might have happened to the bunch of yobbos I left there on my last visit. The herd of Hells Angels were having a knife throwing competition when I left Hickok to return to the Duchy. They have most likely buried their dead and long gone by now.

Ma had enjoyed the old chap being around here and she made it clear. "You did what you had to do, Maccy. You did good letting the old man stay in the yurt. Didn't they all used to live in Tepees?"

"Yes, but not anymore, ma. Nowadays they all live in caravans and mobile homes and own oil wells or bars and gambling joints. Sad when you think about it!"

"You bleddy hypocrite, Macdonald Tamryn. Take a look around you boy, it's like a bleddy holiday camp around here. You've got people living all over the place. It's like a bleddy youth hostel here some days."

"It's hardly my fault, mother!"

What ma says is true. We do live in a commune. It just got a tad smaller recently. We are suddenly minus a tart, a dog and an Indian witch doctor. These things happen all the time probably! The old boy never did find himself a squaw, it was a shame really but then there aren't many around this way. We should have taken him to Indian Queens.

I did notice the witch doctor looking longingly at Lavinia more than once. Alice too caught his eye a time or two. "Ma, you were lucky he didn't come chasing after you, he might have whisked you off." To be fair, maybe we should have taken him to Spec Savers. They might of thought they needed glasses if he walked in. I suppose some people don't mind feathers and warpaint. Lil the Tart used to look similar but only on a good day.

"I was thinking the same thing, Maccy. That would have been all we needed around the place, a sex mad Comanche chasing me all over the bleddy village. What would the neighbours have thought?"

"It doesn't much matter now ma, he's gone to the happy hunting grounds out the back. Nice guy though, kept me on my toes a time or two. I'll miss the old feller. I do need to get these rooms let out now they're finished. We need them to make sure the Mermaid stays afloat, and the taxman doesn't get his hands on the tiny amount they might make. It does get me to wondering what has happened to the tramp. I was thinking she might be useful as a cleaner and throwing people out when they don't want to leave. She looked like she could handle herself!"

"You know I don't abide by violence, Maccy."

"Me neither ma. I mean, I didn't thump my father in here that time, you did. Dusty and I just minded our own business while you imitated Lennox Lewis. It didn't work by the way, for obvious reasons. He stayed, which was exactly what he wanted to do and I'm not forgetting you wanted him to."

"It was inexcusable, though he did deserve it at the time. I was knocking him into shape for the future."

"Yes ma, course you were. You knocked him through the bleddy pub door!"

"I don't need reminding boy. He did deserve it. Why don't you go do something useful and get out of my kitchen?"

"I hate to remind you mother but legally it's my kitchen."

"If you don't like to remind me, then bleddy don't!"

"Michael! What the bleddy 'ell do you want bud? I don't have time for you today, I do 'ave important things to do."

"Nothing much, Maccy. I must be mistaken, I thought I was in a charitable, friendly, roadside hostelry. I will need to pray for you, Tamryn, if I remember. Any food on the go, any Sunday roast left, Ms Tamryn? I can't remember your new name."

"No surprises there, Mike. You did actually take a leading part in the wedding service."

"I can't bleddy remember everyone."

"Any food? So, you're here for nothing much but a free meal. Can't you feed yourself. Try calling your boss, maybe he'll have a fish sandwich going spare. Don't bother with the praying bit, it'll all go wrong anyway."

"I wasn't talking to you. Why should I call my boss when I can come here?"

"He has a takeaway as far as I remember. It's what they told us at school. I did go sometimes. Bread and kippers should sort you out. We don't have any proper fish!"

"I've no idea what you are talking about, blasphemist. Ms Tamryn, Joy, do you have any food you don't need please?"

"I'll make you something, what do you want, Michael. Joy will do fine."

"Give the reverend a bleddy luncheon voucher, ma. Isn't it you who is supposed to be feeding the needy, Mikey?"

"That's what I'm doing, I'm bleddy needy! I can't eat a bleddy book, I can't do miracles. If I could, I wouldn't be asking, and I would have a better paying job."

"Why don't you get yourself someone to cook and clean for you, Michael? It might be best. I don't believe a cook and cleaner would think so."

"Like who?"

"A wife perhaps, then you'd have someone to swap frocks with?"

"Very funny if I got myself an actual wife it would mean she is already married. Don't lead me into bleddy temptation, Maccy. You knaw better than that."

"Then like I said, speak to your boss man. He did used to do takeaway. Didn't Jesus get a load of fish and bread that one time? Surely you can do the same. Just ask him for your fish battered, with chips and mushy peas, you'll need something to wash it down with."

"More blasphemy, Tamryn, sorry Joy, Maccy you can't talk like that in the house of god. Anyway, that time was a miracle. I'll need one of my own to get anything out of you."

"We're not in the house of god Mikey, though yes, I suppose I am god-like, so you're partly right."

"Naw, but I'm in yours. Would you turn me away when all I need is a nice steak and kidney pie with chips peas, gravy and a crust or two, oh and a pint of Guinness on the side. Good job you reminded me, Maccy. Bit of bread and butter wouldn't go amiss!"

"I won't turn you away, Michael. I'm a Christian, my son is a heathen."

"I wouldn't say that Joy. I would think of something much more appropriate. A tight arsed tosser is my thinking."

"Jesus Michael, stop going on. Ma just feed him for god's sake. * Talk about 'behold the rider on a pale bleddy horse'!"

"I don't have a pale horse, I walked here."

"Doesn't matter, 'he brings death'."

"Yeah well, he will be doing if you don't bleddy feed me soon. I'll starve to death and it'll be on your head, Tamryn. Who taught you about the bleddy bible anyway?"

"You did. Just give him leftover scraps ma, my friend doth think too much of himself."

"Do you want runner beans and mint sauce with your lamb, Michael?"

"Yes, please Joy and a pint of gravy. That would be grand. May your god work with you always. May he forever look down on your heathen son."

"Give him whatever he wants, ma. He'll most likely explode with any luck."

"Not very charitable, Maccy."

"Charity begins at home mister preacher. This is my home."

"Well Maccy, you're welcome into the house of god anytime, in a bleddy coffin. I'll do the service for nothing. I'll even nail the lid down for you! You too Joy, not in a coffin obviously. You will surely get your reward in heaven though."

"You just make sure I do, Michael."

"I will, but don't bring the heathen with you. He'll eat all the bread, drink all the wine we get from Looe and empty the collection plate. He won't leave a bleddy tip."

"Oh, I'll give you a tip my friend, don't bleddy come back empty handed."

"Philistine!"

"Tosser! Michael, I need a favour."

"Yes mate?"

"When you're finished eating me out of house and home, would you mind blessing my lake and the engine house please?"

"Get stuffed, I'm on a break. I don't do freelance unless there's something in it for me. I don't do stuff on the side."

"Hang on, your boss worked six days a week."

"Yes Maccy, but he didn't work on Sundays. Neither do I. There was no one at service this morning. Might as well have cardboard cut outs like the bloke did on bleddy Bodmin Moor."

"Typical. You'll be forming a union soon."

"I will, a mothers union. You'll be most welcome, you'll fit right in."

"That reminds me Michael, how's your dad?"

"Yeah he's okay Joy, still seeing far too much of the cleaning lady at the chapel. When I say 'far too much' that's exactly what I mean. It's not good when your father's at it at the same time you are, or in my case, want to be. Not in the same room obviously, it wouldn't be appropriate."

"Michael, stop bleddy complaining. You've done worse, might I remind you."

"Not in front of your mother if you don't mind, Maccy. So, tell me, do ducks walk to the oven nowadays. I suppose it saves you having to go to the butchers, Joy."

"Are you on something mate?"

"I might be. You do have three fresh looking ducks in your kitchen. Are you training them for when they're older? Don't you have to take their clothes off before roasting them?"

"It's time you left, Michael. You weren't supposed to see them. Put them out when you leave mate, I'll bring them back when you're out of sight. I'll go to the shops and get some orange sauce! You can get stuffed!"

"Shouldn't you be saying that to your bleddy livestock, mucker?"

"Don't you have a sermon to write?"

"I do, I came here for inspiration. Inspiration so I can remind my parishioners of how not to live!"

"Give it a rest you two, go to the bleddy pub."

"What do you think this place is, ma?"

"I'm beginning to wonder boy!"

"You're right Joy, come on Maccy, it's your round."

"I'm not standing at a bar with a man in a bleddy dress."

"Don't worry, I'll take it off once I've had a few."

"You do that and I'll 'ave to bleddy ban you mucker."

"You wouldn't dare Maccy, I know too much. I'm also on good terms with Twotrees!"

"I won't if you tell me why you buy your holy wine from Looe."

"That's easy mate, it tastes like piss. That way, no one asks for more, we never 'ave lock-ins in the house of god!"

"Fair enough Michael, drink up."

"Oh, I will mucker."

Michael has forever and ever been a close friend. He is one third of Lenny and I. Believe it or not, he was the worst behaved kid in our class at school, there was nothing saintly about him in the good old days. Now he's following in his father's footprints and has stolen his job from him. To be fair, his dad was retiring, and Mikey was already learning the trade, so to speak. My mate really was the worst behaved kid of all of us. There was much competition between him, me and Lenny. The three of us made a hell of an effort to be remembered when and after we left our education. He's a half decent snooker player. He ought to be, there is a full-sized table in the loft above the altar at the Methodist chapel. We had spent a great deal of time in there when we should have been learning. Some of us can still be found in there on occasion even now. It's where we are if we don't want to be found. Our bolthole has a bolt on it, that way we won't get disturbed so often whilst having a scotch or two.

As for Lenny? Lenny is Lenny Copestick. There is no other like him. Lenny is different. Lenny can eat while playing snooker, he can eat whilst downing a pint. I have heard he eats in bed; I can't divulge my sources. It used to be, if Lenny couldn't be found, it was only by a member of the male species. Any of the opposite can find Lenny quite easily, he used to advertise. Lenny can eat whilst scrapping. It's true, I have had first-hand experience. There was just the one time when he was unable; Lenny lost his teeth while we were scrapping in the quay. He had them previously as he took a piece out of my ear! On occasion we still get into a physical fracas.

My mate Lenny does stipulate one thing, 'never tinker with my women'. These include his sister, his girlfriends and even his mum. It's a good thing he doesn't know who the father of his own nephew is. He is not about to find out from me nor his sister. Not many do know, just me and his wonderful sibling, Alice. It should stay that way. I almost did have a run in with Mrs Copestick once. I backed down as I wasn't in the mood for having my features rearranged.

I wisely put a stop to it before it occurred. As for Danny, the youngster, he is thriving and doing well at school. Alice keeps me up to date, on the quiet of course.

So, there you are, as they say, birds of a feather flock together! Alice and I did just that once, fifteen or sixteen years ago. It's all water under the bridge now. Mervyn is happy in his ignorance of being a surrogate father. I was sure he would be, he isn't actually aware!

"Thanks for lunch, Joy. You'll most likely be rewarded, at some point in time."

"I can wait, Michael."

"One thing Joy and I hesitate to mention this, but the leg of lamb was a tad sparse."

"Bleddy 'ell, you got it for a song you didn't even sing. There's plenty of the beast left. We didn't want to use it all in one go. We can eat the rest once it's feeling better. He's starting to perk up already which is promising. Mind your stomach on the way out, Padre!"

"Well wife, no more visiting the nursing home now Bert has gone on his merry way."

"There's nothing to stop you visiting someone just for the sake of it, even if you don't know who they are. I intend to."

"Have fun with that. By the way, Michael says he's gonna get married."

"He is, who to?"

"Says he doesn't bleddy knaw yet."

"How does that work then, husband?"

"No idea Tex, we'll find out if and when he does I suppose."

"I guess we will!"

There's more chance of Bert getting married again, I'd say. St Peter will have to officiate unless Michael snuffs it early. There's every chance the way he necks his beer. He'll walk under a bus or something. Though to be fair, no one knows what time buses are due anywhere in Cornwall or on which day. They just appear occasionally. He'll almost certainly have to go to Truro to find one to accommodate him. Around here he would have to chase after one to throw himself under, they hardly ever stop. Putting one's arm out to a bus driver around here constitutes a wave. The driver thinks he knows you and waves back with abandon. The women bus drivers are even worse, they are particularly good at digital sign language!

Bus stops are a complete waste of time. The lean-to's have no seats in them, the roofs leak and some are even imitating libraries. I did see one with seats in once. There were two seats and a picnic table with a bunch of flowers on it. What the hell is that all about? It would make more sense if someone put a bed in it. That way you won't mind waiting a whole day before a bus eventually turns up. Don't even get me started on telephone boxes. I saw one of these where a couple were reading the Kama Sutra whilst indulging in live role play. The problem was, there were so many onlookers, I could hardly see a thing, let alone learn anything!

They don't have telephones in them anymore. In the old days, the youngsters used to celebrate getting ten people and a dog in one. One of us would ring the police and then give the already howling mutt the receiver.

Now you can get twenty kids and a dog inside. There's nothing else in them. If they painted the windows out they could be used for an emergency toilet, just like they were whilst still having telephones in them. Failing all of this, chuck an ATM inside? It would save folks having to drive to the bank. They won't need to be insured as they won't have accidents. I suppose a courting couple might have the odd one. There would be no overtaking and just the one light. It's unlikely anyone would ever see a telephone box reversing. Windscreen wipers could be an optional inside extra, useful for clearing any steam and condensation away. A telephone might come in handy for breakdowns. Breakdowns in the sense you might personally have one, because the bus never turned up. If telephone boxes had a handset in them, one would be able to call a tart who might have left her business card blue tacked to the glass.

People should think laterally about the possibilities. That way, a bed in the bus stop would become more useful. Bunk beds could even be employed, might as well make the most of any available space. If the bus stop had a bar, a courting couple could have two glasses of wine before getting down to business. In fact, they could have a bottle or two. They could get a bus home afterwards and pick up the car next time they meet. The possibilities are endless, unlike the bus stops and telephone boxes. On second thoughts, just call a taxi, ask the driver to pick up the tart of your choice and she can be delivered just like a pizza. The driver, depending on which gender or even species – I'm thinking visitors from out of space here – can take him or her home and he or she can give him or her a freebie. No money will need to be exchanged. The whole thing would be completely legal, almost. I'm just saying!

Disclaimer: Absolutely none of the above would be of interest to me under normal circumstances. I would rather stay alive by doing as I'm told but only in the presence of the Texan. My wife has made it crystal clear by constantly demonstrating the art of cleaning a Colt's 45 Single Action revolver whilst extolling the virtues of remaining married. I'd like to stay in one piece and not look like a colander. I am always dutifully impressed by her dexterity. I already know what a good shot she is. So does a large – it's a bit smaller now – headless ** Catfish!

Author's notes:

* 'Behold the man who rides the Pale Horse'. A phrase taken from the book of Revelation. Thought by some to signify the coming of Armageddon.

** See 'Little Petrock' by this author.

Chapter Four

It must be a Sign.

Too the subject of signs for a moment, it seems there is a pilferer of such in the village somewhere. Yes, it was firmly nailed down, at one time. When I catch the culprit, he or she will be nailed to the wall next to the weathervane!

Is it April the First? It might be April Fool's Day! I suppose it's all very well discovering the date, it isn't going to help me to find the sign. One minute it was there, the next it was gone. With a few hours of darkness in between obviously. It's huge, how did they do it? I think I would have noticed if it had been stolen in daylight. My problem is it could have been any one of a dozen who did the deed and now has the sign for the Maltsters Arms. We have a felon in the village of Little Petrock, but who the hell is he, or she? Who would have known the vicar owns a ladder? Why does the vicar own a ladder? I doubt he wants it to be closer to his boss. I've got to admit, I have always been slightly suspicious about our other local holy man, all of them to be fair, except Mikey. I've never been suspicious of our Methy minister, Michael, having always been fully aware of what he is capable of. Suspicion would be pointless. He is always guilty of something, we all are. Chris at the Ring O Bells? Nah, surely not, he wouldn't, he might!

It has actually been almost a week now. No sign of the sign has been noted, no one has come forward to accept liability. Maybe it is a prank. On the other hand, maybe the disappearance is malicious. Again, I ask the question, why? If it was a prank, why is it still missing? It makes no sense at all. What's the point? If you don't have a pub called the Maltsters Arms to hang it on, why steal a sign suggesting you might have? A pub can't be stolen to go with it. I'm not happy. Why do the words 'Dusty' and 'ransom' keep popping into my head on a regular basis? Dusty might have in the old days, there was nothing he wouldn't do for cash. I should know, he laundered plenty of my own!

"Lenny, call a staff meeting. We need to tell everyone to keep a look out for it."

"What have you lost now mucker?"

"I didn't lose anything, someone has removed the Maltsters sign, I believe, for nefarious reasons. I do not think it has blown away. I found it missing earlier."

"How can you find it bleddy missing. It makes no sense, listen to your bleddy self, Maccy!"

"You know what I mean, Lenny."

"No sorry, tell me again."

"It means some git has stolen the bleddy pub sign."

"It wasn't me mate, I was with you."

"When were you with me?"

"When I was nowhere else. I didn't find it missing, you did, I knaw it wasn't either of us. I don't know how better how to say it. See, if you found it missing, there's no need to keep bleddy looking for it, is there! You 'found it'…. 'missing. End of!"

"Lenny."

"What, Maccy?"

"Shut your bleddy rabbit!"

"Sorry, mate, was just trying to be proactive."

"That's what you call it! Lenny, someone from here or more likely St bleddy Issey, has taken my bleddy sign mate. Just call the staff meeting and tell everyone to keep their bleddy eyes peeled."

"I will do as you ask but it sounds a bit bleddy painful. Why would anyone want to do that mate, you knaw I bleddy wouldn't? They would be forever open. How would I sleep?"

"Correct, if they are forever open, you or some other bugger might see the bleddy thing, mightn't you, that's what it does mean. Only one thing, I mean two things, stop you sleeping, Lenny."

"Ais, I suppose, I can't bleddy help it!"

"Just please do as I ask, Lenny."

"I will Maccy, I promise. Can I go back to sleep now mucker, tis bleddy nigh gone midnight and I be a tad knackered. I will 'ave my eyes peeled tomorrow. I idn't looking forward to it mind!"

"Sorry Lenny, you knaw what I'm like with clocks, mine is upside down and hanging from the curtain rail. Tell 'er I'm sorry for calling so late."

"Tell who mate? Why is it hanging from the curtain rail?"

"It's where it landed one time and don't act so bleddy innocent."

"Okay, Maccy says he is sorry for calling us so late, Lavinia."

"Lavinia? I thought she was seeing Peter."

"Not at the moment Maccy, she's busy."

I don't want to know any anything about Lenny's nocturnal pleasures. I have no interest in what the staff do unless they are being paid by me for doing it. I do know what the girl is capable of, I'm trying hard not to think about it.

"I won't say a word, Lenny."

"Neither will I mucker."

"I sure won't either, Lenny."

"Thank you Miss Dona."

"You're welcome Lenny, goodnight Lavinia."

"Ffs Maccy, soon everyone will know!"

"Everyone will bleddy knaw maid!"

"That's what I said!"

"T'wadn't, go back to sleep maid."

"Not yet."

"Lenny, put the bleddy phone down for Christ's sake, this is fast becoming the 'Walton's revisited'. Grandma will chirp up from her grave any time soon."

"I will, Maccy. Are we on speaker phone?"

"Yes, Lenny."

"How does it work then?"

"It's simple Lenny, you just talk normally and the whole of Cornwall can hear everything you bleddy say, most likely

Devon and the Scilly Isles also. They won't hear you on Lundy Island."

"What if I was to only whisper Maccy, how would that be? Why won't they hear me on Lundy?"

"Same thing, everyone in the Duchy will hear you whispering. The thing is you don't have to shout so much. stops you getting a sore throat. Lundy? They will be too busy out chasing sheep I expect."

"Why?"

"No idea mate."

"Come back to bed, Lenny!"

"Come back to bed Maccy, turn the damned phone off."

"Goodnight Lavinia."

"G'night Maccy J!"

"G'night yank!"

"Go to sleep kid!"

"Is that everybody?"

"Billy the goat says goodnight too."

"Who said that?"

"What?"

"Nothing, forget it."

"I did already!"

"Put the bleddy phone down Lenny, it is set to explode in ten seconds."

"I 'ave passed it to Lavinia, she 'ave put it under her pillow for safety."

"Excellent, good work, she must have read my thoughts. Lavinia is so conscientious. Off you go then."

"Maccy dear, why would anyone want to steal the bleddy pub sign do you think?"

"How in hell should I know, firewood mebbe?"

"Why don't you change the darn name?"

"What, you're joking? Half the village will be up in arms, that's why. There would be hell up! By the way, there's a pub for sale in Padstow."

"Why would you want another pub Maccy, you have two already. You can't be in three places at once."

"It's not a pub now, it's been closed for donkey's years, *The White Hart at the bottom of Padstow Hill. I do okay with two."

"There you are then, what's the point in buying a pub that idn't a damn pub."

"I didn't say I wanted to buy it. I just said it's for sale."

"Same darn thing! I knaw what you're thinking, remember that."

"Could turn it into a sex shop."

"No, you couldn't!"

"Not me, someone else. I'd be far too embarrassed."

"I'm not surprised, you get into bed with your bleddy socks on. Nobody will want to know about that. If you got any darned customers, you would bore the hell out of them!"

"I thought everyone did it, this is Padstow remember. Why would anyone want to steal the bleddy pub sign, that's what I would like to know? There's no point if you don't have a pub with the same bleddy name to put it on. I suppose if you swapped a sign with someone else's it might work. Or, maybe someone has bought the White Hart and gonna change the name!" That did it, I got her to sleep in the end. Now I can talk to myself for as long as I like.

"No, you darned well can't!"

"Anyway, it's haunted!"

"It has a ghost?"

"Apparently it does."

"No such thing! They'd soon move out if you moved in."

"I'd bleddy move out if I moved in, maid!"

"Me too."

"Who was that."

"Who was who?"

"Someone said 'me too' it wasn't me."

"It wasn't me neither!"

"Sleep!"

"Was that an echo?"

"Yes."

"There's another one."

She's right, I don't need another pub. What I need right now is a full Cornish breakfast and something to keep my eyes open. I wonder if my mate has peeled his eyes yet.

"Morning Jill, same as yesterday and some matches please."

"Why would you want matches, Maccy?"

"To keep my bleddy eyes open maid."

"You can't have the same again Maccy, you ate it all yesterday. You can only have similar."

Maybe I should go back to bed. Now a twenty-five-year-old is telling me what to do and what not to do regarding my breakfast and my sleeping habits. She reminds me of me when I was a twenty-five-year-old. Actually, maybe she doesn't, she's far more sensible and has certain things I never had nor wanted to own personally. I'm thirty odd and I still haven't got the hang of it all.

I do keep getting to thinking about the Welsh woman. My family grew by three the day I got married, Rio Dona, Padraig and Lyndsey. She has been a godsend to be honest, just by doing the accounts and keeping the office up to date. On the downside, her filing isn't so good. It should be, she spends enough time on her nails! Lyndsey has fitted in pretty well. Even Lavinia seems to be behaving herself better now she is hanging around, for want of a better description, with Lenny. It's even an improvement in him now he is hanging around with her. The pair have plenty going for them, the fact they are both insane provides a common interest.

The Maltsters is paying its way. The eels are breeding it seems. Not sure the ducks aren't getting free takeaways. Not so much a takeaway, more a take unawares. Can't argue with nature. The new season is almost upon us. Dusty has the campsite ready to roll. He has kept his word regarding numbers, just twelve tents at a time. No caravanettes. My bet is he has put up a sign saying no single males under the age of thirty! Even Rio Dona is learning to make a pasty. A pity she calls them 'Patties'. It's scary when she cooks, she says 'taste this' every time. I say, 'I can't taste anything' and get a filthy look and she will put pepper and salt in whatever it might be.

Still there is no evidence of the stolen item. It might be a sign I shouldn't have bought the Maltsters. Chris at the Ring O' Bells might indeed have it and is using it for a wallpapering table. I wouldn't put it past him. All's fair in love and ale! I did see young Glenda pushing a pushchair the other day, it must be at least her third by now. It might have been her stroppy partner who took the sign. He did get a tad upset last time he was in and instantly out of the Maltsters some time ago now, most likely because he had to be carried home by Glenda after we showed him and his mates the error of their ways. I don't think he had to go to outpatients. Glenda is a big strong girl. Put it this way I wouldn't take her on at arm wrestling, I value my life too much. She's the sort of girl who could strangle someone accidentally, probably more than once. She should be a vet, she wouldn't need a rope to help a cow calf, she could just shove her arm in and whip the poor youngster right out. I heard she was a bellringer in St Issey church for a while, until she pulled the bell down. I'm not sure what my brother Dusty saw in her in the first place, he was a braver man than I. I'd hate to ask him. Obviously I wouldn't contemplate asking Glenda anything! If I was to ask her for a light for a cigar, she would most likely take a blow lamp out of her pocket.

Peter has moved on. I don't mean he has left us, he is no longer seeing Lavinia. I think he's chasing after my cousin, Lyndsey. Lyndsey I like, I have a sneaking respect for her. She can glare a tad when she feels a need. Trouble being she gives no warning. One look from her and you could suddenly become a granite gate post and have a cow scratching its arse on you. It's no way to make a living. Lyndsey is good with cooking my books. The chef didn't teach her, the Birdseyes did. The Admiral and his cockney wife have finally got off this mortal coil. They lived on a boat on my very small to medium sized lake, or if you prefer, my very large pond. I prefer lake, anyone can own a pond! The Birdseyes were living in the quay at Padstow and were evicted, so we brought them lock stock and bar here, to see out their later years in comfort. They did put out a very good gin and tonic with ice and a slice whenever I went aboard. Alma had many times tried to get aboard me over the years. I don't believe she did ever give up. She might once have been employed by 'Innuendos are Us.'

I call Lenny. "How's it going bud?"

"Yeah, we're getting on well, Maccy."

"I don't mean your bleddy love affair, I mean how's trade for goodness sake!"

"Yeah, we're getting on pretty well mate."

"That's cleared that up then. Plenty of food trade?"

"Yeah, I'm getting on with that well too, especially the seafood stall. I've called it 'Seafood Eat Food'."

"Excellent, but remember it isn't what you have to do personally. For you, it needs to be: See food, sell food, don't bleddy eat it all. Ignore the 'eat food' bit completely, please mucker. The bleddy emmets will think it's Eat Food, don't pay for food, scarper!"

Dear Lenny and I have been muckers since we began annoying primary school teachers. We aren't what might be called inseparable, as it could be embarrassing if one of us had a maid hanging about. I'm no prude but I do draw the line at being a sideshow. As for Lenny, if my mate has nothing to do, he will eat!

"Any news on the sign yet, Maccy?"

"Not yet mate, nobody seems to know anything."

"What did the sign 'ave on it mucker?"

"It had 'The Maltsters Arms' on it Lenny, oh and a lot of seagull shit and a phone number."

"So, some bugger has stolen the pub sign that does 'ave its name on, a load of gull shit and a telephone number for booking a meal. I wouldn't bleddy eat there Maccy, it don't sound too great."

"Thanks mate."

"I do 'ope you remember the number, Maccy."

"Why?"

"Easy mate, if you don't, you won't knaw if anyone is calling you to book a table. They won't knaw if they are calling you either will they!"

"Got a bad line 'ere Lenny, call me back if the Russians start kicking off."

"Do they 'ave a game?"

"No, Lenny." I'm warn out. I might get more sense out of Jill. "Two fried eggs please darlin'!"

"Get stuffed, you weirdo!"

"I'm not talking to you Lenny, I'm talking to Jill. Put the bleddy phone down!"

"What's she got that I 'aven't? Down where?"

"Isn't it bleddy obvious you moron?"

"Knaw, not straightaway. Oh yes, I understand now. Gotta get on, Moron!"

"Ignore that, it was a verbal typo. Are you still in bed, Lenny?"

"Yes, we are, now bugger off, you're getting on my bleddy nerves!"

Charming, you just can't help some people. I mean not even in an advisory sense – that doesn't work either, obviously. I wouldn't want there to be any confusion. Lenny doesn't need help in the bedroom as far as I knaw. Whoever he is sharing it with might need counselling, glasses, a brain insertion, etcetera!

The decorating at the Mermaid and here at the Maltsters is now fully completed, the lads have done well. Now we just need someone to stay here. One of these days it will be the Copper Mine renovation, a long-term project. For those who might have any doubt, it isn't a retirement home for redundant constables. I'm looking forward to it, I have a plan. Where was I? Oh yes, the engine house will remain as it is, an engine house, but in name only. It might become a restaurant eventually called, wait for it: 'The Engine House!' The pit, which is historically and technically described as a 'Hot Well' will be a pit barbecue. It will be big enough for the potential eaters to cook their own steaks. It'll save me a fortune on paying chefs. So basically, we sell the customer a piece of uncooked meat, they cook it themselves, which will lead to food poisoning by self-infliction, they get a free ambulance to the hospital at Truro where they can even do their own nursing. A dictionary will be available for those who have no idea what Salmonella is. Obviously, the emmets can eat all the veg they like. Another thing, the National Health Service will also save money. The Royal Cornwall has always encouraged patients to take part in their own curing. All they need to do is have someone on the door delegating rooms and operating theatres, making sure the tools are clean – though I suppose it isn't really that important on thinking about it – for the next accident victim who can still walk into A and E. It all lends itself to 'D I Y', they won't ever need to go near a D I Y store ever again. I have left out the V D clinic intentionally. I am all for adventure holidays!

I believe it all has potential. We'll give it a try anyway. If it doesn't work out, we can fill the pit with water, throw a load of trout in it – can't put Sea Bass in it as they only live in the sea – and they can all fish for their supper. Just the one snag, as I stated once before, fisherman spend ninety-nine percent of their time not catching anything. The anglers will just need a permit – you have to have a permit to fish anywhere now – and a bulky wallet. We can supply the rods and stuff ourselves. Another thing, I don't think we could expect customers to dig their own potatoes if they only want fish, chips and mushy peas. That would be taking things too far. Emmets can stay in one of our great rooms, come down in the morning, catch breakfast and smoke it. Sounds like a plan to me!

One thing in the clients' favour, especially the northernmost Celts, is they would not have to tip. Claymores and Bagpipes would need to be left at reception without exception. Anyone not obeying will receive a William Wallace forfeit minus the hanging bit. I don't hold with overkill.

We could keep chickens. The emmets can catch their own, pluck them, pull their guts out, barbecue what's left and Bob's your uncle, most likely! Ffs, I scare myself sometimes. Genius at work, again. There are redundant engine houses all over Cornwall. I'm thinking chain here. I'm not serious, I prefer roast duck with black cherry sauce for one thing. A chicken wouldn't even know it was wearing it. An old chef friend of mine showed me how to make it; he said, just get a load of very dark cherries, boil them, mash them, shove it up the bird's jacksy and dribble. Sorry, 'drizzle' the remainder over the breasts! He worked at the Savoy in London for a short while, a very short while unsurprisingly. I am surprised the Savoy was happy employing people who constantly dribbled over breasts while working!

Still nothing to be seen of the sign. Yes, I know, it makes me sound like a moron. It is a worry to me. Signs don't come cheap, especially new ones. No receipt of a kidnap note asking for fifty quid. I would pay fifty quid to get it back. I'd hand over the cash, take the sign and retrieve my fifty quid by particularly violent means a short time later.

I know Chris wouldn't really have taken it; he might have suggested someone else take it. I don't think so. Glenda's chap has a score to settle. Her man did spend some time in a vacant grave plot, as you do. We left him there for safety reasons. He might have got hurt more in the fight otherwise. He did in fact get a tad damaged beforehand so he's a possible. I can't think of anyone else who doesn't like me, not offhand anyway. It's a mystery right now. I'm not prone to a sense of humour at such times as these but I suppose it could be ash by now. It was an ancient sign and so unlikely to be made of plastic.

The problem is it could be anywhere. Signs are like that. There is a sign for everything these days. Half of them are too grubby to read. I actually did read about a bloke the other day who actually goes around cleaning road signs. Nobody pays him, he does it for nothing, he just has a sign cleaning fetish. Maybe he took it away for a thorough spruce up. 'Spruce', get it? Never mind! There's plenty more, I was in a good mood. Right now, I am perplexed. I suppose I could ask Jack if he's seen any odd lumber lying around. See what I did there? No? Never mind. It'll all come out in the 'Wash', which is somewhere near Grimsby according to my Geography teacher.

One thing I do believe, a pub without a sign is almost as bad as a pub with no beer. Exaggerate, me? As if. In any case, coach drivers would never find it! They have enough trouble as it is when they turn up with fifty already half-pissed oldies singing: 'show me the sway to go home!' They can be a randy lot, well why not if you're eighty and with not much else to do. An aged lady stopped me once in town, she said, 'would you like to see these' and groped herself as she spoke! I have no idea why she asked, they were already resting on her kneecaps!

"'Ave you finished, Maccy?"

"'Ave I finished what, Jill?"

"Your bleddy breakfast."

"I'm not sure, did you bring it?"

"Just before you started talking to yourself, boss."

Authors notes:

* The ancient White Hart building just situated off the harbour in Padstow has been closed as an inn for many years. Records show the White Hart operating as a coaching inn in the nineteenth century. Reliable witnesses have stated it is indeed haunted and has been documented as such.

Chapter Five

In Mysterious Ways

I still have no indication of where the missing item might be. I think about calling Twotrees, but if he found it, he would immediately lose it again. It's hard to believe but Twotrees and I do get on much better nowadays.

There was a time when we lads would plague him to hell and back, we ran him ragged pretty much. * I so remember, there was one time when he thought I was up to no good with Mrs Twotrees. It was all a misunderstanding obviously.

A Constable, as he was back then; a sergeant as he is now, Twotrees actually convinced me himself. Anyway, all was well that ended well. Neither of us were caught by the fuzz that day, me by him, her by him and him by his wife. The local copper had pretty much been up to what I had been up to, with one difference. I can't say anymore, I promised to keep my gob shut. We both did, it made good sense. His missus and I are still on nodding and winking terms but that's as far as it goes. I never did go inside their greenhouse again.

Back along when ma and I needed a license for the Mermaid and Bow, we needed Twotrees on our side. To be fair, a minimal amount of bribery – I mean blackmail – was employed by me. It did help, even though no money change hands. The copper still couldn't find his arse with half a dozen sheets of luxury toilet paper! Anyway, a landlord should show common sense and keep on good terms with the local constabulary and of course vice-versa.

I suppose I'm not much better, I can't find the pub sign and it's around four feet square with a load of fancy writing and my phone number on it. How difficult can it be? It is starting to bug me a tad now. If it is a prank, it's time to call it a day and put things right. We have asked everywhere for information on possible sightings or admissions of guilt. No such undertaking has been received. So from now on, we are at war with the thieving bastard! I meant to say, 'the sneaky perpetrator of the heinous crime' but never mind, I'm sure you get my drift!

Maybe it's just me but don't folks usually just steal glasses and ashtrays from pubs? I suppose a toilet roll and a bar of soap, even a beer mat or an A frame garden bench from the beer garden. It's expected, but why the sign? What is the point?

My main suspect is the local vicar. He's weirder than the next most weird person and owns a very tall ladder. It couldn't have been taken down without one. He also wears very dark clothes, a bit like a dress I suppose. On thinking about it, so does Michael. He wouldn't steal it, my mate wouldn't know what to do with a ladder! I'm pretty much the same. Actually, I did use one once to get on the church roof. When I wanted to get down again, my brother had stolen the means to achieve my descent. I did get it back, in exchange for five quid. It was the way my wayward brother operated in the good old days unfortunately for me. Dusty is much more honest these days. He just asks if he can borrow my cash. To be fair, he doesn't even do that. My brother now has a thriving business, he is doing well. Dusty still owes me a tidy sum.

My younger sibling has grown up a tad. He still continues to be an idiot, only on a part-time basis. He isn't as bad as he used to be. A smack in the eye can change people if it happens often enough. I wouldn't have him any different. Dusty and I get on. I'm certain he would say the same about me. He had better!

Not long ago our father turned up, he had only been away eighteen years or so. Dusty had not even been born when he disappeared. We two showed him the error of his ways when he did finally show his face. In all honesty it was ma who eased him back into line with a great right hook. I just had a quiet but strong word, Dusty beat him at pool and told him to leave town. Actually, Padraig was beating Dusty until he threw the one-off challenge match. The old man had to lose.

He never did leave town though. As for ma, I can't be certain, but I do believe it was the first and only time she ever punched someone's lights out. Padraig took it as a sign ma still held a candle for him, he stuck around and eventually married our mother. Now he's our dad and we're playing happy families. It's not a bad game and better late than never! I was a teenager when he returned and Dusty was a year younger. It's all good now with our father which is just as well as he has a lot of repairs to carry out on the family front. Dusty had been intent on giving Padraig a smack in the eye when he first appeared. Kids eh, who'd 'ave 'em? It does seem neither of us follow our father in looks and habits; though Dusty has a slight Irish lilt whilst talking under the influence, so pretty much most of the time!

Padraig constantly wears a Shamrock badge in his lapel that looks more like a cloverleaf in my opinion. Neither of us have ever done that before, nor do we believe in the 'little people'. Padraig has tried his hardest to convince us they do exist. Personally, I believe they do but only at the bottom of an Irish whiskey bottle. That's what I think. They sure are little, shy too. They do tend to stay out of sight. Here in Cornwall we have our very own home grown Piskies. Now they can be spotted on occasion. I've seen them myself on a Friday night or early Saturday morning trying to hitch a ride home. I've never stopped for them, I'm not that stupid.

Suddenly it hits me, the sign is either in a caravan with wheels or a gold-plated Chelsea Tractor whose owner might well be a Romany who lives in Billionaires Row, a Finchley backstreet. An emmet has got the lump of plywood. I'll never see it again. The tosser will most likely build his own bar in his postage stamp sized rooftop garden and hang my sign over it. Like dear Clementine it will be 'gone and lost forever' my darlin' pub sign! There's nothing wrong with a bit of lyrical waxing, I can do waxing lyrical almost as well as the next man! I did not once say I am capable of singing. I have never accused myself of being vocally melodic. In fact, a plumber who once turned up while I was in the bath abusing my vocal chords, refused to enter, deciding he would come back when I was in better health. I can only assume my chords were temporarily out of synch! It is strange that these anomalies only tend to occur in bathrooms that have an open window.

It's time to put Bessie to work. Bessie is my odd job man and a damn good chippie. If anyone can duplicate the pub sign, I'm certain he can.

"Bessie mate, we need us a new pub sign."

"What do you want it to say, Maccy."

"Erm how about ** 'The Maltsters Arms', it'll be a good start and will give folks a clue what we're about."

"That wouldn't be too difficult. How big do you want it?"

"Big enough for the emmets to see it from the middle of the road. About as big as the one we had previously and are bereft of now. I need the phone number on it. I need it to say we have rooms, as in bed and breakfast. Get the idea mate?" Pub signs aren't necessarily always self-explanatory, and I've forever had a sarcastic streak running through my veins. Bessie never catches on anyway. None of my staff tend to. It's their loss, I tell myself regularly.

"I do, Maccy. Tis a tad puzzling mind. I will do it if it's what you want."

"What's puzzling you Bessie, it's simple enough, isn't it? Lump of wood, couple of screws and the bloke is your uncle, probably, maybe not in your case!"

"Just my take on it bud but why don't we put the phone number and stuff on the sign we already have, it would save you money and I could be getting on with something more useful?"

"Because some tosser has removed it."

"No way, that idn't on. Maybe whoever it was will put it back."

"I don't think so. It's on the roof of a skyscraper by now, maybe even shipped abroad. Some kind of weird collector has it over his mantelpiece, might even be a local. You have to make a new one mate, a pub needs beer and a sign that says so. I'm wondering if the vicar might have borrowed it on a permanent basis, he's known to be untrustworthy. Put another way, I don't bleddy trust him!"

"I wouldn't have thought so, mate."

"Anyway, we need a replacement sharpish, Bessie!"

"Okay, I'll take the old one down then shall I? It'll be useful for a template for the new one. You should have told me before, it just took me a bleddy hour to put it back up."

"It would be best. Wait, what do you mean?" I am easily confused, it's a requisite of the job. No, a requisite of being a Tamryn, most likely both. At least it wasn't the vicar, I knew it wouldn't be. Apparently the shiny advertising board is back.

"I've just now put the bleddy thing up. Had to wait for the bleddy varnish to dry proper. Now I have to take it down again. If it were me, I'd just leave it as it is."

My sign is back. It looks almost brand new. It has everything I need. I could lamp Bessie. I do think it only right to give him a bonus, even if he did take the piss a tad. I won't be forgetting that misdemeanour.

"Tosser!"

"Thank you, Maccy."

"Good work, Bessie. If only you had told me, it would have been useful mate. I have had better things to do than pull my hair out and worrying about a bleddy plank for the last twenty-four hours."

"Well if the varnish hadn't taken so bleddy long to dry, you wouldn't have even noticed it had gone! What's Dusty done now, Maccy?"

"Now now Bessie, not that plank!"

"You should hear what he calls you."

"Yeah yeah, I am fully aware!"

Self-inflicted drama over. A pity I can't see further than my nose. If only the rest of my staff had their brains in the necessary places. If I want normality to return around here, it might take a while.

"Wosson Maccy, what can I do for you?"

"Not much Lenny, it's been done."

"What 'ave been done mucker?"

"Finding the sign. Bessie had the bleddy thing in his workshop." The workshop itself is the old milking shed we use to make our own potent brand of rough cider in. Four pints of the stuff can easily make you forget where the 'old milking shed' is. A person could walk in the front door and straight out of the back door without remembering why he or she went in there at all. This manoeuvre usually denotes that person has only had three pints, which is just under the health and safety guidelines which are only to be adhered to in accordance with cider pubs. Just the Maltsters Arms really. As for five pints, this convinces the cider drinker that instead of three Muscovy ducks, there are in fact six. I won't divulge my source. They will however look as if they are twice the size they were when last seen. I refuse to even mention pink elephants, self-incrimination isn't good for the soul despite what we were advised as kids.

"The thieving git. Should I 'ave a word with him, Maccy? Tidn't on stealing your bleddy sign that way."

"No Lenny, it wadn't lost, nor did he did steal it."

"So, it just went invisible for a while. A bleddy invisible sign idn't no good mate, I'd chuck it out if it idn't bleddy working proper. If it won't tell anybody we sell beer. Coach drivers will just keep going to bleddy Rock."

"Bessie was doing it up. He was giving it a clean and a fresh coat of varnish."

"Why didn't the bugger bleddy tell you?"

"He did, just now."

"So why are you telling me then?"

"I don't really know mate, can I go now?"

"Yes mate. Now let it be a bleddy lesson to you. I would tell Bessie, don't take down the wood tonight, you might get a big surprise. Get it?"

"Ffs Lenny, what will I do when you're gone?"

"Gone where, I idn't going anywhere."

"Are you certain sure?"

"Ais, I'm bleddy stayin'. You might need me for something important!"

"True enough, I'll go then." 'Need you for something important?' that'll be the day!

"You can't go, Maccy."

"You said I could just now."

"That was then."

"That's what I thought. Where shall I go now then, mate?"

"Round the back might be best."

"Around the back of where, Lenny?"

"How the hell should I bleddy know, I don't have to bleddy go there!"

How difficult is it to convey a message? If only he had given me a sign, not Lenny obviously. It wouldn't be worth the plywood it's written on. Anyway, Bessie did right, that's why I hired him. It's a pity we two spent so many years at loggerheads and often came to blows. Lenny and I have also fought regularly, even in our infants school and still today. Not actually today but I suppose it's possible, it's early yet. Scraps between us can go on forever, trouble is we can never remember why they had begun! It's better than going to a gym, we think so anyway. It's cheaper too! Long may they continue. I will admit to having a playful scrap with Lenny's sister more than once but that's another story. Lenny doesn't know and that's the way it will stay, please god. The strange thing is, Dusty, my younger brother and I, never scrap. We never have, we never really had to. We have a simple way of dealing with any such situation: I tell Dusty 'no' and he takes no to mean, do what the hell you like.

So, mystery solved. On to the next one. Oh definitely, one will occur. And she does, instantly.

"Maccy, have you found the sign yet?"

"Yes and no, Lavinia."

"What's that bleedin' mean?"

"Affirmative and not affirmed, maybe unconfirmed up until just a few seconds ago."

"What's that mean?"

"Well, it sort of means yes, no and pretty much more than likely."

"Where is it now then?"

"I thought I just explained."

"So where is it now then?"

"It's over your head, Lavinia. Sotto voce – like most things really."

"There ain't no need to be bloody sarky, I'm showing a bloody interest! Why do I bleedin' bother?"

"Bleddy, it's bleddy. I think you need a bleddy refresher course."

"And I think I bleddy don't."

"Okay, we'll start again, it's over your head Lavinia, up there, on the wall. Where it says, 'The Maltsters Arms' and all the other bits, blah de blah."

She follows my pointing digit, near enough.

"Why didn't you say, you dick head?"

"I'm sorry, I thought I did. Is there anything else I can do for you; frontal lobotomy, that sort of thing? I feel sure the doctor would have smacked your bleddy mother's arse when you first appeared!" Lavinia can easily be considered as disturbed. My diagnosis can be trusted, I'm on the same ladder myself. Like they used to say, it takes one to know one. I never did understand that when I was a kid, I was a slow learner.

"Frontal, eh? Yeah, go on then, so long as your yank missus isn't around. I knew you would give in one day. Where shall we go? Where do you want me, you won't regret it?"

"I'm not sure I can do it Lavinia, I don't have a drill and all my scalpels are rusty. I need an assistant. Another time, yeah. I'm certain there is nothing I would regret more maid."

"Bloody typical, I don't hold with threesomes, it's not my scene, Maccy!"

"Bleddy!" Just another day when paradise is in no way visible, not even in mirage form. I will continue to live in hope, which in no way can be considered to mean I have suddenly become an optimist. Do not misconstrue my intentions as Lavinia most certainly has at various times. I shiver even at the thought. My fear knows no bounds. By the way 'Hope' is in Devon, a beautiful place. It's wasted on the Devon Dumplings! If you ever go anywhere near Hope Cove, never ask a local where they live. The stock answer will be 'I live in hope'! It's pathetic!

I poured it, looked at it, swallowed and shivered like they do in films. I had no idea what it was. I did feel a tad better.

"What's wrong with you, Brit?"

"I'm formulating a list."

"That bad?"

"Couldn't be worse!"

"Tell me, Brit."

"I was considering a near death experience. After that, a post death experience. Neither have ever been on my bucket list to be honest, they don't sound too appealing."

"Wow Brit, do you think you need to see the doc'?"

"I'm considering it, yank."

"Come into my surgery Brit, I'll see what I can do to help."

"Bleddy 'ell, it's working already."

"I haven't started yet."

"I know, I know, I can't wait."

"Shut the damn door then! Is that better?"

"Not yet."

"So why are you so tense, Maccy?"

"Lavinia, she scares me."

"Man up Tamryn, grow some and pull yourself together man, she's only a poor helpless woman."

"That may be yank, but I ain't bleddy 'elping her and she idn't getting the bleddy chance to help herself. You mean poor excuse!"

"Idn't Maccy, idn't 'elping 'er. I say ain't, you say 'idn't!"

"Do I?"

I have created a monster. That *** Mary Shelley has a lot to answer for with her foolish notions. I would give Lavinia a piece of my mind, but she would most likely pass it on to someone else because she has nowhere to keep it. I can hardly afford to lose any of it anyway. People keep telling me I have a tiny mind. I don't even ask for an opinion. My wife, a Texan, is telling me, a born and bred Cornishman, how to talk and sound like I'm Cornish. Go figure, as they say in the States. What the hell does maths have to do with it anyway?

The yank had worked her magic, I am grateful for that. I didn't thank or congratulate her. She does some kind of fancy foot fighting. I've had my arse kicked before, it was not pleasant. She's done it more than once when she was asleep; she said she must have been asleep. I am now retired from any arse-kicking competitions. I never did win one, unlike the yank, she may never have lost one. I'm hoping she doesn't intend to teach MJ the finer points of Sav'at.

Let there be no confusion here, during the search for the much-coveted sign, no blood nor milk was spilled, just a small amount of cider.

For the record, Bessie did tell a white lie regarding where the sign was renovated. In actual fact he did the work in the church loft. Apparently the mad vicar had made the charitable invitation, providing the carpenter brought a couple of litres of the orange stuff – which weirdly is actually made out of apples – with him! Bessie, being an amiable type, would have readily agreed. I cannot divulge the identity of my source, other than the two are in the same line of work. It was not god. The great one doesn't live around here. However, he does move in mysterious ways, so I suppose he could do by now. I know he's never around when you need him ..... or her. He could have once been a goddess who changed her mind!

Authors notes:

* Maccy's brush with the law is explained in The Mermaid and Bow by this author.

** The Maltsters Arms at Little Petrock may have come into being between eighteen fifty, possibly a little later. It's first landlord may well have been a Mister J Keast who was in situ in eighteen fifty-six. Further research is continuing.

*** Mary Shelley 1797 – 1 February 1851) was an English novelist who wrote the Gothic novel Frankenstein; or, The Modern Prometheus (1818). She also edited and promoted the works of her husband, the Romantic poet and philosopher Percy Byshe Shelley. Percy Shelley is in fact said to haunt a small housing estate in Horsham, West Sussex. Mary's father was the political philosopher William Godwin and her mother was the philosopher and feminist Mary Wollstonecraft. Shelley's mother died less than a month after giving birth to her. She was raised by her father who was able to provide her with a rich if informal education, encouraging her to adhere to his own anarchist political theories.

Chapter Six

Hell in a Handcart

"Did you see Lenny, Maccy."

"More or less. I tried not to. He didn't see me. I'll catch up with him sometime. Did that bloke come?"

"Which one darlin'? Nope, I don't think so. How would I know?"

"An architect, he builds things."

"Nope, no one has built anything here while you were gone. Can I go back home to Texas now? I sure don't feel too well."

"No sorry, it's closed for renovation at the moment. Go shopping at Asda, that'll make you feel more at home. You can pretend you're in * Walmart. Or better still I can give you a complete examination to see what the real problem is, what was the name again? Lie down on the couch please while I check your notes and pulse. Racing, that's good."

"Go away, you dirty old man. I've read about folks like you."

"So have I. At least you recognised me anyway, it's a good sign. Eyes working properly near enough, that won't matter, it's not too important. Attention span limited. It's a good start, now breathe deeply, oh, come on, heavier please. That's much better. Now please remove any unnecessary clothing."

"Patient, Brit, I only have two pairs of hands."

"That's helpful, thank the lord! Better, more please. Let the dog see the rabbit."

"Pardon me, I thought you weren't supposed to say 'rabbit'."

"Only on a boat love. I was only saying rabbit as I didn't know what else to say, so it doesn't count."

"I sure don't own a rabbit."

"Good, say ahhh."

"Again only louder."

"If you say so. AHHH."

"Quieter."

"Ahhh."

"Very good. Now concentrate."

"I'm bleddy trying to."

"Look, it's easy maid, just one yank and they're off. Now what did I say?"

"That isn't remotely funny damn you, Tamryn!"

"You're right." I did think it was amusing, I decided to keep my thoughts to myself. "Concentrate again please, say thank you. Good, you can go now, next patient!"

"You can go to hell in a damned ** handcart mister!"

"Well, thank you ma'am. Now all I have to do is find out what a handcart is and I'll be on my way. Will I need a license?"

"Goes without saying husband!"

I've never heard of such a thing. I doubt myself by admitting it, it might have been better if I had stayed talking to Lenny longer. She eventually went off looking slightly bemused, nothing new there. Either the yank has been taking lessons from my mate, or she's going down with the same affliction, better known as constant confusion syndrome. Either way, most people around me seem to have become zombies but without the dead bit possibly. How can one be sure? Maybe all the others are normal and I'm not! I could have moved in with Bert, that way I wouldn't have had to go far when I'm old and unable to think straight. If that's the case I might just as well go now. The old feller was still cutting a rug at the old folks home until the day he demised. My old confidante was so close to his century, he only had to hit a single. Bert was one run short! I'm not far off with the amount of funerals I've been to recently.

"Why is this architect coming?"

"The engine house."

"What's happening with the engine house?"

"Erm, it's gonna be a restaurant."

"I thought about that myself, Brit"

"Why didn't you say something my 'ansome?"

"I thought it was a ridiculous idea."

"Really? I think it's a great idea. I have it all planned. You just need to let me have me the money maid!"

"Do I? I don't remember you asking."

"Nor me, sorry love. Can you let me have twenty grand?"

"Pounds or dollars?"

"Yes please, maid."

"I ain't a maid, I told ya before. You were there when I said it. In fact, you were totally to blame."

"I was, where?"

"Do you want me to lend you money or not? You ain't doin' this right, Maccy."

"I am trying."

"You got that as right as the weather, Brit! Now if y'all would like to get out of my darn kitchen!"

"It's my bleddy kitchen!"

"Out!"

"Fair enough." She sounded determined. One small worry for me, for her really, is will she remember to get fully dressed again? Ah well, not to worry. "Just one other thing maid, how will I ever know when you're angry with me?"

"There are two ways, Brit. First comes the glare, if that doesn't work or you miss it, it's mister. Mister is a derogatory way of addressing a man where I come from. When I call you mister, you darn well better run."

"Mister what?"

"Just mister. Make sure you never hear it."

"What about the glare?"

"Make darn sure you never see it!"

"Sounds easy enough."

"Don't get complacent, Brit."

"I won't. Please make another appointment with my receptionist on your way out." I think I handled all this rather well.

"You sure did not."

"I was talking to myself."

"Then don't, I'll get jealous. You know what that means, Maccy Tamryn?"

"Which?"

"Most likely both, Brit."

If she thinks I knew what she was talking about, she needs to think again. I didn't have a clue. It was all Texan mumbo jumbo. From now on I will keep my voice down to zero when I am thinking aloud. I don't like pain, particularly my own. It doesn't sit well with me. Coward? Yes, I most likely am. I can live with it, it's not like I have a choice.

"You do, Brit!"

"Maccy!"

"Yes, Pete."

"It's Peter."

"I thought it was you, Pete."

"There's some bloke outside Maccy, something to do with an engine or something."

"No idea mate. Are you sure it isn't something to do with you?"

"Um, come to think of it, it might be. He said he is a mechanic and my engine is missing."

"I'm sure you had it when you arrived, Peter."

"Yes I did, but it's not that kind of missing,"

"There's more than one kind?"

"Yes unfortunately, the expensive kind when it involves my car."

"It's a good job you don't have your own plane mate, it would cost you a bit more. What's wrong with the motor anyway. Why did you buy it if the engine is crap? There is nothing expensive about your car. It's worth twenty-five quid at most."

"That's why I bought it. It was going for a song, twenty-five quid."

"It must have been a crap song then."

"I'm wetting myself here from laughing so bleddy much."

"So am I, Peter. You best go and see what he can do then."

"About what?"

"No idea, your car maybe, just a thought." Yes, I can certainly pick them. From now on I'll let someone else do the picking. I don't do well at it. I'm not even sure how he got it here. Bits of string and super glue plus gaffer tape I guess. Peter should go to a hardware store and forget about mechanics who aren't completely rich yet. This latest one will be by the time he's sorted the old banger out. Peter will need a mortgage!

More trouble. I can smell it a mile away. "What?"

"Can I have a car, dad?"

"No MJ, you have to be a certain age to have a car."

"I am a certain bleddy age, I always have been."

"You're fifteen boy."

"See, I was right. Now about a car?"

"You have to be seventeen to get a car license, it's the law."

"I know that, but don't you have to be twenty-one to have a pub license?"

"Correct."

"So, how did you get one for the Mermaid and Bow? My gran, Joy, told me you were only eighteen when you got the bleddy Mermaid."

"It's different." I knew this was going to come up one day. MJ is not fobbed off easily. For one thing the lad is smart, too smart!

Peter has returned. So Peter, what's the damage mate?"

"All of it pretty much. Best I scrap it."

"You'll have to pay the scrap merchant mate."

"It's true, Maccy."

"Tell you what I'll do, I'll take it off your hands for twenty-five. How's that?"

"Fifty!"

"Twenty-five pounds fifty, okay, but don't try to fleece me for more. I don't have any small change, you'll have to wait. Give me the bleddy keys. There you go MJ, Pete will show you how it all works. Actually it doesn't all work, not much of what's there does not all work. Show him Pete, don't let him go out on the road. Stay on the field. Don't let him squash the ducks, don't upset the eels and don't let him run over Stan's grave or the old Comanche will get annoyed and make an appearance. Make sure he puts a seatbelt on."

"About the seatbelt thing, Maccy. The only one that works is on the passenger side."

"Then you're safe, Peter!"

"I don't need any teaching. dad."

"How's that boy, everyone needs to learn properly. You can't just get in a car and drive it, despite what your gran thinks. She's the exception to the rule."

"I already have, Peter and gran have already been showing me what to do. I can't go on the roads anyway, it's shagged out!"

"Knackered, MJ."

"Okay, it's knackered, it's shagged out too!"

I'm beginning to believe there is such a thing as a past life. I'm living it. I was driving ma's Cortina thirty years ago. I was about six when I started to drive. I had to sit on my ma's lap, she worked the pedals and I did the rest. We did chase a few stray cows, I think they came back eventually. They weren't our cows. The postman was only bruised, the same as his bike pretty much. I'm not certain he ever came back. Probably got a transfer to somewhere quieter, Lundy Island most likely. When he retires he'll probably get a card from the landlord of the Marisco Arms and a small herd of sheep. I wonder if the Marisco Arms is for sale. It's a non-starter anyway, MJ won't need a driving license on Lundy, there aren't any roads. On thinking about it, it would save me a fortune on road tax and petrol.

"Tex!"

"Corn!"

"Very amusing, yank."

"What do you want?"

"Nothing Tex, forget it."

"I already did."

I call her 'Tex' as it's easier to remember than all the other names she has. It's better than 'yank'. She didn't like it much the last time I said yank, I was temporarily in hot water. That'll teach us to bath together. Not that we needed much teaching to be fair.

I don't like being in water anyway unless I can the see the bottom. If it gets deep I get out. I can swim, any Padsta kid that can't swim isn't a Padsta kid. That's what I was told. I just don't see the point unless I'm drowning. If I'm drowning then learning to swim must have been a waste of time. If I don't go into deep water I won't drown. Why take unnecessary risks? I know I have flown over water and I have looked down at the water. There is far too much of it for my liking, especially in the Atlantic! I get nervous in the bath when I'm alone. If I am not alone there isn't so much water in it and there is someone to help me if I'm struggling to keep my head above said water, which I mostly am. Another thing, the sea is already so badly polluted, it would be best I stay out of it. If I was meant to swim I would have been born with gills, fins and a tail. I don't need either as I just don't swim. I confess, I do like watching the ladies swim – keep it to yourself - who doesn't? Other ladies I suppose. Obviously some might, but we won't go into that here.

If anyone wants to know who the 'Padsta kid' was, it was any of them. I taught my brother Dusty to swim. I didn't get in the water, I just told him what to do. I must have done something right, he's still alive and kicking.

"Yes Lenny, what now mate?"

"We need to 'ave a yack, Mac."

"We need a Yashmak?"

"Do we?"

"I've no idea Lenny, we might do."

"Shall I look out for one for you?"

"You could do, have you been to Turkey recently, Lenny."

"I 'aven't and I don't have any holiday left to let me go. Why do I need to go to Turkey?"

"To look for a yashmak mate."

"Bugger that mate, I wouldn't know one if it was right in front of my bleddy face, Maccy."

"You're probably right, Lenny. Put the thought out of your head mate. Anyway, what do you want to talk about, is it important?"

"Um, yes, Lavinia says it is. She told me, I 'ad to talk to you about it."

"You said it is important. How can anything be important when Lavinia says it is?"

"See, she says we do need to buy a house, Maccy."

"What for mate?"

"Ffs Maccy, she wants to live in it. She says we can't bring a kid up in a bleddy pub."

"What kid, you don't have a kid. Does she 'ave a kid I didn't know about?"

"Yes sort of, she do."

"What does it look like, this kid?"

"No idea mate, I 'aven't seen it myself yet. It 'aven't been delivered."

"Where's it coming from, Iceland? Or do you mean the bleddy goat. It idn't a kid no more Lenny, it 'ave grown up. It's just a goat that vaguely looked like a puppy dog once."

"Naw, not that kind of kid, the other kind. Like us but smaller. I'm gonna be a dad to it."

"Right, so how did that happen, Lenny?"

"Well, you knaw. You do 'ave one Maccy."

"Yes, but I knew what I was doing most of the time, some of the time anyway."

"I don't think I did mucker."

"You shouldn't meddle in things you know nothing about mate. What 'ave I told you and with Lavinia too. What the bleddy hell were you thinking mate?"

"You knaw what I was thinking, Maccy."

"Lenny, chuck Alice out and stay in the bleddy flat at the Mermaid."

"Where will she go, she's my sister."

"She can come here and live and work there."

"Where?"

"There!"

"Where there?"

"At the bleddy Mermaid, where you live now. Problem solved and I've saved you a bleddy fortune mucker."

"Thanks Maccy, you are a real friend. We're gonna get married mate."

I am as my mate says, but Alice won't appreciate it. Neither will Lavinia when she finds out. She'll separate him from important working parts. No bad thing I suppose. I'm all for Lenny having someone, it's about time. I know my mucker like no one else. He'll make a great dad, he'll make a great husband. When the time's right, he'll have a great wedding, I will see to that.

"Cows are in the pond husband, I mean lake, cows are in the bleddy lake, Maccy."

"No way, they'll eat the bleddy eels or trample them to death. What am I gonna do maid?"

"No idea, Maccy."

"I'll have to go in there and get them out. How will I do that?"

"You could maybe saddle me a horse Brit and one for yourself, I'm not doing this alone. We'll see what we can do. Ain't making no promises, I'm a mite rusty."

"Not as rusty as me. Rusty? I can just about ride in a straight line if the horse agrees."

"Just ride to my right flank Maccy, stay about ten feet back. Only move when the beasts do and when I do. I'll find the boss beast. If we turn her round, she'll take to the point and the others will follow. It may take a while, they don't like to be hurried. If they stop, we stop, okay? Stay to my right, cowboy."

"Cowboy? That's not very nice!"

"What shall I do, Rio?"

"Best you get a first aid kit, Lenny. For now just wave your arms about like a fairy. Not yet, in a minute or two when we have horses would be best."

Once aboard my pony, I watch as she walks her nag into the water and approaches the nearest cow, which looks to be the ringleader. I hear her talking in a whisper to the beast. It must be listening as it reluctantly turns full circle almost at once. I do as I'm told and stay just behind and to her right. I have been called a 'cowboy' before but never under these circumstances.

"Quiet back there greenhorn."

"I've never been called that before."

"Shhh!"

The Texan knows her stuff. If she's rusty, I'm a greenhorn, whatever it might be. Dusty and I rode cows once upon a time, I've never even thought of herding them. There is just twenty or so and they allow the first cow to take the lead. They move forward at a snail's pace, it's fascinating to watch. I might have seen the odd cowboy film where there might have been hundreds or thousands of cows but there were always dozens of riders steering them in the right direction. She is doing this all on her own and it's damned clever. I've only had to chivvy the odd one or two forward so far. It made me feel pretty good. I believe I got it right too as both returned to the group. As she had predicted, it was slow going. I don't ever remember following a cow around for so long. I don't believe I have ever once followed a cow around. I could take to it. I did get the opportunity to slap one once. The thing was standing in the middle of a road one day. It was just standing there minding its own business and holding up a bunch of emmets waiting to go back to England. I stopped the car, got out, walked up to it and gave it a slap in the face. It went off like a bull at a gate. Okay, like a cow coming out of a milking shed. I didn't even attempt to follow it! I actually felt sorry for it afterwards, it hadn't done anything to me. I have heard they are intelligent, I'm doubtful. I am talking about the cows here, not the fast disappearing emmets. On second thoughts!

Cow to cow:

"I hate that bleddy place."

"Which place?"

"Where they take our milk."

"Why dear?"

"It makes my tits sore!"

"Yes, mine too. You've got shit on your feet again, dear."

"That's nothing, you've got shit on your tail. No bull will want to come near you looking like that."

'That's good, I'm gay!'

'So am I!'

'What shall we do then?'

'No idea love!'

'We could go and lie on the grass.'

'Okay, race you!'

'Fuck off, I'm too tired!'

'It's always bothered me how we can stand up straight on a hillside.'

'Gravity love.'

'Isn't that what they put on roast beef!'

'I'm a Friesian."

"You silly cow. You should have been a Jersey, you could keep yourself warm!'

"Concentrate damn it Brit, if they get away we'll have to start all over again."

"I will, don't you worry."

"You'd better or I'll make you do it on your own next time."

"We could bill farmer Bird for this."

"Could we?"

"Not really darlin', it was a joke. 'Bill' bird, see?"

"God dammit Maccy, enough already!"

"You're the trail boss!"

"You know it! We don't get much mud in Texas."

"You could send them some Tex, we have plenty here to go round."

"Ain't that the truth, Brit. You did good out there."

"I did?"

"You sure did!"

"You didn't do so bad yourself, Tex."

"Been doing it since I could walk."

"You can't walk and be on a horse at the same time, maid."

"Very amusing Brit, you're so sharp you'll cut your ownself."

"I'm not sure I can walk right now anyway, I've got lumps behind my ears."

"You need a hot bath, Maccy. So do I."

"You took the words right out of my mouth, yank."

"You're having the tap end! *** Colonel Charlie Goodnight would have been proud of you today, Brit."

"Who on earth is Colonel Charlie Goodnight when he's at home?"

"Never you mind."

"Can I stop waving now please, Rio?"

"Best you do Lenny, put your arms down."

Authors notes:

* A wholly owned division of Walmart, Asda is not required to declare quarterly or half-yearly earnings, but it submits full accounts to the U.S. Securities and Exchange Commission each November. Despite being a subsidiary of Walmart, the company has more autonomy than any of the other supermarket chains within the Walmart International division and has retained its own British management team and board since the 1999 takeover.

** "Going to hell in a handcart", "go to hell in a bucket", suggesting sending someone to hell in a handcart a variation on an American allegorical elocution of unclear origin, which describes a situation headed for disaster inescapably or precipitately.

***Charles Goodnight (March 5, 1836 – December 12, 1929), also known as Charlie Goodnight or Colonel, Goodnight was an American cattle rancher in the American West. He was sometimes known as the "father of the Texas Panhandle." Essayist and historian J. Frank Dobie said Goodnight "approached greatness more than any other cowman in history."

Following the end of the Civil war, he became involved in the herding of feral Texas Longhorn cattle northward from West Texas to railroads. This "making the gather" was a near-state-wide round-up of cattle that had roamed free during four years of civil war. Goodnight invented the chuckwagon, which was first used on the initial cattle drive. Charles Goodnight helped get Texas back on its feet once the war was over. On March 5, 1927, his 91st birthday, Goodnight married Corinne, who was young enough to be his great-granddaughter, he died two years later aged ninety-three. 'Colonel' was an honorary title.

Chapter Seven

Seeing Double.

Thank God for Texas, my own personal bit anyway. A bunch of tame beasts could easily have outwitted me. They won't get another chance. I'll just borrow a gun from Annie Oakley next time and shoot the buggers. The lead cow – she calls them steers – had no idea he was the lead cow, it's obvious steers can't do what their name suggests, they were all over the place!. The lead 'steer' suddenly decided it was a competitor in a high-speed ballroom dancing competition. As for steering, forget it. MJ has a better sense of direction and that's saying something. The beasts didn't have a clue! A bit like me pretty much, though she did tell me 'well done.'

It all makes sense. The kid must have scattered them whilst driving around the field in Pete's jalopy, which did, for less than five minutes, belong to me. I inadvertently caused the mayhem by giving him the keys to the heap. Once again I am the architect of my own demise. The beasts must have stampeded just before the kid did a disappearing act. I need words with my son, they will not be pleasant. Although I did enjoy every second of the 'round up' he does not need to know that. It would only water down the forthcoming bollocking. It's obvious now the beasts and the boy can be compared, they are both totally useless at anything connected to the right direction.

"Good afternoon, Mister Bird." It looks like I'm about to get my own bollocking first. I didn't even do anything!

"Afternoon, Tamryn. What's been occurring here then, bit of a bleddy mess. It's a bit of a bleddy mess."

The old git spreads his arms like a scarecrow. My weird imagination visualises one of the said birds sitting on top of his head even as I look at him. I must stop sniffing glue. Half the lake bank looks like it's just been seriously and badly ploughed up without the aid of a tractor driver, just the driverless machine. According to the scarecrow, it's been done twice. How the hell can he tell? It does look like the army might have been holding tank manoeuvres.

"Rabbits Bird, it's that time of the year when they do get fruity and kick off a bit too much."

"Okay Tamryn, that's alright then. That's alright then."

I can't remember if I've ever seen the bloke wearing glasses, I might have done. I'm not about to suggest he finds any right now. I'm about to be let off lightly, why spoil it? I do wonder if we have a colony of rabbits living out here. As for the old farmer's repetitive speech problem? I can't be certain, he might have double vision too, which would make the mess here look twice as bad. Maybe there were forty cows after all. I admit I was as much good as a chocolate fireguard, but the yank sorted everything out beautifully. Bird scratched his head and wandered off seemingly pecking at the ground.

If the yank hadn't helped, the beasts would be running around the Ring O' Bells car park chased by rampant and angry rabbits by now. That would wipe the smirk off Chris's face for a while. Not for long as he might think his butcher is delivering the topside for his Sunday roast lunches. Fresh is good! He'll be totting up his discount for having to kill the beasts himself with his own bare hands. Actually, Chris only has to look at an animal and it will begin to whimper. I've almost done it myself on occasion.

As for Bird, from now on when he comes into the Maltsters to perch on a barstool I'll pour him doubles. If he starts saying things three times, it'll need to be trebles and so on. Well, why not. If it's good enough for him. I wonder what causes it. Does he have instant dementia, does he forget the very last thing he utters. Is the old farmer distantly related to a family of Goldfish? He, with his friends and relations, are going to have a pretty boring life. I said …, oh never mind!

"So Michael, what are you gonna do about Lenny and Lavinia's wedding, I take it you will be officiating at the do?"

"First things first Maccy, can I get a pint, this is a pub not a bleddy chapel, or a confessional. I'm off duty. It'll be ages away yet anyway if it ever happens. You knaw what Lenny is like, he'll just go his own way as usual. He most likely won't even mention it until the day after it's bleddy happened."

"True enough. I thought you people were always on duty."

"Think again mate. You're on duty right now, I'm not. Get me a bleddy pint, I've had a crap day, it 'aven't stopped yet!"

"What's happened?"

"I had to rescue a bleddy cat."

"You have rescued a cat. Had it sinned Michael? You've been preaching to a bleddy feline! Did you read it the riot act, has it promised to behave itself in the future?"

"Probably I did when it tried to bite me and claw my eyes out, Maccy. I wasn't trying to rescue its soul though."

"Too far gone then, mate?"

"Yeah, too far gone up a bleddy tree. I did 'ave to steal the vicar's ladder for a while and climb up it. It wasn't my best position. I prefer ground level mostly."

"I'm not surprised when you're wearing a dress. Why didn't someone call the bleddy fire brigade? Is there anyone in this village who hasn't stolen the vicar's ladder?"

"Most likely not, Maccy. Someone did call them, but they said they were away putting a fire out, that's what they said."

"You didn't think they were?"

"I knaw they weren't, they were playing bleddy cards for a big pot. They refused to leave the bleddy table, the buggers. They would have been off like shit off a shovel if someone was burning bleddy toast or the roast dinner has been over roasted or a naked woman was trapped in a bedroom screaming and when they get there her husband tells them to 'piss off' and mind your own business."

"How do you know then?"

"Lenny explained it to me."

"How the 'ell did he knaw?"

"Because the bugger was in there playing cards with the bleddy fire brigade. He was holding all the big cards and wouldn't let them go out until the hand was played out."

"That's a bit strong, Michael. So you've seen Lenny since then. Why didn't the bugger 'elp you with the bleddy cat?"

"I asked him and he told me to bugger off."

"Watch your language reverend, you're already on a yellow card for coming in here with no bleddy money. So Lenny did tell a man of the cloth to bugger off? That's not like him. Hang on a moment, course it is like him! He told Twotrees to piss off once. The copper didn't know where to put himself. We made various suggestions of course."

"Anyway, I wasn't wearing my bleddy frock at the time, I don't bleddy live in it."

"What were you doing then?"

"I was playing bleddy cards with Lenny and the other boys!"

"Who won the bleddy pot?"

"'Ow the hell should I know. I was up a bleddy tree doing their job. I was being a bleddy Christian!"

"Is that what they mean by friends in high places?"

"Don't take the mickey, Maccy. I lost every penny I 'ad in that bleddy game. I 'aven't got two halfpennies to scratch my arse with now. I'm poorer than the bleddy mice in the chapel."

"That's bleddy unfortunate Michael, maybe we should 'ave us a whip round?"

"It is for you, Maccy. I'll write you an IOU."

"You come in my pub with no money and order a bleddy pint and you want to write an IOU? I don't need any more i o u's, I've got loads already. I have me enough to paper a bleddy big wall!"

"I confess that is what I have done my son. I am suitably ashamed, they idn't all mine are they?"

"Mostly! How would you bleddy like it if I came in your bleddy chapel and took the bleddy cash off the collection plate and left a note in it? Dear God, I O U twenty-five pence and five francs!"

"I would 'ave to call the police. To be fair there wouldn't be anything on the plate anyway and it idn't valuable so there wouldn't be much point in stealing it."

"That's right Michael, anyway, out you go then."

"You wouldn't do that Maccy, not to a mate, would you?"

"Yes I would old buddy. You come in my house, eat all my food, drink all my beer and don't 'ave any bleddy money. You're always on a bleddy freebie, you scrounging git."

"Shut your face you tight bastard. Guinness please. How's that lamb coming along?"

"Bleddy scrounger, getting there. We will need to eat it soon or it will be too tough. Not even sure where it is right now. It was wandering around the kitchen earlier."

"Oh that's nice, calling a minister of the lord a bleddy scrounger. Wait 'til you bleddy snuff it and want burying. I will say no way you tight-arsed git. Dig your own bleddy hole and bury your bleddy self! Tough? So you think you might have to fight it?"

"I hope your boss can hear you Michael, he will be displeased for sure. I'll give it a rabbit punch!"

"He idn't around tonight, Maccy."

"Where's he buggered off to then?"

"Last time I saw him he was picking up his winnings at the fire station."

"Now why doesn't that surprise me. You religious buggers are all the bleddy same, self, self, self. That's all you ever think about. Charitable my bleddy arse!"

"Just pour the friggin' Guinness and stop bleddy whining. You knock back enough of my Scotch in the loft, you tight tosser. You invite yourself in, play snooker, beat me on my own bleddy table, drink my whisky and you're complaining because I can't pay for my beer for Christ's sake."

"When you put it like that mate, yes I do and I'll do it again too, every bleddy time. So what about Lenny then, Mike?"

"Forget Lenny, he most likely wants to get married in the bleddy registry office, if he knows such a thing exists."

"He can't do that, 'tidn't on. He's another tight tosser, nearly as bad as you!"

"Jesus Maccy, stop bleddy complaining, you're like an old woman!"

"Language vicar!"

"I'm not a bleddy vicar. 'Ow many times do I 'ave to friggin' tell ee for Christ's sake? Ah, now, here's a decent bar person, I might get some respect now. Evening Rio, you're looking rather edible tonight dear lady. Give me first refusal when you get fed up with this moaning git."

"Bullshit reverend. Don't bother, it doesn't work for me either dammit. So, am I right in guessing the Church of England didn't think you were up to the job?"

"I turned them down actually, Rio. The pay was crap. The hours were long, and they didn't have a bleddy snooker table! As for this place, it is slowly going downhill fast! I might have to take my bleddy business somewhere else after you've fed me obviously."

"Be my guest, Padre'. We'll be pounds in."

"I already am. Rio, do you 'ave any decent food going spare? I need something to be washed down by my Guinness."

"And I need to wash my hands under the faucet."

"Under the what?"

"The damn faucet, there!" She points and my friend has no idea what she is talking about.

"It's a bleddy tap woman."

"A what?"

"A tap, Rio."

"Faucet. It's a bleddy faucet."

"Tap, it's a bleddy tap."

"Michael, you'll have to cook your own darned steak if I can't wash my darned hands under the bleddy faucet."

"Maccy tell her, it's a bleddy tap."

"Bugger off and do something useful. Leave the poor Texan lady alone. I give up. Wash your hands wherever you must then give the mother whatever he wants sweetheart."

"Father Maccy, I'm a father not a friggin' mother."

"You're wrong Michael, you're what I said you are, I'm far too polite to give you the full title in front of a lady."

"I forgive you, Maccy. You know not what you say. You never bleddy do."

"Yes I bleddy do! Cook the tosser something to eat Rio, give the bugger his steak just so he can't speak while he's trying to chew. We might get some peace and quiet, I won't hold my breath."

"You cook, he's your darned mate. I ain't no damn skivvy."

"I don't care who cooks it, just decide and bleddy cook it. Today would be good."

"How do you like it done Michael, medium?"

"Just wipe its arse and wash its feet Rio, make sure it's bleddy fresh maid."

"Wait while I saddle my horse and I'll go and catch one for you. Oh sorry, my horse is broken."

"I thought that's what you did with all of them. It's what you told me. You definitely said, 'I break horses'."

"Just the youngsters, husband. Now leave me alone, I have a non-paying customer to deal with. I ain't likely to get a tip now you've put him in a bad mood."

"Dearest Michael has never tipped in his life. He doesn't carry money. His wallet, or purse, is always skint!"

"Now that is what I call service. Maccy, you could learn a lot from this woman, she knows how to treat a real man."

"Yeah well Michael, first we'll need to wait for one to come in to find that out."

"Do you want steak, Maccy?"

"I can't afford it darlin'. I'm a poor man thanks to my mate here."

"No Maccy, you do 'ave it wrong. You're just a poor man, full-stop. There is so much room for your improvement."

"Shut your gob, reverend! What does a decent man have to do to get decent friends around here?"

"No idea! Being a decent man might be a help, Maccy. It's worth a try. Don't go bustin' a gut mind, I can't eat proper with blood and gore all over the bleddy place."

"Rio, burn his steak to a cinder. He might as well get used to it when he goes to hell, as he most likely will. He's heading that way pretty smartish. Michael, you should give your boss a call and book your room. At least you won't have to cook for yourself where you're going."

"Rejoice in the fact I'll see you down there, Tamryn."

"Down where, mate?"

"On your hands and knees and kiss my ring!"

"Charming, I'm betting the ol' Devil can't wait for you to turn up, sinner."

"If I'm a sinner, what does that make you?"

"What do you want with your steak, Michael?"

"Just more steak, lady. Oh and mushrooms, tomatoes, pepper sauce, some chips, peas and another pint of Guinness please, do you do starters? Maccy has made this pint go sour. Can you follow that with a lump of cheesecake, or even two if you can spare them without my mate going into liquidation!"

"What are you, a friggin' hamster for god's sake? You won't be able to get in your bleddy frock the way you're bleddy going mate. You'll be too fat to get into your bleddy pulpit buddy. You'll be a damn porker soon enough!"

"Go to hell, Tamryn!"

"After you rev', I do like to learn from an expert as you know."

Michael and I are the closest of friends. In fact Lenny, Michael and I could not be closer. We started school together, left school together and have just about done everything else together ever since. We might scrap some now and then but it's only play fighting, there is never really a winner. I did go off to London for a while to learn the culinary arts, Michael went to some other godforsaken place to learn a bit of ministering. Lenny, well I'm not sure where Lenny went. Lenny isn't sure where he went. We three have stuck around together through thick, thin and thick again. It will always be this way, I'm certain. Unless Lenny finds out we are accidentally related. There could be a parting of the ways if he learned such a thing. It's unlikely because Lenny's sister, Alice, is married to Popeye Mervyn these days. They have done a good job over the years bringing up my, I mean their youngster. Mervyn got his nickname whilst out night fishing many years ago. Night fishing is another name for poaching in these parts. The lad had an accident while casting a line and caught himself. I don't believe Mervyn eats spinach from a tin.

As for the delightful Alice? *One morning she appeared before me like a golden-haired vision, as if an angel had descended. Dear Alice, got herself caught in a manner of speaking whilst we two happened to be in very close proximity. It has all worked out fairly well. The boy doesn't know and most likely never will as far as we're concerned. Best to let sleeping dogs lie pretty much. If Lenny ever did find out, he'd likely explode, and it wouldn't be a pretty sight. Neither would I be, I suspect. Lenny is rather possessive towards the females in his life. I think Michael knows, he did give me a strange, knowing look at the christening. He didn't preside over the affair, he was far too young at the time, his dad performed the head wetting as he was the current Methodist minister back in the day.

Michael took over from his parent when he retired. Mike's dad still watches over the local flock, the female section mostly. He likes to put it about a tad if you get my drift. Michael would like to; he's still waiting in line. My mate will get what he deserves at some point, I'm sure. At least I hope he will. He's a good all-round bloke and not half bad at snooker. He should be good because the only proper snooker table in Padstow is in the loft of the Methodist chapel. How they ever got it up there is beyond me. I guess maybe some divine intervention was called for and received. God does look after his own it seems. Is god a snooker fan, who knows? Only him I suppose. Mind you, there's little point in him playing by himself, he could cheat all the time. He could spend all day snookering himself, it would be easy to get out of it if no one's looking. Would he cuss and swear if the white went in accidentally? More than likely.

Most of us play pool when we get the chance. My brother Dusty and my father Padraig can claim to be two of the best pool players around these parts. We won't let Rio Dona Marina play if we can help it, she's from Texas and a bit of a hustler on the quiet so she says. There's not much else to do in Texas. To be honest, she's not quiet when she beats any of us, she's downright noisy. Like most yanks pretty much!

My cousin Lyndsey plays a good game too. I like to think I helped her in that respect but to be honest she was pretty good when she arrived here. She does all our office work and helps out behind the bar, but only reluctantly. She states 'barmaiding' is below her; I just tell her it isn't true, it's in front of her. Anyway, she has a mind of her own and lets us know it. We had never even met until the day I was getting married to Rio. Lyndsey arrived, stayed and is still here. The jury is still out!

Lyndsey turned up here with the news we are half cousins, she is welsh, it's not her fault. We all have our cross to bear. God help anyone who crosses her, she can turn a man to stone with one look. Locally, we call this the 'stone frog effect'. It's probably why there are so many standing stone circles in Wales. Her forebears may have inadvertently engineered Stonehenge.

Joy, my ma, does the same thing in a way. She produces concrete mushrooms. The good ones are everywhere. I found one in a front garden in Fulham once. I knew it was one of hers, it had the MMF Co stamped on it. MMF are the initials of the Magic Mushroom Farm where my brother Dusty and I were brought up. The bad ones, the mis-shapes, are all around the place. They make good dry-stone walling. You can hardly melt down concrete mushrooms and have another go. Ma doesn't need to work, she just doesn't want to stop. At least she has Padraig to help her now. The old man is a grafter. He had no choice, large amounts of humble pie were consumed upon his belated arrival as a parent, he had a lot of catching up to do. My little brother Dusty and I both had faith in our father, so did ma.

Author's note:

* How Maccy and Alice first became closely acquainted is told in 'The Mermaid and Bow' by this author.

Chapter Eight

It's a bleddy Pig Sty, Lenny!

I have no idea why this is down to me. Seemingly, Lenny is to be a dad. Why should I be involved? I had nothing to do with it. He didn't even ask my advice.

"Now Lenny, don't worry about it, I'll sort it all out." I'm beginning to think it's why I was put on this planet, to look after my friends. It's all I seem to do most of the time. Maybe I'll get my reward somewhere, I'm pretty sure it won't be at the place most people seem to end up.

"Well you'd better, Lavinia doesn't want to sleep on the floor."

"You'll be best to stay at the pub for now. The boys will need to take off what's left of the roof first."

"Look Maccy, we can get in and out of the bleddy doors just as easy, they don't 'ave to do that."

"Yes they do. If they take the roof off they can make the walls higher and therefore make the doorways bigger. It's no good 'aving small doorways when Lavinia is gonna be huge. Another thing, you won't get concussion every time you wake up and have to feed the babby in the middle of the night!"

"I'm with you mate. What about the garden, will they need to make that lower? What do you mean, 'feed the babby', Lavinia will do all that won't she, how the hell can I do it?"

"Worry about the feeding later. One thing at a time. Roof first, windows and doors next, garden last. What bleddy garden? That's not your garden Lenny, it's the bleddy carpark for the Pickwick next door. Are you sure the estate agent didn't sell you a pup mate? Maybe it's best you don't feed the little one. Just tell the maid to do it." I hope I won't be around for the fallout when that subject is raised, every night.

"I don't believe he did. I do 'ave a goat which I thought was a pup but I didn't buy it at the estate agents. I didn't even know they had any bleddy goat puppies for sale. What kind did they have Maccy?"

"Not sure but the kind that crap a lot and eat good footwear I guess. They are like baby dogs, Lenny. It's a good job you got the goat."

"I'm not so sure mucker, Billy did eat most of our bed, almost half of it."

"Bleddy 'ell mate, he must take after you. Where is Lavinia sleeping now then?"

"On the sofa."

"Have you bought a sofa mate?"

"No, not yet, she is sleeping where it will be when we do get us one."

"You're getting the hang of this co-habitation thing really well mate. Anyway, if you did have a sofa, the goat would have eaten it by now. Do you know something, Lenny?"

"Depends what it is I need to know, I might, I mightn't."

"It would have been easier if you'd bought a stable. It would've been taller, we wouldn't have to go through all this bleddy malarkey."

"But what if it was only a little horse?"

"It isn't, is it. There is no horse mate, which is good as you don't have a stable to keep it in."

"Where did it go then?"

"France mate, they eat them there."

"No Maccy, you're pulling my bleddy plonker!"

"That isn't something that has ever crossed my mind mate. No offence. Let's just stay friends, yeah? You know it makes sense. I do anyway. What you and Lavinia get up to is your own affair!"

"Do the frogs really eat them, Maccy. I thought they ate frogs."

"Yes mate, they do, both."

"Why would they do that?"

"Because they're tasty mate."

"It would turn my guts Maccy, I'd get the bleddy runs if it was me."

"I don't think you would mate."

"How do you know?"

"Easy buddy, they don't eat racehorses, they can never catch the bleddy things. Something is bugging me, Lenny."

"What?"

"How come the goat only ate half your bed and whose half did it eat? Why was Billy inside in the first place?"

"I did have to let him in Maccy, he don't like the bleddy rain and it 'ave been chucking it down a lot lately."

I wish I hadn't asked my mate now. A goat who doesn't like the rain can come in the house, eat her half of the bed and Lavinia has to sleep on the floor. It's none of my business. All I know is, I need to help Lenny and Lavinia and I believe I can, I must!

"Anyway mate, I believe you 'ave bought yourself a pig in a poke."

"What's one of them mucker?"

"Lenny, it's like you have bought something you thought was something else. It isn't the first-time mate."

"I never knew it was a pig in a poke or a pigsty, Maccy."

"There you are then, I'm right. You must be pig sick!"

"I idn't happy Maccy, stop it. You know how it is with me, but we 'ave bleddy bought it, it'll be alright."

"When it is rebuilt Lenny, you'll be as happy as a pig in shit!"

"Maccy, I am gonna have to lump you if you don't bleddy stop. I idn't 'appy about you taking the bleddy mickey out of this. I wadn't to knaw, tidn't on."

"Stay your hand Lenny, I don't 'ave anything else to say mate. We will get you another floor to your house I promise. I didn't mean to get your goat!"

"Maccy, I am bleddy warning you. You did bleddy promise. Just one more time and that's it."

"I can't, I don't know any more Lenny, honest. Anyway, there's no need to worry, Jack and Peter and you will soon have this place shipshape mucker."

"Thank you Maccy, I know what you are doing is bleddy wonderful."

"Lenny, we have been friends all this time mate. You have done plenty for me over the years, I'm just happy I am able to save your bacon!" It is all okay, I knew what I was doing. Lenny never could run unless he had an oval shaped ball in his hand, and I had a head start as I knew what I was going to say before he did. Oh come on, it was bound to come out sometime. Better it was me than someone else who isn't so nimble on their feet. It's done now anyway!

I think it would be good if Bessie and Jack take the roof off, build up the height of the walls and put the roof back on. Lenny's no builder, he'll need to labour for the other two, god help them, god help all of us. It won't be as simple as I make it sound but it is the only way the two can live in the pig sty without getting fractured skulls every feeding time. Lenny has helped me so much over the last two or three years. If it weren't for he and Alice, the Mermaid and Bow would have closed long ago. I owe them both plenty. Not sure which I owe the most to, my close friend or my friend who got too close once, quite a while ago.

"Maccy, is that you mate?"

"Pretty much Lenny, wosson now mate?"

"I didn't rightly tell you all the truth, Maccy."

"What about?"

"The bed thing."

"The goat didn't eat the bleddy bed?"

"Oh yes, he did eat some of the bed, only the quilt mostly and a pillow, but that idn't it. See, I idn't truly letting Lavinia sleep on the floor, I wouldn't do that."

"Then why did you say she is, Lenny? I was a tad shocked."

"I didn't want you to think I 'ave gone soft in the head, so I made it up."

I don't have the heart to suggest Lenny has always been soft in the head, I would never state it. To be honest, I'm not so sure he is really. My mate is just different, but we can all be that. I wouldn't ever want him to change. Lenny is

Lenny, I hope he always will be, I would hate him if he wasn't. My guess is the two will be as happy as pigs with piglets when the work is finished. They will have to be as that's where they will be, at least with one piglet anyway. Jack, Bessie, even Peter and I will do our best to make them a home fit to live in, one that cannot be blown down!

"Never mind Lenny, all's well that ends well. Can't stop mate, the yank is just about to dish up my dinner and I have to talk to the lads and fill them in."

"She is good to you mucker. What are ee 'aving? You idn't gonna fight them all at the same time are you, Maccy? You will need my help mate."

"Not before I've eaten my Pork chops mate."

"Bastard!"

Suitably sustained, I get the team together. "You two with my help will rebuild Lenny's house. Jack, you're on the stonework, Bessie, timber. When they get here, Lenny and Peter will help wherever they are needed. We'll make a start first thing later!"

"You two concentrate on getting the slates off the roof trusses, don't break any. Those that aren't broken must go back. We'll replace the damaged ones. Lenny, you start clearing some level ground so we can stack the slates. They must be leaned upright so lean them along the longest wall. We have to chip off any remains of cement from them. I'll get on the phone, order the new trusses and struts. Take measurements Jack and let me have them as soon as you can. Let's get this done."

"You're the boss, Maccy. Whatever you say."

"We've got a slate loose, boss!"

"I knaw that Peter, can't be helped. It's most likely the result of mass interbreeding in Devon!"

It is the oddest thing; I feel as if I am walking in someone else's shoes, wearing another's footsteps. Once I built a shed, okay not so much a shed, more a bit of a chalet effort. It's strange, I know what we must do but I don't know how I know. I would be crap at building a Lego house, I don't have the first idea how to rebuild a house. I do know planning permission isn't needed, we're going up an arm or two, not out. I suggest the 'arm or two' simply because I am fed up with trying to use my feet as a standard measure. Well, why not? I wouldn't check for building regulations in any case, nobody else around here ever bothers. Jack can turn his hand to most things, Peter told me when we first met, he did whatever comes along and Lenny? Lenny has enthusiasm. Me? I can bang in a nail until it bends double. I could turn a screw the wrong way. DIY is not really my forte. * When Lenny, Dusty and I put the old railway carriages back together, it was pure unadulterated bullshit in action. We three were teenagers and didn't know any better. Is it possible I can suddenly oversee the building of something for someone else to live in, we'll find out soon enough? I would most likely fail to erect even a canvas home by myself. Cubbing or scouting was not for me as a youngster, I was much more at home with girl guiding if you get my reasoning. I did catch one once but didn't know what to do with it. She was a bit older than me and gave me a wedgy, I'm not quite sure why. I believe she did it to make my eyes water.

I cannot allow Lenny to believe his faith in me is misplaced. So if there is no such thing as a supernatural input, it is wing and a prayer time pretty much. I wish I could state I am fortunate enough to have a smidgen of knowledge to construct an abode, I don't! We will indeed wing it. If we need divine help, there is always Michael to call on, unless he is busy at the betting shop.

This is one of those times when I need to stretch my legs. It has been a hard day, we have managed to get all the slates down and not much more. It wasn't as easy as it looked. At least we didn't need to employ a ladder, I wouldn't be surprised if Michael hasn't put it back where he stole it from yet.

The walls of the sty are only five feet high. It was tough going all the same. I walked a mile or two and suddenly realised how much I miss my four-legged friend. The old Alsatian had departed a while ago now – that tells how often

I used to walk him – he would follow me everywhere, in fact he mostly got to where I was going before I did. He had an uncanny knack of knowing my moods. He was with me for years before I named him Stan. Every time I called him he would do just that; stand and little else. I didn't buy him, I wasn't given him, the ugliest dog in Cornwall adopted me one day and never left my side unless I was on a plane or asleep in bed. When he was a youngster the poor bastard had a head-on collision with an outboard motor in the Quay at Padstow. He came off worse and was most likely uninsured. Obviously, the motor was connected to a boat of some kind during the impact. In recent years some have suggested the dog was swimming much too fast. Anyway, the old feller passed on a while ago. It should be said I never once suggested to the dog he should exercise more, he would make up his own mind and would mobilise at every opportunity. Stan had the ability to give the impression he was two faced. It's a pity he didn't look both ways whilst in the water. He was vile looking, but he was mine and I became his!

Mostly, by a huge amount of luck, we had managed to get all the roof slates off on the first day, obviously not all in one piece, but it could have been a lot worse. There were very few accidents, nothing serious and all in all, we had achieved as much as I hoped we would.

I was feeling quite content as we two walked the lanes that evening. As Lenny's goat and I approached the junction, I noticed a newly erected roadside sign: **'Hals Grave.' I have no idea who Hal is or obviously in this case, was. I make up my mind to find out one of these days. The sign is new. I have passed here a thousand times and never seen it before. The indication that someone is buried around here somewhere is weak, but that is the suggestion amongst the half dozen other roadside signs that litter the confluence of the two roadways and direct the traveller to either Padstow, Wadebridge or St Columb. It does occur to me that burials are almost always sited at some quiet little corner and mostly in a graveyard, so it is rather odd to have one so close to two of the busiest roads in the Duchy. 'Rest in Peace' does not seem to apply here in this lonely spot. It is unlikely any other will be deposited here near Hal's internment, but you never know. I don't think I would want to be one of the any other, I'd most likely die of lead poisoning being so close to the road.

I hear voices! I turn towards the road sign in time to see two people approach each other. One is male, the other resembles the alternative. I would swear it's the vicar. The woman, I can't be sure, looks like someone I've seen before, not that long ago. She is recognised, by me obviously, unless there is someone else about I can't see. Hal may be. To be fair, 'Hal' sounds like he might have been a man. I'm no Miss Marple!

We turn and wend our way back as far as the Maltsters Arms, wondering who the hell is Hal, all the while knowing that after a handful of pints, I would almost certainly be unable to ask myself the same question due to the age old trauma of being totally tongue tangled.

At my entry I am surprised to see how busy the Maltsters is, but unsurprised at the stare from my wife who is coping alone admirably. My bet is I'm in for a bollocking due to my newfound interests in ambling and road sign recognition, whilst accompanied by a goat.

"Good of you to pop in, landlord."

"I know maid."

I'm not certain she did actually mouth the words; the angry movement of her lips suggested she might have extended to 'where have you been you lazy bastard' and 'I've been working my damn butt off while you've been admiring the countryside in the bleddy dark'! I intend to plead guilty at some other point in time. For now I will just play it by ear. As she is mostly only miming it should not be a difficult task!

"Sorry yank, I have been checking the veracity of our work so far. It's important. It's all looking as it should do."

"'Veracity' huh? Fancy words don't pull pints, Brit. Get your arse back here where you can check the veracity of your bloody elbow!"

"Bleddy, love, it's bleddy elbow!" The unusual usage of my word must have been correct as if not, she would not have reciprocated with the same. Something good has come about on my return anyway. The silence didn't last long as I knew it wouldn't.

"Why don't you take a break my beautiful Texan? I think they are showing re-runs of Dallas on the box."

"I will, though I'd rather watch Corrie with the sound turned down, Brit."

"What's the point of watching it with the sound turned down?"

"Simple, I can't understand a damned cotton pickin' word they bleddy say!"

"'Tis the same for me yank. Try the other channel, EastEnders is on."

I did not understand her reply, it did serve to shorten the less than gentle bollocking somewhat. I am particularly grateful for that. I get off pretty lightly. The power of prayer is alive and kicking!

"You did well, Maccy."

"I believe I did Lyndsey, thank you."

"You wouldn't have got off that easy if it had been me, Mister Tamryn."

I believe her, I've witnessed the stare that can replace a thousand curses. Even the 'mister' made me shiver a tad. Do you ever get the feeling you're being manipulated by every woman in the village? I do! First one hits me hard, square on the jaw, second one comes in with a low blow.

"Where the bleedin' 'ell 'ave you been, you lazy git?"

I can't even manage a stutter as Lavinia follows up with the knock-out. These three have almost certainly planned a three pronged counter-attack while I have been surveying our day's handiwork. I can call it that whilst I am talking to myself. I can lie to myself as often as I like. In all honesty I only took the goat rambling so I could smoke a cigar or two.

"No, you bleddy can't and what's that damn smell?"

She is definitely psychic, I never uttered a word aloud. Her last words remind me of an epitaph which hasn't been written yet.

"Yes vicar, what can I get you?" Odd how he keeps popping up, I mean in. I mean materializing!

"It seems Mister Tamryn, I can be of more use to you in your present state. May I suggest a psychiatrist?"

"Do you know of any that can help vicar?"

"I'm afraid Mister Tamryn, you may be beyond help. Try asking the minister of the other persuasion. He's far more likely to aid you with his vast knowledge of the female of our species."

"You could be right vicar. Do you know where I can find him?"

"Yes, he is most likely in bed, giving instruction to some other poor member of the local coven. If you do go in search of him, I would knock loudly before entering the confines of the vicarage. He won't thank you for interrupting his teachings, as I would not myself in his position, whichever it might be!"

"Charming." Punch-drunk? Not quite, but I do know how it feels, even when I'm completely sober which is more often than not nowadays. "Is that lady with you vicar?"

"Um, yes, I mean no, she isn't Maccy."

"She looks like she might be vicar."

"No, no, never seen her before in my life, landlord."

"Okay, have it your way vicar. You do know he's all seeing?"

"I am well aware of that, thank you."

So the vicar is behaving shiftily. I'll keep it to myself for now as the lady in question kept herself to herself whilst sipping her gin and tonic.

"No you won't husband, you'll tell me all about it after we close."

I have no idea how she does it. If I myself was all seeing, I still wouldn't know where she is.

"It's for me to know Brit, not you. Now Brit!"

"I don't know any more than you do maid."
"You got that right mister!"
"I'm gonna have an early night."
"You are, husband?"
"Yep!"
"You ain't!"
"I idn't!"
"You see, I told you!"

Authors notes:

* This is described in 'The Mermaid and Bow' by this author.

** Hal's Grave is situated at the junction of the A 39, the trunk road which separates Wadebridge and Padstow

Chapter Nine

Who the Hell is Hal?

"Yank, what would you say if I told you the vicar might be misbehaving, rather badly in my opinion for what that's worth?"

"I guess I would ask; in what way Maccy, has he been stealing, burgling, has he been flashing his wanger about the village?"

"None of those as far as I knaw, but maybe. No, like you knaw, as in a woman, sort of. I suppose he might have been, not as far as I knaw. How would I knaw maid?"

"He is a man Maccy, like, you knaw, a bloke but a mite different."

"But, how can I put this? I think she is Lil's daughter, Lil the tart's daughter. The vicar is connecting with a tart's daughter and I think they are or have been, maybe were in the same line of business. Obviously Lil isn't now, I shouldn't think so anyway, I bleddy hope not. I hope the vicar isn't into necrophilia. He's only a bit mad I wouldn't call him stupid."

"How do you knaw – know – he is and she might be? He wouldn't. Neither would I, Brit."

"I saw them together, last night. They met at the end of the road, near Hal's Grave, up down that way near the campsite."

"Who the hell is Hal, I guess I mean, who on earth was Hal, he or she must be here somewhere, or you wouldn't have seen the sign. One of 'em is dead or they wouldn't need a grave, would they!"

"Make up your bleddy mind Rio, which is it?"

"How the heck do I know, I sure have not met either of them as far as I'm aware, wherever they might or might not be."

"Me neither, I hope I don't, and I hope you don't either yank. Can you stop talking in bleddy riddles maid?"

"Amen! I am not talking in riddles, if I am it's because you darned well started it!"

"How did I?"

"Easy Brit because you were, are, talking in damned riddles quite perfectly. Anyway, if it is Lil's daughter, she might be paying him what she owes."

"It doesn't work that way darlin'. He might be paying her what he might owe, or not, as the case may or may not be."

"Maccy, what did I bleddy tell you?"

"No idea. I thought I did for a moment earlier, I did, now I'm not so bleddy sure. I am easily confused by you."

"Godammit, spit it out, Maccy!"

"Is that all you yanks ever think about?"

"What?"

"Bleddy spitting!"

"Are you sure you're a Cornishman? Seems to me you would be better off in Holland or a sanatorium, either way no one will know what the heck you're saying!"

"It's a thought maid, I might consider it. Look, the vicar and the woman at the funeral met tonight at the end of the bleddy road."

"Which end?"

"It doesn't bleddy matter which end, does it? Why Holland?"

"I guess not. I'm a woman, I like to know these things. Because you're talking double Dutch."

"Me? I'm beginning to wish I hadn't walked to the end of the bleddy road now."

"Why did you walk there? Were you meeting another woman, Maccy Tamryn?"

"No, the bleddy vicar was. I told you. I was walking Billy."

"How did you know the vicar was meeting another woman, why were you walking the darned goat?"

"I didn't bleddy knaw! The vicar did knaw and Lil's daughter – if it was Lil's daughter – did knaw. I didn't have a bleddy clue who was meeting who if anyone was. I was walking the damn goat as I don't have a bleddy dog."

"Sure you were Brit, I believe you, hundreds wouldn't."

"It's thousands love."

"There you go then, it's even worse than I thought mister."

They might have stumbled on each other accidentally. I only wish now I hadn't seen anyone on my walk. In future when I go for a walk, I will put on shorts, a vest and trainers and will run instead. That way, I might get where I'm going faster, or slower – most likely slower – and not meet anyone at all. I will become a jogger like more than half the other people on the planet. I bet they don't meet anyone they would prefer not to! It must be why they do it.

'I'm just going for a run love.'

'Okay but don't meet anyone you shouldn't.'

'Oh I won't.'

'Make sure you don't!'

All I wanted to do was take my dog – who is no longer with us – for a walk, which I had never done before and can't now as he has passed away and I'm up to my neck, or throat – whichever it arrives at first - in brown thingy. I did not do it intentionally, it was a whim. Next time the dog can go without! Serves it right. Anyway I was out with a damn goat. The vicar was playing vicars and tarts with the daughter of a tart. To be fair, she might not be a tart at all!

"Are you talking to yourself, Maccy?"

"Yes and no!"

"You went out to smoke a darned cigar, didn't y'all. I can smell it, stinking bleddy thing. Go to sleep!"

"Give me some of the bleddy quilt and I might be able to."

* "It's my quilt, I made it. You might as well stay awake, either way you'll still bleddy talk your damn butt off."

"Head!"

"Same thing, it's where you keep your brains anyway."

"I'll sleep, it's the only way I can get a bleddy word in edgeways."

"Make the most of it Brit, I'll soon put a stop to that. Now get out of bed, you wanted an early start."

"It's twelve thirty."

"It's six o'clock."

"How do you know?"

"I know because the damn clock is hanging upside down on the bleddy curtain rail. Why is it doing that, Brit?"

"It's where it landed when I threw it one time because it was making so much damn noise, which on thinking about it, reminds me of someone."

"Out! Now Maccy!"

"I was just about to go maid."

"Wrong, you are just about to go and sort the damn clock out before you leave the bleddy room."

"Yes maid."

"Stop the damn mumbling for Christ's sake!"

"It wasn't me darlin', it was you. Why do I have to get up first?"

"Dammit, because you're supposed to be a gentleman."

"I am gentle. I'm soft in the bleddy head anyway."

"Out, now!"

"Morning Jill, where is everyone maid?"

"Gone toiling. Shouldn't you be doing the same, Maccy?"

This is life for me now. Last thing at night, first thing in the morning, probably the space in between, I am nagged to perfection. The women around here must have a rota system stipulating who takes over from who. Official Application for job. Duties: Must know how to take a deep breath no more than once every five minutes, be inflexible, most importantly chatter (nag) incessantly to all males in close proximity. Only mind readers need apply. Hours, twenty-four/seven. Pay, non-negotiable. Training ongoing. Some experience necessary but not a lot.

"Soon as I'm done, I am sorry for disturbing you maid!"

"Be sure you are, here's a dishcloth you spilled your bleddy tea man. Bring that mug back when you're done. Don't leave it lying around on a the bleddy building site and tell the others the same. Have you paid?"

Jill has completed her training and is in possession of flying colours. I would just like to mention I do employ her and even pay her wages, obviously I am not as completely certain as I thought. I rest my case in the knowledge I could be suitably beaten senseless if I repeat any of this information within earshot of any female of the species.

I took the hint.

"Right you lazy bastards, do us have any electric in here?"

"Yes, Maccy."

"Then get down to the supermarket Peter, buy a kettle, some tea, coffee, milk and plenty of sugar. Pinch a couple of teaspoons and mugs from any café owned by a Midlander as they have a tendency to fall asleep while pretending to work; they should be particularly vulnerable and get your arse back here soon! Don't mess about mate, we'll need it all in an hour, you won't you're already on a break. One other thing, leave the waitresses alone. Biscuits, plenty of biscuits and a copy of the Sun for my back pocket. Pack of cards too for when it's raining. Sticking plasters, five packets maybe a dozen, that should be enough for today."

"Did you miss anything, Maccy?"

"I don't think so."

"Pasties, ffs man, you're a crap building site boss."

"You're right. Tell them to have them ready to collect, steak, not bleddy mince."

"Gotcha! What about beers?"

"Peter, we have our own bleddy pub across the road."

"Can I borrow your car mate, my battery is flatter than a witches tit!

"Same as the tyres, roll it off down Little Petrock Hill, it will most likely bleddy start drekly."

"Lenny!"

"Yes Maccy."

"Music. Get a radio for tomorrow. When Peter gets back we'll bring my car over and put the stereo on."

"Maccy."

"Yes, Bessie?"

"We don't have any bleddy hard hats matey."

"We don't need any, the walls are only five feet bleddy high. The only thing that can fall on your heads today is rain and then we'll be in the Maltsters waiting for it to stop, won't we. You idiots wouldn't feel anything anyway."

"Yes mate, I wasn't bleddy thinking. Good job you're here boss."

"I knaw, that's why I'm here. You're here to mix cement, lay stone and keep sanity prevailing, Bessie. It's a shit job mate but I know you can do it best!"

"Thank you Maccy, I won't let you down very much."

"That's it, you got n!"

I think I have everything organised pretty well on my first day as a foreman. I admit to never having worked on a building site. I certainly don't believe in blowing my own trumpet, I do like music but couldn't possibly play an instrument of any shape, size or sound. I reckon I have covered everything pretty much. Obviously we will have to find some shovels, or we won't have anything to lean on when we're not sure what to do next and need to have a conflab as to what direction to take. Tomorrow it will be shades, spades and shorts. Shorts will be pulled down to half-mast at the crack, oops, I mean at the back. We will need woolly hats and baseball caps to support the shades. We will also need a small van with a comfortable bucket and a toilet roll. I can't think of anything else apart from a stolen biro for filling in the crossword and defacing blonde models in the newspaper. That's it I reckon, I'm sure I haven't missed anything. Maybe I should order a family pack of toilet rolls. It is time to get grafting.

"Excellent lads. We'll meet back here in an hour, I need to go and make some phone calls. I'll be back in ten, so no slacking. Any questions?"

"Yeah, ten what?"

It seems like I have acquired a barber shop quartet! Fair play, at least they are already working in unison. It's a good sign. I wouldn't be surprised if we're throwing trowels at each other tomorrow. It's all about building team spirit, camaraderie. One of the quartet seems to be missing already. I forgot, it's Peter. He's probably making pastry!

If there is any doubt, we will eventually get into a routine and prepare ourselves to take the walls a couple of courses higher tomorrow.

We enter the Maltsters with pride. What comes before pride? Lack of!

"No workmen! No boots, no jeans, no bonking on the bleedin' pool table. Piss off to the Ring O' Bells you lot and tell your dirty bleedin' jokes there and don't come back in here like that in bleedin' future. The sign says smart casual. Hang on, none of you lot could carry it off, so tidy please. I ain't putting up with the likes of you bleedin' lot. No smutty talk and no swearing when you do decide to look like bleedin' human beings, I doubt you could if there's a Y in the day anyway. Get out, sling your bleedin' hooks."

It seems we may have over-trained Lavinia. I should blame myself, I'm still lacking in experience. Even the men don't talk to me like she does. It won't be long before they stop talking to me. I need a map, Coventry here I come.

"Right lads, round the back and take your boots off, we'll go through to the kitchen. None of us want to drink our beer and look at you at the same time maid, you'll turn it sour. I shouldn't think anyone would do unless they are partially sighted. I'm thinking maybe you should be working in the kitchen and manning the dishwasher. While you're there you can wash your mouth out at the same time. Do you have German ancestry? If you don't, you can get rid of the bleddy moustache. Four pints please and bring them through to the kitchen, if you can remember where it is."

Seriously? I'm proud of Lavinia. She does exactly what I pay her to do. She keeps the riff raff out.

"Peter, did you get everything I asked?"

"I did Maccy. I got extra plasters, just in case. I got some smelly stuff for the bog too."

"What for? Waste of bleddy money. We already know what it'll smell like, waste of time."

"Okay, I'll keep it. I might find it useful."

"So Maccy, wosson?"

"Graft brother, hard graft. Nothing of interest to you, Kid. Don't get involved in things you don't understand."

"Yeah well, tell me who done it and I'll put them straight for you. Why are you necking it in here?"

"Lunch break!" I haven't seen my only sibling for a day or two. Dusty is in the tourism business. He is a bit of a tour guide. He shows folks the easiest way to get to Newquay and back without suffering drowning, so far anyway. The Sea Bus business is thriving for him and I am proud of what he has achieved in the last few years. It took a while for ma and I to redirect his attentions away from the female form – not completely obviously – to making an honest attempt at making money instead of using all of ours. He is turning over a good amount by all accounts.

"We were asked, almost politely, not to frequent the bar area in our condition bro."

"Correct me if I'm wrong, you've been banned Maccy, from your own bleddy pub!"

"Sort of, not quite. We have received certain ultimatums regarding the smooth running of the licensed premises, technically and by an operative who is looking for a new job."

"You've been banned from your own bleddy pub brother, don't give me excuses!"

"When you put it like that, yes I suppose we have. It's only a temporary measure brother."

"Ffs, you can't drink in your own bleddy pub. I love it. Only you Maccy, only you. I'm gonna have a look for my Guinness book. If it isn't in there, I'll give them a call and see if they're interested."

"Okay, while you're at it, see if there is a section for the biggest tosser in Cornwall. That might bring about two new entries." I doubt my brother is joking. He does have the book somewhere and I wouldn't put it past the bastard to do just what he has suggested. Wait! It's no joke on my part. We are both of the same ilk. I guess it still stands even though our father has in recent times returned. Our parents are married now but it wasn't the case when we first appeared. I like to keep the record straight!

I pull my brother to one side. "Dusty, have you seen the vicar knocking around lately?"

"Not that I remember Maccy, why?"

"Just interested brother."

"What's the bugger been up to now?"

"I idn't sure but …."

"So he's up to something then?"

"Could be."

"Spit it out, Maccy."

"Don't you bleddy start." I tell my brother what I had witnessed the other night.

"You are joking, who might be Hal?"

"No idea, not joking, Dusty."

"You think the vicar is bonking Lil's daughter on a financial basis, really?"

"Looks that way but we don't actually know it's Lil's daughter do we, it does look that way to me kid."

"Maccy, I 'ave seen her with Twotrees."

"What, you're 'aving a laugh."

"Naw, seen them twice now in closeness."

"'ow bleddy close."

"Close enough but not that close if you get my drift. Smiley close. I do reckon she is Lil's daughter, why else would she have been at the old girl's funeral?"

"That's my thinking, brother. She has to be who we think she is mate."

"I believe so."

"I feel a tad sorry for the vicar, no more than a tad but Twotrees, that's another kettle of, bleddy thingy."

"Fish?"

"That's the one."

"Tidn't none of our business, Maccy."

"No, not at all, but it's useful to know such a thing. Keep your eyes open, Dusty."

"I will, but not too far, I don't want to see more than I need to."

"Me too, it makes me shudder a tad. Dear old Lil used to make me shudder regularly. Maybe it was guilt but there was no reason, never did I cross her palm with silver or anything else of a valuable nature."

"That's what I meant Maccy. the thought of it starts me off."

"You're always thinking of your bleddy self, Dusty!"

"I'm qualified!"

"Dusty, you're many things. I don't think I ever connected you to 'qualified', delusional I can easily accept."

"You lot, out of the bleddy kitchen now, darn it!"

"We're 'aving a bleddy site meeting, Rio."

"I have to cook meals for customers Maccy, serious stuff, shift your butts outta here now, git!"

"Oh dear. Okay boys, in the bar. We don't need nor want to witness anything which might upset our stomachs do we? I hate cremations!"

"Maccy, that reminds me, don't forget extra bog rolls for the van we don't have yet."

"Yes, tell you what, steal some from here but don't let the landlord catch you, he's a miserable bastard. He'd stop it out of your wages if he knew. Until we get the small van, just crap in the pigsty. The previous occupants used to, I doubt it bothered them. We're mostly working on the outside for now anyway."

"Can't do that, we'll all smell of shit."

"That's right Lenny, so you won't notice the bleddy difference will you!"

"What did I tell you lot?"

"Sorry Lavinia, you should flush out the culprit easy enough."

"Very funny Tamryn, you crack me right up. No, don't even think about it or else!"

"Get yourself a drink and chill out woman."

"I will, thank you boss, I'll have a double with loads of ice."

"So will I Lavinia, good idea. Actually Lavinia, you just did me a favour."

"I bleddy didn't, that ship has sailed mister."

"Not that kind of favour, I need a plumber."

"Don't bleddy look at me."

"Don't worry, I won't, I've never even considered such a thing."

"Bleedin' liar!"

"Bessie, do you know any plumbers mate?"

"I do."

"Can you talk to one about plumbing stuff?"

"Shouldn't be a problem, Maccy. He said yes, he can do some plumbing jobs but as it's a specialty job it'll cost you a wad."

"Tell him it doesn't matter, you'll have to do it."

"Fair enough, but it will cost you extra, I'm a trades person."

"So's Lil's daughter but I wouldn't pay her anything for any bleddy reason."

"Neither would I" The chorus girls have struck up again. It seems they have added to their number.

"I would!"

"Who said that?" No reply is forthcoming. I know it wasn't me, that's about it. Another of life's mysteries.

The afternoon shift went well. There were lots of tool cleaning operations which was odd as we had hardly used anything apart from the kettle. To be fair the roof space is now open to the elements. We will be able to begin the replacement soon enough. As we meandered down the hill, we were all content with what we had achieved.

The evening quickly became one of a celebratory nature as we all bragged about what we had and hadn't achieved through the day. There was some exaggeration of course but we have made a decent start all things considered. Fun's over, tomorrow will see some real graft. I told them so. I fear my voice fell on deaf ears. I will remind them at every opportunity. It's good none of them need to drive to work, myself included. I did warn Rio not to drink Vodka – she's more used to American Rye – she took no notice so it's a good job she prefers to ride horses. God help the horses I say! The vicar wandered in for a late night short. It was difficult to tell but it seemed he had a look of fear on his face. Neither I nor anyone else enquired why it might be. I believe he had once again spent time with Lil's daughter.

I leave the lads to their bragging and think back in time to my arrival here as landlord. When I took over the Mermaid and Bow at just eighteen years old, I had the crew. I was a member myself. They only became my crew once I became their landlord. So many of those dear friends had drunk in the Mermaid and Bow before I was even born. Now so many, just about all of them, are no more. They have pulled up their anchors and have sailed quietly away into their individual sunsets. Here, in the Maltsters, another crew has signed up it seems. I hadn't realised until tonight it is happening right in front of my eyes. It is gratifying. The same is happening at The Mermaid in Padstow. Lenny is forming his own crew there. When we have finished his little hovel and turned it into a posh pig sty, I must get back to Padstow Town and find out who they are, let them know who I am, which I believe is just as important. I hereby make myself the promise. It must be kept whatever happens. All over the country pubs are closing down. I must not let it happen to my own. Not just 'my own' but theirs. The aged couple who had left the Maltsters – I didn't know them well, but ma did – had been here for almost a half century. Bligh and Blencathra had held the wheel at the Mermaid and Bow for only half that time but they did keep it going and allowed me, Maccy Tamryn, to take it on further. Rio Dona and I must do the same. It's a responsibility that cannot be shirked, it will never be on my watch! The Mermaid and the

Maltsters must continue on. It is down to Lenny and I and our respective crews to make it happen.

* There is a long tradition of African-American quilting beginning with quilts made by slaves, both for themselves and for their owners. The style of these quilts was determined largely by time period and region, rather than race, and the documented slave made quilts generally resemble those made by white women in their region. After 1865 and the end of slavery in the United States, African-Americans began to develop their own distinctive style of quilting.

Chapter Ten

A Site for Sore Eyes

Considering everyone lives around here or at least very close by, I am both surprised and disappointed they have all turned up late. Not me of course, I was almost on time and here on my own for a quarter of an hour. As none of the others were here on time they wouldn't have known if I was late.

"Kettle!"

"On."

"Toaster?"

"No, we don't bleddy have one mucker."

"Bugger, Peter get the spare toaster from the pub kitchen. No, better still, Jack you go."

"Why me?"

"Because your missus is in the bleddy kitchen grafting."

"She's not my missus, we're not married."

"That's different, don't ask her for it, she'll say no. Wait until she's not looking and steal one, I mean borrow it. Shove a frying pan down the back of your shorts too if you get a chance, that way Jill can kick your arse and get a sprained ankle and won't be able to do it again for a few weeks. See how I look after my bleddy workers!"

"Okay boss, no worries. What about bread and butter?"

"Don't mention butter in there for god's sake, everyone will want some. Ffs Jack, just steal anything you think we might need. If you do find any butter best you bring it."

"What about a sharp knife?"

"Don't worry about a sharp knife, if you get caught by your intended, you'll have one sticking out of your back, we can use that. We won't need ketchup or jam to go on the toast then either!" I really do scare myself sometimes. I'm taking to this like a Muscovy takes to eating cigar butts.

"Why can't Peter go? I don't really want to."

"He's a bigger target than you Jack, he'll come back with far too many knives, it'll make the washing up harder. Why do I have to think of every bleddy and stop bleddy whining Jack, you only have to do that when Jill's around."

"Sorry, I forgot boss."

"Then don't forget or you'll forever be subservient to her. She'll walk all over you."

"Like Lavinia does to Lenny boss?"

"Pretty much like that Jack, but without the leather boots."

"I'll get an ashtray too, Maccy."

"What the hell would we want with an ashtray lad?"

"Bleddy 'ell Maccy, to put the bleddy used teabags in."

"Fair enough, get a big one, we should keep a building site tidy I suppose. Best you bring a dustpan and brush too mate, maybe a duster and a fresh air spray."

"Ow the 'ell will I bleddy carry it all?"

"Tell him Lenny, I don't have the heart. Another thing Jack, mate, stop with the quaint bleddy Cornish dialect out here, it's only to be used when we're working in the pub and there are loads of bleddy emmets around. It's bleddy wasted on us lot. Give it a rest, knock it off for now unless some holidaymakers wander past, comprende?"

"Don't mumble at me under your bleddy breath kid. This is a building site, we're hard men, you can't go around acting wuzzy all the time, it idn't done. When you work on a building site you have to get hurt sometimes, a broken bone or two, missing teeth, get a six-inch nail stuck in your foot, maybe lose an eye. Don't worry we'll knock the nail out for you with a rubber hammer. Even your newspaper can suddenly burst into flames while you're sitting on the can in the back of the van. You just carry on regardless and when you get home with your chin on your chest you tell the missus all about what happened and she'll say; 'oh my poor little soldier, let me take a look at it, I'll get the TCP and bathe it for you my love. Shall I run you a hot bath my luvver?' You say hardly anything, just look really pained and sad with just a little bit of whimpering and nodding as if you're a toy dog on the shelf in the back of a car. Sound effects are good but don't overdo them too much or she'll suss you straight away, you have to be convincing. Try and get a half tear in your eye, that's always good if you can. A half tear means you're trying to be manly. After your bath and she's dried you off and put talcum powder all over you, you say; 'where's my bleddy tea woman', get me a beer and turn the bleddy tele' over, put the football on'! Last but not least, it'll be 'shall we have an early night love, it'll do me the world of good'. See, that's how it's done mate, you take my advice and you won't go far wrong. Everybody's happy! Ask anyone except this lot, they wouldn't 'ave a bleddy clue!"

"But ...."

"Most importantly Jack, don't ever say 'but' slowly, it's a sign of weakness, it's giving her an opening. She'll be on to you in seconds mate, you won't stand a bleddy chance. You'll be cutting the grass with one hand and doing the dishes with the other. Idn't that right lads?"

"Okay, but don't say I didn't warn you all. Jack, don't take advice from these two bleddy tossers. Now get to work you bleddy slackers, I've got important phone calls to make. I'll just be five or so."

"Five what?"

They're at it again. I don't know why they don't go on the stage. they're always looking for new talent in comedy. Suddenly I realise I have the answer all along, they don't have any talent. I would stand more chance than they would and that is saying something!

The walls are coming up. All being well, we'll have the roof on the place before the week is out. Once this is done, the upstairs floor and the downstairs ceilings will be next. I'm not even sure which should be done first. After that, the downstairs flooring, window and door frames, followed by plastering the whole place. Yes I know, no one wants to be followed by plastering not even a plasterer. Not even me. Lavinia might be content under such circumstances.

Lenny and Lavinia will be in here within a month by my reckoning. They will be as snug as the proverbial. The bugs are most likely already outside waiting for the new rugs to be delivered. The loved up pair can do their final titivating in their own time. They won't want us lot knocking around and they're capable enough. I'm sure Lavinia is anyway. I don't envy them, but I wish them all the luck in the world.

Lenny and I go back so far I don't even think they had invented dirt when we two first got together. My mate has always been there for me. Some lumps of wood and a few bags of cement won't break the bank. Damn it, I need a cement mixer, we need a cement mixer. We don't need it for mixing render but will do for the flooring. I think I know just the man; I use the term loosely.

"Brummie! Is that you, are you awake buddy? I need a favour mate, urgent."

"No, no, no, and no chance Cornishman."

"It's Maccy, that bleddy freezer didn't work. I will need recompense mate."

"Get stuffed, Cornishman."

"That's not very nice."

"Are you surprised? You said my chiller was crap."

"Shut it you bleddy furriner. I need something fast."

"You're right, a psychiatrist would definitely be favourite."

"No mate, I need a bleddy cement mixer buddy."

"Hang on, I'll see if there's one in the cupboard under the stairs …. no sorry. Got a hoover and an ironing board, I think it's an ironing board, some of them mucky magazines, will they do, no one ever uses them and just the one unknown owner?"

"And there was me thinking comedy was bleddy dead. It is now by courtesy of a rat-arsed Brummie!"

"What do you want it for and don't call me 'rat-arsed', you tosser?"

"My washing machine has packed up. I want it – I know how daft this might sound – for mixing bleddy cement in. It's all the rage on a building site I hear."

"Why didn't you say, Cornishman? Two hundred and fifty quid!"

"Listen mate, I'm not in the market for a second-hand Rolls Royce. I want a giant food mixer to mix cement in. Two hundred mate."

"Where am I gonna get a bloody cement mixer for that money."

"Robbie, if I knew the answer I wouldn't need you, would I, I'd just get it myself and a lot bleddy cheaper. So, you don't have one then?"

"Not right now, but I might be able to get one. I'll get you one for two twenty-five mate. I'll even deliver it for twenty-five."

"No you bleddy won't, you'll deliver it for two twenty and scampi and chips in a basket with tartare bleddy sauce."

"Nobody does scampi and chips in a basket anymore you Cornish peasant."

"Fair enough, no basket then, you'll have tartare sauce on your trainers, Brummie."

"Where did you say your pub is?"

"Just behind me."

"How do you know, can you be more precise mate?"

"Just outside Padstow mate."

"Padstow? They eat their young there, don't they?"

"No, not anymore, we were told to refrain from doing it. Apparently it's heavily frowned upon in the European Union whatever that is."

"I'll be in touch, Maccy."

"Cheers Robbie. By the way, what are you like with cooking stuff?"

"Best there is I'm told."

"Not what I heard. What about Pig Roasts!"

"Same to you. What about them, Cornishman?"

"I'll tell you when you get here, Brummie."

The manky Midlander appeared within a couple of hours with the very item we needed. It looked surprisingly good. Surprising as I hardly know the bloke and Lenny wanted to punch his lights out at our first meeting.

"I knew you wouldn't let me down, Robbie. Nice motor, is it yours?"

"No mate, I borrowed it."

"Good mates round your way then."

"No idea, Maccy."

"Who did you bleddy borrow it from then?"

"No idea, I didn't ask. The keys were in it and it had a full tank. Seemed a shame to see it sitting around in the street doing nothing. If I hadn't borrowed it the fuel would have just evaporated. I did them a favour I reckon."

I don't believe any more questions would be a good idea. I don't ask them. This Brummie is a man of means. By any means!

"Maccy, we do 'ave a problem mucker."

"What problem, Lenny?"

"It's a petrol mixer mate, that idn't any bleddy good. We do only 'ave electric 'ere. You can't plug a petrol mixer into the electric, it'll make a hell of a bleddy mess."

"Shit, I never thought about that. You better take it back, Robbie."

"Lenny mate, do you have a garage around here. I know it's a lot to ask in this bloody backwater."

"It's not bloody, Robbie, it's bleddy. Don't they say 'bleddy' in your neck of the woods, are you living in the bleddy dark ages?"

"They might do Lenny, but people are different in Millbrook. Do you know what I mean?"

"Ais, on thinking about it I believe I do. What did you ask me before?"

"Is there a garage around here where we can get some diesel to make the mixer work?"

"Maccy you bleddy idiot, why didn't you think of that?"

"I don't know Lenny, I just don't know. Anyway, Bessie is in charge of that sort of thing."

"I'm not, Jack is. I only do electrical appliances, like toasters, kettles, sharp bleddy knives and stuff."

"Where's my scampi and chips then, bread and butter too."

"Good thinking, dinner lads. Polish your boots before you go in. Lavinia will spill your guts open if you don't"

"Who's this Lavinia then, Maccy?"

"You don't want to know mate. Whatever you do, don't look her in the eye. Actually, today's a good day, do what you think is best." I'm just testing him out, I won't let him come to any serious harm.

"She only has the one eye. I think I will give her a wide berth mate."

"Up to you, that's why I said don't look at her. She'll probably turn you to stone mate. You'll end up standing around in a field waiting for cows to come along and scratch their shitty arses on you. One day folks will come and marvel at you, thinking you're a stone age leftover. They'll carve their initials in you and come back twenty years later to see if they are still there, they will be and you will be."

"Which one is it? It could be any of them."

"That one there is the yank, she's my missus, she has a bowie knife inside her boot so don't even think about it. That's Jill. I know he looks like a female but that one is Jack, the weird looking one is my cousin, Lyndsey and that my friend is Lavinia." I am even nervous of pointing at her myself and pretend not to. "Remember what I told you. You don't want to go home with regrets mate. Just don't get within touching distance and you should be okay. There are no guarantees Robbie, be quick on your feet if she gets close. Keep your hands down in front of you."

"We don't have anything like that in Millbrook."

"Think yourself lucky then. Actually, you could take her back with you instead of me giving you the cash. A straight swap! She has to be worth a mixer at least."

"No, no, I don't think so. No one in Millbrook would ever talk to me again."

"Lavinia will! Thanks mate for taking the trouble. Wait a minute, she's Lenny's slightly better half, I forgot. You're safe for now, probably. Just don't get complacent!

We pack Robbie off back home with a wad in his back pocket and everyone's as happy as a pig in a pigsty. No bones were broken, no limbs were lost as far as I know. Now we have just about all we need to push on with the job, except a gallon of diesel obviously. We'll fire it up tomorrow, it'll keep the lads happy for an hour or two and then they might actually do some work. I hope Robbie gets the pick-up back in one piece, I wouldn't want him to come to any harm. Maybe they all borrow motors and stuff from each other without asking in Millbrook:

'Is this yours'?

'Yes, what's it to do with you'?

'Nothing much, I borrowed it yesterday.'

'That's okay, any time. Look out for the brakes.'

'Why?'

'I lost them the day before!'

'Is the engine missing'?

'Not as far as I know. I think it's still there.'

'That's okay then.'

It could be the same with wives and kids. They might get bored and just pass themselves around.

'Just popping out for a few days love!'

'Okay, don't be late back.'

'I won't.'

'Hello, I've got a wife and a few kids!'

'What are their names'?

'Sorry mate, I can't remember.'

'Doesn't matter, come on in.'

'Is this your house.'

'No sorry, I live across the road, I'm just about to leave.'

'Which road? Ideal.'

'I'm not actually sure.'

'Never mind!'

As for the Brummie, I quite like the bloke; no airs and graces, no pretensions, no sense of direction, no idea who his neighbours are, pretty much no clue about anything. He definitely reminds me of someone, I can't quite put my finger on it. I'm sure it'll come to me. I doubt I've seen the last of him. I'm not sure if it's a good thing or not. Only time can tell.

"I got the diesel Maccy, what shall I do with it?"

"Erm, put it in the mixer, Lenny. It'd be best."

"Which end does it go in, front or back?"

"In the fuel tank mate, it's on the top, where it says 'fuel'."

"Maccy, what's a pottle?"

"It's a hole mate."

"Where?"

"In the road, it's a hole in the road that you can't see until after you hit it and your tyre pops."

"I wasn't sure. I think I hit one and some old bloke in the garage said, 'that's a bleddy pottle mate.' I didn't know what he was on about."

"It must have been a pothole, Lenny."

"Why didn't he bleddy say so?"

"He most likely thought he did. I expect he's a famous chef from Rock or Wadebridge."

"That would explain it then."

If I say it myself, I get a nice surprise when the mixer starts first time. I got me the feeling Robbie was doubtful it would. The speed of his departure in somebody else's pick-up was a clue. Anyway, money well spent it seems. It will still be useful even when we have finished the pig sty. The lads will be fighting over who will use it first but only because one of them will have to load it. It won't be me. They can fight it out amongst themselves. All we need now is some sand and cement and a * Cornish shovel, so called as only the Cornish know how to use one. Emmets wouldn't have a clue. They would be using the wrong end most likely. There is a knack to its use and one that should not be shared with anyone who resides outside of the Duchy.

Just why is it everybody and their dog wants to poke their noses in when building work – yes, another loose term for what we're doing – is being undertaken? I could do without this one. It's true, folks are like bees around a honey pot if someone lifts a shovel.

"So then Tamryn, what's happening here, it all looks pretty industrious, it all looks pretty industrious."

See what I mean. 'If you build it he will come.'

"Weem gonna breed chickens, Bird. This will be their home until they're past it and we have to wring their necks. Tidn't big enough for anything else." I don't call him by his first name, I can't without smirking.

"Very substantial, very substantial, Tamryn. I wouldn't mind living in it myself, I wouldn't mind living in it myself."

"Funny you should say that Bird, I do believe your ancestors lived here once."

"Really, I thought it was an old pig house. I thought it was an old pig house."

"Naw, folks were much shorter in the old days."

"They were, they were?"

"That's right, that's how twenty or thirty people could live in one house back then. Like in that film with the girl. She had seven little adults all living in her house. Now what was her name? Anyway, must get on Bird, bleddy chickens are waiting to get in here. Good stock too, double yolks all round."

"Good work, Tamryn. Good work, Tamryn. Carry on."

I'm still waiting for him to finish. He's missed a bit. "Bye Arfur. Bye Arfur." What were his parents thinking? Snow White, that was it! I don't know how I do it but I crack myself up sometimes. I watch Bird as he walks away, hands behind his back, pecking at the ground.

"Tea up guys, come and get it!" Well you have to spoil them sometimes once a year won't hurt. Christmas is just around the corner.

"Lenny, get the biscuits wherever you've hidden them."

"It's not a tea break, keep going, I want this finished in one month, no longer. Ratchet it up now. Not a word to Lavinia. We do the lot and nothing bleddy less. Got it?"

"Yes boss."

"What's this, given up the choir have we?"

"Yes boss. 'We do the lot'!"

"That's it. Not a word. Lenny won't realise anyway. Rain or shine, light or dark. Now, I'll be back in five."

"Is he serious, Jack?"

"What back in five? I believe he is, Peter. He looked that way when he left. What's your bet, Lenny?"

"He'll be back!"

"I guess we'll know in about four minutes."

"Christ, he's back!"

We worked solid almost day and night. It's what Lenny deserves for all the loyalty he has shown me since we were kids and not forgetting that of Lavinia, a woman I had decided long ago is a complete nutcase. She makes Lenny happy and that is enough. The lads buckle too and never stop. We don't skive off to the pub when a whiff of rain is in the air, or even a gentle fluttering of snowfall. When the roof was on, nobody hid inside painting. Eventually Lenny realised what was happening, he too worked on and sometimes was the last to put down his tools. A fond camaraderie grew throughout all of this. There is no bickering, no skiving and no shirking. We are all working for one cause. It was a delight to be a part of it. The women from the pub brought out food, hot tea, coffee and sometimes a beer, if it was too cold they brought brandy or whiskey. No one got rat-arsed, we have a job to finish and finish it we will. Then we'll fill our necks.

Heating is installed before emulsion is laid on render in order to help the drying process of the plaster skim. Water is plumbed in by one of the Maltsters regulars at little charge. A path is laid where pigs once walked into the warmth of their shelter. Their cottage – as cottage it is becoming – is taking shape. Lenny and Lavinia will have their own Christmas tree, they will sleep inside their own home on Christmas Eve, it is my silent promise to both my friends.

"I doubt they'll sleep!"

"Yes, I mean no boss. What was the question?"

"Can't remember!"

So the choir has reformed. It was just a matter of time. I think I'm just glad they don't actually sing. We do manage to trail back down the steep partly cobbled hillside lane that passes by the side of the pub and is hardly even wide enough for a small vehicle. We get inside the Maltsters minutes before closing time. Lavinia immediately starts firing questions at anyone. She is not impressed with some of our answers. Telling her the new roof had fallen in was not a good idea. She wasn't best pleased at the story of finding the skeleton of a pig under the earthen floor. 'Earthen' being a polite way of saying hundreds of years' worth of pig shit. She has been banned now from even bringing us drinks to the site. She isn't happy, though she does solemnly agree to stay away. Lavinia, the sex mad barmaid I met at Tredinnit only a few months ago has changed almost beyond recognition. Maybe it's down to Lenny. Maybe it's all down to her. I'm beginning to take to her. I realise that deep down, she is a nice, decent hippy lady with a mouth like a Victorian sewer underneath a large city.

The roof is on and it is complete. The porcine skeleton was Lenny's invention. He'll regret that at some point! There is still plenty to be done but now we aren't hindered too much by the weather. We have the smouldering remains of a fire to return to every morning now and it allows us to get a good start. Standing around for ten minutes with scolding coffee and toast splattered with Marmite is positively encouraged now that we are on the homeward straight, though the finishing line is still on the horizon and so a distance away yet.

The ladies have put up the Christmas decorations in the pub and it looks just like it should look at this time of the year. They haven't been standing around doing nothing during the long days. Jill, Alice and Dusty with the help of Selina, who is an old friend – posh totty – of Dusty's and home on leave, have done the same at the Mermaid and Bow apparently. It has been all hands to the pumps and not one has shirked their duty. It seems that once again I am part of and part owner of a crew! I couldn't ask for more than they have given me. They haven't asked for anything in return. Tell me where else that could happen!

"How long have we got off for Christmas, Maccy?"

"You lot will all get a sore throat at the same time, I hope!"

"Thanks boss and we hope you do too. What time does this place close?"

"When I bleddy say so!"

"Are you sure, Maccy?"

"I am fairly sure. As sure as I can be!"

Authors notes:

* The Cornish Shovel is a round mouthed open socket shovel. It has its origin in specific areas where long ash shafts are preferred because of the extra leverage they generate. The timber used for the handle and shaft has a very low moisture content to avoid shrinkage or splitting. The open socket blade is hardened and tempered, so it can be used for light digging as well as for moving loose materials such as shingle, sand and gravel. The key to usage is to keep the back straight and take the strain in the arms and stomach muscles. Some people also turn the shovel over their upper leg to operate.

Chapter Eleven

The Goat Hunters

"Maccy, I can't find Billy, have you seen him about anywhere this morning?"

"Check the milking shed, mate."

"I did that already, he idn't in there mucker."

"I don't want to worry you, but he might have eaten himself, Lenny. Just a thought!"

"I don't think so mate, he'd be bleddy sick as a dog, I know I would."

"Don't worry, we'll look for him later. I still think he could have eaten himself accidentally Lenny, you knaw what he's bleddy like. Anyway mate, he can't get as sick as a dog, only dogs can. On thinking about it Lenny, you have come close a time or two."

"Billy doesn't eat everything, mate."

"That's only because he haven't had time yet. He did try and eat your best jeans, Lenny."

"That's bleddy different, 'ee wasn't to knaw they were my bleddy best ones."

"One good thing came out of it, Billy did save you 'aving to wash them."

"I do 'ave a bad feeling Maccy, the bugger is always about here first thing, tidn't like him. Lavinia made them into shorts."

"He could be in a Moroccan stew somewhere, maybe in bleddy Morocco? Shorts, are you sure that's a good idea? I wouldn't want to be in your shorts when Billy gets hungry again. He might not like meat, but he might take to your two veg."

"Don't start Maccy, I idn't bleddy 'aving it."

"Sorry mate, he'll turn up. We got stuff to do here. I'll help you look for him when we're finished. We can knock off early for a change."

"It'll be dark Maccy. Billy's never been out in the dark on his own."

"No, but he has been out in the dark mate."

"When?"

"The other night. I wanted to walk the dog but as he isn't here anymore, I walked your goat instead. He was good as gold too, never barked once and kept away from every single lamp post he did. There is only the one in the village. No one wants to not walk their dog on their own, Lenny, it wouldn't be the same thing. If I hadn't 'ave walked him, I wouldn't 'ave found out about the bleddy vicar and the daughter of Lil the Tart. If she is the daughter of Lil, we still don't knaw do us! I put him in the shed and read him a story when we got back. The yank read me one too, 'twas called 'the riot act', 'twas for being away so long!"

"Maccy, if she looks like a Lil, walks like a Lil and works like Lil, she's probably a thingy, a daughter of Lil the Tart."

"So, a bit like a goat then!"

"I'm warning you, Tamryn!"

"We'll finish up here and go find him mate. He won't be far away, I doubt he will 'ave a map and a torch."

"So if 'e don't have a map and he's lost, he won't find his way back, will he."

"I doubt he will mate. I'll get the lads together and we'll get going. Best we start at each end of the village and work towards the Maltsters to meet up. We'll find him Lenny, I promise. You and Peter can start at the top end, no wait, we'll start in the middle and walk to the ends and cross over and come back on the other side. Then we'll do the back lanes if we need to, yeah?"

"Thank you Maccy, for what you are doing and the other boys too."

"Does he come when you call him, Lenny?"

"Maccy, I never call him Lenny, you know that. I 'ave called him some things mind, none good, especially when he ate my pants."

"I hope you wadn't bleddy wearing them mucker."

"I wadn't, they were on the radiator."

"They were 'hot pants' then. What did you call him?"

"Um t'was a bit like 'you little bastard, give me my bleddy pants back'. Lavinia thought I was talking to her and lumped me one!"

"And did the goat do what you told him mate?"

"Yes and no. They did come back the next day, but I couldn't wear them because they were full of bleddy girt holes."

"Lenny, they were most likely full of holes before Billy ate them. Anyway, it could have been worse mate, look on the bright side, they could 'ave been full of you if you know what I mean."

"Mebbe, are you taking this bleddy seriously, Maccy?"

"I am Lenny, let's get going lads."

"I idn't so bleddy sure."

It's a tad weird. I have heard of ghost hunts, I've even been on a couple myself; only in the Mermaid and Bow, we pretty much knew who they were anyway. They used to come in and out of the front door all the time. None of us was scared, all sorts came in and out of the front door, sometimes through the window in Stan's case. Mostly live folks went out through the window to be fair. Alice helped that crazy woman get out the window I remember. Anyway, I will admit I've never been on a goat hunt before. Change is as good as a rest I suppose. Where's an old wife when you need one?

I did write to Most Haunted about the Mermaid and Bow, I never did get a reply. I suspect they were a bit nervous of discovering the supernatural. I know I was! Apparently it is the dearly not quite departed One-armed Frank who was a one-off in every sense and his dad George who wander in and out of the Mermaid and Bow. I never did come face to face with George. I am pretty sure he is around at times. I won't even go into what happens around the village, we're all miserable enough already. And it's a shitty night.

"Over here!"

"It's a sheep Jack, look, there's dozens of them, we're only looking for one bleddy goat. They've got different feet."

"I couldn't see its bleddy feet. Different to what?"

"Goats have cloven hooves just like the devil, Jack."

"Like the bleddy devil?"

"They have horns don't they, the devil has horns they do say. Look Jack, there's nothing to worry about, he doesn't live around here, he lives over in Rock, always has and Billy isn't old enough to have any horns yet. They'll grow and then bleddy look out, he'll butt you into bleddy St Issey most likely! Keep bleddy looking lad."

"For the Devil?"

"No, the bleddy goat!"

"Don't go too far away, Maccy."

"I'm not holding your bleddy hand kid so forget it. The only thing you should be scared of around here is Lavinia, you don't want to meet her on a bleddy dark night."

"Shut it Tamryn, I bleddy 'eard you from 'ere, you git!"

"Sorry Lenny, only joking mate. Any luck over there?"

"No mucker, 'ee have disappeared. Billy is gone and lost forever."

"Just like Clementine! Don't give up mate, he'll turn up, you'll see. He's bound to turn up when he wants some food. Wave your jeans around your head, that might get him back. Don't leave your wallet in the pocket though."

"Maccy, the bleddy thing will eat anything. He idn't likely to go bleddy hungry is he, ffs. Who the hell is Clementine?"

"Good point Lenny, I hadn't thought of that. She's a baby orange! We'll have to call it a day lads, we should go back to the Maltsters and see if he do come home. I'm bleddy starving."

Thankfully we were all in agreement. I do feel sorry for my mate, but I think Billy will return when he's fed up with eating the feet off scarecrows. It's not like they can run away with a goat hanging on to a leg stump, is it. It's just a matter of patience. He'll come home when it rains heavier.

"Listen Lenny, Billy will find his way home mate. It's starting to rain harder. He'll find his way home safe and sound, at least he will if he has an ordnance survey map, not forgetting an umbrella. It's time to get warmed up, it's bleddy cold out here. Billy does have him a fur coat, I wouldn't worry."

"I suppose you're right mucker. I'll go out again in the morning before we start work."

"What do you mean, you never turn up until bleddy lunchtime anyway." I seemed to have joined the choir myself now. At least it put a smile on my mates' faces for the first time in hours. It's not a pretty sight but better than nothing.

"I've never tasted goats milk."

"What are you talking about. You idn't about to either."

"I know that Lenny, I was just saying. And another thing, Billy's a boy kid Lenny, he can't give milk."

"Right, keep it down everyone, we'll end up in the kitchen again else. Just look at all of them, aren't they the most beautiful women in Cornwall."

"That's it Tamryn, get out. I ain't bleedin' serving you."

So now we have a female chorus line. Very soon the whole village will turn out to watch them doing the Can Can. I'll emigrate. I can take a bollocking from anyone but not a Rio trio. Rio, Jill and Lavinia are treading on very thin ice.

"Is that the way a man gets treated when he pays a woman a bleddy compliment? Think I'll go to the Mermaid and Bow in future ladies, Alice knows how to treat a good customer. Lyndsey, you can serve us maid. By the way Lyndsey, whatever did happen to the tramp, I mean your mother, sorry maid, has she emigrated or something? Lundy Island maybe? There are plenty of Viking descendants over there, she might like that. Has she still got her beard?"

"We've had the bleddy 'maid' conversation before Maccy, I'll hear no more of it. I am not used to compliments from you, shouldn't think anyone is. None of your damn business! I think she lives in St Columb. I don't know any more than that."

"Ahh, Michael, get a round of drinks in mate, one for yourself. You just can't get the staff around here buddy. You haven't seen a tramp in your travels, have you mate."

"I will, it is nearly Christmas after all. Chance would be a fine thing, Dusty."

"Put me in there Michael. I'm not missing out on you buying a round. I know he's superstitious and he wouldn't want to be buying thirteen drinks and a Baker's Dozen is said to be unlucky. Some bleddy puddin' burnt down London when he went off to borrow a cup of sugar for his bleddy cakes from a neighbour."

"Padraig will want a pint, he's putting the goat to bed. Will be here in a minute he said."

"What bleddy goat, brother?"

"Billy!"

"Padraig is putting Billy to bed. Where is he putting the bleddy goat to bed?"

"In the yurt, he likes it in there, especially when it's cold and wet and miserable, I mean the weather, not the yurt."

"Dusty, how long has he bleddy been in there?"

"Couple of hours brother, mebbe three. He should be dry now, he don't half stink."

"Lenny, talk to my brother will you. I don't have anything to say to him at the moment, there are far too many ladies in the house. Present company accepted, obviously."

"Dusty, have you stolen my bleddy goat you tosser?"

"No Lenny, he wandered in all cold, wet and smelly, so I let him sit in front of the log burner to dry out, then he began to bleddy steam. No, there's no need to thank me Lenny, my pleasure. Padraig is settling him down for the night. He said to get him in a Guinness, for him, not the goat obviously."

"Very funny. Tell him to get his own and tell yourself the bleddy same. Tell yourselves we're bleddy shut. No bleddy drinking after hours!"

"Tell me your bleddy self, son!"

"I'll tell you something in a minute father ... What are you bleddy lot laughing at, don't you have some bleddy work to do? Piss off to the Ring O Bells, Chris will tell you to get stuffed too. He will do it much better than me." The significance of my statement is not lost on anyone present. I suddenly realise I have finally called my old man, 'father'. This is a turn up for the books. More than a medium shock if I am honest, about a five on the Richter scale. For the very first time in thirty-five years, Dusty and I have an actual dad. I'm not sure if I should laugh, cry or ask for a recount, maybe a refund. I think I will just take it in and process it for now. Of course I have forgotten what I was going to say. Now what do I do? A headless chicken springs to mind.

"What do you think you're smiling at Dusty, you tosser?"

"Nothing at all brother nothing at all. You just carry on yakking, take no notice of me."

"Then bleddy stop it. Oh, I won't, don't you worry about that, I'm not about to change a habit of a bleddy lifetime."

"Correct me if I'm wrong Maccy, but I think you just now did."

"What did I just say to you?"

"I'm going. Think I'll go sleep with the goat, he's not as bad tempered as you."

"Give it a kiss from me."

"You can kiss my arse!"

"Nobody's kissing my bleddy goat, get your own you bunch of bleddy weirdos."

"Can we just get this bleddy pub shut. Twotrees will be wandering in for breakfast with half a dozen of his mates in a minute. He'll probably nick us for giving him a snotty egg."

"He doesn't have that many mates, Maccy."

"Don't worry too much about me asking but who's looking after the bleddy goat?"

"MJ, he didn't want another beer, said he don't feel well after the last one."

"Who gave him beer, he's only sixteen or something. Oh that's it, you've all gone bleddy quiet all of a sudden behind there. It's okay, if MJ has fallen asleep, I wouldn't want to be in your bed Dusty, most of it will be in Billy!"

"Bugger, I wasn't thinking."

"You never are brother. You left him on his own."

"I did not, Padraig did. Dad? Weird isn't it. I never thought it would happen."

"Me neither, it just came out. What do we do now?"

"Just do what feels right Maccy, can't go wrong."

"There's another first, you giving me advice kid."

"The old man didn't make too much of it, why should we. It's done now. Done and dusted."

"So brother, can't be many punters around. Why don't you come and give us a hand to finish Lenny's place tomorrow, still a bit to do."

"I will Maccy, I'll see you in the morning."

"We 'ave got to lay the floor."

"How many rooms does it have?"

"Four."

"How did you manage that?"

"We went up in the world and a bit out too. We pinched a bit extra. Made it higher, wider and plenty more handsome."

"Did we get permission?"

"Erm, permission for what? I'm sure we would have if we had asked brother. The council was busy, they are all at a golf tournament I believe."

"What's it like then, this pigsty, bro?"

"Well Dusty, it's a bit like a bleddy pigsty, only bigger. There's lots more room in it now."

"Because you extended it?"

"No, because there's no bleddy pigs living in it."

"It'll be good for them to have their own place, Maccy."

"They won't be completely on their own, Dusty"

"Why not?"

"The goat, Billy will be there eating stuff."

"I can't believe Lenny's 'aving a baby, Maccy."

"Well technically he isn't, but I know what you mean. I hope they aren't too alike, I'm not sure there's room for another like our mate."

"See you in the morning Maccy, what time?"

"When you get there, before lunch break might be good. In a way, today was a big day for us Dusty, you know, calling Padraig 'dad, father.' Massive, in fact."

"I know Maccy. I'm good with it. It was a good job I didn't hit him the night of the pool match at the Mermaid, my bet is he would have gone if I had."

"He surely would have brother, goodnight."

"Night, Maccy."

What a day. I never thought I would see it happen, not yet anyway. It was all about luck. Not forgetting Billy. If the beast hadn't have wandered in when it did it wouldn't have happened. It might still have I suppose but it was something Dusty and I hadn't talked about. In the end, no talking was needed. It all fitted into place perfectly, couldn't have been better.

"Early start in the morning, Brit?"

"Will be, Dusty is gonna give us a hand."

"That's good isn't it, Brit?"

"Yes it is maid, real good."

The next morning brings another surprise. "What are you doing here father." As if I couldn't tell. The old feller is in shorts and boots and all the necessaries obviously. I watch as my brother allows it to sink in. I'm surprised he even turned up. He'll be glad he did. We three have never worked together before. Like I said, there's a first time for everything. This is the time.

"Worth getting up for, Dusty?"

"Don't go all soft Maccy, get your damned finger out, there's work to be done already. Yep, course it was. New day, new dawn, etcetera."

"That'll never catch on brother but yes, it does seem that way. Long may may it continue.

Another thing, it's a good job you didn't lump the old man, brother."

"Why?"

"Think about it, he might have lumped you back. It would have hurt!"

"I know, but he would have deserved it at the time."

"You I mean, you pillock."

"I know, Maccy. C'mon, all is good. Work brother!"

"Bleddy 'ell, you had a personality exchange?"

"At least I have one. So what are we doing then?"

"Floor, Dusty. We mix, Peter and Bessie lay. Jack learns, with luck. Dad will carry on with the garden. I might give him a hand."

Once the floor is laid we can't do much inside, in fact we can't do anything inside for a couple of days. My father is bringing in a Rotavator which will not only break up the rich soil, it will allow us to make the garden much more level than it is right now. Lenny and Bessie will put up the fencing once Padraig has finished his work. It is good to have all of us working together. There has been a real change for Dusty and myself with Padraig. He's been around for a few years but not as our father until now. It has been a subtle change and it is for the good. It is all very different now. Ma has said very little to me but it's obvious it has had an effect on her too. It's true what they say, there is nothing that counts as much as family! Padraig even takes his turn at making a brew and without being asked.

Tomorrow I will make my visit to the Mermaid and Bow as I promised I would. It's been a while and I want to make some plans regarding the changes to the bar area there, as I do at the Maltsters. I have one other call to make while I am in Padstow; it is a visit of a sentimental nature, I don't believe it will be anything more. I intend to see inside the one building in town that, apart from The Mermaid and Bow, has forever fascinated me. The White Hart! There have been many stories surrounding one of the oldest of Padstow buildings just a short walk from the harbourside. I'm not really sure why but I have to go inside the old place. The name itself suggests it was once an inn. My visit is arranged, I will even have a guide. No, not a young girl in a blue uniform, a man who as a child, once lived inside the huge old building that dominates its surroundings. I can't wait. As a child myself, the building had fascinated me and I never knew why. I intend to at least find out more if possible.

Tomorrow comes and I wait impatiently at the far corner of the building that points outward and into New Street on one side and Padstow's still partly cobbled Strand Street, on the other.

"Maccy, Macdonald Tamryn. We spoke on the phone I believe, I made an appointment."

"That's right, shall we go in?"

"Sure, I didn't catch your name …."

"I never threw it. Shall we? Just one thing Tamryn, be alert but do not be nervous and you'll be fine, most likely."

This man is a local, easily noted due to a feeling of a suspicious nature approaching me from his direction. I could be wrong of course. Anyway, I'm using his time and I am thankful he has it to spare. I have walked past the White Hart many times even as a short-arsed urchin. I have stretched my neck at each pass just to get an eyeful of what might be inside the ever grubby windows. I'm much taller now and I still don't have a clue what might be lurking inside the four walls. There is far more than four, I'm certain. I am about to find out. The White Hart is a large building and at first glance it looks to be L shaped with possibly a courtyard at the rear. Maybe the remains of stables out of sight but I wouldn't mind betting they, or their remains, are still there. I have no idea if this was a coaching inn, I would not be at all surprised. I wait impatiently while the stocky, early middle-aged bloke unlocks the large door, which allows access to the interior passageway that runs almost the length of the larger L shape of the ancient building, standing solemnly in its silence.

I am certain it will look nothing like I imagined it would. It doesn't matter. I need to see inside and perhaps imagine what it was like in its heyday. As for the warnings? Any nerves I might have should be balanced with pent up adrenalin.

I take in a deep breath as I have one last question for my guide before we enter. I don't need to ask as he offers the information I had been looking for.

"Mac! Everyone calls me Mac, I call myself Mac! We have the same name more or less, Maccy Tamryn. Yes, I've heard of you. * You won the Padstow Chase a few years ago if I'm not mistaken."

There's a surprise. I just knew there was something, I didn't expect that. Now I need the adrenalin, I'm suddenly nervous and not sure why. He's got his facts right. I hardly won it, the others lost it, I remember I was the first to get my clothes back on!

"Just 'Mac'?"

"It will do for now, Maccy."

So far, the man who might remind me of a jovial jailer has called me by three different variations of my name. I can't help it but wonder if he knows there is another. I have no idea if the jailer does or doesn't. I wish he would stop jangling the keys in his hand, I'm nervous enough as it is. I don't expect my teeth to stop chattering any time soon. I wouldn't be surprised if the bugger isn't doing it on purpose.

"So Mac, what do you think, are we related in some way? It isn't impossible, is it? My great grandfather Henry Tamryn, he was from Queenstown, yours was from Cork, you say. It's the same place more or less. It would make sense, wouldn't it?"

"It is as you say, Maccy. It's possible, who knows? Mind the steps there Tamryn. Ffs, I warned you, you bleddy tosser. I never told you he was from Cork!"

"It wasn't me. Someone bleddy shoved me in the back mate." I don't even know why I blurted out where his ancestors hailed from. I believe he would have already known.

"It's likely he was." Mac seemed a tad suspicious. Not surprising to be fair, he's not the only one! I already have the feeling I don't want to be here.

Author's notes:

* The Padstow Chase occurs in the Mermaid and Bow by this author.

Chapter Twelve

The White Hart.

"What did I bleddy tell you, tread careful, Tamryn!"

"I thought you were joshing me." Fair enough, I will be in future, I'll be more careful. What am I saying? I won't be coming back. I'm not sure what's the most creepy, the house or Mac, he wears the haunted look well!

"It's happened to me and plenty of others. I did warn you to mind the bleddy steps."

"I didn't expect to be shoved down them, Mac. Good job it was only a half dozen. Are you sure you didn't bleddy push me?"

"Yup, weren't me. We won't stay long, I don't believe they want us about here today. They are being mischievous!"

"They who, I mean who they, who don't want us about the place?"

"Best you don't knaw. They're here mind, you can be sure of that. Listen Maccy, if you go in any of the other rooms, block the door open so it can't be shut. I mean by itself, no, I don't mean that, just block the bleddy doors open, it would be best."

"Bleddy 'ell, it's not even Halloween."

"They don't take any notice of all that shite. These are real, not real, sort of real, but they are here, take it from me. That's all you need to know. Just respect their presence Maccy, you won't come to any harm, hopefully."

"So you don't know who they are, Mac. Harm? I almost bleddy died of bleddy fright!"

"Is that a question or an answer?"

"How the hell do I know, bit of both? I didn't come here expecting to be spooked out. I wadn't good at schooling either."

"You get used to it after a while. My father did, me too, plenty times. I lived in here as a young tacker don't forget, I knew they were here then."

"I didn't realise that. What was it like?"

"Varying. Different things happened but at my age, at the time, I suppose I thought most of it was normal. I didn't know any different back then."

"Rather you than me, mate."

"They're alright when they get used to you being around if you're lucky. You weren't today. They were most likely just pre warning you not to step out of line. Best we make tracks."

"The sooner, the better. I'm not sure I want to be around again, no offence to them, or you." I had seen enough. Actually, I never saw anything. Mac says they're here and I'll take his word for it.

"Oh, you'll come back Maccy Tamryn, wait and bleddy see."

"How do you know?"

"This is between me and you, I don't warn everyone. Almost all who come here come back sometime unless they have passed on. They that have returned don't knaw why either. That's why I have a key. You aren't the first, you will not be the last. I believe it is the curse. I keep coming back because others want to. Tell you what my friend, you can have the key – there is only one and I have it – then you can come here any time you like, or not. I've had enough of being a bleddy jailer."

"I don't want the bleddy key, you keep it. Think it best you keep it mate. I wouldn't know what to do with it. I won't return, I'll just continue to look through a grubby window. You keep the bleddy key."

"I don't bleddy want it, it has me and it won't let me go. I don't do it for bleddy fun you knaw! I have a life, this isn't it. It is, but I don't want it, I have stuff to do. I can't keep coming here every bleddy day wasting time with the likes of you, I have better things to do. Sometimes I wish I had never set eyes on the blasted key."

"Why don't you give it to Twotrees?"

"Can't do that, he'll only bleddy lose it. I'll find it and be back where I started. I lost it plenty of times. It's cursed, I'm telling you, mark my words."

"Well don't bleddy give it to me then."

"That's bleddy nice. You wanted to come here and now you don't want any bleddy responsibility. It's typical, you're all the bleddy same, you people. I bet you idn't even a bleddy local! I bet you idn't even local."

"That idn't very nice, Mac. My father is from Cork, I think that's why I became a landlord ….. Cork, get it?"

"I get it, very funny. I'm sorry but I 'ave 'ad enough of the place, I just can't do it anymore. It's time someone else took it on."

"So why do you have so many keys then?"

"I can't always remember which one it is."

"Look Mac, chuck the bleddy lot away, throw them all in the quay. Chuck them down a bleddy mineshaft."

"I did that, but some bugger found them and gave them me back."

"Throw them out in the estuary, get on the Jubilee Queen and drop them out on the Doom Bar."

"There's no bleddy point. I 'ave tried everything over the years, it's no use. The bleddy Doom Bar? It's where I found them, where it all started. There was a neap tide and you could see the whole thing. I was treasure hunting with my metal detector, first time it ever worked!"

"There you are then, you found your treasure. I do 'ave to go now. Thanks for showing me around." I have not the slightest idea why I said that! I couldn't take any more. I turned away and went through the door. It was a serious mistake. I think I'm in a cupboard. "Mac, Mac, get me out of here man, bleddy 'ell!"

"I bleddy told you to prop open any doors, didn't I!"

"I wasn't to knaw it was a bleddy cupboard, mate."

"Nor did I when the same thing happened to me. It was a good job I had the key. Here, you have it."

I said something quite rude before I left in a great hurry. I felt sorry for Mac as I walked away, I do believe he saw me as his replacement. It would have been like getting a chain letter without the chain and the letter. I shivered all the way up to the carpark at the top of Padstow Hill. I didn't look back, I hope I never have to. The poor man is more haunted than the White Hart. I believe he is exactly that, or he could just be mazed. Otherwise, he was pretty much affable. I looked back and saw the look on his face as he looked down at his hand and the key, I swear I saw a tear welling up in his eye. I couldn't watch anymore and walked away. I must admit that while I was inside, there did seem to be something of a heavy atmosphere. It was as if someone, or something was watching, even following me as I had looked around. I had seen every room and it was enough. Creepy doesn't really cover it. As for the building? It is huge, even bigger than it looks from outside. I had exited through the side door and past the previously imagined stables now serving as storage sheds. The cobbled courtyard had allowed access to an overgrown vegetable patch. I need a drink!

"What's wrong with you, Maccy?"

"Don't ask Alice, I hardly want to think about it. I need a drink, two, a double, in the same glass."

"I knaw how it bleddy works. What's got you all het up then? You idn't yourself, which is useful."

"You got that right. I 'ave been in the White Hart, Alice. I will never go in there again, please remind me I should not return."

"Right Maccy, never ever go in the White Hart ever again, how's that?"

"Not now you idiot, later, when I don't remember."

"How the hell will I knaw when you don't remember, I'm not a bleddy thingy, psychic, as far as I knaw. No one knows what goes on in your head if anything at all. I might not bleddy remember! Let's start again. It's nice to see you too, boss."

"I bleddy knaw that maid, you don't need to tell me."

"Try this one, what do you bleddy want, boss?"

"Nothing, I just came into my pub for a drink. I 'ave had a bit of a shock. So, is everything good here, are we making any money?"

"You bleddy are, I'm not sure I am."

"Is Jill learning the ropes alright."

"She is a bleddy good barmaid Maccy, like me, pay rise, hint!"

"What?"

"I'm hinting about how good I am at my job, Maccy."

"Alice, I know how good you are at most things, but all that was a very long time ago. How is the lad maid, I don't see much of him these days?"

"Engaged, engaged by post. He met some girl in the summer, and they are considering a future. I think she lives on Pitcairn Island, somewhere like that."

"Considering what, he's only bleddy seventeen for god's sake. Pitcairn? Everyone on Pitcairn is related to each other. I heard the kids all go around asking all the men if they are father. Another thing, I wouldn't trust Royal Mail, he'll end up with the wrong bleddy girl!"

"I think he and she are considering meeting. The girl found him on the internet. She's far enough away for now. If she lived here there would be hell to pay, I wouldn't see Danny at all."

"Why not maid?"

"Because they'd be in the bleddy bedroom all day, wouldn't they."

"And there was me thinking the boy took after me."

"Very funny Maccy Tamryn. Anyway, now about my pay rise?"

"What pay rise?"

"That's the one, boss."

"Wait until we do the new bar Alice, I'll sort it out then maid, one way or another, is that okay?"

"I suppose. Don't bleddy forget or I'll sort you out, one way, painfully."

"And in what way would that be my luvver?"

"In a way that bleddy 'urts my bird!"

"I won't forget Alice, promise, you knaw me."

"Yes I do, that's why I'm asking you not to forget, my luvver!"

"I bleddy won't forget! I will make things right."

"Ah, Tamryn, what are you doing here, slumming it?"

"You could say that, I own it as you probably know already."

"I haven't been in here for years, you reminded me it was here. It was a while ago Maccy, the good old days. What happened to them?"

"Not sure mate, I wasn't there. I had some of my own to deal with, they weren't all good in all honesty."

"And did you?"

"I'm getting there Mac, there's no rush. Might be a while yet." The haunted look still prevails, rather like my own possibly.

"Where have I heard that before?"

"This one's on me, Alice."

"Cheers mate, not stopping, just the one and back to the bleddy grindstone. You know how it is. I've got another bleddy appointment later."

It's always useful to have a spare brave face and Mac certainly has, even if it is edged with fear. I watch out of the corner of my eye as he slides the bunch of keys nearer to me than they are to him. I back away slightly, I wouldn't want him to think I'm considering picking them up. I wonder why he doesn't go to Scorrier and chuck them down a mineshaft? Better still, Illuggan, he wouldn't get them back then; folks from Illuggan never give anything away for nothing, I suppose the women might. It's the main reason I never go there myself, I can never refuse a bargain. I can make an exception in Illuggans' case, anyone with any sense can. For those not in the know, Illuggan is like Rock but with more class. Biased, me? Never! To be fair, it might have improved since I was last there.

As for Rock, it isn't as bad as it seems, especially when there's a particularly thick fog on the Camel. *Even the

German Luftwaffe couldn't be bothered to bomb the place when they had the chance in nineteen forty two. Waste of a good bomb, I suppose. They did in fact let a couple slip just up the road from the White Hart in what is now New Street, pity they missed. They dropped some on Bodmin, turned right and moved on to Truro where major havoc was caused. I did hear there are one or two unexploded in the Fal river at Truro. Apparently, they just sploshed and didn't go off. I've known of folks who have fallen in the Fal and not gone off. There's something to look forward to!

As for the Germans, they didn't know Truro had three rivers, so they didn't know which one to drop their bombs in. Most likely it was a case of eeny meeny miny mo and they went for the middle one! My guess is they were aiming for the Pannier Market, which at the time was full of Spitfire parts. Why anyone would mistake a large river for a load of Spitfire parts is totally beyond me. Anyway, there were no shoppers in the market at the time as there was no room for shops.

"See you around, Maccy."

"Not if I see you first sotto voce yeah, cheers Mac and thanks again."

I have a feeling I will be seeing more of Mac'. I have no idea what his first name is – he never disclosed it other than 'Mac' - what he does or where he resides. He made me nervous in his own obvious nervousness. Affable, edgy and an overall feeling of dread, quite a combination. For myself, I made a joke to Rio regarding the possibility of acquiring the building. I don't think so, it comes with far too many side-effects! I have always wanted to see inside its walls and now I have. Another visit is out of the question.

"I think I will forget the sex shop Alice, I don't believe it would be accepted."

"By who Maccy, the locals?" Alice comes alive whenever the three letter word is uttered. Rather than encourage her, I don't reply and exit the bar with speed.

"Been anywhere nice, husband?"

"I have been in the White Hart my little Texan."

"You've been inside there, did you meet any of the occupants?"

"I have been inside. I didn't meet any of them as such, they were around but a tad on the shy side I believe."

"More darned riddles Maccy, forget I asked."

"I will try, wife."

"Good. Maccy, we have someone on the Birdseye's old boat, you'll never guess who. Sounds like he's staying a while."

"How long a while?"

"He asked how long it is empty for and laid down a substantial amount once I told him no one is booked into the place. He's a bit odd according to Bessie, who showed him around the boat."

"Odd? He must have felt right at home with Bessie showing him around. You haven't seen him then, maid?"

"I sure have. His money is as good as anyone else's I guess, he must have a lot of it in cash."

"He paid in cash and it was a lot?"

"Sure did, enough to pay for all the work on the bleddy pigsty."

"I like the sound of that yank, I could never have asked Lenny to cough up. So who is it?"

"Michael!"

"Makes sense, there's no one odder. Where did he get that kind of money?"

"How should I know!"

"Bookies more than likely! If he's paid long term, we can't charge him holiday rates. He can stay out there as long as he likes. He must have fallen out with his old man again."

"Apparently the father has moved a woman into the house. Michael and her didn't hit it off, so he moved out."

"That's good and even better for Mike."

"Why is it good?"

"Easy, he can practice walking on water every day and nobody will bother him. It's good all round. He might even make the eels multiply quicker while he's out there."

"You darned blasphemer!"

"I knaw. I can't see him baking bread mind. I suppose we'll have to put up with a queue of strange women coming and going every day. He might even get to nail one of them down permanently, who knows? Seems to me we have almost as many folks living out here as there are in Little Petrock. We'll need a school and a doctor's surgery here soon enough."

"There's a new doctor living in the village by the way."

"Is there?"

"There is, strange bloke, rides a bicycle to the surgery in Padstow and back again every day. A foreigner I think."

"So you've seen him?"

"I have, sort of."

"How do you mean?"

"Hard to tell what with him in a woolly hat, gloves and scarf."

"It is winter, Rio."

"You got that right, don't I know it. The damned pond has thick ice on it."

"That's good, it means Michael can walk on the water easier. It's bleddy perfect. He'll feel right at home out there."

"Not that thick."

"Oh, I don't know, he idn't too smart."

"I meant the ice, you damned fool!"

"Speak of the bleddy devil and he shall appear!"

"That idn't funny Maccy, I have had to move out, the old man has lost the bleddy plot. He's playing loud bleddy music all the time. He should grow up."

"He's always been a crackpot mate. He is a grown up Michael, he's older than you are anyway."

"I should bleddy hope so, it would be wrong if he wadn't."

"I suppose you're right. So, you're gonna be a neighbour, Michael."

"Only if you don't play loud music all night."

"Michael, it's a bleddy pub."

"I knaw that Rio, but a working man needs to sleep at night."

"Guilty conscience, Michael."

"Shut it Tamryn, or I'll move out."

"You haven't moved in yet."

"It will make it easier then, won't it!"

"I'll help, just say the word."

"I'll say two, you know which ones."

"Just trying to be helpful to an old friend, Michael. Right, as you're getting mate's rates to live here and most likely eating out of the kitchen when you aren't too busy, you can help the lads at the pigsty. Another pair of hands would be useful, so long as they aren't pressed together all day long."

"Pray for me, Rio!"

"Pray for your damned self, Michael. You're the darned expert."

"You're wasting your time yank, he's supposed to be bleddy forgiving. In his case, it's for giving to himself."

"Get stuffed, landlord."

"Get lost cross dresser! You should carry a handbag mate. It would have to match, otherwise people will think you're a man!"

"Jealous?"

"Not in the slightest. Michael, just one other thing before you go looking for your hobnail boots. Don't wear your bleddy dress on the building site, the lads will start fancying you, they idn't too smart."

"Who can blame them, mate."

"I meant to say their eyesight isn't up to much."

"Much as I would like to stand around saving your soul all day, I have better things to do."

"That's okay my friend, just keep your hands where they can be seen, or you'll end up like Saul. Figuratively speaking of course."

"More bleddy blasphemy Maccy, where will it all end."

"Damascus mate and you'll have to go on a diet for three days!"

"Why don't we swap places, Maccy? You know more about the good book than I do. You wear the bleddy dress and I'll chuck good folks out through the window and pour beer."

"That was an accident, Alice that did it, not me. Yeah, you'll pour beer, down your bleddy throat. I'm not letting you get behind my bar mister, you'll be giving everybody broken biscuits and I won't have any Russian wine left."

"Wrong church, mate."

"Is it?"

"I think so. Maybe not. It's not important and anyway, you used to drink cider in the chapel and most of my bleddy whiskey."

"Shouldn't you know these things? Not at the same time."

"I'm off. I don't know everything, I'm new at the bleddy preaching malarkey!"

"Fancy a few frames, Michael?"

"Yeah, why not. I don't have to marry or bury anyone today as far as I know. It will be Christmas soon of course; party time!"

"Are you sure you're cut out for your line of work?"

"I have references, Tamryn."

"Yeah, me too, I'm coming with you."

"It's not allowed Rio, men only."

"Don't you bleddy dare try that on me, Tamryn. Either I can go or you can't. Make your damned mind up."

"She's right Maccy, you can't stop her boy, it's sexism. It's frowned upon these days, you bleddy dinosaur."

"Well, I'll tell you right now, I'm bleddy frowning. When did this all happen?"

"Not long ago since the beginning of time I think. It's just been slow in gathering popularity amongst us male heathens."

"Well it could have been a tad bleddy slower, it would have been more popular with me."

"You're pushing your luck Maccy Tamryn and I'm your luck!"

"Yes you are, maid."

She's right, he's right I know it. In all honesty, I'm not biased or sexist and I know the ladies do play snooker. It's just that even when we were tackers, Michael, Lenny and myself had used the loft as a safe haven and most times whilst skiving off from school. We would buy cheap beers or out of date cider and spend many hours in that great room, where there was never a female of any shape or size or colour present.

We did all play snooker and Rio enjoyed it as much as Michael and I did. It's what it should be all about. Nothing counts more than friends and families after all is said and done. I seem to have more than my fair share of both. I count myself lucky in that respect.

Author's notes:

* On Thursday, August 6, 1942, the unspeakable happened as Nazi air raids took place over Truro. German planes shot at Truro railway station with machine guns and bombs were dropped on the old Royal Infirmary Hospital, destroying the south wing. The first hint of trouble from the air was a report at around 7.31 pm that two German planes had been spotted near St Issey, coming in low and fast down the Camel Estuary. Reports suggest that 100 houses were left damaged and three demolished, with at least four people having to be pulled from the rubble. As well as the dead, more than 65 people were injured. On departing the Truro area, the same two planes machine gunned several farms, including Golden Manor Farm near Grampound, where two cows were destroyed.

Chapter Thirteen

Winds of change

"Where 'ave you been, Maccy? I thought you were gonna be here early today mucker."

"I did have to see a man about a bleddy dog, Lenny. Only the dog didn't turn up. The man did though, so it was half successful and a tad unfortunate."

"Oh, that old bleddy chestnut."

"No, it was about a dog mate, I did say, you were here when I said it."

"I heard you Maccy. I just don't believe I believe you."

"Firstly, I have been to the White Hart Inn, they didn't have any beer in there, they did only have some spirits. I wasn't impressed as I have a bit of a downer on spirits. Well I do now, unless they are in a glass, so I went to the Mermaid and Bow for a pint. It's a pity you weren't there mucker."

"Why was it a pity, Maccy? So you did have to drink out of the bottle then!"

"You could have bought me a pint, that way I would be better off by a couple of quid. T'wadnt them kind of spirits mucker."

"The old White Hart, eh. I heard it does 'ave a ghost or two mate. Is it true?"

"I believe you may have heard correctly Lenny, certainly about one anyway, there might be more. I did say 'spirits'. There was no actual proper introductions. I didn't 'ave time to count the buggers!"

"Bleddy 'ell Maccy, did you see any of them?"

"Naw mate, I didn't, unless push comes to shove. I don't really want to talk about it mate, t'wadn't nice. The old place would make a great bleddy strip joint Lenny, but I don't think the occupants would be too happy. I can't say for sure, I don't hear voices." I might, but I wouldn't tell Lenny, he would most likely get jealous.

"I don't knaw, I 'ave never been in a strip joint, Maccy. Anyway, I don't think you'd get away with it around here, mebbe over to Rock you would but you can't, can you mate. The White Hart is over here with the ghosts, I meant the bleddy ghosts are over here with the White Hart."

"They wouldn't know what to do with it in Rock, mate. Another thing, they might not want to live in Rock, they would take one look at it and come back on the bleddy ferry, same as I bleddy would. I have seen as much of Rock as I need to."

"Yeah, I hadn't thought of that Maccy, who could blame them."

"I went into a strip joint in Plymouth once, it was bleddy sad."

"Do you mean not good matey?"

"Naw, like in sad. We came home bleddy skint. T'was me and an old buddy who went, you know, the one who went off, Honkin Tonkin."

"I remember him. Where did he go off to, Maccy?"

"He went off girls and stuff, he went the other way. He was batting left handed I believe. It didn't make him a bad person mind."

"Which way did 'e go off to? Them poncy bleddy cricketers, you never know whether you can trust the buggers waving lumps of wood around for days on end and chucking stuff at just about anybody who gets in the way. What's the bleddy point of it? They play for days and no one ever wins the bleddy game, I don't get it."

"That idn't quite what I meant Lenny. Somebody does 'ave to play the bleddy game; unless it's raining, otherwise them that make cricket bats would be out of a bleddy job, balls too!"

"I wondered what happened to Honkin. So he became a weatherman, Maccy. Wait 'til I see him, he's bleddy crap! It's time he got a proper job like us. Did he turn into a woman mucker? Last time I saw the weather forecast 'ee was a woman. I thought it was bleddy strange at the time. Balls?"

"Them too! Anyway, I don't think so Lenny, he stayed what he was. What you might 'ave seen was an actual woman weatherman, a female. Honkin is still a man more or less. He was last time I saw 'im anyway but 'ee wadn't a weatherman, he was a labourer on a building site, a bit like us too. He was crap at that I did hear, he didn't knaw how to make tea."

"But you said ….."

"I did not Lenny, I said different to that. I meant different. I might 'ave confused you a tad, it was not my intention."

"I think you might 'ave, mucker."

"I didn't mean to, I was trying to be subtle you see."

"You idn't no good at it then mate. Maybe you should try and be like Honky, different."

"I don't wanna be like Honky. If I went like Honky I'd be just the same as Honky, not different at all. Us would be like twins!"

"Like a labourer on a building site, Maccy?"

"Yes Lenny, like I am now and like you are. I do reckon we'll 'ave to knock off early, it looks like rain coming in mate."

"So you do 'ave two jobs mate, like that bleddy politician, 'ee did 'ave two Jags. What looks like rain?"

"A bit like that Lenny, yes sort of, watery. As they say, 'if it looks like rain and it sounds like rain, that's what it is most likely'." Sometimes I wonder why I do this. I suppose it helps pass the time.

"If you're sure, Maccy. So, what did happen at this strip place then mucker?"

"A bit of this, a bit of that and almost a bit of the other, Lenny. There was a lot of multi-tasking going on if you get my meaning!"

"I idn't certain I do."

"I idn't what you might call certain either. How did we bleddy get here?"

"We did walk up the hill from the Maltsters buddy, don't you remember?"

"So, Honky got married then. Why did he do that, Maccy?"

"Bleddy 'ell, Lenny, wasn't it enough, I do 'ave a day job. He was a tad confused, still is I suppose. He reckoned he didn't know if he was coming, going or on the way back by the end. He did find out eventually. He gave himself away one night in the Mermaid and Bow when he had drunk too much, said he thinks his boyfriend is gay! The cat was out of the bag then sure enough!"

"So what did 'appen to the bleddy dog then, mate?"

"What bleddy dog?" I had completely forgotten about the animal.

"The one with the man you went to see."

"Bleddy 'ell, I told you before, the dog didn't turn up, it wadn't there."

"So what did you do after that, mate?"

"I went home mate, wouldn't you?"

"I most likely would, Maccy. So, Honky was never a weatherman then. You could be a weatherman Maccy, you know plenty about rain."

"I suppose I do but it doesn't mean I like it. In any case, it's better if it's a woman and she says heavy rain is coming in."

"Why is that, Maccy?"

"It's bleddy obvious mucker, she might change her mind. The women can do that at times."

"So ….."

"Stop right there Lenny, it's enough for one day."

Thank god that's all over. I was beginning to bore myself to death after a while. It isn't a suicidal way forward I had ever considered before. In fact, I have never considered suicide before today, it would just be a waste of time. I doubt I could put my mind to it. I firmly believe boring one's self to death would make a lot of other people bored! They would get bored etcetera and it could turn into a mass suicide. Where would it end? I almost wish I'd never mentioned Honkin Tonkin at all, it was hardly worth it.

"So mate, what are we supposed to be doing today?"

"If you make a start, I'll be back to give you a hand. I just need to make a couple of calls. Dusty will help out for now, at least while he's still more or less awake." I nearly said reliable, thank god I stopped myself. Dusty and reliability have never really worked well together. My brother never has got the hang of it.

"How many?"

"Fifteen."

"Ten!"

"Ten then but I might be a tad longer."

"Ten!"

"Lenny, if it idn't too much trouble, can you tell me just who is in charge of this building site?"

"Us lads boss, every one of us. We all thought you knew."

"Okay, I do now, mucker. I wouldn't want to step on anyone's bleddy toes."

It's official, the lunatics have finally taking over the asylum. Personally I wouldn't call swinging a pickaxe at a tree stump building site work. What I know about working on a building site could be written down on a postage stamp, but not by me, I have trouble writing on a postcard. Doesn't everyone? They must do, either that or I don't know anyone who ever goes on holiday. Which reminds me, the yank and I must think about a return to Kansas and keep some past promises made. Christmas needs to be used up first. The Kansas trip had completely slipped my mind. We do need to get the lovebirds into their nest before the Christmas celebrations. I need to instruct Bessie and his team – of which I am supposed to be a member – on how to obtain certain fittings for kitchen, bathroom, etcetera. I have just the place in mind. The milking shed is in line for stripping out, it's used for little else these days apart from brewing scrumpy, as they mostly only call it in Somerset. Not much of that has been done recently. The golden liquid can be produced easily in four or five weeks from scratch. It won't be happening this time of the year. They will have to go without as I will myself.

"Please don't step on my toes, Maccy."

"I won't Lenny. I'm going home now mate, best you do the same."

"Shall us walk together then? Maccy, wait for me buddy. We didn't get much done today mucker."

"We will work faster tomorrow, Lenny."

"How do you knaw?"

"Not now mate. You live that way mucker."

"I do?"

"You do." Lenny doesn't need help, just encouragement!

"So maid, we need to go away once Christmas is over and Lavinia has produced whatever it is she is lugging about with her. Not forgetting yourself of course. Might be best you don't take your time, yank."

"I'm pleased you remembered, Maccy Tamryn. She idn't much further on than I am so you best get to thinking about it."

"How can I forget. We will need a bigger bed soon enough. Have you told anyone?"

"Nope, I don't have any family to tell. We'll get to Kansas when the babby is a tad older. Do you know when Lavinia is due?"

"No idea, that's a woman's subject, isn't it?"

"Not in your case, husband."

"I could ask Lenny, he will most likely know, maybe not. No, I'll ask Lavinia. Any port in a storm!"

"If he's anything like you, he won't, so it might be best."

"I'll know when you bleddy tell me, maid."

"I ain't no maid, isn't it bleddy obvious? Why am I asking these stupid questions?"

"Habit maybe?" I realise I'm not doing myself any favours here.

"Damn you Brit, I'll ignore that! I need to clean my guns, I never know when I might need them, Tamryn."

"Did I tell you about the * White Hart? I went there today." It's wise to change the subject when the subject could have lethal consequences.

"You didn't bleddy buy it, tell me you didn't bleddy buy it."

"I didn't and I won't. I suddenly went off the idea and twice according to you. It's not for us maid. There's too many folks in there already."

"We don't need another darned pub, Maccy."

"We don't need the White Hart that's for sure. It's spooky as hell in there. The guy that showed me around was spooky enough before we even went inside." It was all far too creepy and enough to put me off. I have seen inside now, I don't need to do it again.

"In what way was the place creepy, husband?"

"I was pushed down half a dozen stairs kind of creepy."

"The guy pushed you downstairs, why would he do that?"

"No, the bloke didn't push me, he was nowhere near me. I was shoved down the stairs by someone I couldn't see. Whoever it was must have been behind me I suppose."

"That should teach you. Serves you right for meddling in unnecessarily in things. There were others in the building while you were there, Maccy? Did you go to the pub first?"

"No I didn't. I went to the Mermaid and Bow after. The bleddy place was empty of anyone but the two of us, empty of anyone we could see. So was the Mermaid. I suppose she was empty!"

"So, you're saying something, or somebody pushed you down some stairs but you didn't see anyone do it? You're plain crazy, Brit. So who else was in the Mermaid with you?"

"Mac, the bloke who showed me round the White Hart. He tried to give me the keys for the place. I told him I didn't bleddy want them."

"I don't blame you, you have enough trouble with living people."

"That's the truth!"

"So you're saying a ghost pushed you down the stairs, that's what you're saying, right? If it's as you say, I'm sure glad you didn't buy it. I wouldn't go in there my own self!"

It makes me feel like an idiot to say all this but there was no other explanation. It has got me to thinking that if the White Hart is haunted, then maybe the little the Bridge of Tears is also. It isn't the bats that live under there making all the noise, it's the children, poor little tackers. I'm not sure I really believed it until now. I will need to think again. The creek is as the rumours have it. It's not easy to say but I have always hoped it is true, which if it is, makes the place even sadder now. I should tell Lenny he doesn't cup his ears for no reason whenever he walks over the bridge. I have always said my mate is not as daft as he makes out. Lenny has been right all along, who would have thought it?

"Leave the light on, Brit."

"No way, there's no ghosts around here. ** Did I ever tell you about our grandpa? Dusty and I found him down the old quarry, stone cold. He looked as though he had been fighting with someone, but he wasn't killed, he just died there, so we were informed by the authorities, a heart attack."

"I don't think you did. You can tell me in the morning, no more tonight. Maybe best not to tell me any more at all."

"You scared, yank?"

"No Brit, just tired, tired of your constant yakking."

"I believe you yank, thousands wouldn't. Are you sure you aren't scared, yank?"

"Go to sleep Brit, remember my bleddy condition damn you."

"I'm not likely to forget yank. I'm not scared either, I've been shoved downstairs more times than I care to remember. I have been shoved upstairs more than once, mostly by you." Jen did carry me upstairs one time. I thought it best not to share any further information. I believe some things should never be shared. A guilty conscience is only acceptable when it is fully deserved. Only then can it be shared with friends but not with immediate family.

"Make sure you don't!"

She who should be obeyed will be, more or less. What I have to do to keep everyone happy. Just how is it possible to bend over backwards. I have made every conceivable effort, it just doesn't work for me. Can anyone actually bend over backwards whilst keeping a straight face and a straight back and not receive a double hernia? Many times I have heard false claims of this phenomenon. I can only assume the world is full of liars! Think on. The next person I hear make such a claim will receive this answer; prove it by taking a photograph, a 'selfie', whatever that means. I have no idea, but it seems everyone's saying it. I just think it shouldn't be too difficult; one might put a camera between one's legs point it upwards, snap and Rob's your uncle!. Personally I don't believe it is something which will catch on but what do I know? Just remember, you heard it here first.

"Rio."

"Now what?"

"Is ours your first?"

"Can I think about it, honey?"

"If you have to, I suppose. Shouldn't you remember, maid?"

"I guess I should at that husband, I will surely try."

"Um, so?"

"I'm trying to remember, give me a damn chance."

"Oh, how long do you need, maid?"

"Ya see, you gave yourself the answer all by your ownself. As long as it takes"

"I did?"

"Sure you did!"

"What was it?"

"Never mind, husband."

Peace at last and it allows me to think about today's excursion into the supernatural. I doubt I will ever visit the White Hart again, I'm certain I won't. Why would I need to be shoved around by someone who's been dead for years? It's bad enough being manhandled by the living. To be fair, it might not have been a man at all. My bucket list just got shortened by one. I think it might be non-existent now. When I think about it, I've done bucket loads of stuff that was never on it at all. I've been doing unpaid overtime in effect.

"Serves you right, Brit!"

"Don't you ever give up, yank? I don't read your bleddy mind!"

"Best you don't try, Brit."

"Oh I won't, it's bad enough listening to you talk in your sleep!"

"Don't listen and don't believe a word I say."

"Don't worry yourself, I never do!" I felt I had to lie, I don't get the chance very often.

Author's notes:

* At the corner of Strand Street and New Road, Padstow stands what was once the ancient White Hart Inn. Records suggest the Inn may have ceased to trade in the late nineteenth century. Records of only three incumbents can be noted: Around 1830 the landlord was a William Ibbott, 1844, one Moses May and almost certainly the last person to hold the post at the inn was Mary Bennett circa 1856. There may well have been others but no record exists as far as this author is aware.

** This is explained in the 'Mermaid and Bow' by this author.

Chapter Fourteen

A Tramp, a Lady and a Vicar

"Mister Tamryn, Maccy, can I talk to you if you're not too involved in whatever it is you're doing if anything. I wouldn't ask, it is important."

Just what I need first thing in the morning, a serious conversation. "Sounds official. Sure, what can I do for you? By the way Lyndsey, what's happened to the tramp, sorry, I mean your mother, my aunt. Is she really my aunt, is she really a tramp? Where is she anyway?"

"It's what I wanted to talk to you about and no, she isn't a tramp. She's just a bit eccentric, a bit like yourself pretty much. Having said all of that, she is in a bit of a mess at the moment. I am pretty sure she is your aunt, I'm not that certain myself. Anyway, that's not important right now. What is important is I believe that she is in a bit of trouble. I can't tell you everything right at the moment as I don't know much myself. I will tell you when I know more if that is acceptable? You might need to know, it may concern you. We will have to wait and see."

"Eccentric, me? Yes I can see why you would think that. Anyway maid, does she need money or something, what kind of trouble, serious?"

"Serious, as I said. I don't know what she needs, I need to see her and find out what exactly is going on."

"So where is she living then, I haven't seen her for bleddy months, longer."

"It's a bit difficult. She is seeing Peter and it seems they may be getting serious. That's as much as I know right now. Tell me, what do you know about him, Maccy?"

"Our Peter? So that's where he's been sneaking off to, the dirty git. In all honesty Lyndsey, I don't know a lot about him, I did give him work, I don't regret it, he's more than useful. He's a decent bloke too as far as I know. I can't tell you much about him apart from he's from Devon, it's not his fault, it should not be held against him, somebody has to come from there." I'm just glad I am not a Devonian, I couldn't be doing with all that malarkey. They don't even have pasties there, they're not allowed. Devon is officially not a 'Cornish Pasty' producing county.

"Yeah, yeah, they have been seeing each other for a while, Maccy. You would hardly recognise my mother since she moved to St Columb. I saw her a few days ago, Peter was there. I had no idea until then. I very quickly made myself scarce. I need some time off to go back and see her, to find out how serious they are. Mother can be easily led, she can also lead just as easily."

"I have news for you, so can Peter. Sounds like they're two of a kind. I thought only opposites attract maid! Okay, you get to doing what you need to, we can manage for a day or two if you need that long. Will you get back for when the big day arrives? We're gonna need you then most likely."

"A couple of days Maccy, that is all I will require, I don't tend to waste time."

"Rio can do your work while you're away, she needs to keep busy, so get going maid. Keep in touch yeah, let me know what's happening."

"I will, thank you boss. Can you keep Peter busy while I'm gone, I want to see her on her own, it would be better that way. By the way, is Rio pregnant?"

"Tis a mystery to me maid but I would put money on it. I don't think you have anything to worry about, I believe he's a good man, I'm sure of it. How did she snare him? That wasn't very diplomatic of me. Anyway, Rio wants to keep things low key until after Lenny and Lavinia's expected arrival."

"It's a mystery to me to, Maccy. Like I said, you would hardly know her now the beard has gone. Obviously it wasn't actually a beard cousin, it was the fur collar on her coat, which reminds me, half of it was missing, so I put it in a black bag for collection. You wouldn't know what happened to it would you?"

"Maybe, maybe not. It came away in my hand, her beard was in her pocket. It was an accident."

"Your secret is safe as far as I am concerned, the coat has left the building."

"I know that maid, thank you. I didn't know who she was when she turned up at the wedding."

So you're about to be a father again?"

"I only have the one."

"One what?"

"It's a bleddy secret. If I tell you, you'll know."

"Maccy, don't think I don't already. The boy with Alice, he is yours, isn't he?"

"What makes you think that?"

"I'm not stupid despite what you might think. You might as well put a sign on him or yourself. So can I borrow your car please, let me rephrase that, give me your car keys!"

"Help yourself, maid. Do you need my wallet, cousin? There's little in it. Believe me, stupid is the last thing I would take you for."

"I assumed that and took the possibility into consideration, I decided, rightfully. It isn't right to ask you for anything more than I need, I have money thank you."

"You best get to doing whatever you need to, the car is out back, not a lot of fuel in it."

"Wallet please."

"Sure maid, help yourself." What could I say?

"It's okay, I was just testing the water cousin. Keep it, I'll let you know if and when I need it."

I am not at all nervous regarding what she thinks she knows. On second thoughts I might be. The pigsty is almost complete. Another couple of weeks or so will see Lenny and Lavinia with their front door key. It will allow them to name their day and a short time after that, they'll be able to name the baby. Why do people do everything the wrong way around these days? Anyway, it doesn't really matter, I'm all for them getting together, it's about time my mate settled down. I know he will be a great husband and a brilliant dad, I just wonder if he knows himself. My mate does have the perfect temperament. I can't wait to see his face when he has a baby in his hands. He doesn't know it yet but it will have company. Rio and I are keeping quiet for now, not wanting to steal their thunder. We both agreed to wait a while before making an announcement. Rio is keeping a low profile for a while. It hasn't been easy, certain comments have been made by MJ already. Bribery is always a good fallback, I should know, though I would rather it didn't become common knowledge. It will be my fault Lyndsey knows.

"Alice, is that you?"

"Why don't you come here and find out? I could answer all your questions at the same time"

"Stop it woman, I'm a married man in case you'd forgotten."

"So am I!"

"Yes, you probably are maid. Never mind, I'm sure you'll be fine in the morning."

"You know very well what I'm like in the mornings, Maccy."

"I still remember, even though it's so bleddy long ago."

"Seems to me you need reminding mister."

"No I don't. How are Mervyn and the boy?"

"Have you become a saint, Maccy Tamryn?"

"I don't believe so, I thought about it and decided against it."

"A good choice, it wouldn't suit you. Let me know if you change your mind."

"I will maid."

"Make sure you do. What do you want anyway, I'm bleddy busy."

"Nothing, just calling to see how things are."

"Pretty quiet, we haven't had a decent fight here for months."

"We don't need fighting Alice, what did I tell you. We need to be pukka now, those days are gone. Not spending time in A& E or the bleddy police station for hours on end has allowed us to get the pigsty almost finished. Not long now. We're saving money in bribes and fines."

"Do you have to call it a pigsty, my brother has to live in it you know."

"It'll be like a home from home Alice, they should take to it perfectly. Lavinia's okay once you get used to her, maid."

"Damn you, Tamryn."

"You don't mean that, Alice."

"Can you go and annoy someone else now Maccy, I'm too bleddy busy to argue with you."

"Yes Alice, thank you for the chat. Is there anything else I can do for you?"

"Are you still bleddy there?"

"Charming!" Alice and I get into these heavyweight conversations now and then. We both know we're joking, a bit of playful teasing, so no harm done. She is a great bar manager, an even better manageress, as is her brother, who is of the opposite sex of course. When it all started, Lenny was coming in with me. I knew he wouldn't go the distance, but it did no harm to ask him. Almost ever since, Lenny and his sister have built up the Mermaid's trade. It's still going in the same direction even though we've lost a lot of our regulars along the way. One by one, long serving members of the old crew have disappeared into the serene silence of * God's Half Acre, the Padstow cemetery that lies on the very edge of the old town.

I'm not sure what to think regarding Peter and Lyndsay's mother. It doesn't matter, it's none of my business. I clearly remember when Lyndsay's mother arrived, it was my wedding day. In fact, both mother and daughter appeared for the first time that day, neither knew the other would be present from what they both told me later. Fair to say, Lyndsey took it all in her stride. I have no reason to think she won't handle this current situation equally efficiently. I would not be at all surprised if 'efficient' is her middle name, no situation seems to faze her. I believe it to be a useful attribute, one I doubt I could ever aspire too.

I firmly believe she will solve any problems regarding the two protagonists. There may not actually be a problem in any case. From what I know of her already, she is ultra-careful about most things. The happiness of her mother will be uppermost in her mind and rightly so. Nothing wrong with that, Dusty and I were much the same before our father, Padraig, returned to the fold. As it turned out, our ma was able to deal with everything herself. Dusty and I would most likely have gone in a bit heavy handed. Instead, ma went in heavy handed and flattened our errant parent! Since then he has behaved impeccably. I expect everything to turn out for the best for Lyndsey, as it did for us.

"Is everything prepared, Bessie?"

"Yes and no, Maccy. Some of this stuff is a bit past it to say the least, mate."

"Do you mean the stuff in the milking shed?"

"Yep, mostly scrap crap! I wouldn't be surprised if a scrapyard turned it all down, mate."

"I had a feeling it might be. Best get whatever we need ordered then buddy. I'll leave it with you."

I knew it was a bad day to give up smoking cigars. Just when you need one, they're on a shelf in a shop. As there is no shop within a couple of miles, it would seem ridiculous to drive a six or seven mile round trip to buy something I'm only going to set fire to and let smoulder for ten minutes. It would have burnt away by the time I got back and I'd have to go and get another one. I refrain from even continuing to consider it. That and the fact Rio has forbidden me to smoke anywhere near the Maltsters Arms due to the fact she is carrying a 'tiny child'. There was no need to remind me of the tiny child, it is the way they always tend to be in my experience. To be fair, ma has always insisted that isn't the way they always tend to be. I won't go into it but suffice to say, Dusty is around sixteen stone bone dry and I'm close at seventeen stone soaking wet. Needless to say, I am rather pleased I am about to become a father again. Dusty hasn't decided to take that road yet. I guess his lady friend, Selina, has decided the same. She is still about the place on her time off and it is hoped that one of these days, the day will not be a day off for the usual reasons and that the two might spend an hour or two of it vowing stuff to Michael the Mad! That is if Michael feels like doing any work. Most of the time he seems to be working from home, not his usual workplace. The cause of this might be down to my mate suddenly becoming human again and spending said time with an opposite version of a human in a boat on my lake. I refuse to draw pictures, just work it out for yourself!

As for Lenny's plumbing for the pigsty, I did wonder if lead piping might have gone out of fashion these days and it seems it has. Something to do with folks going a bit round the U bend from drinking the water supplied from such. Apparently it became a no no around nineteen seventy. No bugger told me. It's a good job we aren't still keeping cows, they would all be as mad as cows by now. I'm very sympathetic as I like cows very much, they are docile even when noisy. A cow has never offended me even if I did have to slap one once. It was standing in the middle of the road and holding up the traffic. It was not attempting to direct traffic at the time, it was surely just bored with standing around in a field directing other cows, I suppose. Nothing wrong with that, one cow is more likely to take notice of another one, even more so if the other one doesn't seem to have udders – or bagpipes as we used to call them as kids – dangling down to the ground with all sorts of insects crawling over their supply section to the food chain. How can that be better than drinking from a lead pipe?

Lyndsey was as good as her word and returned within the two days.

"So maid, how did it go with your mum?"

"I am not sure Maccy, I don't really know. I think it is all okay from what I learned."

"Is she seeing Peter then?"

"Yes she is. He is moving in with her. I am okay with it, I think. If she is happy, I should be. Peter is my biggest worry."

"Why's that, maid?"

"Mother is a bit changeable. I don't know if he knows what he is letting himself in for."

"Think of it this way Lyndsey, Peter can be different too. Just let them get on with it and see what happens maid, it's all you can do."

"Mother is a naturist, Maccy."

"Well, there's nothing wrong with nature. We all like it, don't we."

"No, no, she's a naturist, she tends to walk around completely naked. Do you see what I mean?"

"Well thankfully Lyndsey, I don't see what you mean. I do understand, I wouldn't worry, Peter might be okay with it, mightn't he."

"Oh he is! When I arrived there, they were both mostly naked but eating and drinking tea at the table thankfully."

"And you're not happy with it, is that right?"

"That is correct, Maccy."

"Lyndsey, when I was a tacker there used to be an advert on the TV. Chimps sat at a table eating and drinking tea, they were pretty much naked too. Everyone in the country watched them for years."

"You're not taking this seriously, Maccy."

"Yes I am, it's just that if that's what they like, who can say they shouldn't? To be fair, the chimps most likely got paid. Unfortunately, they probably didn't know what to do with the cash. A trip to the zoo perhaps!"

"Yeah yeah, that's very good boss."

"Live and let live maid, we're all different. Let them get on with it. If they're happy, then so be it."

"I took mine off too!"

"Right, okay, well done. So, how did you feel?"

"Fucking cold, Maccy!"

I did not expect that comment. I almost wished I hadn't asked. So it seems Lyndsey has a mild case of Tourette's.

"Well there is little else to say after that, Oh, except one thing."

"What thing?"

"I'm just glad she didn't do it at my wedding maid, she would have put us off our bleddy food!"

"Very funny."

"So, will you do it again, maid?"

"Not bleddy likely, once is enough!"

"Fair enough. There you are you see, we're all different. You did something you've never done before today. Variety is the spice of life!" I learnt something myself from Lyndsey's story. I wouldn't do it either. What was I thinking at eighteen when I ran up and down the quay completely starkers half a dozen times on a freezing cold night? I must have not been thinking too well that evening. It may have had something to do with the fact I was half pissed. It was my eighteenth birthday. I did win the 'Padstow Chase' for the only time in my life! There has not and will not be another.

I remember an old friend of mine running around in her home town dressed as a cave woman on her birthday. She was looking for a club apparently, 'club' get it? I guess we don't think too much at eighteen. I know one thing, Lyndsey at thirty five or whatever she is, has guts! Got to give the nutjob her due. I've never heard the welsh woman swear before today. Well done to the Welsh for using the same word we do!

Her mother may have once been a tramp, whose daughter may once have been a lady. A reassessment may now be in order, it's not my job, it's none of my business!

My present task is to get the pigsty finished, get the Maltsters and the Mermaid through Christmas, become a father for the umpteenth time – actually for just the third time – and make sure everyone has a good time without getting arrested or pregnant. Actually, I won't get involved with curtailing any horizontal pleasures that may occur, or any that aren't in fact horizontal. I will look the other way, turn the other cheek in fact. None of this should be too difficult. I am kidding no one.

It's all hands to the pumps. Myself, Bessie, Dusty, Jack, Lenny and the old man will complete the pigsty. One other will join us as soon as I've had a chance to talk to Peter. So far, it has all gone to plan. If it continues, the sty will no longer be vacant, it will be engaged for want of a better term. Quite apt really as Lenny had proposed and had been accepted by Lavinia just last night. There was a celebration of sorts, everyone got pissed pretty quickly and all, but one went to bed before midnight with the knowledge the pigsty should be finished before Christmas.

I decided to take the goat for a late night walk. As I approached a sign telling me that Hal had been buried somewhere close by, the vicar approached me.

"Evening vicar!"

"Maccy, you're out late."

Now after this short, friendly greeting, I decided it was an ideal opportunity to mention what I had recently seen, the meeting between him and the daughter of Lil. I was careful!

"I often am vicar. I used to walk the dog this way after the pub has closed. He's gone to the great lamp post in the sky now, poor old thing. I still do the walk vicar. Actually, I saw you last time I did it, you were chatting to a lady."

"I remember. You are wondering why a man of the cloth was out late with a, shall we say, a 'lady of the late evening'. Nice goat!"

"It crossed my mind, vicar. It isn't my goat, I'm looking after it for a friend." The vicar is stalling somewhat to explain his actions.

"Good man! Maccy, I know how it might have looked to anyone who was about at the time, I will explain."

Instantly I decide I would not push him. Something in his tone tells me the meeting must have been completely innocent. It has to be, why else would he want to explain it to me now?

"As you might be aware Maccy, the minister and I are friends, always have been. It's very much the same for publicans, isn't it?"

"Pretty much vicar yes, in a love hate sort of way."

"I will continue my friend. The minister has been seeing the lady for a while. I talked to him about it and advised he should cease. He agreed with a heavy heart but has been too afraid to tell her himself. I should add here, no money has ever changed hands, that's what he has told me and I believe him. The two had a friendship that got out of hand so to speak. I offered to be his mediator. Tonight she called me and asked that we might meet and discuss the decision."

"It all sounds plausible, vicar."

"It does and it will be. The lady has decided she will back away and put it all down to a hopeless fling."

"Okay, so it has ended?"

"It has Maccy and no harm done, I hope. One can't be certain of course. It may depend on who may have seen the two together."

"No one will hear about it from me. The Texan already knows obviously but only I know she knows, I hope."

"Thank you Maccy, that would be a perfect result for everyone. I won't mention seeing you out with your goat to anyone."

"I think it will vicar. Shall we walk back, a nightcap maybe?"

"Capital Maccy, why not. Lead the way old son."

I am becoming a pillar of the community. The vicar is asking me stuff, almost requesting favours. I never thought this would happen. What will I tell people. My reputation is slipping, the locals will notice. The old feller will be sending me a Christmas card next, I'll be drinking sherry in his drawing room or his study; the two are probably the same thing anyway. Now the vicar and I are about to have a lock in! That is a worry. There is no going back now, I have become responsible, maybe even a pillar of the community, albeit a short one.

"Come in vicar."

"Reg."

"Come in Reg, park your arse, brandy mate?" That just about does it! Reg the vicar and I are bosom buddies, we're on first name terms, me and a man of the cloth, fancy that.

Another man of the cloth. How can I forget Michael, who could forget Michael?

"Capital Maccy, nicely put landlord. Always wanted to do this."

"Sorry vicar, Reg."

"Not at all Maccy, this is just perfect. I'm slumming it in the boozer with the landlord and we're having a lock in, oh joy of joys, me old mucker. Jingle bleddy bells, jingle bleddy bells, oh what fun it is, get me a sleigh and a donkey Maccy, and another brandy while you're up!"

"What have I done? Jesus Christ, I've ruined the vicar, I will become the unforgiven! Shit, I thought I was only thinking that, sorry Reg."

"Can I have a packet of pork scratchings Maccy, and a cigar too. Drink up mucker, take it out of that? So, is it your goat?"

"What goat?"

This is a dream, it must be. The vicar is giving me money, that can't be right. I'll get run out of the bleddy village. The vicar has turned into me! I've turned into reasonable and respectable. Okay, I'll concede, respectable. The vicar has become a yob and I am a snob. Why am I bothering, he's already asleep.

There is only one thing for it. After checking the locks, I throw a throw over him and leg it to bed. What am I going to tell people? I will have to be first up in the morning or my life won't be worth living, I'll be a laughing stock. I can see the headlines now; 'Maccy gets vicar pissed!' God help us all, God help me!

Authors' notes:

* God's Half Acre is how most Padstow locals describe the serenity of the cemetery on the outskirts of Padstow. They continue to do so at time of writing. MB

Chapter Fifteen

A Vicar's Redemption

The funny thing is, I have been told the vicar is mad. He will be when I wake him up. He'll be bringing down the thunder, that's what he'll be doing. One stupid night and I have ruined it all, my reputation will be in even more tatters. The lads will crucify me if the vicar doesn't do it first. No, no, he will forgive me, that's what they do, it's their job, isn't it? They wash away your sins. I'll need a bath or an hour under the shower, I'll shrink! Knowing my luck it'll be an acid bath! Stupid is as stupid does. It was Michael who told me the vicar is round the bend. What the hell is the mad minister going to say about me when he finds out the opposition and I are bosom buddies? 'Sinner', that's what he'll call me. 'A damn heathen sinner'! What are my mates going to say. I won't have any after this.

"Shouldn't you be dressed when you come down, Maccy."

"I had to let the dog out maid."

"We don't have a dog, we have a goat and he's already out."

"That's what I meant, I had to let the bleddy goat out but I couldn't find it to let it out so I wasn't able to. I should go and look for him."

"Liar, you bleddy liar Maccy Tamryn, stay here and tell the truth now."

"Alright, I'm actually looking for a vicar, Jill. I think I might have mislaid him. He might still be here somewhere with a hangover. Have you seen him?"

"There was a spare one in the bar with a fry up. He looked like he might be a spare something. Do you want what he's having?"

"Me, I want forgiveness Jill, I don't need the back door bleddy trots. I'm not sure I want to share a plate with him."

"You know what I mean. I've got bacon and scrambled eggs ready but if you don't want them….."

"Okay, I'll start with that. Then I will need forgiveness, a large helping please."

"Forgiveness is between you and your own god, Maccy."

"That's all very well but I don't have my own, I just have Mikey."

"Blasphemer!"

"I'll likely be struck down by a lightning bolt drekly, I wouldn't be surprised maid. One good thing, I won't know much about it, will I? Every thundercloud has a silver lining I guess."

"I expect you'll deserve it, Mac. Anyway, your vicar is in the bog at the moment. It's the same one, not another one. You can go and tell him his breakfast will go bleddy cold!"

"I'm not his keeper!"

"The vicar should be thankful for small mercies!"

"Can I have some bread with this maid."

"Stop it now, that's enough. You're pushing your luck boss. I don't want to be anywhere near you when it arrives."

"When what arrives?"

"Your bleddy lightning bolt!"

"I suppose you're right. It wasn't my fault maid, I was talking to the vicar up the lane last night and innocently asked him if he wanted a nightcap. That's all it was. He had a couple of brandies and turned into Cliff Richard at bleddy Christmas, without the mistletoe. He just had the one brandy and almost a bottle of wine. I didn't do anything but be hospitable, it's my job. He's a crap singer. I doubt he can play tennis or the guitar. To be fair, neither can I but I wasn't pretending to be Elton John."

"Cliff Richard!"

"Or him. What will I do maid?"

"Firstly Maccy, you should see if the vicar is okay, after that you need to be toiling with the lads at the bleddy pigsty."

"Shit, the lads. They're gonna make me suffer, I know they are. I'll have to go begging without a bowl."

"On the street, Maccy?"

"No, on the bleddy building site maid."

"Maccy my luvver, where are you?"

"In the kitchen my dear Texan, having breakfast with Jill."

"So, who's in the bog then, Brit?"

"The vicar my love."

"That's just great. I just told him 'pull your trousers up and get to bleddy work you lazy shyster'. I'm gonna be struck down Maccy!"

It just gets better at getting worse. "Why didn't you just say, 'get your arse in gear you lazy tosser'?"

"I said that too Brit, there was no answer. There's still no answer."

"Oh hell!"

"He did say that, Maccy. Why is the vicar in our rest room husband?"

"I can't really say dear."

"Yes you bleddy can. Is he volunteering to help with the pigsty then?"

"I bleddy hope not, I'm praying he won't, missus."

"Please don't call me that, Macdonald Tamryn."

"Morning vicar, sleep well?"

"Morning mucker. Not really, my back is playing up and some bleddy skivvy just told me to piss or get off the bleddy pot. What kind of people do you have working here for heaven's sake?"

"I have the dregs of society, Reg. Have you met my wife? I don't know who could have said such a thing. I will give whoever it was a verbal warning when I find out. I will leave no stone unturned until I get to the bottom of it."

"Maccy it was ….."

"Yes please maid, more coffee, thank you. Off you go now and feed the goat."

"About the goat Maccy, oh dear, oh dear, a sign of the devil old son."

"Funny that, I had a feeling the bugger had been around recently."

"You might need a cleansing old boy."

"Nah you're alright Reg, he'll be gone to your church to steal the collection cash now."

"And so must I mate. Thank you all for your hospitality, must fly."

"I wouldn't do that if I were you Reg, isn't it witches that do that?"

"No such thing Maccy, no such thing old son."

"Okay, on your head be it vicar. Have a good day, don't do anything I wouldn't do."

"Oh I will Maccy, I will."

"Cheers Reg."

"Damn and blast it to hell, bleddy seagulls!"

"You okay vicar?"

"No, I need some toilet paper, Maccy."

"You didn't shit yourself, did you Reg?"

"No Maccy, I didn't, a bleddy seagull just crapped on my Uncle Ned."

"Well Reg, let's just hope it was a seagull, eh? It couldn't have been a witch could it, there's no such thing!" Oh god, Reg is employing rhyming slang now, I will never hear the last of it.

"Pray for it Maccy, I'm off to buy a twelve bore. We'll see how it likes a cartridge up the bleddy jacksy. See you later mucker. Thank you again Maccy for releasing me, I feel rather liberated!"

"No need Reg, you did it yourself."

"Nevertheless."

"Bye Reg."

This is a bit weird. The vicar and I have just grunted at each other occasionally over the years, now he's Reg and I'm his mucker. It will all take some getting used to. He'll be wanting me to go to Wimbledon with him next summer, eating strawberries and cream and calling out 'love' every two minutes. It'll be life in the fast lane from now on, actually more like life in the church aisle I reckon. I'll be singing in the church choir this time next year. We'll be holding the harvest festival in the Bar of Doom next. I have to shake myself out of this quickly. I do seem to have damaged the vicar.

"MACCY!"

"Yes, my lovely yank."

"Are you calling the vicar Reg now?"

"Yes dear, but I think it's always been his name."

"You'll be singing Christmas Carols in the choir next. You can't be calling the vicar Reg."

"Don't be so bleddy daft wife, the vicar told me to call him Reg. It's far better than calling him Rev' isn't it? I didn't ask to, he insisted." I can't believe I have solved the vicars problem as well as the methy ministers dad's problem, both at the same time in one late night drink. I could be an agony aunt. If the yank gets her way, it'll be my own agony, she will be seen cleaning her pistols again. I don't like it when she does that, she can be rather thorough!

"Right lads, how far have we got?"

"About as far as you did with the vicar last night boss."

I knew it, if one farts at one end of the village, it's known about at the other within just two minutes. These lot remind me of old Bert, the cleaner at the café next to the Mermaid and Bow. Now Bert was always one for gossip. If he didn't hear any, he would make some up and everyone would be talking about it ten minutes later, even in the godforsaken place the other side of the estuary most likely. Bert was my friend and confidante back in the day when I was just past being a kid. If I wanted advice Bert would give it without even being asked. Bert was a psychic, floor cleaner and cash collector. He also had a large collection of hearing aids. Pensioners from a tour bus would drop them, Bert would pick them up and not know who they belonged to. Then none of the pensioners could talk to each other because none of them could hear what they might be saying, except Bert of course. He would have one in each ear while he pointlessly collected gossip about people who had travelled from Shepherds Bush, Manchester and even Devon. We don't get many Devonians here, thank the lord. I miss Bert, he was a good friend and mentor.

Now even Lil is still visible by her daughter. I don't know her name but I will find out. She will always be welcome in our pubs as was her mother. Lil the Tart was one of us, one of the Mermaid's crew. The new woman may take after her mother. That's her choice, I don't judge anyone, I don't have the right. No one has the right. 'He who casts the first stone'! I'll be safe, no one would pay for my body, maybe Alice would!

"We need to get on with some work lads. Lenny says he is cheesed off with sleeping in the draughty bus shelter."

"So where's Lavinia sleeping then boss?" The choir are at it again, why can't they just speak individually?

"In the other one across the road, it doesn't have a hole in the roof. Think on, it could be you lot. Let's get to it you bunch of useless tossers."

"Yes boss."

"That's more like it, we're all on the same hymn sheet more or less." It's a pity none of us can actually sing anything worth a damn. It's not for a lack of individual literary or vocal skills; most of us can read. It really comes down to faulty vocal chords and the lack of evidence of their existence. Nobody present will complain of my speaking up for them.

"Who is painting inside and who is painting outside? By the way, who paid over the bribes to the bloke at the …., never mind, so long as they were paid, he'll keep quiet probably."

"You did boss."

"I'll see him later and pass on a gentle reminder. Then I couldn't have been off skiving every day, could I?"

"No boss, anyway, hardly any of us said you had."

"What does a man have to do to get some respect around here?"

"Nothing boss."

"Once more and I'll quit and get myself a proper job, just one more."

*"Cornetto, boss?"

"Koff you tossers!, put the kettle on someone. Who got the milk, why is there a dirty trowel in the bleddy toaster?"

"Bread got stuck boss, we couldn't find a clean one."

"You know you should use a screwdriver or a chisel, bleddy 'ell, can't any of you get anything right?"

"Sorry boss."

"Maybe you would all like to try and get it out. Wait a mo, I'll plug it in for you first. Right, there you go, carry on."

"Thanks boss."

"Maccy old son!"

"Reg, have you come to lend us a hand?"

"How's it hanging mucker? No, I'm on official business, I've come to thank you all for what you are doing for your good friends, Lenny and Lavinia. It is wonderful to see you all working together for such an excellent cause, my children. You are a great credit to yourselves."

"So you're saying he knows what we are doing and he is all for it."

"Of course he does Muccy, sorry, I mean Maccy."

"Mucker? Children? We don't employ kids here. On second thoughts you could be near the mark. Look, we're a bit pushed for a minute vicar, can you see if you can get that slice of bread out of the toaster please, it seems to be stuck and we've all got grubby hands, building site hands you see. We'll only make it all dirty and won't be able to eat it."

"Even god has a sense of humour my children. He'll bleddy need it when you lot turn up at his door, gate. Where are your paracetamol?"

"Fair play to you vicar. We hope your congregation shrinks. In the back of the van next to the toilet roll."

"Pardon?"

"Nothing vicar."

"Maccy, best you unplug it, we can't electrocute the bleddy vicar, boss!"

"Fair enough I suppose, I wasn't thinking straight."

"Thanks boss. By the way, hope you're guts aren't complaining, there's no toilet roll left in the van. The paracetamol are all gone too."

"I've got some spare paper you can have lads, only three sheets though, sorry. I had better get going now. Thank you for your welcome. By the way, if you see a strange ladder knocking around, please let me know. The bleddy thing has gone walkabout again. I should have bought a longer one, it would be easier to find, harder to borrow without my knowledge. It always seems to be going missing."

"We will Vic. Dusty might have borrowed it."

"Why would Dusty borrow it?"

"To go up it vicar."

"That seems to be okay then."

"Thank you vicar, for all your help."

"Oh dear oh dear lads, it's raining in your tea. I think you should unplug the toaster now or cover it up. Never mind. Ciao and Hasta La Vista boys. See you down there!"

"Down where vicar?"

"Down on your hands and knees, kiss my ring."

"That's bleddy charming."

"Reg? Bleddy Reg, everything's Bleddy Reg now! 'Morning Maccy, morning Reg, ffs!"

"Shut it you lot, paint, paint like you never have before. Oh I'm sorry, I see you already have. My bleddy kids could do a better job than you lot. One of them hasn't even arrived yet. Sort it out lads, we don't have long before it's bleddy New Year's Day and the county is full of a fresh load of emmets."

"That's all very well boss but do you know where they are? Do you know who they are?"

"I don't need to, I'm just bleddy pleased it's none of you lot."

"So are we boss."

"Koff the bleddy lot of you. Wait, one of you can stay and put the kettle on. You can toss for it, you're all fully qualified tossers." My days as a building site manager may be numbered but I have put everything I have into it. It's just a pity I seem to have damaged a vicar in the process. You can't build an omelette without cracking some heads, I mean eggs, or do I?

"Jill, why was the vicar in the restroom this morning?"

"I think he was a bit poorly Rio, Maccy got him drunk last night, he was throwing up, so I believe. It sounded like he was talking to his boss on the big white telephone, he definitely called someone hands free. He isn't very happy with you either, Rio."

"There sure is no end to my husband's talents. One of these days he'll go too bleddy far. Why me?"

"You told him to piss or get off the pot."

"The vicar, did I, surely not, darn it!"

"Afraid so."

"It may have been someone who sounded like me, Jill. He seems to have gone off the rails a little."

"The vicar?"

"My husband."

"It would seem so."

The pigsty's kitchen is in the kitchen now and working pretty much as it should. The first coats of paint are drying. The garden is drying out after all the flooding, not by heavy bouts of rain, someone managed to leave the hose on all night. The cement mixer has completely seized up, most likely due to all the banana skins and teabags that have been thrown into it. I will refrain from mentioning whatever else went into it. Boys will be boys, girls too by all accounts.

"So Lenny, what do you think of it all mate. Sorry about the smaller bedroom, well I suppose you would just call it a landing really. If you were to put the cot under the second bit of staircase that doubles back over the kitchen next to the shower, it should be alright. So long as the baby doesn't grow too fast and keep banging it's head on the ceiling, should be okay. Maybe it's a good thing it isn't twins. The shower will work better once it settles down, just a couple of slight teething problems. Bound to get them in a new place. Bit of movement here and there, nothing to worry about, it's always good for the foundations to settle down."

"The foundations have been here for hundreds of years, mate."

"There you are then, can't get better than that. Safe as houses, I mean pigstys!"

"The nipper hasn't been born yet, Maccy."

"Which, yours or mine?"

"Both, either mucker."

"We should have a sweepstake on which one is born first and what its first words will be."

"Probably 'it's a bleddy pigsty' might be favourite boss."

"I'll have a couple of quid on that."

"There's not much point if we're all gonna bet on the same thing. Anyway, shall we get started, please?"

"Yes boss!"

"Lenny, once the paint is dry inside mate, you can start moving your stuff in."

"How will we know when it's bleddy dry, Maccy?"

"That's the easy bit mate, you just have to watch it until it isn't wet anymore. You will knaw then. Do I have to tell you everything?"

"What bleddy stuff?"

"Anything you've got that you need inside, Lenny. Like curtains, more goats, maybe a pool table and a television, a dog and a beer fridge."

"You don't like televisions mucker, I don't have a dog. I'm a pub manager!"

"I won't be watching it, will I, nor do I! Nothing I can do here now mate. Thanks, Lenny."

"You get on then mucker. Thanks for what?"

"For letting us all build your erm, house and the entertainment."

"What entertainment?"

"Later on when you throw a party for us all, for getting shot of your pigsty. What will you call the place anyway?"

"Lavinia reckons we should call it 'The Sty'."

"That's great, all you need is a pig, then it can have its full title again. I'll give Sargent Twotrees a shout if you like, he might have a spare one or two."

"Does he have some pigs then, Maccy?"

"Yep, there's always one or two knocking about around the station at Wadebridge, most police stations."

"That would be grand Maccy, I do like my bacon as you knaw."

"Me too, though personally I much prefer it on my plate. See you at the party after we close. Twotrees will be there with his mates most likely."

"How do you knaw, Maccy?"

"I invited them Lenny, it's always useful to have a few coppers around."

"Yeah, you're right, they can be handy mucker."

"Definitely, especially if you have them in your pocket, Lenny."

"I don't knaw what you mean, Maccy."

"Don't let it worry you, Lenny."

"You knaw best!"

"Later mate."

"What's for tea, maid?"

"Steak and chips and more steak. It's not maid, damn you!"

"Lovely, did you wipe it's arse dear?"

"Yes and I washed it's bleddy feet, same as I always do."

"You're too good to me my love."

"You got that right. Is the pigsty ready yet?"

"It's finished, we just need to let it all dry out properly."

"The lads did a good job then, husband?"

"Not really, they were a bunch of bleddy cowboys pretty much."

"No they weren't, they are nothing like cowboys."

"How would you knaw?"

"Maccy, I come from bleddy Texas remember! We have real cowboys in Texas my luvver."

"Are they any good at building maid?"

"You should go to Las Vegas husband, you'll feel right at home with all the other damned comedians. They'll just love you there. They'll eat you alive, with luck."

"What about the men?"

"Shut your bleddy mouth and eat your damn food."

"Yes ma'am, I sure will try to do what you suggest. It might take me a while yank."

"I need to clean my guns, wash up after you, Brit."

I can't wait. She, Jill and Jack will play and sing all evening and then some. Dolly Parton might as well retire from singing and get a nine to five day job. Another thing, Rio has something to rest her guitar on tonight, her belly. She'll have to make the most of it, it will be gone soon enough. Sometime in the future it might return. 'Wash up?'

"No it damn well won't."

"How do you bleddy do that yank?" She's not even in the room. I don't have any privacy at all. I didn't even say anything.

"Mind your own business Brit, it's for me to know. Some people are all seeing, some people are all hearing, that's all you get. Even a damned Limey like you should be able to work it out. Privacy? Think again, you gave that up a while ago, check with Methy Mick the mad Minister if you don't believe me."

"We shall all have to help out at the pigsty maid, they don't have much to put in there I reckon. Lenny is hiding it well but not well enough, I could tell. Can you think of anything?"

"Yes I can, for one thing the goat should stay here. If they have a goat in the house, the baby won't know where to get its food from."

"It's a bleddy male for god's sake."

"Oh sure, I forgot."

Oh dear, she's going down with Lenny's disease. It's a worry, I don't think I can cope with another one.

"I am not! Don't you dare say that."

She is still two rooms away and I was hardly even talking to myself. It's like having a ventriloquist without anyone holding the dummy, she's working herself. I fear for my future.

"I fear for your future too Brit, it's getting shorter all the time. You'll soon take it over."

"Overtake it, that's what you mean, yank."

"Yes it is, thank you Maccy."

"You're welcome."

"I know that husband. Thank you once again."

"Once is plenty Tex, I don't want to have to owe you for one."

She has turned my life upside down this yank. One minute I was paddling, washing anyway, in a stream in Kansas, next minute I'm married and expecting. A goat wanders in and out of the pub half a dozen times a day, Lenny has bought himself a pigsty to live in; what does that say about him? The vicar gets pissed after going out with a tart's daughter and starts effing and blinding all over the shop, Lenny is expecting, so is Lavinia his partner. Dusty has done some physical work without pay – he doesn't actually know about the second bit yet, Ma has retired. Lyndsey has been visiting her family whilst stark bonkers naked. Ghosts are flitting around all over the village. The yank has become a part-time one woman band. Padraig has gone missing again. As for myself, I have had to stay completely sane throughout it all while the rest of the world has gone totally mad.

"You don't seem to have managed it very well, Brit!"

"Sorry love, I have been trying." I bet I'm sounding like a beaten dog. I've just about had enough of this. She knows what I'm thinking all the while. How the hell can she do that? She must be breaking some law of the universe, her vows even. 'I promise to love, honour and obey', there was no mention of mind reading as far as I remember, I'll check with Michael.

"Well you darn well got that right on both counts, Brit."

"I know you mean well, Tex."

"It's my job, have you forgotten already?"

"Forgotten what?"

"The Comanche, my grandfather, was not only a Dog Soldier husband, he was a medicine man."

"A bleddy witch doctor?"

"Don't you dare mock Maccy, don't ya'll think you've had enough bad luck already?"

"I'm not answering that, you don't catch me out with that one maid."

"Oh I will Brit, I will.

Chapter Sixteen

Pillow Talk

"All you ladies are now required at the pigsty, no exceptions unless you don't like pigs, that's why we men are keeping out of the way. We are to become as scarce as bacon rind! Curtains are needed, we lads don't do curtains, on account we don't do curtains. We can open them and we can draw them, we don't stitch. Before you find something to complain about, there isn't anything, so there!"

"Bit uppity today, ain't you, Brit?"

"I don't think so, just making our position clear, nothing more yank. Pretend you're making a quilt if you have to!"

"I'm not a yank!"

"You're a yank according to we Brits maid. It makes you a yank, yank."

"Okay, I'll accept that. What do you know about the North and South anyhow, Brit?"

"More than you might think, Tex. I know North is at the top and South is at the bottom, Texas is at the bottom, more or less. I also know that in your Civil War, your guys wore grey and the other bunch wore blue. Maybe they all wore brown trousers when they went into battle, I'm not actually certain of that, I wouldn't be surprised. Your president was General Robert E Lee and theirs was Ulysses S Grant. The war kicked off in eighteen sixty one and they jacked it in five years later. If there is anything else I can help you with just shout and I will happily do my best to put your mind at rest. Sorry, to rest, I wouldn't like to think I have bored you to death, wife."

"I'm impressed Brit and darned surprised. Damn, you could be a yankee your own self underneath all that Cornish stuff, you must have Confederate blood in ya, darn it!"

"I'm surprised too yank, I was joking about the brown trousers bit but to be fair, most soldiers way back in the past wore * red jerkins so it wouldn't show if they were wounded. Well thank you Ma'am but if it's okay with you, I'll stay as I am. I might be wrong but I am just a simple country boy at heart, Tex."

"You'll do, country boy, but I think you must have been swotting up on our history, you might know more about it than I do."

"Well thank you most to death, country gal. Not so, I just spend almost all my time listening to you rabbit on. However, as you now well know, I do listen maid." I dare not!

"And so you bleddy should. I have to listen to all your gibbering about how you Brits won the bleddy war and all that talk about football, soccer whatever you call it! Stop talking under your damn breath, what did I bleddy tell you?"

"Pretty much everything wife, I'm sure you never left anything out, I could be wrong."

"When you two are done bleedin' drooling over each other, you'll be cooing like lovesick pigeons next. Can we get started on some bleddy curtains and what-not?"

"We sure will Lavinia, sorry maid."

There was me thinking I was in charge! Rio did remind me once before not to push my luck. I'm not about to ignore the warning while Lavinia is about. I'm cutting down on 'stupid is as stupid does'. I am not cutting down on cigars.

"Wrong decision husband. You're learning pretty damned quick, or as we would say back home, PDQ! Now, as you would say around here, bugger off and take that danged smelly cigar with ya!"

I might just have won a battle, I'll never win the war. I've also decided not to go down the suicide route, there's no future in it and I know I would most likely fail miserably. If I didn't fail, I would still be remembered as miserable!

"You got that right, Brit."

This is not the least bit funny. Mind readers should be on the stage, preferably the first one out of town.

"So, as I was about to say, Padraig will pick you all up later when you call him and bring you back to the Mermaid and Bow."

I am beginning to accept the semi-psychic conversations as a part of the norm'. What's the point in my fighting it? Even if I wanted to, she would know. Does it bother me, no it doesn't, it suits me down to the ground. I'm as happy as a pig in a pigsty which hasn't been cleaned out in fifty years! One small thing that does worry me is the lack of family planning around here. Two babies are about to make their first appearance around the same time. It could be a recipe for chaos, no doubt about it. Lenny and I will most likely get to fighting over names, we might both choose the same one. There will be hell up if they are both of the same sex and both are named the same. The best thing that could happen is they are one of each but I'm not sure which I would want; a maid is favourite with me I guess. I haven't asked the yank and she hasn't given me any idea. With just a few days to go to Christmas both are likely to be New Year nippers. At least it saves us all from Christmas names such as Noel, Holly and Rudolph. Eve is out too, at least I hope so. Eve sounds like the day before finality, that's the end of that and then you start all over again if you're lucky. The last thing we want is two new-borns kicking up a stink on Christmas Eve or New Year's Day. It should only be the Maltster's and Mermaid's regulars who can do that; you can be sure they will.

I am glad Lenny is in line to be first, obviously Lavinia will be too. I won't have to get in a panic before he does. My mate will most likely fall apart once he sees what he has. No one will hear the last of it. Lenny won't say 'it's a baby Rodney' like Del Boy famously did, Lenny will say 'I'm not sure, how can I tell?'. It'll be his first words. Then he'll be speechless for a couple of minutes. After that it'll be like the youngster is the very first one ever to be born to anyone, anywhere – it could be Adam or Eve after all. I can't wait to see my mate melt, he will blub. Why do men have to do that?

I won't blub when it's my turn obviously. I do see a problem occurring in the not too distant future. Now that Reg the mad vicar and Michael the mad reverend are both my bosom buddies, who will I ask to perform the christening shenanigans? It might be best to let them fight it out between them. 'Winner takes all!' We will have to wait for them to come out of hospital, the religious blokes, not the women and babies. Forget 'women and children first' it'll be a case of women and children last, a bit like the survivors on leaving the Titanic. One thing about that caper has always puzzled me; why did the skipper just stand there watching the chaos unfold? All down to the director I suppose.

So, the ladies are doing what they may not consider to be their best. I won't be accused of sexism, other isms can be obtained from over the counter, or more likely under the counter from other well-known suppliers. Or so I was once informed by one that wasn't too well known!

I might hastily arrange a pool match at the Mermaid and Bow in Padstow in a 'while the cats away' format and against the Maltsters Arms. Ma and Padraig will hold the fort here for the evening when I inform them. Padraig will transport the ladies to Padstow where they can for the whole evening tell us how tough it has been to attach a few flimsy curtains on tiny hooks and hang them from a piece of wood stuck to a wall. They will also point out we are taking 'no bleddy notice' of them whilst complaining about the cloudy cider that isn't actually supposed to be cloudy and has most likely not even been invented yet, apart from the stuff we used to make in the shed which was always cloudy!

The ladies toilets will be 'disgusting' forgetting it is only the ladies who actually use it, mostly anyway. Those who have to return to the Maltsters will be yelling and shouting all the way back to Little Petrock how they are cold and it's 'bleddy pissing down out here'. Thank god it's 'out there', if it wasn't I would be needing a new roof!

Padraig will have to stop the people carrier to allow these ladies to get down from the roof rack. It's all fair in love and war when you're a Padstownian. The trouble is, half of them aren't. It's not their fault they were born in the wrong place, I blame the parents!

The Mermaid isn't quite the same as it had been when I was a teenage tearaway and on some particular rampage. It has slowly but surely jumped a century over the last year, just one more to go before it's up to date. Lenny and Alice have worked wonders at the pub. I knew they would turn it round. It's not the same as it was when all the old crew were here, it never will be. Everything must change sometime and the Mermaid has. Soon it will have its new bar 'The Bar of Doom' maybe. Am I pushing my luck, am I tempting fate? No, I don't believe I am. The Mermaid cursed the estuary not herself. If the Mermaid had not been murdered by the dastardly Archer, the Mermaid and Bow would never have existed. The crew would not have existed as a crew. Every member would have drunk somewhere else. Blen and Bligh would never have been here. They weren't even Cornish, they were from Devon. They got away with it though and well done to them. They had us all fooled most of the time.

The Blighs didn't take the Mermaid very far. They did allow it to meander along but with hardly a breeze. I nearly said 'prosper', I'm not that naive. The place still needs to skip another century but the previous one only passed a handful of years ago. It has plenty of time to catch up and I will make sure it does!

"Ah, Lenny, we need a new pool table in here mate."

"There idn't enough room buddy."

"Not enough room, why isn't there enough room. What do you mean?"

"It's bleddy obvious Maccy, idn't it?"

"Not to me mate, no I don't see it."

"You best get down to the opticians then, Maccy. It's there, look."

"I don't think so, Lenny. There's no need to point, I know what a pool table looks like."

"Maccy, the place idn't big enough for two bleddy tables."

"True Lenny, you're right."

"If you get a new one, we will need to push the other one out of the way, see."

"Bleddy 'ell mate, I hadn't considered that."

"That's why you made me manager, Maccy."

"Bleddy 'ell, so it is, I hadn't thought of that either."

"Pay rise, Maccy?"

"Yes please Lenny, but we'll get a new pool table first don't you think?"

"Where will we put it?"

"Where the old one is Lenny, right there mate."

"That's just what I was thinking!"

"There you go, it was easy really mate."

I bet you're all wondering why I did make Lenny manager of the Mermaid. The answer is really very simple, Lenny is the most trustworthy bloke I have ever known. You can't improve on perfection, it is enough.

"Get some music on Lenny, let's get this place decorated. Put the tree on the table until we get the new one, no one plays pool at Christmas."

"Everyone, get these decorations up!" We managed it and just before the ladies arrived.

"Dammit Maccy, get that darned tree offen the darned table. I'm gonna play pool."

"You won't be able to get near the bleddy table, maid."

"No, you guys won't get near the table. Set 'em up! Who's up first?"

"After you Dusty, show her the error of her ways brother while I move the bleddy tree."

"No chance, brother."

"Padraig?"

"No son, you first, I insist."

"Damn it, I'll play her first! Rack 'em!"

Just as I am about to take my first shot a familiar sound stops me. I don't know when he came in but somehow the phantom fiddler is here. Thank the lord for that. Rio hates the sound of a violin and she hates the sound of the accordion even more. His timing is perfect and so it proves. The accordionist has been here before, somehow he is just available when required. I haven't seen him since the day I took up the keys for the Mermaid. It just seems like he is a lucky omen. I remember asking him years ago how and why he does it. Guess what he said? 'It's my job'! The bloke who reminds me of Elvis – he must remind himself of it, though he doesn't need to - is still doing his job all these years later. He still wears the shades and his hair still shows a deep, shiny black tinge in places. A smoke ring rises as he smiles and winks in my direction. I nod and he continues. I just bet he will play 'The White Rose' before the evening is out. If the White Rose isn't the anthem of Padstow, it should be. We have the May song of course but you can't spend a Mayday in Padstow without thinking of the White Rose; somehow the two just go together. One always reminds me of the other and vice versa.

Rio, after taking a couple of frames by luck, lays down her cue and produces her guitar as all thoughts of continuing to play are wholly forgotten and the sound fills the room. The musician takes a break and comes over.

"Maccy, how are you mate?"

"All the better for seeing you buddy. How did you even knaw?"

"I told you before, it's my job. I go where I need to be."

There is something about him I can't seem to pin down. On thinking about it, why should I need to know? As he says, he is just doing his job. Nobody does it better. The guy knows his task perfectly as we all join in to sing the words of the beautiful ballad. No other tune can make me shiver like this one. I would be surprised if it didn't affect everyone else in the same way.

With the excellent music, the decorations are eventually completed. Some half-hearted pool did get played later with no level of seriousness, much to the disapproval of my wife who had been chomping at the bit to thrash someone else. Padraig forfeited his Guinness until we returned to the

Maltsters where he made up for the shortage. It was a good night, we don't often allow bad ones.

Suddenly all hell breaks loose. Lenny calls in a state of fear and obvious panic.

"Maccy, is that you?"

"No mate. Is there anything else I can help you with?" Who the hell invented the telephone?

"Maccy, it's me."

"I'm sure it is but I'm not sure I know anyone of that name."

"Maccy, she has wet herself."

"That's great, so you're calling to borrow a mop and bucket?"

"No, no, it's the baby, Maccy!"

"The baby has wet itself?"

"Naw, it's coming mate, what do I do?"

"First thing Lenny, get an ambulance, then find a nappy. No, seriously mate, ring off and get an ambulance. No, I don't mean go out and find one, you don't have to do that. Just ring for one, nine nine nine might be best mate. And find a mop!"

"Get off the bleddy line then as I can't while I'm talking to you!"

"I'm sorry mate, I wasn't thinking. Let me know what's happening when you can. Don't worry about the Mermaid, I'll sort that out, just lock up and go."

"That was Lenny, yank."

"No, really? Thank the lord you told me, I would never have known, Brit. Is everything okay?"

"As right as it can be."

"Shouldn't you go to the hospital, Maccy?"

"No, Lenny has to deal with this himself. He'll be okay, it'll be the making of him, eventually. He'll do just fine."

"You get down there in the morning Maccy, he'll need you. There's enough of us to deal with everything here."

"Send Peter to Padstow, Lyndsey too. Alice can go hold Lenny's hand, it'll save me having to do it."

"Good idea, you Brits do know how to dig up trouble when you need to. Does her mother really wander about naked?"

"Peter too, so I'm informed."

"Can't argue with that, they're both old enough to do what they like. I'd say they are of an age with nothing much between them."

"Maccy, is that you?"

"Same answer matey. What?"

"What's your middle name?"

"Olyver mate, why?"

"Mind your own bleddy business."

"Are you in the ambulance, Lenny?"

"Ais, I am and Lavinia is here too, she keeps calling me bad names, Maccy."

"Call her some back then, Lenny Should you be using your telephone in an ambulance?"

"I'm not mate, I forgot mine, I borrowed this one off the driver."

"Of course you did. Goodnight Lenny, call me when it's all over."

"Call you what, Maccy?"

"Call me a lazy bastard for not answering the bleddy phone."

"Okay mate, I will do as you say."

"Maccy, he's your bleddy mate for goodness sake!"

"I knaw, we idn't that close."

"Maccy!"

"You got the right number this time mate, what more can I do for you?"

"What's Rio's middle name?"

"It's Rio, mate."

"So she's called Rio Rio then."

"I suppose so." In an instant the phone rings once more. I am not at all surprised.

"Mucker!"

"Has she dropped it yet?"

"I bleddy hope not. My mother bleddy dropped me once, I was lucky it didn't cause any serious problems. They say it idn't good to drop a baby on its head, it's what I 'ave 'eard."

"Then you were lucky Lenny, anything could 'ave happened. Goodnight buddy, say hello to the baby for us when it turns up."

"I will mucker. She's calling me bleddy names again now."

"Well pick one of those then!"

"What did Lenny say, Maccy?"

"He said they're gonna call it a little shit!"

"That's nice, goodnight Brit."

"Goodnight yank."

My mate has hardly ever caused me to lose sleep, this is one time he has succeeded. Though the phone had finally gone silent, it doesn't stop me worrying.

Jill is up and about and primed to replenish my food intake. I remember the call of late last night and return it for an update.

"Has she stopped swearing now, Lenny?"

"She have mate. She is asleep so best talk quietly, Maccy."

"So you aren't asleep then mate."

"I'm not now, I was 'til you bleddy phoned. She 'ave been asleep for hours."

"That isn't on, she should be bleddy busy."

"Doing what mate?"

"Having a baby, she won't do that while she's asleep."

"That's what I bleddy thought, you know what er's like, she's bleddy skiving."

"Right mate, you go back to sleep and call me when you know something."

"I will, I wouldn't be awake if some tosser hadn't called and woke me."

"No really, anyway it wasn't me it was the phone that did it. That's why I don't like phones. See you later mate."

"It's alright Jill, nothing have happened maid."

"No news is good news, Maccy."

"No it idn't maid. It's a useless saying if you're waiting for some bleddy news, you bleddy want it. Standing around scratching your arse and waiting idn't much good."

"Maybe you're right, Maccy."

"My yolks are broken maid."

"That's useful boss."

"How do you work that out, Jill."

"Well it will save you from having to cut them and spread them all over your bleddy plate, won't it."

"I guess it will Jill, good thinking maid. When you think about it, you have to break the shell to get them out, might as well start as you mean to go on, I mean might as well carry on as you started. What's the worst that can happen?"

"No idea, what's best with Lenny, Maccy?"

"Potential mother and father are sleeping like babies."

"Don't you think it's lovely when a family do things together!"

"Um, I suppose but the baby will most likely be awake when it makes the breakthrough."

Authors notes:

* Maccy may be correct regarding the red tunics. It has been suggested lives could have been saved by their use. Some retreating armies might have killed their own troops if they had been previously wounded so that they would not be slowed down in their retreat. Troops not only needed to look to the front, they also had to watch their backs.

Chapter Seventeen

Lily

The Mermaid and Bow is finally entering the twentieth century. Just one more to go and it will be up to date more or less. That sounds a tad like me, we have something in common. I don't do fashion, I let fashion do me, it does it well enough as far as I'm concerned.

I have thought of calling the Maltsters 'The Texas Chainsaw Inn' but it might be a tad on the tame side for the likes of Padstow. Amityville Arms. No, I don't think so, it will remind people too much of the Texas Chainsaw massacre!

"Phone, Maccy."

"I don't like phones."

"Then why do we have one, Brit?"

"Remind me, Tex."

"For emergencies and someone who might want to book a bleddy room. We do have rooms to let, don't we, we did the last time I looked."

"When they're empty."

"They're all bleddy empty, Maccy!"

Saved by the bell. "What now, we're bleddy busy Lenny. It's a what?"

"How much?"

"She called you a what, I wouldn't have put up with that, mucker!"

"You're bleddy joking."

"When?"

"She did what?"

"You didn't, that idn't right, Lenny."

"Yes I will, no I won't forget."

"Where is it?"

"Okay we will, don't worry about that, mate."

"I am blowing her a bleddy kiss. I'm not sure she will know mate."

"Yes and the baby too but don't bleddy tell anyone for crying out loud. I'll be down later, probably tomorrow."

"For crying out loud, Lenny."

"It's a bleddy saying mate, what do you expect it to do. I was not taking the micky!" I think I might have been taking the mickey.

"Yes I know babies do that, they are allowed to, it's their job to scritch, get used to it mucker. I gotta go change a nappy mate, sorry I mean I gotta change a barrel!"

"What did he say Maccy, my bird?"

"I told him I didn't have time for all this." I didn't even know she was behind me. "Lenny said it's a Rio, Rio. It's a bleddy porker at nine pounds. She called Lenny a tosser, not exactly a tosser, something similar – which he can be at times, obviously, - when she was in labour. He won't be back to work for a week. She punched him and he slapped her because she was hysterical. Then she punched him again when she wasn't but he was. He said he thought about putting a pillow over his head, she said she would let him have one of hers. Lastly maid, I asked him how he felt about being a new dad, he said 'I can't stop now Maccy, I'm being sick."

"That's nice, he's taking to it well, so quickly too!"

"That's what I was thinking maid. Like father, like son. Lenny did say he wants the heating turned up full and a hot water bottle in the bed for when they get back. I had to blow Lavinia a kiss down the phone. I had to blow the baby a kiss down the phone. He said, 'have a good night' and all the drinks are on him. He said he has a slate; I don't know anything about Lenny having a slate. What's a slate? Why don't I have a slate?"

"You bleddy liar, Maccy Tamryn. What the hell are you asking me for, I have no idea Brit, I thought they were on the roof, you seem to have one or two come loose, if you ask me."

"Thank you muchly, Tex. Now tell me what a slate is!"

"A tab ya damned fool."

"Okay, I give up, you have totally lost me now, yank."

"Yeah right, good try husband."

"Oh, by the way, he did nearly get arrested for not giving the ambulance man his phone back but he says he had inhaled a lot of gas and didn't mean to keep it. It could be true. I bet they ran out of gas."

"He stole the ambulance driver's phone?"

"No he didn't, he forgot he had it."

"He's no * Bonnie and bleddy Clyde that's for sure."

"He couldn't be, could he? He'd be shy a Bonnie. He would just be a bleddy Clyde. They couldn't make a song about Bonnie and Clyde if there was only a Clyde, it would be like Morecambe and Wise without one of them, it just wouldn't work the same. On second thoughts, we are talking about Lavinia, she's not all there most of the time anyway, neither of them are when you think about it."

"You're so darned sharp, be careful you don't cut your damn self. Who the hell is Morecambe and Wise?"

"I was just saying maid. Don't worry about it, not is, was. We don't have either now."

"Whatever, I don't intend to husband, I'm far too busy being a wife."

"You are? I have to take him a clean pair of trousers too, Lenny pooped while he was throwing up!"

"It would be best husband, best take him a brown pair in case he does it again."

It's only right people should have something cheerful to talk about over a nice breakfast. It will be a long day; Christmas is one day closer and the new bar needs stocking, the champagne needs chilling and the buffet needs cooking and arranging. Blencathra and the Cap'n should have been here. It's a shame they won't be but I bet the two will be looking down and criticising anything and everything. Blencathra couldn't make a sandwich without reading a cook book, I don't believe she ever owned a cookbook. She might have but probably ate it which pretty much proves my point.

"Jill, who is that woman, she seems familiar but I can't put my finger on it. I've seen her before somewhere."

"Yes you have Maccy. I'll give you a clue, shaving cream!"

"Don't be so bleddy weird girl. Useless, something bleddy relevant maid or just pretend I didn't ask might be better."

"Wedding?"

"Don't bother, I'll go and ask her who she is and why she is climbing all over Peter."

"Bleddy hell Maccy, it's the tramp, you remember!"

"Don't be ridiculous!"

"It is."

"No way."

"It's her I tell you. Stop staring. What's her name, Maccy?"

"I thought it was tramp. We didn't set a place for her at the wedding, she chose her own. Ask Lyndsey she's her daughter, the tramp is Lyndsey's mother. I thought she was her bleddy grandfather when she first turned up. I didn't know she was a stripper either. More importantly I still don't want to know. She is called Elizabeth!"

"Face it Maccy, your eyesight isn't great, you only have to look in the darned mirror."

"She should be naked!"

"What are you talking about?"

"She's a naturalist."

"She's a naturist!"

"It's what I said."

"No sir, it isn't. A naturalist likes plants and suchlike. Read a dictionary, oh I forgot, you can't because of your eyesight."

"If I didn't know better I am being chastised. I most likely don't know better. Rio does it all the time I guess. Another thing, what's the point of looking in the mirror if my eyesight is crap! I did stop myself from pointing out the fact my crap eyesight might have culminated in my marrying the Texan. I feared it would not go down too well.

"What are you doing here mate, shouldn't you be feeding baby Rio?"

"I had to get out of the hospital, Maccy."

"Why would you do that?"

"She told me to. She feeds the baby herself, I can't do it you see, I don't have the necessary bleddy equipment apparently. She told me to bugger off as I was useless. She did tell me I was a tit in a trance. T'was good of the maid to let me go. Maccy, what do the womenfolk mean by being under the thumb?"

"It means we do everything the womenfolk tell us to do but only when we feel like it! Anyway, you're supposed to be on maternity leave."

"I knaw, that's why I did leave."

"It's not that simple mate, nothing ever is. Did she say you can go then?"

"Not in so many words, she did just use the two."

"Well then it all makes sense now mate. You can help me with the stocking up here, you knaw as much as I do where we want everything."

"You're right, Maccy. I won't be here for a while tomorrow mind, she says I do have to go and bring her home. I thought the big bird did do that."

"You're right mate, it's only right you do. Maybe Storks don't come to Padstow."

"Why wouldn't they?"

"No sorry, it's a mystery to me, Lenny. Anyway, don't worry, I will be here to get the Mermaid open."

"That'll be grand, Maccy."

"Lenny, you will need to bring them in here before you take them home mate."

"Why would I do that, Maccy?"

"Because the women will need to see the mother and especially the baby."

"Haven't they seen one before?"

"If they haven't their kids could explain everything."

"I didn't think of that."

"The ladies will need to make ridiculous bleddy cooing noises, they will all turn into pigeons. They'll want to hold the little one and tickle under it's chin. What is it again?"

"It's a Rio. Why would they do all that, Maccy?"

"It's what they do, some kind of bleddy female ritual mate. It's part of the job description due to being a woman, you'll get used to it, you had better or your life will not be your own, you will be reminded regularly. You'll be in the shit for the rest of your days trust me mate, just do as I tell you for your own sake."

"How can't my life not be my own, it can't be someone else's Maccy, tis mine."

"Don't listen to him Lenny, just do what you think you should do and we'll just make suggestions when you're wrong. I mean we'll just tell you when you're wrong. It's as simple as that, there ain't no darned mystery about it."

"See, I bleddy told you mucker, it's already begun."

"Yes Miss Rio. Shut your mouth Maccy, you don't knaw what you're bleddy talking about."

"Okay mate, don't say I didn't warn you, on your head be it!"

"I thought everything had to be on the baby's head."

"Lenny, it's not that simple."

I did my bit, I had warned my mate as best I could. It's a slippery slope from now on. There's nothing more I can do. The women here will be playing pass the parcel and cooing like doves for most of the day, most of the week more than likely. Later the men will start doing the same thing and there will be large amounts of said head wetting performed, even by people who don't even know whose baby it is or even if there is a baby at all. Total strangers will make suggestions regarding middle names. At least fifty people of all shapes and sizes will get a free celebration and have no idea what they are celebrating! Drunken men will go home to their wives or more than likely other's wives, there won't be so many of them, they will ask if they can have one. Occasionally it will be the other way around. There will be pregnant people, women everywhere. Totally useless advice will be dished out by all and sundry. It'll be the end of mankind for ten minutes, then we'll be the best thing since sliced bread again. Maybe not the last part.

Just take my word for it, nothing else of any use will get done here tonight. I'll be washing glasses and chucking away half eaten food until two O'clock in the morning. I will forget to lock up and will most likely find a stranger or two asleep in here in the morning, one will most likely be a well-known vicar. He might be found holding hands with a lesser known Methodist minister who has forgotten he lives out the back on a boat. Lenny won't remember a thing until Lavinia reminds him he has invited two hundred people to a christening, nobody knows where it will happen or even when. His mother-in-law will do the same, so it will add up to three hundred.

In just a few weeks' time it will happen all over again. It'll just be a different baby with different potential names and different parents; maybe the same names and with all the same people in attendance and without them hardly knowing why they are present. Their own names won't be remembered but it will happen all over again in exactly the same way. 'Ground Hog Day' may have been a totally boring film, it does have an awful lot to answer for, a bit like myself really. It's far too late now, I don't know all the answers.

So now my mate has turned against me. It's a good thing Lenny has grown up finally. My oldest friend doesn't need me to hold his hand anymore. I couldn't be happier for him, he deserves it all more than anyone I know. Lavinia is a lucky lady, Lenny is a lucky man, hopefully anyway. Lenny now has what I think he has always wanted. In a short time we both will. We two have fought many times in the past, just for the hell of it more often than not. The two of us have always been up for a knuckle swapping. Good times, now the times they are a changing. Apologies, Bob Dylan!

Great, it's Bird. The odd old farmer is most unlikely to be here to make my day. "Dicky, what can I do for you pard'?"

"I'll tell you in a minute, I'll tell you in a minute!"
"Time's up!"

Maybe he will or won't tell me in a minute. I can't wait, I suppose I don't have a choice. He may have come with a message referring to the end of the world which might only be in thirty seconds time and could happen at least twice. Bird will be late. If I'm going, I can think of better company to go with. I don't want to die with, or of the commander in chief of boredom.

"Maccy, get the damn bag now!" She is screaming particularly loudly from the doorway and gripping something she wouldn't normally grip in mixed company. Don't let your imagination run away with you, she is trying to pull the door handle off. The Texan is early!

I had been idling my time today and thinking of everything but this moment. Lenny and I didn't quite manage to get the Bar of Doom operational. I'm thinking it will have to wait a while now.

"I think you're gonna need my help Tamryn old chap."

"Not me Bird, I think my wife might want to have a think about it for a while as well." It is a decent offer from the old sod, I just don't think the yank has the patience to hear him repeating the same thing twice every two minutes for eighteen hours. It would be okay under certain circumstances but we are not expecting twins as far as I know. She would have told me, probably!

"Plymouth or Truro, Yank?"

"My ancestors came from Plymouth, Brit'. Let's try Truro, it's nearer for one thing. Just start the damn car."

"Yes dear. I need to make a call, yank."

"It's me, Maccy, I need a favour, I need a car."

"What is it this time, we don't run a bleddy taxi service, Maccy."

"I need to get to Truro very quickly, it's really, really important."

"Have you been drinking Maccy, it's Christmas Eve mate."

"Nope but it's life or death."

"That's bad isn't it, life or death, best you don't panic."

"Just the life bit to be fair."

"ETA, seven minutes, mate."

"Thanks sarge." One of these days I will find out what his first name is. Maybe I won't bother.

I knew Twotrees wouldn't let me down. Not so may years ago the station Sergeant at Wadebridge would have gone through hell and high water to nick me. Over the years we have become friends, not close, but friends. As I write, they arrive. Just the two cars are waiting outside looking and sounding like musical Christmas trees – very apt when I think about it – covered in flashing lights and making a lot of noise. There was a time long ago when I took it upon myself to drive from Padstow to Truro in around twenty minutes; I think this time my long standing record will be broken. My staff are organised and have had their orders. We're on the move thanks to my friends in blue and yellow and looking like giant Battenberg cakes. We are sandwiched between two very fast cars. Twotrees did offer to put us into one of his motors but to be honest I thought he might get carried away with old habits and take us to the station and lock us up for the night.

No cars were injured or damaged during the making of this visit. I didn't have time to time the twenty mile journey as I was attempting to time contractions, rather haphazardly whilst concentrating on not becoming squashed between two pretty nippy beamers. I do know it was quick. Quick as in very fast, as in maybe a fifteen or sixteen minutes. I well remember Jen' expanding her vocabulary many moons ago in a similar way to my own general usage tonight. The yank did well, she didn't let the side down. There was a little cussing as she likes to call effing and blinding, which was hardly useful as I don't understand a word she says half the time. Not even in normal times.

I did have time to recall reading once ** the British Grand Prix had been held at the old aerodrome at Davidstow. It makes me wonder how we all would have fared in comparison. Rather well I would like to think considering the circumstances. It was a tad disappointing the yank wasn't interested and complained loudly about various obscure things as we made our journey without any serious mishap.

To be fair to her, flashing lights before the eyes, coupled with blaring sirens can be a cause of the onset of a migraine but this is not the case thankfully. We'll be suffering from semi-permanent headaches soon enough. As for Twotrees, he and his mates took care of us pretty well. We weren't stopped and fined by any of his other mates. It was good to get some of our council tax back. To be fair I never did pay any for a year or two when I lived in the carriages. Nobody but a select few knew where I lived, I wasn't always certain myself. I didn't bribe the local postie, the occasional free pint does not constitute bribery, not in my book anyway.

She is a girl. I am hooked and landed, thankfully I am not at all gutted. Another potential barmaid will eventually become useful. My new daughter and Rio junior will get along fine. I'm pleased my mate used the name. If he hadn't, Rio might have wanted to. They will go to school together and become friends for life I'm certain. I'm also positive they will not grow up to be anything like their fathers. They hadn't better! Lenny, Michael and I had terrorised the neighbourhood as much as we could manage when we were kids. It wouldn't be fair to put the locals through it all again. I would bet some of our victims still haven't fully recovered, most especially those in the teaching fraternity. For clarification, no one teacher was singled out, each victim was treated equally between eight forty-five and 4 pm. I can safely say no tutor was physically damaged during their education; mental damage may have occurred. Yes, we taught them a few things. What on earth am I doing? I'm a dad again, I don't have time for the past!

She wants to name it after the nurse who tended her; Lily has landed!

Authors notes:

* Lawless duo Bonnie Parker and Clyde Barrow were an American criminal couple who travelled the Central United States with their gang during the Great Depression of the nineteen twenties, known for their bank robberies although they preferred to rob small stores or rural gas stations. Clyde Chestnut Barrow was born in Ellis County, Texas 1909. Bonnie Elizabeth Parker was born in Rowena Texas in 1910. Both were shot many times and died on a back lane at Gibsland Louisiana in May 1934. The two were still in their mid-twenties.

** Davidstow Circuit is a now disused motor racing circuit and airfield built in Cornwall, in the United Kingdom. The circuit was built on the site of a World War II RAF Coastal Command base, RAF Davidstow Moor, opened in 1942. Davidstow circuit opened in 1952 and held three Formula 1 races between 1954 and 1955. The circuit hosted its last race in 1955.

Chapter Eighteen

Christmas Presence.

Instead of a ten pound Turkey Rio and I now have a nine pound child of the female variety, not sure about giblets nor self-basting. Just what is 'self-basting? In all my years I have never once seen a turkey with a ladle in its claw! It's never happened. So anyway, I'm looking on the bright side here and there is one, it's not in the oven anymore, it could be worse. Worse? I'm certain we are about to have a particularly disorganised Christmas Day, beats humdrum every time in my opinion, which I'm certain will be backed up with plenty of vocal evidence. The other thing is Christmas is blown all out of proportion. It starts in July and ends late January. While I think about it, one good thing, at least the quilt will fit the bed again and I will try not to scream so loudly in future.

For weeks and possibly even months everybody – not me obviously, I am far too busy – has nothing else on their minds but stuffing and a small coin of some sort. What's the coin all about? I'll tell you, it's about making young kids eat Christmas pudding, Lenny being one, he'll never grow up! It's awful food and the kids eat it on the off chance they will gain a tiny financial reward. Only one victorious kid will get the coin even though he or she might have ten brothers and sisters. How can that be right? They can't stand the pudding, I never could. Lenny and Lavinia will be fighting over it this year, next year all three of them will. I try not to think about anything connected to Lavinia. I believe I would suffer further bouts of sleeplessness, even depression. Anyway, she's Lenny's problem now! He can keep her on the straight and narrow. Good luck with that, Lenny!

The thing is Christmas is only two days. One to get rat-arsed on and the other to sober up and look forward to New Year's Eve when we will do it all again. It's like the wind;

one minute it's there; next minute it's somewhere else. Blame it on the Sprouts! The second day after New Year's Day is almost always crap. All we think about is where did Christmas go and how long is it until we do it all again! I can't do that. In the interests of honesty, I know there is more to the holiday than just getting stuffed but does everyone else think the same? Please don't reply; it'll only get held up in the Christmas post. All I ever wanted for Christmas was a cowboy suit! I've been to Kansas and almost to Texas and hardly saw anything that looked like a cowboy. I never saw a rattlesnake that wasn't sleeping. I never saw one that was!

I always seemed to get my wish until I grew out of the suits, which in fact means they didn't make them in my size anymore. I went all the way to Kansas and Texas and didn't see one man riding a horse and carrying armoury, just a bunch of pretenders spitting everywhere. Cowboying isn't what I thought it would be. I must admit I always felt comfortable on the back of a horse, cows too, exercise is good whatever the species of the mount. I do wonder what my great grandfather, Henry would think if he had met me. Most likely he would have said: 'fill your hands you son of a bitch'! I would have had no clue as to what he was talking about and would most likely end up with a third nostril! The nearest thing to a cowboy I've seen is my wife!

My great grandfather was for all intents and purposes a gunfighter, a shootist. Not a cowboy as such but a gunfighter. Imagine that? It is true, he was. To be fair; he did only kill one man according to the family history which is sparse to say the least. It is good to know the skeleton in our cupboard wasn't a mass murderer. Another thing, I read somewhere the feted lawman, Wyatt Earp only ever killed one man. I bet he wouldn't admit it was a lucky shot! I heard somewhere the deceased might have been dead drunk so he was already halfway along his final journey.

The early emergence of the tacker is partly, actually half my fault, and so I have no room to complain, not that I had contemplated complaining at all. I'm not sure what my great grandfather would make of me if he had an opportunity to comment. I hope he would approve. Henry had won a saloon in a poker game apparently. I have two pubs so we were in the same line of business it seems. I want them all to approve of me, even Renee; I want her to be proud of me. We'll see! No we won't; as she's long gone now. Henry McCarthy is even longer departed; having lost his life in a fire while attempting to save the life of his friend. I'm not sure I could rise to my ancestor's heady heights.

"Jill, put some hot water on maid. Plenty of it."

"There isn't another baby coming is there, do you need towels."

"Naw maid, I need tea and plenty of it, find me a cigar!"

"Bleddy foolishness! Find your own damned stinking cigar."

"Thank you Jill, I'll manage."

"Damn right you will boss, breakfast Maccy?"

"Might as well, Jill. Don't you ever sleep maid?"

"Better than you do. Better than you're about to for a while."

"You're most likely right maid. How's the ducks doing?"

"Keeping out of your way. They don't want to be your Christmas dinner. Your reputation has gone before you it seems."

"I best go and steal one of Bird's cows then. Come with me; you can steer it and I'll kick its arse if it goes in the wrong direction. Wear thigh boots maid!"

"I will not take you up on your cruel suggestion I don't hold with animal cruelty, Maccy and I don't own thigh boots, you can put that out of your mind right now, you dirty old man."

"Fair enough, thank you maid. I'll chivvy it along quietly then, how would that be?" 'Dirty old man', I think she is getting me mixed up with someone else. Still, I can take a compliment when it's offered.

"You wouldn't really steal one of his beasts, Maccy, would you. Why thigh boots boss?"

"Of course not, they are so old; they should be turned into leather jackets rather than a lovely, tasty Christmas dinner. That way Lenny's goat can eat the jackets, the cows can go commando! They might be useful with all they leave behind, not forgetting the mud. I wonder what Rio will be eating today?"

"Her words I expect. Get out of my kitchen and take this with you, fool!"

"Yes maid!" I do have an annoying habit – it annoys me - of doing as I'm told by any female. It might be a wimpish trait but it can lead to a quiet life. It is unlikely I would argue with the girl while attempting to carry an extra-large Cornish breakfast. If anyone is even mildly interested; the stated meal can only truly be described as a 'Cornish' breakfast if it contains lightly fried slices of Hog's Pudding. It's got to be better than Black Pudding. Our delicacy would need to be produced west of the Tamar, anything else should not be tolerated nor accepted as a substitute. In fairness other similar products can be obtained on the eastern side of the river and should only be consumed in that place. I suppose to my way of thinking only average standard food is sold and eaten in Devon. Actually I have never eaten a meal in Devon as far as I know, it's unlikely I ever will. I just know I won't ever eat a Lancashire breakfast, I'm not keen on dried blood at breakfast time.

As for the sainted Cornish Pasty, I happen to know a genuine Cornishman who once borrowed a friend's kitchen while visiting New York. This gentleman produced a number of our Duchy delicacies and sold them on the street under the pretence they were in fact Cornish Pasties. I am reliably informed he did indeed completely sell every one. As far as I know the amateur baker and salesman – he was in fact an estate agent, you know what they're like – anyway he was never apprehended nor punished for his misdemeanour in Manhattan. I'm pretty sure he won't attempt anything similar in the future. I must admit respect for him for teasing the yanks by only appearing the one time. I would like to point out; I have never visited New

York personally. If anyone reading this happened to be one of those lucky purchasers I would be most grateful if you got in touch. I would also never disclose the identity of the pasty purveyor; though I am not averse to some forms of bribery under the correct circumstances; which of course means either the provider or members of the press can participate.

"I need you Jill."

"Behave yourself for goodness sake, don't you ever think of anything else? Your wife just got out of hospital dammit."

"Not that kind of need maid."

"What then?"

"The tree is still almost naked maid. If you make a start, I'll get Lyndsey to help you. It needs more."

"It's a bit late. It's already Christmas bleddy day."

"Doesn't matter, it's not over yet."

"Then you've already missed some."

"It was hardly my fault maid, I blame the new nipper."

"Yes it bleddy was!"

"I'll concede that. You're partly right. I wasn't on my own."

"Are you sure?"

"I don't know what you mean!" How many filthy looks does one reasonably innocent man have to endure from a young female at breakfast time? On second thoughts I don't think I want to know. Ignorance can be bliss!

"What shall I do with this, Maccy?"

"Hang it by the balls at the top, Jill."

Sotto voce "Mind someone doesn't do the bleddy same to you!"

"Pardon?"

"Nothing, Maccy. There it is done, happy now boss?"

"Yes maid, well done, good work." It is too. "Now maid, have you seen my mistletoe?"

"Stop your foolishness and go check the gents to make sure there isn't a bleddy vicar sleeping in there. Check the floor for dropped cash while you're there, half each!"

For just a short while I had thought the Maltsters to be my pub. It just goes to show I know next to nothing. "What do you need dropped cash for maid?"

"To make it worth my while being here, it will supplement what you laughingly call a fair wage."

"Morning Maccy, happy erm thingy, Christmas mucker!"

"And the same to you, Michael. What do you bleddy want. Shouldn't you be polishing your candlestick and chilling cheap wine.?"

"Don't be disgusting, you'll fry one of these days and it'll be your own fault. Talking of which; any breakfast going spare Jill or has he eaten everything?"

"Tell him no maid!"

"Bleddy liar!"

"Do you talk to all your flock that way?"

"No, only you, Tamryn. You bring out the worst in me, always have."

"You should find yourself a good woman mate. I did."

"I don't want a good woman, Maccy, if you get my meaning. If I wanted a good woman I would consider Jill here. How's the babby then?"

"Sleeping like one, same as her mother. The yank has already got her into bad habits. I knew it wouldn't take her long."

"Your turn will come mate. I didn't see you at Midnight Mass."

"I was in the bleddy hospital, Mike. Many there. It's always my bleddy turn."

"Not really. I wound it up early, it was all over by half midnight and I went to the pub. Why were you in hospital mucker? Was it the one where you can do your own operations?"

"You got n. Which pub were you in and why?"

"The Ringers. You know what Chris is like. He doesn't turn good decent people away on a cold bleddy night, not like some I could mention. I didn't have to walk home hungry either. He's a proper host, he knows his stuff which is more than I can say for some hereabouts."

"He knows everyone's stuff. If he's that bleddy good why don't you go there for your bleddy breakfast? Santa give you a lift here, did he?"

"No the bugger ignored me and flew right over towards Rock."

"They'll need more than one Santa and a double-decker sleigh in that bleddy place, it's full of effluent folks. Where did you sleep then?"

"In Dusty's yurt if it's any of your business. It's affluent, you moron!"

"I know what I bleddy mean. You slept with my brother in my bleddy garden!"

"No I said I slept in Dusty's yurt. I have never slept with your brother, god forbid! He was somewhere else with someone else. Last I saw of the kid he was giving some sad, defenceless woman the kiss of life. I think he missed a bit while he was at it."

"Poor maid, let's hope she doesn't remember a damn thing when she comes around!"

"So, about my breakfast?"

"See Jill and ask her. Only I would stand back a bit if I was you, she's a tad feisty this morning. She may have had a premonition you were coming here."

"I'll ignore that. Bit fiery is she?"

"Volcanic mucker. She could give Joan of Arc a run for her money! Good luck with your request, you could be wearing your bleddy breakfast." I didn't think so, I didn't believe myself what I was telling my minister friend, I just wanted him to believe it. Jill is far too mild mannered and docile. She wouldn't hurt a fly. I wouldn't tell Michael as much.

"Michael, eaten?"

"Oh yes mucker. The maid can cook. I want one like that. She is rather edible looking."

Best thing you can do is pray then. You only get what you deserve in this life. You don't stand a chance bud. You might be a man of the cloth but you're still doing bleddy penance for what you did before you joined his team. You still have a way to go yet."

"You can go to hell in one of those thingies!"

"Handcart! After you vicar."

"Minister, I'm a damn minister, how many bleddy times?"

"Of course you are. Now get to church and do your stuff. It's Christmas, you should be bleddy grafting, not skiving. You'll be farting and belching all through the service for sure. If you ate the Hog's Pudding your dress will be flapping above your head."

"Chapel, it's a bleddy chapel, you moron. Jill said there's none left, you finished it off."

"What's the bleddy difference, you'll still be stinking the bleddy place out!"

"No idea!"

"You should go to confession, you bleddy Philistine."

"Are you doing it on purpose?"

"More than likely."

"Thanks for breakfast, Maccy."

"Just leave a couple of quid in the dish by the door on your way out. No wait, a fiver. Christmas prices, Mikey. I'm letting you off fifty percent. If you were family and I thank your boss you bleddy idn't, it'd be the same price so don't try that one on."

"Why don't you …."

"Now, now, Padre, peace on earth and goodwill to Maccy Tamryn. You know the drill. Make the bleddy plate rattle on your way out."

"I'll make your bleddy teeth rattle if you don't give it a bleddy rest!"

"I'm so scared, I believe they may have begun without me. Mind your bleddy dress on the way out. A seagull crapped on the vicar last time he left here. He said it was a seagull. I thought it was Old Mother Ivy practicing for the next Halloween."

"Serves the old git right. He shouldn't have been in here in the first place. Cassock, it's a bleddy cassock, Tamryn. Jesus, don't you ever listen to anything?"

"You're so caring, I like Reg, he's a good chap, can I say the same about you Michael, I need to think about it. I'll let you know my decision in good time. I hope you find what you want, I mean need, god help her."

"I will. I'm a patient man, he will, Reg? So, you're getting friendly with the vicar now!"

"Yeah, yeah whatever!"

"What's that all about?"

"No idea Mike don't ask, it's just something nasty I picked up from the yank I think. I most likely will need antibiotics jab."

"You be careful, you know she has good hearing, anyway I would like to say I hope you get better soon but I'm not about to. You need something. I'm not sure a little prick will help much!"

"The best thing you can do is become a catholic, Mikey. That way you can get rid of all your pent-up guilt. Now go away and wash your mouth out. Don't you dare talk like that in front of my staff. There's a babby in the house too!"

"That was not what I meant and you bleddy know it, Tamryn. The babby has my sympathy."

"Yes I do but I like to get my side of the sad story in first when possible. Now bugger off potty mouth."

My religious friend mumbled quite incoherently as he left with his tail between his legs, which is pretty much how he arrived.

"Yes Peter, what can I do for you? You left the bleddy door open mate. Were you born in a bleddy barn?"

"Yes, I was actually, how did you know?"

"You must have stayed a while. You don't live in one now mate. Where did you live while you were in Padstow?"

"In a skip mate."

"I said where did you live while you were in Padstow?"

"In a skip mate."

"Okay, I'm not gonna get anywhere with you."

"Maccy, I lived in a skip. Why do you think I came here, I heard you had plenty of bedrooms full of crap, I thought I would feel more at home here, more importantly I would be warmer."

"I hope you had a cleaning lady in."

"Not quite, I moved out and came here."

Who am I to criticise, I lived in a cattle car, mostly alone of course. There were no animals apart from Chalky. The cat turned up one day and stayed, he must have thought I was a soft touch, he was right, I was. "I hear you're going out with my Auntie. You better behave yourself buddy."

"Actually she has asked me not to. I haven't yet."

"That's enough information thank you."

"Just think, we might be related one day. It'll be like all your Christmases turned up at once."

"No chance, keep smiling. Did you lend her your razor? There's no need for that kind of language, Peter, I was just enquiring, showing an interest. There's no pleasing some bleddy people. Send the next one in and shut the bleddy door behind you!"

"Maccy, are you there?"

"Nope, please leave a message after the beep and I might call you back. Don't hold your breath."

"Don't bugger about, Maccy this is serious, what beep?"

"How serious?"

"Very."

"How very?"

"The bleddy gulls keep stealing the seafood off the stall."

"Shoot them mucker."

"But the emmets will get in the bleddy way."

"Shoot them too. There can't be that many around this time of the year. Who's gonna miss half a dozen? Bring me a gun I'll shoot them."

"I would if I could, I don't have a gun."

"Buy one, Lenny, have the bill sent to me."

"Who from, Maccy?"

"Someone who has a gun for sale would be favourite. I'll ask Robbie, no that's no good, he'll be using it if he has one."

"To shoot gulls?"

"Nah, he likes the gulls, he'll be shooting emmets. Get a catapult from the toyshop."

"Is the toyshop the one that sells those things, you knaw, toys."

"No Lenny, not that bleddy shop, the one that sells kids toys mate."

"I didn't knaw there was one."

"How did you knaw there idn't, how did you know there is a toyshop that idn't for kids?"

"You told me Maccy!"

"Just make yourself one mate."

"One which, Maccy, I'm confused."

"A bleddy catapult, Lenny. You know how to make them, don't you. It's either that or a gun. Wait a minute, do what we used to do in the good old days; use the baking powder and silver foil ploy like we used to."

"They idn't gonna like it mate."

"Who idn't gonna like it?"

"The bleddy emmets!"

"Not on the emmets, Lenny, in the bleddy gulls man. You can't really kill the emmets, they have bulging wallets, the bleddy Padstow gulls have bulging guts. It makes them harder to miss."

"I gotcha Maccy, that would be best and it will be less messy too."

"Next time listen to my answering machine. There idn't no emmets here anyway. I have enough trouble listening to my bleddy alarm clock. I don't think I need it anymore."

"Why's that."

"I have a three day old baby and a bleddy hairy goat to feed every bleddy morning Maccy. Why did you let me get the bleddy thing?"

"The baby, I didn't have a say in it."

"Not the babby, the goat!"

"What did you say you're gonna call it?"

"Bleddy noisy!"

"You knaw where you went wrong mucker."

"Yes mate, I do."

"Don't do it again!"

"That idn't bleddy fair."

"Then see the doctor, he'll know what to do. He's very good, he did his own vasectomy once."

"No way! Wait, you can only do it once!"

"Tell you what, I'll go with you and wait outside. I can drive you home after. You won't be able to bleddy walk in a straight line, you won't be able to see with your eyes watering so much and you'll need to get smaller trousers. I caught one of mine in my zip once."

"Just the one?"

"I thought it best, Lenny. I didn't want both my eyes watering!"

"I idn't going, she bleddy can."

"Good thinking, that should do it." My mate does tend to get to his destination in the end, he just doesn't always know when and where he has arrived. He never knows how long he is staying.

I am tempted to build a stable and whatnot, obviously the little ones will need bunk beds! Just one thing stops me, where would I find three wise men and a donkey in Little Petrock? No-one springs to mind and there is little point in my volunteering, I'm far too busy in my attempt to impersonate an innkeeper and the baby is already here. My old friend and crew member has a lot to answer for. Dear Lil, was a serving member of the oldest profession, I believe she might well have been the oldest purveyor of said profession. I'm fairly sure I never did encourage her services in a financial way, I bet there are plenty who can't say the same. Dear Lil didn't make much, rumours suggested if business was exceptionally quiet she would actually pay her regulars for their services and even supply the paper sacks. Lil wasn't what you might call a beauty. She did show dedication to her profession. One other member of the crew who has now sailed on would never refuse the monetary gift; One Armed Frank would snatch the cash without blinking, Frank would snatch the sacks and sell them! Rest in peace, Lil, you too Frank, though you did have some pieces missing.

"I'm sorry Peter, I forgot you were there. You can go and carry on with your Christmas now."

"Thank you, Maccy."

"Wait a minute, Pete. Write out a note asking all staff to come to a meeting when we close tonight. Anyone not here, find their phone numbers and make sure they are."

"Where will I put the note, Maccy. We don't have a noticeboard."

"Get Bessie to make one."

"What will you be doing?"

"I'm going shopping in Wadebridge mate."

"Christmas shopping, Maccy? There's nowhere open!"

"Everywhere is open to me, Lenny."

"You could say that.

Make sure no-one eats. We all eat here after closing time tomorrow afternoon."

"Boxing day?"

"Exactly mate. Make sure you tell everyone at the Mermaid and Bow. I want all of them here at three for a comfy chat. They can close early."

"I'll do my best, Maccy."

"You do that!"

"What about the goat?"

"Does it work here?"

"No but it gives us plenty to do."

"What does it give you to do?"

"Clean up after it."

"Okay, tell Lenny, to bring the bleddy goat."

"The queen does a speech on Christmas Day mate, at three O'clock. Every year."

"Does she, no-one told me, what about, Peter?"

"Anything she likes."

"Yeah, a bit like the queen, Peter. you're right. It will be a bit like her but I don't dress up."

"That's not what I bleddy 'eard!"

Chapter Nineteen

Sleepless in Little Petrock

Would you believe it? Just when you think it's safe. I'm about to find out it just isn't the case. It is most unfortunate. I seem to be faced by a visitor with a serious head-shaking problem.

"Good morning, Reg!"

"Is it Maccy, is it? Not in my neck of the woods it isn't, I can tell you."

"But we live in the same place more or less. So what's the problem, Reg?"

"Maccy, the bleddy worst has happened mucker, it idn't bleddy right."

"I'm beginning to believe you, Reg, In what way?"

"The bleddy worst way, that's why I said it."

"Fair enough, so how bad can it be?"

"I already told you!"

"Tell me again I'm thinking I must have missed it in the translation."

"They want to close my church, our bleddy church, your bleddy church. Actually not 'your' church as you never bleddy go. My congregation has shrunk."

"Maybe you should try a different laundry and stop eating so much cheese, Reg?"

"It's no laughing matter, Maccy. Where will everyone go if the church is closed? Why cheese?"

"You just said no-one goes there mate. They won't have to go anywhere else, will they? Forget the cheese!"

"But they might and if they want to, they won't be able to."

"Maybe you could find another job, Reg? Let's put the cheddar and the laundry to one side for the moment mate."

"I'm a bleddy vicar, Maccy, what else could I do? I like a bit of cheddar."

"I see your problem, Reg. I like cheddar too but I'm trying to cut down due to the massive side-effects."

"Do you see the problem, Maccy, do you? Do it if it's best for you mucker."

"I do but I have no idea how you can rectify it unless you bribe people to attend."

"How would I go about doing that mucker?"

"Easy, you just give the villagers money for turning up on a Sunday instead of the other way around." Thank the lord the cheese has gone off. I have almost forgotten why it came up in the first place.

"That's not how it works, Mucky. They're supposed to come and give the church money."

"Is that what happens? I've always wondered what the attraction is. Brandy, Reg?"

"Oh yes please erm, Maccy. Have one yourself old chap."

"I was planning on it. It's my bleddy Brandy!"

"Yank!"

"Pardon?"

"Not you Vicar, keep your flies done up, I was talking to the wife."

"Whose wife?"

"I thought mine would be best. You don't actually have one that I know about. I didn't realise the Texan was there. If I started saying things like that to other men's wives, my wife wouldn't be very wifely any more. She's listening to us from outside the door but she's not all there."

"It's not me and I didn't hear a darned thing!"

"So who is it wearing your perfume then wife? Reg, whatever you do now, don't think about anything while she's about."

"Why shouldn't I?"

"She will know, she reads minds. Some kind of Texan hocus pocus mate."

"I'm not listening husband."

"Yes you are. I can hear you listening, it isn't polite to read the vicar's mind so stop it now or you could be excommunicated, probably." I never thought it could be possible but I now have absolute proof she can in fact read minds; in my own case, a tiny one, the vicar only has a half. I hope my daughter doesn't have the gift.

"No you don't Brit! Oh she will!"

"You see, Reg, I never said a word and she still did it."

"I'm thinking maybe a séance, perhaps a cleansing, Maccy?"

"What did I just say, Reg? Don't bleddy think for Christ's sake. I'm trying to keep you safe here mate. You're only encouraging her."

"She made me do it my son."

"So now you're a firm believer, Reg. Welcome to my world."

"Just give me another Brandy and I'll be on my way back to the office to pray for her."

"I'll come with you mate. What sort of wine do you have in stock?"

"The wet variety! I think it's a Russian rouge."

"I need to go out maid, can you look after the baby? I won't be long."

"I can and yes you won't."

It's all we need around the village. A vicar with a sense of humour, I didn't expect it! I might even pray for him myself. "I suppose all Russian wine would be Red, Reg, even the white!" Personally I think Reg is in his own dreamworld. The Russians only make Vodka surely. Where the hell can they grow grapes on the Tundra? I have never even seen Russian Red Vodka, I don't believe I would want to be acquainted, not without lime juice anyway.

"Another, Maccy?"

"Are you trying to get your own back, Reg?"

"As if I would young man?"

"I'm not sleeping in the church bog vicar."

"That's good as I don't do fried breakfast. Churches don't have bogs, Maccy"

"And I don't like to antagonize armed Texans, Reg. I best be off mate. She's a good shot! So just one thing then,

Reg, where do you go when you need to go for a splash and you're in the middle of a sermon?"

"Isn't it obvious, Mucky; behind a bleddy gravestone like everyone else does around Padstow. Sometimes they just do it even if they're not at a service. Except for Midnight Mass. At midnight mass half the bleddy town is in church and the other half are in the graveyard waiting for a bleddy space."

"Fair enough. It's not the sort of thing I would do."

"Maccy, what do you know about the old bridge my son?"

"Not a lot Reg, to be honest. I know it's been there a long time otherwise I don't think it would be called the 'Old Bridge', do you? Oh and it keeps your feet dry! That's about it." What else could I say?

"It's not quite what I meant, Maccy."

"Bats, there are loads of bats living under it and more importantly it stops the cars and lorries from falling in the water. Gotta run, Reg. Talk some more later."

"Later, when?"

"After now mate. I need to get some food. I think it will be Fish and Chips from Wadebridge."

"What's wrong with the chippy in Padstow mucker?"

"Too expensive, Reg. Their fish doesn't have batter on it, it just has gold-plating, it's why it costs a bleddy fortune. It's just Cod or Haddock, not bleddy caviar. It comes out of sea-water just like any other bleddy fish. If it was down to me I would let the fish decide what it's worth, sort of out of the horse's mouth."

"True enough, Maccy. Adios!"

"See ya down there, Reg. You know where so don't ask!"

"That reminds me, I must clean my ring!"

I still can't get my head around being the vicar's best buddy. It can't do any harm I suppose. It's odd; there's Michael, Lenny and now Reg. Reg is the vicar, Michael is a minister and Lenny is a Philistine. Best to cover all the bases I guess.

Wadebridge as always is bustling and with all the holiday shopping going on parking is not good. I glance all around the Platt, an area which occupies the centre of the town, and spot a stretch of double yellow lines not yet being utilised. The Chip shop is close-by as I decide to take the risk. Twenty minutes of standing in a line sees me leaving with my parcels of grub and makes me wish I hadn't decided to make the effort to visit the town.

I receive a long-distance glare from the largest traffic warden in England. As I watch she is writing a ticket. On the bonnet of ma's car is what can only be a half-opened package of what I have in my carrier bag. She is struggling to stick the ticket to my windscreen. I wait while she tries to lick the frying fat from her fingers. I now realise the ticket will cost me more than if I had bought fish and chips in Padstow. No salt and no vinegar. Sea-salt? What's that all about, surely all salt comes from the sea. Salt doesn't grow on trees. Salt marshes were part of the sea once, weren't they? Why do we have to pay three times as much for it just because it has Sea in front of salt?

"Do you really have to?" I asked her with something I believed to be akin to friendliness.

"Yes and no!"

"If it's yes and no, why are you despoiling my windscreen?"

"Simple Mister Tamryn; last time I was in your pub you offered me two chairs to 'park my bleedin' butt' on."

"So, I was being attentive and affable and caring for your unusually large welfare. I was rightfully attending to your own parking problem at that time. It's my job!"

"And this is my job, I absolutely bleedin' love it!"

"Well if you're sure maid. When you've finished wiping your hands all over my windscreen let me know so I can be on my way. Before my supper gets cold.

"I will when I'm good and ready Mister Tamryn."

"Have it your way."

I put the key in the ignition as she still attempts to decorate the screen in black and yellow. I give diplomacy one more try. "Are you sure you can't overlook it just this once maid?"

"Positive!"

"Okay, on your head be it!" I tug at the bonnet catch, knowing it has a particularly powerful spring below the lid, the half-eaten fish and chips are now settling about the Platt. A slight exaggeration I agree but my action did have the desired effect on the now disgruntled lady in black. It's not often I am pleased to see more than a half a dozen gulls circling and waiting to pounce on the now descending supper. For once I am overjoyed, she is wearing a tad of soggy batter like a crowning glory. It reminds me of the oldest of sayings 'what goes up must come down.'

I can't resist a parting shot. "At least I'm helping you with your diet Miss? No, no, don't thank me. Glad to be of assistance." I get out and shut the lid quietly and smile at her in a friendly way. Of course I do!

I refuse to translate her reply. A smug smile eagerly crosses my face as I drive back towards Little Petrock whilst thinking about the audience of locals who had gathered and obviously appreciated the street entertainment. The ever-expanding traffic warden once again has a chip on her shoulder. The applause from the locals was rather pleasing as I pulled away whilst peering through the smudges of solidifying grease. I've heard 'street entertainment is a new fad and catching on in lively fashion in the big cities these days. Anything new can take a little longer to get to the West Country but we do catch up eventually, especially when it comes to unplanned participation in score settling. Takeaway supper? More like flyaway supper. I bet the cockneys don't do it better than we do. Nobody does it better! I decide that if she ever comes into my pub again, I'll offer her three chairs.

I won't forget the last thing I heard as I moved away from a bystander with a whippet. "Bet you don't know where she comes from mister!"

"Do I want to?"

"She's a cockney!"

My day is made. I should have realised but didn't. Never mind, I can live with it: West Country One - Bow Bells Nil!

"Thanks mate, so where are you from?"

"Yorkshire, but I love Cornwall as much as you do. We have been here five years or more now."

"No you bleddy don't, nobody does. Keep working on it mate. Another fifty years here and you might be able to get a permanent passport, Pudding Tosser!"

"Guess what wife!"

"Now let me think; you had to wait for the darned potatoes to grow and the fish to get bigger?"

"I'm not about to tell you now maid. Don't even think about asking."

"Thank the lord for small mercies. Oh I won't, where's the darned fries?"

"No 'fries' dear, I got chips."

"Fries, Maccy!"

"Bleddy chips. Only the French have French Fries, Yanks have American Fries. Here we have chips, you should know that by now."

"In the USA we call cow droppings, 'chips'."

"There you are then. It amounts to bullshit! It's what you said maid." Who am I to argue? I believe I am on a roll today: Maccy Two – Every bugger else Nil!

"No you ain't, think again mister!"

"What you yanks know about potatoes isn't worth knowing. Where the heck do ya think they came from?"

"Out of the ground, American ground."

"Walter Raleigh was a Brit!"

"And a darned thieving pirate!"

"I'm going to the pub, can't be doing with all this."

"Brit!"

"Yes yank?"

"It's through that door."

"Ffs, why do I even bother?" I can't even creep off with my tail between my legs now.

"Yes you can husband."

"Dusty, buy me a drink brother."

"I'm not made of bleddy money! What do you want?"

"Something strong and in a glass. Are you gonna marry the pilot?"

"No idea, mind your own business. It's nothing to do with you."

"Suit yourself. I was just gonna point out some pitfalls you might not have thought about."

"Why didn't you do it before, Maccy?"

"I didn't know about them before. If I had known before, I wouldn't be talking to you about them now. Anyway, I'm not going to put a restaurant in the engine house now brother."

"What will you do with it then, Mac?"

"Fish and Chip shop. That way I won't ever need to visit Wadebridge again and I won't have to frequent the jewellery shop in bleddy Padstow."

"Jewellery shop?"

"It might as well be the prices they bleddy charge for a pickled egg."

"You got it bad, Maccy!"

"Extortionately kid."

"Lock up when you go kid. I'm for bed!"

"Sure!"

"Do I scare you Brit?"

"I thought you weren't talking to me, knaw maid."

"Are you sure?"

"Knaw maid, I idn't."

"That's a good answer, shame about the other one. At least you're on the right trail now"

"Thank you yank."

"No need Brit."

"Damn!"

"Pardon me?"

"Nothing my yank!"

"Tell me the truth now."

"I did yank."

"We'll talk about it in the morning mister."

"Yes dear!"

"Where else did you go?"
"I went to see a mate of mine."
"Why husband."
"To get some Christmas gifts for the staff maid."
"Hey Brit, smart move. They have all worked hard for you. I'm glad you're about to show your appreciation to them all. They sure deserve it."
"You know me. I don't like to let things slip. Is that our baby crying?"
"I hope so, if it isn't we must have someone else's."
"It's stopped now."
"That's because you stopped gassing. So what did you get for them all my luvver?"
"Something I know they will all appreciate yank."
"You're so kindly Brit."
"I know that wife."
"Will you hand out their presents tomorrow, Maccy?"
"It's the plan, maid. Peter has put up a sign for everyone to meet here after we kick out all the locals. We'll shut at half two and eat first. We can hand them out after the meal."
"You really do care about them all don't you husband."
"I know that maid."
"You are a very kind boss, Maccy."
"I know that maid."
"I love you boss."
"I know that maid."
"Goodnight, Maccy."
"Goodnight maid."
"Are you asleep yet husband?"
"Not yet maid."
"Maccy!"
"Yes maid?"
"Can I tell ya something?"
"Yes maid, will it take long?"
"Nope."
"Go ahead maid."
"How do you think you would feel if you won the lottery?"

"I think I would feel like I would if I won the lottery."

"Dammit Brit, be serious."

"I already feel like I would if I had won the lottery maid."

"That's good, you did a mite better than that. You gotcha the winning ticket."

"I did, how much did I win, twenty-five, do I have to share it with you?"

"You don't have to if you don't want to. Not twenty-five, Maccy no, just twenty-four. It might be twenty-five by now with the interest. You don't sound real interested, Maccy. Would you like to see the cheque husband?"

"I'm certain they don't send out cheques for twenty-five quid maid."

"I don't believe they do Brit."

"I'll look at it in the morning maid, then we'll put it in the charity box for the donkey sanctuary."

"I don't think you should do that, Maccy."

"How about for veterans of the Boer war?"

"There ain't no-one left who was in the Boer war, is there?"

"Really? Okay, we'll keep it for a rainy day then maid."

"It might be best."

"I'll leave it on the bedside table for you to look at in the morning shall I?"

"Thank you maid."

"Don't thank me, thank your Aunt Renee, husband. She left you the goddam town."

"Can we just get some sleep maid."

"Sure we can white man. Get yourself some shut-eye, I have a feeling you're gonna need it if and when you wake up."

"I always bleddy need it maid."

The suspense is getting the better of me. I never have been able to let a good dog lay. What the hell has the lottery got to do with Renee anyway. She most likely never knew there was such a thing. Another thing, I just never buy lottery tickets. The yank must have bought it but if she bought it, she won as I don't buy lottery tickets. I don't think I ever will in all honesty. I never win anything. I did win the Padstow Chase but there wasn't even a prize that night apart from Lil the Tart and she was only hoping she could be the prize. I just knew there was no way I was about to unwrap her. I'm not even sure why I entered the race. Yes I am, I was half pissed and it was my eighteenth birthday shindig. What about Bert? Bert was always finding money on the cafe floor, I never found a penny myself. He got rich on it.

I'm certain they don't send cheques out for twenty-quid in any case! I suppose there's a first time for everything. I flick the switch and the room lights up. I look sideways and she was as good as her word. The slip of paper is there. I can't be bothered, I know what it says. It's a shame she didn't just tell me in the morning at breakfast. I would be well asleep by now. Bloody yanks get everywhere!

Twenty five quid, I knew it and don't know why I even bothered. Still, it's better than nothing I reckon. Will I put it in the charity box on the bar? No bugger that, will I hell! I'll pin it up behind the bar, it will remind me never to buy lottery tickets. It might put others off from wasting their money, so at least it will be put to good use. Maybe I will even spend it on lottery tickets. Then it will all be lost and I can give them up again. Not that I ever started in the first place. What the hell has Renee got to do with it anyway? If she had won twenty five quid she'd be off down the road to the Spar or the Circle K to buy half a dozen bottles of scotch, or Bourbon and would have drunk a half bottle before she had even paid for it.

Renee was a great lady as I remember her. Her eyesight wasn't 'great', she shot at me with a rifle half a dozen times and hit a barn door the same amount. Worse still, she missed Dusty too! I don't think there ever was an opticians in the old town. There's no use for one now. There's no-one left there to wear glasses. Last time I was there, twenty hell's angels were planning to trash the place.

"Sleep Brit, you're wearing me out here."

"It's not my fault maid, you started it."

"Did ya'll look?"

"I did, very nice. I'll take you out for some more fish and chips tomorrow and have enough change for a nice cigar."

"I reckon you should see an optician Brit."

"I was just thinking the same maid."

Why am I even having this conversation, she always knows what I'm thinking anyway!

"Yes I do! Put the damn light out. I got me one big regret Brit."

"What's that maid?"

"I just wish you could know what I'm thinking, then I wouldn't have to tell ya to shut the hell up and let me sleep. Ya'll would already know."

"That's nice maid, Thank you. You can forget fish and chips now."

"I already did that husband!"

"It serves you right! I'll take you out for a bag of chips and a pickled gherkin instead."

"Fries, you mean fries goddammit husband. What the heck is a Gherkin?"

"Chips! We don't eat fish and fries. We eat fish and chips, you bleddy knaw that. I told you! It's a bleddy Wally, a Gherkin!"

"Which is it, a Wally or a damn Gherkin?"

"It's both ya wally!"

"Do I have to clean my Colts at this time of night, Maccy?"

"Chips and a wally!"

"Fries!"

"Maccy, you might not want everyone here tomorrow."

"Why wouldn't I?"

"They might see you blubbing. You wouldn't want that, would you?"

"I don't mind, they might feel sorry for me."

"I doubt that Brit. I suppose you could give them all their presents."

"All except Peter."

"Why not Peter?"

"It's simple my tiny yank, I asked Peter to let everyone know to be here."

"And he won't?"

"Oh yes he will tell them and they will come but he'll just forget to tell himself."

"Gnight, Brit."

"Gnight wally!"

"Damn you, Tamryn!"

Chapter Twenty

It's only money, it don't make the grass grow.

So I learn the yank has received her paperwork pertaining to the financial winding up of the sale of Hickok which will facilitate receipt to my brother and I the proceeds of the sale of a Kansas ghost town named, Hickok and a cheque for twenty-four quid plus interest. To be honest I did think it might be worth a tad more than the cost of a dog license. I have no idea what happened to the paper payment, last time I saw it, it was on the bedside table.

"Here husband, this is yours and Dusty's too. He doesn't know yet. You'll need to tell him gently."

"Why should I tell Dusty, it's only just worth a tad more than the cost of printing it."

"Look at the damn cheque, Maccy. Jesus, it's like talking to a damned schoolkid here."

"What does it say, it's in dollars? Twenty four dollars. What's all these bleddy ooooo's mean then?"

"They ain't ooooo's, they're zeros. 0's are different."

"What's the point of them?"

"Listen, Maccy, there are one hundred million cents in a million dollars. That means you two have twenty four times one hundred million cents between you."

"So it's more than I thought then. We didn't get twenty four quid or even twenty-four dollars at all."

"You didn't Brit, no."

"So how much do Dusty and I have to divvy up then?"

"I can't rightly say as it keeps going up every hour or two husband. Shall we just say around twenty million dollars?"

"That's easier maid. So what is twenty million dollars' worth then."

"A lot more than twenty-four quid, Maccy."

"So how much do we have then?"

"Too damn much. Stop asking your stupid questions and tell your brother."

"How much, Rio?"

"How the hell should I know?"

"Do you think it might be enough to buy, Rock? We could buy it and tidy it up a bit and sell it on for a small profit."

"Why would you do that, you don't even like Rock, husband. You called it a darned lump. You told me it was a bleddy meteorite and the folks who live there came down with it."

"It is, they did, maybe you're right, let's buy somewhere else then. Lundy Island might be worth a punt"

"Where?"

"Lundy Island maid."

"Where is that?"

"In the water, that way."

"So, you didn't sell Boot Hill then?"

"I did not, it still belongs to you."

Ma comes within earshot. It's now or never.

Rio Dona Marina stands back clutching my daughter and wearing a nervous smile. She leans against the wall in silence, she carries her nonchalance well. The remainder of my family, minus my brother, are seated with a maximum of fuss. It must have been something unusual in my tone of voice as they suddenly quieten. My baby is already asleep. There is one missing, Padraig is absent but we need the old feller here.

"Ma, can you get the Irishman please?" She yells; my father appears instantly. I ought to talk to him about that, it's a bad habit. He isn't doing Dusty and I any favours by jumping to attention in this way.

They all three stare at me impatiently, they aren't used to me being serious about anything. I'm not used to being stared at, apart from by Alice. I'm nervous. Unsure, I wait for the Texan as she begins to explain to everyone why we are here.

"Dusty, sit down and relax bro'. Actually what I meant to say is shut your bleddy gob boy!" I can only do diplomacy up to a basic level. It's like basic hygiene without the hygienic bit. It seems to work pretty much with my brother, apart from the scowling. To be honest, he almost always looks like that unless there is a young woman present. The silence allows Rio to again take the floor.

"So I had a brother who died of an illness very young. My dad began to look upon me as an absent son. I attended my schooling and when I was old enough I left college to help my parents on the ranch. We built it up over the years until it was almost too big to handle. I guess you all know my parents were killed in an automobile accident. I'm all alone now grandpa has passed on, apart from you folks. I would have been here sooner but for the accident."

"My folks had already decided to sell up and move to something smaller. Anyhow my grandfather, who ya'll met and I had to arrange a funeral and other stuff. The ranch is sold now, all bar the signatures. Everything we had as a family in Kansas is now mine, mine and my husband's. In case you're wondering, I would rather be here obviously or I wouldn't have let the big galoot put a ring on my finger. I intend to stay as long as you'll have me. This is my home if anyone is in any doubt, I sure ain't."

Even Dusty has quieted as she continues with this sadder part of her family story.

"Like I said, the ranch is sold and has brought a tidy sum. I am not one to splash money around, so I intend not to change my ways much. Neither will my husband. I get the feeling he would rather earn it his own self, which goes for both of us pretty much. It's not all I have to say, there is one other item. Let me introduce you to Lily Tamryn, she will only ever be known as Lily!"

This is a complete and utter surprise to me, one which is most acceptable and after a few seconds I chime in. Champagne I think. I could not be happier. "Dusty, do the honours please brother."

"I don't work the bar, Maccy. You know that."

"Brother!"

"Sure, Maccy."

"Everyone meet my beautiful daughter, Lily, Lily Tamryn!"

I have only ever known one other lady named Lillian. I couldn't be happier and was in no way consulted before the Texan made her sudden proclamation. Dear Lil the Tart was what she was and is no more, now the lady will only be known simply as Lil in the future. I could not be happier as Rio and I both smile and wink across the room.

"Maccy, what was all that about, I had a bit of a late night."

"Nothing really, you didn't miss much, Kid! No wait, little brother, what would you do with a million or so boy?"

"A million what?"

"Fleas, boils on your arse! For Christ's sake boy, dollars! Pounds but a bit less! You'll need a bigger wallet either way. Not for long obviously, it'll all be gone in six months with your track record. You invented the saying; 'splash the cash', trouble being, most of it was mine at the time!"

"I dunno, whatever. I don't have any boils or fleas, I'm a bit skint as a matter of fact. If you're looking for a handout, you're out of luck. On the other hand, if you're feeling flush?"

"I'm not looking for anything brother. I know better than to ask you for bleddy money."

"It was a crap bleddy question, Maccy."

"It might have been a crap question; it is a serious one bro'." The kid is getting me mazed now. I've been in a good mood for a while. It's not going to last. There may have to be some physical contact with my brother by me to do some convincing.

"I dunno, what would you do, maybe I would buy some of what you've been smoking most likely."

"We both have the same problem kid. Right now I have no idea myself what to do with ten million pounds either."

"Ten million pounds, Maccy, you said one. You're serious. You're bledny serious, you nutter, you never once said ten."

"Yep, I'm bledny serious but only once. Saying it twice won't make it more so. It'll still be the same amount of money. Don't call me names. Anyway you can't have it unless you agree."

"I need to think about it, Maccy."

"Best you start now then, I wouldn't take too long."

"Why."

"Why do you think? Anyway, we don't have it yet. It could be a while, it's in dollars right now."

"How come it's dollars?"

"Maybe because it is dollars."

"A million dollars times ten, yeah? What's that in old money then bro'?"

"No idea. Lots of paper. You stayed on at school, little brother, why did you bother, why did the school bledny bother? I remember now you didn't bother and neither did the bledny school. I know how they felt! I hope you're listening youngster. Money comes with much responsibility; you best remember that kid."

"Okay I agree to everything, where is it?"

"Good, it's in the Bank of Yank right now. When it does appear you can pay off all your debts, your bledny credit cards. The full deck, all fifty-two, I'm guessing you have fifty or more not including the Jokers. It should almost clean you out brother. Oh and not forgetting all you owe me!"

"Ten million!"

"Might be more by now kid."

Ma and Padraig sit in silence. Ma already knew thanks to my telling Padraig after Rio showed me the cheque. The yank says nothing, she has known a while, she knew before me for obvious reasons. We agreed to do it this way at her suggestion which sounded pretty much like an order.

Ma speaks, I knew it wouldn't take long. "Maccy take your own advice boy or you'll answer to me. It's only money, it don't make the grass grow, don't let it go to your heads, you boys."

"Yes ma, maybe and you can pack up making concrete bleddy mushrooms." I said the wrong thing. I could tell by the look on her face.

"I won't be doing that boy. It's yours and Dusty's money. I won't discuss it"

More silence, the quiet lasted longer this time. Padraig does what he finds easiest, he smiles. He owns a building company in Cork. I doubt he is short of a few quid, thinking about it; I have no idea what he has. It's none of my business. Dusty appears to be sleeping, it's likely cash induced shock. A late night wouldn't have helped and another one to come for certain. I'm going to miss my brother conning me out of cash. Every time I see him I will instinctively take my wallet out and ask him how much he needs. It's been a fact of life for so long. Give my brother his due; he's tried every which way and almost always failed to fail. I would take my hat off to him but he'd only sell it. I shake him out of his stupor just for the hell of it. "Come on brother, let's see what that water is like in the lake."

"It's a bleddy pond brother, how many time do I have to say it? It'll be bleddy freezing Maccy. So what's her gaff worth, Maccy?"

"A bit more than the old town was brother."

"Jesus! It is a pond, Maccy."

"It's a lake sometimes."

"It's a muddy pond!"

"That boat says it's a bleddy lake. No-one puts a boat that size on a pond."

"You did!"

"I didn't. We did and just by luck mostly with your atrocious bleddy navigating. You missed Rock by miles! One last thing kid this is family business and it stays that way. This place must stand alone. It has to pay for itself. What you do is up to you, brother."

"Kid, you'll be able to get your new boat now."

"To be honest brother I was gonna sit on my arse and count money. Then I thought again, you're right, Maccy, new boat. Two new boats, maybe a third later."

"That's it kid, you got n!"

"Lily Tamryn, Maccy. It has a ring to it brother. I like it."

"Thanks kid, it sure does, so do I, it's perfect."

Everyone who needs to know knows everything there is to know. I haven't realised the enormity of it all myself. It is a good time for a swim in the lake. I'm not going in for a wash like my brother most likely needs to. I just need to bring my heart-rate down. It is only now sinking in for me after all the talking and head scratching, sometimes even my own. My brother is about to come into ten million dollars plus, now he is napping on Michaels home. My biggest worry is he can't even look after two hundred quid for more than forty-eight hours. Twenty-four most likely! What the hell will he do with ten million quid; give or take? It's scary!

"Darlin', will you get me a towel?"

"Get your own damn towel. I ain't your damn skivvy, Englishman. We stopped slavery in eighteen sixty-six, we don't do it no more. Slavery don't go around here."

You see, I said nothing would change, serves me right though it was only a friendly request, I don't do demands on her, I don't push my request. I don't like watching my wife clean her guns. She takes so long at it; I get particularly nervous at such times. Did I say she murdered a fish once?

My brother wasn't napping, he was in a trance. Nothing new there, he's spent most of his life in such. We two swim and laugh all the way to the bank, the lake bank that is. I had other things occupying my mind. How will I keep control of myself? Eventually the excitement will wane, things will quickly get back to normal. Dusty might continue to chill a while longer. Thank god for the heating installation on the pond!

I have one more duty to perform but first we will eat as a complete family. I notice the bar is quickly filling up with everyone who works for me. No-one is missing it seems, even Peter has remembered.

Meal over and it is time as I drop a sack on the floor of the almost finished Doom Bar. "I know it's a tad late guys but I have something for you all in here." I stoop and take out a handful of the packages passing one to each of my gathered staff. When the sack is eventually empty I issue the order. "You can all open them now."

"What's this all about, Maccy?" Jack asks as he holds up the contents of his package.

"I didn't know what to get you all. Then I thought every single one of you have one thing in common: your nuts! Wait, wait, don't start throwing the chairs around guys. Inside each bag is an envelope. Happy Christmas!" I had been planning this even before the cheque appeared.

A single fly landed in the ointment. Lyndsey came to me with a request.

"I would like to come to Kansas with you Maccy when you 're ready to go. Like you, I may never return there, there would be little point I think. My great grandfather is also buried in that cemetery."

Not so much a fly to be truthful. The ointment is bereft of any insects. The Welsh woman is right as she always seems to be, it makes sense. There is no good reason she shouldn't make the trip. She had made it once before and alone. Both Rio and I agreed. MJ will stay as will the recent addition, the beautiful infant, Lily. It was ma's suggestion she would look after her as she will Lenny and Lavinia's child while the two continue to ponce up their home, which presently looks something like a smart pigsty. Their first child is named Laura Rio and is already a couple of days older than Lily. She always will be of course.

Ma eventually had a change of heart, her business in the Magic Mushroom Farm will in fact be slowly wound down. She has decided to close the business up. You can only have a certain amount of concrete mushrooms about the place before the novelty wears off. My mother will have plenty of time to devote to the little ones as Padraig will devote his time, with Lenny's, to oversee both pubs while we are gallivanting around the bottom bit of North America without a care in the world.

Both pubs have competent management for now but there will be a small change at the Mermaid shortly.

The new bar is almost finished. 'The Bar of Doom' is complete. We had decided each and every member of staff would have the chance to vote on their favourite title. The choices were 'The Doom Bar' or 'The Bar of Doom'. Other suggestions were written on scraps of paper but quickly discarded due to their salaciousness and physically impossible ridiculousness. 'The Naked Lady' was strongly poo pooed by Lyndsey. I shouldn't have done it but couldn't resist. She did see the funny side eventually. 'Rock Inn' was also turned down by all but one, one who will remain nameless. I believe it was chosen by Alice whose husband, Mervyn hails from that dubious hamlet on the opposite side – maybe opposing side - of the Camel.

The Bar of Doom won heavily and so it was decided upon. It was my own first choice and I was pleased it was supported by the largest vote. The Maltsters Arms now has a bar named 'The Bar of Doom', very apt in my opinion. I did seriously consider buying the White Hart, I was put off by the abundance of spirits. It's a shame, as with three bars in a line I would have been in line for a jackpot!

The moniker suits perfectly, the name is out of respect born of fear of a certain landlady who no longer scares the kids and their parents collectively. Blencathra Bligh is gone but like the husband, the Cap'n, she is not and never will be forgotten by those who knew Blencathra. It was these two who unknowingly encouraged me to become a landlord. Many who were lucky enough to meet them might have compared Blen' to the Sasquatch or the Abominable Snowman. If you knew her well, she was a woman – I use the term loosely – she was a great woman who would do anything for anyone. If you had an enemy, Blen could turn it to stone with a glance. She was blessed with 'the stone frog effect' – I would be surprised if she's not had a go at Saint Peter already - obviously I don't know the bloke but I do know Blen' and I'm certain she would have succeeded. Blen' would never give up on anything without a fight. Fight she could and more than once she had physically ousted me from the Mermaid and Bow's interior. It was always an honour to be another of her victims.

As for the Cap'n, Cap'n Bligh as he used to tell it, descended from the famous 'Bligh of the Bounty.' The old feller could land a punch too, he may have only been ten stone at six feet plus but he could plant a mean fist, not always on his opponent. Bligh was afraid of no-one once One Armed-Frank had departed this mortal coil. Of course if he did get into something he couldn't handle, Blen was always there to provide back-up. She doted on the old bugger. As for Frank, he was a one-off in every sense thanks to his old man George accidentally blowing off his arm with a twelve bore shotgun. I'm not certain I ever believed the tale.

And so to dear Lil the Tart as she was known with affection, another 'great', she would do anything for Frank, within reason. There were many things Frank couldn't do for himself; for one he couldn't do ambidextrous, he couldn't roll his own ciggies either. I was about to add she couldn't do everything for him but that may or may not be true. I shiver almost uncontrollably at the awful thought. Even afterthoughts regarding the pair tend to make me smile nervously. All of this was from the good old days. Hopefully we are perpetuating more of the same, just with a different cast. Like someone might have once said in a fit of common sense; if it ain't broke, don't try and bleddy fix it. Something along those lines!

Chapter Twenty-one

Pig sick!

"Yes?"

"Yes what? Mostly you say naw mister!"

"I most likely will when I know what it is. I was about to say. I just need to find someone who can give me a clue. For now I am showing a mild interest more or less. It may start to fade anytime soon."

"Why?"

"Once I know what it is yet you're calling me for I will tell you? My interest might improve. I wouldn't bet on it, Lenny."

"Whatever, anyway it's a bleddy caravan, Maccy."

"I don't want one mate. I had one before as you well know. We broke it and it's in the quarry about halfway down, maybe a tad further by now."

"Tidn't that one, tis another bugger."

"Like I said, I don't want it, Lenny. I'm pretty much off caravans mate. I doubt I will get back on caravans unless I get to live twice and even then I have my doubts."

"You might need to mate. You've got yourself a replacement at no extra cost to you buddy. James Bond lived twice, didn't he?"

"I don't want to. Once is enough buddy. Tell me, why do you need to ring me about a bleddy caravan this time of the bleddy night?"

"Okay Maccy, we will leave it where it is. I just thought you should know. Sorry to disturb you mucker. It's not night, it's morning. It's ten past six mate. How will you get out tomorrow?"

"Same as I always do, through one of the doors."

"I don't mean that, I mean how will you get your car out of the yard, Maccy."

"Through the gate, Lenny. Can you bugger off now!"

"Yes I can but you can't. Your gate is knackered. It does 'ave a caravan stuck on it, in it, to it."

"Go back to sleep, Lenny. Tell me better when you wake up. If you would stop playing computer games to all hours you wouldn't have bleddy nightmares so often."

"I 'aven't had one. Alice just got home."

"There you are then, it proves I was right."

"About what mucker?"

"Sorry mate, I can't remember."

"Alice did come past the Maltsters before and she saw the goings on. She did say you have a caravan stuck in your entrance. My bet would be it's an emmet that have done it."

"I didn't feel anything. Is there a car attached to this caravan?"

"Naw, she says not. Just your gate really. Which caravan are you talking about?"

"So you're telling me an emmet is driving around the village minus a bleddy caravan? That's a bleddy first and I missed it! Now you telling me there's more than one."

"I believe I must be mate. Is there another?"

"Now I know you're telling porkies, Lenny. Every emmet does have a caravan at the back of their car and a bicycle, sometimes even another car. They wouldn't drive around without at least one and I've never seen an emmet with two caravans. It's early days!"

"This one must be short the caravan bit. Why do they have another car at the back do you think?"

"Then it'll be easy to find the bugger won't it. The one at the back is in case they aren't too good at reversing. It's a bit like a train, trains have an engine at each end. They can go either way."

"So a bit like Honky Tonkin then?"

"That's it, you got it buddy."

"Maccy, can you talk to Lenny another way?"

"What other way is there Rio?"

"Send him a damn letter and go back to sleep!"

"Why would I waste fifty pence when he only lives down the bleddy road?"

"Let me say it different husband."

"Go on maid?"

"I'm giving you the silent treatment."

"Thank you darlin."

"Lenny, what was Alice doing out at ten past six in the bleddy morning?"

"Something she shouldn't be I suspect. I'll ask her shall I."

"I bleddy wouldn't. Not without a suit of armour and a machine gun."

"I'll ask her drekly and tell you what she said."

She will say, 'mind your own damn business you bleddy pervert' is my wild guess!'

"How do you know that mucker?"

"Easy mate, it's what I would say under the circumstances."

"Not on me you wouldn't husband. Give it a try and I'll sure let you know where you failed when you come out of it."

"When I come out of what." I pretty much knew it was a stupid question to ask.

"Your coma husband."

"Now see what you have gone and done, Lenny. You have started her up again, I'm in a bleddy cowpat and I haven't hardly even done anything yet. I should have just let the bleddy phone keep ringing."

"Then you best get to it mucker. No use to being told off for nothing. What will you do, Maccy, by the way it's Meadow Muffin."

"I will consider your advice and get back to you later, probably very much later. So, Lenny get lost and take your 'meadow muffin' with you."

"Like an emmet, Maccy."

"More or less, Lenny, they do like their souvenirs to take home. They don't get to see meadow muffins in London much I reckon. Bye Lenny."

"What the hell did he want husband."

"He did say an emmet has rammed our gate with a caravan maid."

"Why?"

"Why did he say it or why did the emmet do it? Theirs neither one I have the answer to maid" I personally have never known an emmet to lose a caravan before. Usually emmets just tend to lose their way. Then they lose their temper and tell their kids to get lost, which is all very well but we don't need any more parentless kids hereabouts, especially if they come from some godforsaken place in Wales or Liverpool but pretend they're from bleddy England." I won't attempt to explain this phenomenon, just to say it does happen. Actually, scousers don't pretend they're from anywhere. Some don't even know where they have come from."

"Wake up, Maccy!"

"I am awake!"

"It sounded like you were having a nightmare."

"It is night maid."

"It is not, it's very early in the bloody morning and Lily isn't happy."

"It's bleddy my tiny Texan, how many times? If you wadn't yelling, she would still be happily asleep."

"No more mister!"

"I was doing what you asked me to."

"How in hell do you figure that?"

"You just now told me to wake up."

"I was talking in my sleep. I must have been darn it. Why else would I say that?"

"I can think of a couple of reasons wife."

"Think again husband but not the same, different!"

"Sorry, it still came out the same maid."

"You'll wake the babby again."

"No I won't, you will."

"Sleep, Maccy. You know you want to!"

"You're not always right yank."

"I sure am Brit. Don't you go forgetting it."

She who must be obeyed speaks with a forked tongue unsurprisingly.

"I sure do."

"What did I tell you about reading my mind Tex?"

"I wasn't reading your damn mind Brit. It was talking to me."

"How do you manage it maid? What's the secret?"

"It's no secret Brit. You're an open book husband."

"Well if I am as you say, can I have some of the covers back please? I'm freezing my bleddy butt off here!"

"You have your damn socks on, Maccy."

"So, does that make a difference?"

"It does make for a smelly bed."

"Not at all, it's my feet that pong. It's why I wear the socks so as not to smell my feet. I mean so you won't smell my feet."

"Enough now Brit."

So there you have it. I gave my own game away without my even knowing it. I was just minding my own business and talking to myself and she heard every word. That can't be right. It must be against universal law somewhere, - an invasion of privacy - it shouldn't be allowed. I will talk to Michael. He'll have an answer. It will most likely be the wrong one but hey-ho it has to be worth a try before I commit suicide by driving in the middle of the road like an emmet. I would bet it's the very reason there is a caravan stuck to my gate. I would also bet said emmets car is not insured. Why else would he or she drive off without their mobile home? I suppose they might not have noticed it had become detached! I wouldn't be at all surprised if they haven't left their kids inside and they're still watching the television or playing computer games or I Spy with the light off. I doubt the latter as it is dark outside and without street-lights they wouldn't be able to see anything anyway, no-one would win or lose. They should play Hangman it would be much better and would give us all a quieter life.

We do in fact actually have two street-lights; one at one end of the village and one at the other which I suppose is okay if you want or need to continue in either direction. If you don't and stop in the middle it would be rather pointless. You wouldn't know where you are.

"Morning Jill, where's Jack?"

"Jack is a cook today, Maccy. He is being usefully employed as a grill chef in the kitchen right now."

"Really? I thought he was an electrician."

"So did he! I pointed out the error of his ways."

"I bet you did, poor man, is he in shock? Are you teaching him how to fry breakfast, Jill?"

"That's almost funny boss. I did try to show him how to kill a pig."

"How is the pig now, Jill."

"A bit sore I imagine. It's running around minus it's tail. The animal wouldn't stay still long enough and my knife slipped."

"Neither would I Jill, you can't blame it. Where is it now?"

"He's frying it!"

"He's frying the pig, not while it's still bleddy alive maid?"

"Not the pig, just its tail. He said it would be wasteful otherwise. The pig is still running. When it stops we'll put a plaster on its stump. Full Cornish boss?"

"Obviously, you can't put me off that easily!"

"Coming up, sit yourself down. By the way boss, do you know you have a caravan stuck to your gate?"

"You hum it maid and I'll sing it. Actually I do, Jill thank you for reminding me. I would rather not be reminded. Actually why didn't you just ring me and tell me?" I still haven't looked outside as I am hoping it was all a bad dream Lenny was having.

"I did try but your phone gave me the engaged signal."

"Morning, Maccy, did you know you have a caravan blocking the car-park gate?"

"Yes Lyndsey, I do. Can we change the subject now please, or else!"

"Okay, do you know there is a pig running around outside with part of it missing?"

"Call a bleddy vet maid! I'll call a psychiatrist." What the hell is happening here, I thought Jill was pulling my leg. On thinking about it further, I would rather she didn't pull anything attached which might be attached to myself, not while she has a knife in her hand. I'm happy as I am, whole!

"There is a psychiatrist who lives at the end of the village but he's pretty busy most days. I saw that weird doctor from Port Isaac waiting outside the consulting room earlier."

"Now he really does need a psychiatrist. Which end please maid?"

"He's not certain and taking advice from a colleague, so I heard!"

"Um…...! Never mind, pretend I didn't ask and I will pretend I didn't understand. I don't have to, it is not in my job description. That reminds me, I must finish writing it in between doing stuff."

I am in a parallel universe which might be out of kilter. This is all happening to someone else; somewhere else. I refuse to recognise myself. After I eat my breakfast obviously.

"Thank you, Jill. Please inform Jack he has my compliments. Just the one thing maid?"

"What's that, Maccy?"

"Are we now putting pork crackling out at breakfast?"

"Not as far as I know boss, no. Would you like us to?"

"I had some on my plate and very nice it was too. Jack did good, I should know, I'm a chef, I used to be a chef, right now I couldn't cook a bleddy goose"

"Oh that? I'll tell him don't you worry. He said you'd eat it, I said you wouldn't. Still a bets a bet. I lost!"

"No!"

"Yes!"

"No bleddy way!"

"Oh yes, way!"

"Tell him to find a job centre, you can go with him and help. I'll go and check the bleddy goat!" I actually thought it was a deformed onion ring from a deformed onion, it was more like chewing my own finger.

"Okay, suit yourself boss. You do know what's below every single animal's tail, don't you, boss? Don't worry I did make sure the item in question was well scrubbed! Talking of which; aren't male pigs tails and other external items similar to look at? I'm sure I heard that somewhere! An old wives tail most likely."

"You're not married maid. Another thing while we're on the subject maid, Jill."

"Go on!"

"If pig's tails are so near their arses, why do females of any age wear their hair as pig tails? Game set and bleddy match I believe maid."

"I'm pretty sure you told me a sense of humour would come in handy working for you, boss. Let me know when you say something amusing please."

"I'm off to check on the bleddy goat! Just one other thing, Jill?"

"Yes boss, there is only one chef, it's you."

"Winning a battle does not constitute victory in a war maid, just you remember that when you're cashing your dole cheque!"

"I've work to do. Where do we keep the first aid kit, Maccy? Hang on boss, goats don't have tails do they?"

"Keep it to yourself, Jill, keep it close and tell Jack the bleddy same."

"You certainly have Jill trained, Maccy."

"Your next, Lyndsey. Only my brother gets one over on me and even he doesn't try anymore. I taught him the error of his ways a time or two."

"You're scaring me cousin. I might have to take up self-defence, Kick Boxing might be favourite!"

"Yeah, yeah, whatever!" Now I know what Bligh of the bleddy Bounty felt like. All at sea and completely helpless!

"Still talking to yourself husband?"

"I'm off to sort out this bleddy caravan maid. I may be gone some time."

"You do that and when you come back, don't antagonise the staff more Brit."

"Know-all!"

"Yes I do, if I don't I damn well soon will!"

"You've left it late maid."

"My dear mother used to say 'Never put off today what you can do tomorrow!"

"Are you sure she said that, Rio?" The poor woman has already been living in Cornwall too long. It's getting to her, she has the beginnings of Lenny's disease.

"Don't you dare think that husband."

"I hardly did maid."

"I will talk about it later."

"Someone here to see you, Maccy."

"It's not the rampant pig is it? The one which no longer has its tail between its legs!"

"Not quite, it's Sergeant Twotrees."

"That's what I asked."

"I thought you meant the other one with the tail completely missing."

"This one will do maid. Morning Sarge'. Fancy some breakfast?"

"I don't mind if I do, Maccy and its Ron by the way."

"Ron, bleddy 'ell. We have Ron the copper and Reg the vicar. The world has gone completely mad. What were your parents thinking?"

"Our parents were Vinny Jones fans, Maccy. They liked gangster films."

"Hang on, you said 'our parents', Ron."

"That's right, Reg is my brother and I'm his, didn't you know? I thought pub landlords knew everything."

"Didn't I know? You're the boss of the local underworld and your brother is halfway to becoming a bleddy Saint. No, I don't think I knew that, I'm sure I didn't. You two should have been twins mate. If your parents had named you both Ron you could have been the two Ronnies!"

"You learn something new every day, Maccy. Now then, did you know you have a caravan stuck in your gateway? We are twins, Maccy."

"Is that another caravan, or is it the same one?" I refuse to reply to his last statement.

"The same as what one? I am here on official police business, Maccy. You have a caravan stuck in your entrance. There must be a car driving around without a caravan behind it, it stands to reason. Do you know anything about it?"

"I know plenty about it. Everyone I've seen so far this morning has told me all about it. You mean my exit, don't you? People I haven't seen are queueing up outside to tell me about it. You could have side-swiped them. I would have been grateful,"

"Where's this breakfast, I can't detect stuff on an empty bleddy stomach."

"Jill where's Ron's breakfast maid."

"Coming up, Maccy. There you go Sergeant, enjoy!"

"Lovely maid, I'm sure I will."

"That looks good Reg, I mean Ron. So, this caravan. Will you need to go over it and detect stuff."

"We most certainly will, Maccy. It could be a crime scene."

"Will you have to take it away to get it checked out for finger prints and what have you?"

"Definitely."

"Could you do it right after you finish your breakfast mucker?"

"Certainly!"

"Good, that means I don't have to get it shifted then." That worked out well, now Ron will have a caravan in his entrance!

"Great breakfast Miss, I'll come back again. Lovely bit of crackling that, Maccy. By the way, Mister Tamryn; Reg and I are twins, we're just not identical!"

"You bleddy couldn't be, could you. It's not rocket science, Ron. You wear different uniforms for one thing."

"What do you mean mate?"

"Simple mate, Reg is a vicar and wears a dress, you're a copper and wear a tunic and want to know everyone's address! Catch ya later, Ron."

"Don't give up on your day job, Maccy."

Good god, once upon a time, Ron would have nicked me without breaking sweat. Now we're mates. I never did like his missus that much, a bit too clingy for my liking. Clingy, Ivy, get it? Oh never mind."

"Jill, I need a word with you maid, in the kitchen, now."

"Okay boss."

"Jill tell me, how many tails did that pig have? I take it, it is now deceased?"

"One, Maccy. They all do. It's only dogs that can have two tails! Of course it's deceased. Your ma ran it over earlier."

"Sounds about right. So maid, how come I had one tail and Twotrees had another?"

"That's for me to know, Maccy. Never you bleddy mind."

"Tell me you didn't maid."

"Nope, I won't tell you I didn't and I don't believe I will tell you I did."

I always knew the girl would settle in here. She's like one of the family now. I never knew Jack was a butcher albeit a crap one. It takes all sorts and I seem to have some of each variety. Poor old Ron, not only can he have a pig in a poke, he just poked a piece of pig in a pig. Happy days are here again. I love this world!

"Just a second, Ron, will you be able to make a claim on whoever damaged my gate to get it repaired?"

"I don't see why not. Though I don't expect he had any insurance mate, that's why he legged it I reckon."

"The court can make him pay for damages though can't they?"

"Absolutely Maccy, if we catch him."

"I'll have a word with my solicitor, get the ball rolling for a new gate then."

"Correct me if I'm wrong Maccy, but wasn't your gate already mangled?"

"Yes it was but only slightly, my ma isn't the best driver around Ron, but only we know that, don't we." I decided not to tell Twotrees ma had only just killed his breakfast.

"I believe you might be right, Maccy. Good thinking mucker. I might try and find something twisted or bent of my own and shove it underneath the caravan before we take it away."

"Not Ivy, Ron."

"That was my line of thinking, Maccy."

"Things are still not too good then, Ron."

"Everything is fine mate. She doesn't talk to me."

"How can that be fine?"

"It means I don't have to talk to her."

"Jill get rid of the pig please, in case the food inspector turns up."

"Jack! Maccy says for you to take Sergeant Twotrees outside before he kills him!"

"You do it, I'm bleddy busy. Why would Maccy want to kill the copper?"

"Other way around, Jack."

"Maccy, what are you running here?"

"Why are you asking me, Ron? You're barking, up the wrong tree. My wife is in charge of kitchen duties and that includes the restaurant mate. I don't have a say. I don't want a say. So about the caravan, Ron. Is there anything valuable inside it?"

"I doubt it, the lads would have been through it already. Anything useful will have gone into the boots of their Jam Sandwiches by now, Maccy."

"Bleddy 'ell, is there nothing safe around here, Ron?"

"I wouldn't think so mate, not really. I don't know what the world is coming to."

"Shouldn't you know mate? Anyway, can we get the gate shifted now, Ron?"

"After lunch mate, I'm still bleddy starving after all this talk of food. What else is on the menu?"

"Pulled pork and roast spuds."

"Can't get fresher than that. Where did you get your pig anyway, if you don't mind me asking?"

"It wasn't my pig. I don't keep pigs mate."

"Probably just a stray. Don't forget the apple sauce mate please!"

I have never suffered from boredom since I became a publican, I don't believe I ever will whilst I perform the role. Peace and quiet does not sit well with me. If only it did.

"Another day done husband! What will tomorrow bring?"

"Pretty much more of the same maid I guess."

"That'll be nice, Maccy. The policeman seems friendly."

"What policeman?"

"The one trying to turn himself into a porker. He's made a start. Seems like Jill has the kitchen well organised husband."

"Doesn't it! We only had the one bloodbath in there all day. Can we sleep now darlin'?"

"Did you shut the gate, Maccy."

"Sure and I never even saw one horse bolting or one pig flying Tex! I can't wait for tomorrow. I'm so excited wife. I can hardly sleep!"

"Why? Is the circus arriving tomorrow?"

"Naw, it's leaving."

"I'm a mite confused, Maccy!"

"It's nothing to worry about maid. Maybe I should give you a check up to be certain, just let me find my periscope, I'll be right there."

"Don't ya'll mean your stethoscope."

"I know what I mean maid, trust me I always wanted to be a doctor."

"You're the trainee doctor, cure me."

"It could take a while. I'll give you something to take the pain away."

"Damn, it's already starting to work. Will I need to recuperate doc'?"

"More than likely. Say ahhh!"

"I already did that."

"Again please!"

"Ahhhh."

"Bleddy 'ell, now I'm feeling better. I'm better than I realised."

"I like your bedside manner doc'."

"Thank you ma'am. Send in the next patient on your way out please."

"Don't push it, Maccy."

"That's not what you said earlier yank!"

Chapter Twenty-two

Lenny and the Mermaid

"Lenny is that you?"

"Who wants to know?"

"I bleddy do, shut your face and listen to me."

"Come here and say that."

"I'm busy mate or I would. Lenny, I've got something I want to say to you."

"Was that it, Maccy?"

"No, Lenny."

"What is it then, I idn't letting you stand on my bleddy back again at the back of the bleddy Maypole. It did bleddy 'urt every time."

"Nothing like that mate. I do 'ave to give you something matey. If you could shut your fat bleddy gob for just a minute or two."

"Yeah, I can do that Maccy. Not sure about a 'minute or two' as I might have to come there and lump you drekly. I don't want to keep you waiting."

"In your dreams, if you raise a hand to me, you'll probably bleddy fall arse over tit. You don't knaw where I am."

"I know that. What do you bleddy want, Maccy?"

"It's the pub mate, it's important."

"I knaw that, Maccy. I'm doing my best mate. Are you gonna sack me? Tis quiet at the moment, always is after Christmas. Can't be 'elped."

"Tidn't nothing like that, Lenny. I've got some good news for you, mucker."

"Why didn't you bleddy say so, you worried me up. What is it that's important, Maccy?"

"Lenny, the Mermaid, she is your'n now mate."

"I'm gonna lump you one when I see you. It idn't mine, it's your'n, you tosser. You bought it. I manage it, remember."

You idn't managing it any more mate."

"You just said, Maccy. Now I am sacked."

"I didn't say that, Lenny. I didn't get the bleddy chance to say. You keep butting in."

"Don't matter about that, if you want to get another manager, it's up to you. My sister, Alice will do it."

"Not any more Lenny, the pub is yourn, both of you."

"Ffs, Maccy, talk bleddy proper, I idn't too bleddy clever this time of the day. I might not want her."

"Of course, you will want her. The Mermaid, she is yours now. I'm giving her to you to keep, Lenny. You own her now mate, lock, stock and all the bleddy barrels, oh and the scales obviously. You and Alice are now the rightful owners of a mermaid. You have earned it."

"How did that bleddy 'appen then? Why would I want scales?"

"I don't know mate, bleddy weird idn't it, I can't explain it. If I were you I wouldn't look a gift-horse in the mouth. Maybe because you're a fat bastard, you'll know when you're getting fatter."

"I don't want a bleddy horse as well. Maccy. I do 'ave a goat already, I don't have a bleddy clue where the bugger is much of the time. I might be fat but I idn't a bastard, not all of the time anyway."

"Same applies I suppose. Don't look at the goat's teeth when he does come home mate, it would be best. Okay I concede the fatherless bit and I humbly apologize."

"Thank you mucker. It's probably best I don't, I most likely wouldn't have anyway. Looking inside Billy's mouth is not really my thing. I would worry he might eat my hair while my back is turned."

"Right good, you know it makes sense Lenny. All the paperwork is at the solicitors' mate, so it would be best if you don't kick off about it anymore. One thing though, you might need to reapply for your license, and we shall have to go to the bank and whatnot. How the hell could you look in Billy's mouth if your back is turned, Lenny?"

"Cos I have eyes in my arse mate. What's my driving got to do with it anyway?"

"I'm not really sure mate. I'll ask around, better still; you ask around and let me know how you get on. Tidn't your driving license, it's your license to be a thingy, a proper publican."

"Why would you want to give me a pub Maccy?"

"Um, because it's there and you're there, it makes good sense."

"Okay, well thank you mucker. What will I do with it?"

"Let me think for a minute, erm … Nothing comes to mind. Don't worry mate you'll think of something."

"I'm not stupid Maccy."

"I know that mucker, I've always known you idn't. I just need you to do me one favour in return mate."

"What's that?"

"It's like something you do for people when they ask you to. Even if you might not want to, you still do it if you remember."

"I knew that mucker."

"I want you to not to tell anyone what I told you I knew, and you know now."

"How long for Maccy?"

"Forever might be best, Lenny but it doesn't have to be."

"Yeah, I can do that."

"You don't want everybody knowing your business, do you mate."

"No, I don't think I do. Lavinia knows, she has been listening. She told me to tell you to knock it off."

"Knock what off?"

"How the hell should I know, Maccy. She didn't elaborate an awful lot inbetween the swearing and whatnot."

It is the way real friends do things around here. I am looking forward to seeing what happens at the Mermaid and Bow. I'm not worried, I know how it will turn out, unlike

Lenny, he won't have even thought about it yet. Lavinia will have even less of a clue. She can only concentrate on one thing at a time. It's always the same thing too. I won't keep a close eye on my friends, I don't need to. Lenny will be well aware I'll be here for him if ever I might be needed. I don't expect to be unless of course he needs someone to use as a punchbag. It's always a possibility. We two haven't fought for ages. It is time we stopped now, it's childish and painful.

"I have given Lenny and Alice the Mermaid and Bow wife."

"Good idea, husband."

I might as well give up. I can't even say anything under my breath without her sticking her oar in.

"Yes, you can."

Lenny the Landlord. It does have a certain ring to it I must say. Real friends should be for life, not just for Christmas!

"It's about time to give Lenny what he deserves maid and I have."

"You just now told me you were gonna stop fighting with, Lenny."

"I am, we're too old to fight anymore. I didn't tell you, you bleddy eavesdropped."

"Never mind that."

"The Mermaid and Bow is all theirs now. They have earned it, don't you think?"

"I sure do husband, you did good, Maccy, and his sister?"

"Yep, Alice too. Not forgetting Mervyn and the boy. He'll have Lavinia with him too of course."

"Your boy, Maccy Tamryn!"

"Maybe yank."

"'Maybe' don't cut it with me Brit. Ain't nothing wrong with my darned eyesight, Maccy. You best remember that pardner. It's a good job Mervyn only has the one eye or else he might see what most of us see."

"I better had maid." I should have guessed she would have guessed. There's no sense to trying to pull the wool over the yank's eyes.

"No there ain't hombre. Who all else knows about the boy?"

"Me, Alice, you and Lyndsey I reckon. Dusty idn't stupid. Neither was Bert, he knew, and I never did have to tell him. Can't now mind. I think ma might have had an inkling."

"Then that's the way it'll stay. There ain't no reason for changing it, Maccy. Let sleeping hounds lay is best all round."

"That's what we'll do maid."

"The boy don't know?"

"The boy don't knaw maid."

"What was in all the envelopes husband, them you gave to everyone with their nuts."

"I gave them all a train ticket to somewhere else."

"You did not husband. If you did, where's mine?"

"Of course not. They all got the same maid, a bonus, except Alice. She got a tad more just to help with any extra schooling for Danny."

"That's an end of it!"

"That's an end of it maid. Tis all done. I told Lenny he can call on us anytime if he needs anything."

"No, no, not any time, Maccy, no bleddy way Jose!"

"Yes not any time, anytime Senorita."

"That's okay then, you sure had me worried there for a moment. We all have skeletons in the cupboard husband. Why are you speaking Spanish?"

"I don't know maid; it might have been something you said.".

"Neither do I, Maccy, neither do I! Are we gonna have us a party, Maccy, for Lenny and his little family and ours obviously?"

"Think we should maid. A pool party I reckon."

"Yay, a pool party, I need to get a new bikini!"

"Not that kind of pool maid. Mind you we could take the table out on to the floating dock and have it out there. I'll talk to Bessie to extend it. We never did have a wedding out on the dock maid."

"That's Michael's fault. He lives on it most of the time. You can hardly have a wedding out there now. There's plenty of time for that later."

"No but we can have us a pool party. We might have a fly in the ointment mind maid. Lenny might want to have his party at the Mermaid?"

"That's okay!"

"Well he'll have to have two then, one here and one there. We won't tell him about this one for now, that way it won't be a problem."

"You know best Brit. There's the phone again."

"I know where it is."

"Good, then you can answer it!"

"Maccy, are you there?"

"No, I'm here. Who wants to know?"

"Not me mucker. Some bleddy emmet wants to know where you are. He wants to know where his bleddy caravan is. He said he left it there."

"No, I'm sure I would have noticed it, If there was one, tell him the police have got it."

"You tell him. He wants to speak to you."

"Put the tosser on, Lenny."

"Maccy said, if you want your bleddy caravan, the police have got it."

"Maccy, it's Pablo mate. You remember me, college yeah."

"Mebbe I might, do I have to?"

"You said for me to look you up if I was down this way. I'm doing it now."

"You tosser, you smashed my bleddy gate."

"No, I didn't, it was pretty crumpled already. Anyway, I don't need it anymore. It wasn't my fault mate, I had to swerve to avoid a bleedin' goat. The poxy animal was in the road. Who keeps a goat in the bleedin' road ffs?"

"We do, it keeps the emmets away, though it didn't work in your case, Pablo."

"So, can I come over and annoy you mate."

"You're already annoying me. Is your car fully insured?"

"Not fully, no, why?"

"I need to claim for my badly damaged gate and a copper's wife. They were both underneath the caravan by the time you buggered off."

"Liar!"

"Okay, okay, I might have bent the truth a tad. You did bend my gate though. Stop yacking and get over here. We won't say anything to the local coppers. Let them work it out for themselves. They'll never do it in a month of Sundays."

"Sweet as a nut mate, I'll see you when I get there."

"Tell Lenny not to serve you."

"Who's Lenny?"

"The bloke who let you borrow his bleddy phone, the landlord."

"What phone? I thought this was your pub anyway. Is he the same bloke that threatened to shoot me?"

"Used to be, I gave it to him. Did he threaten to shoot you, Pablo?"

"Yes, he did bud. Bleddy nutter! Why would you give him a pub, Maccy?"

"It was in the way like your bleddy caravan, Pablo."

"Fair enough, see you soon."

"That's all I need, a bleddy emmet who knows all about me."

"Which emmet husband?"

"Some tosser I met when I was at college maid. Don't worry, I'll soon get rid of him."

"When, Maccy?"

"As soon as he gets here with a bit of luck. I don't need reminding of bleddy education. He'll never stop bleddy reminiscing and telling porkies if I remember him well. Whatever you do don't believe a word he tells you. It'll be like a bleddy history lesson only none of it will be true. It'll remind you of home."

"I'll be the judge of that husband."

"That's what bothers me, my little yank. Take him with a pinch of salt maid, when his lips are moving he'll be telling a lie."

"Like I just said. I'll be the judge."

"Dusty, my little brother, we got company coming."

"Who might that be, Maccy."

"Some nutter from bleddy London."

"Do you want me to suggest he goes home again. Happy to help, bro."

"No, just don't lend him any money. I don't know why I'm telling you that. You never lend money; you just borrow it. Actually, I still haven't got used to you not scrounging off me."

"The good old days. I will if you want me to. Old habits do die hard brother, I hate to think you're disappointed in me."

"Just you try it and I'll stop your bleddy cheque."

"When's it coming, Maccy?"

"Soon, Dusty, when you're older and wiser most likely."

"Chances are I'll never get it then! We will need to organise a party bro."

"It's cool brother."

This is all I need, a face from the murky past. I never have liked history, especially when it's my own. It'll be like being on 'This is your life without Michael Aspel.' 'Maccy Tamryn, you won't remember him, but you were at college together and shared a cell for a night after managing to get twelve young ladies into a single bed all at the same time.' It won't be true; it was just ten. 'Do you remember when you drank a yard of ale through a straw, Maccy Tamryn?' 'Once you escaped from a taxi without paying your fare. Tonight, we have found that actual taxi driver and here he is now!'

It's all rubbish, it wasn't a yard of ale at all, who the hell can measure a yard of ale while it's on the move. It can't be done! How would they find out who the taxi driver was, London's full of them. There's more taxi drivers in London than you can shake a stick at. I never did that either! Some old lady will appear all giggly and say I headbutted a concrete mushroom in her garden in The Fulham Palace Road. Actually, that was indeed true, but it was one of my ma's. It had her name on the underside. I was checking out the ten-year guarantee. 'Maccy do you remember when you traveled two hundred and forty miles in a British Rail toilet and never bought a ticket? Well here is that very guard who tried to encourage you to vacate it and insist you find your wallet.' Most of it, I mean some of it is a load of bullshit! Pablo will embellish it all by saying everything happened on exactly the same day, which was when I was in fact in a police cell with him and eleven ladies. We never did find out where the eleventh one came from. I always did like a lady in uniform!

"Pablo, me old mucker, how are you buddy? I'd like to say 'it's great to see ya mate' but you know I'm far too honest. So, mate, what do you think?"

"She's a bit small, Maccy but not bad. Not very old. Where's her parents?"

"I was talking about the bleddy pub you tosser."

"Oh, sorry mate, thought you were talking about the lady with the purple face and the cowboy gun. Does she always carry that around. Nice butt by the way!"

"Careful mister, this is my wife and she don't take kindly to strangers!"

"Sorry sister, I'm only joshing. Take no notice of me."

"I ain't mister and believe me I surely won't! What can I get you to drink, Pablo, cyanide and coke, distilled water with a slice of arsenic petal, a pint of goat urine. Name your poison, nothing's too much trouble at the Maltsters Arms, we got it all here honey. I can get you some shots of liquid Deadly Nightshade on ice if you prefer."

"Wow, Maccy, you got yourself a live one there."

"I certainly have, Pablo. If you're not more careful, we'll have a dead one too. It won't be me. The gun isn't an ornament. Now if you'd like to leave the same way you got here unless you prefer a hearse buddy?"

"What about my bleedin' caravan your gate damaged?"

"I'll give Sergeant Twotrees a call and see if it's available for you to collect, shall I?"

"No, don't put yourself out mate. I know when I'm not wanted."

"Then that's both useful and wise, Pablo. Out you go and don't come back if you value those you don't actually seem to have any of. By the way, shut what's left of my gate on the way out. The bridge is forty miles that way."

"That all seemed to go well maid."

"Sure, did husband. Purple face, my butt!"

"They idn't anyways alike my little gunslinger."

"I know that! I was planning to turn your friend into a damn cullender. It was just good luck for him he saw the error of his ways husband."

"Agreed maid."

"Just a cotton-pickin' moment, Tamryn, are you comparing my face to my butt? I'm warning you; be careful how you answer limey."

"I'm taking the fifth amendment maid, the one you told me allows a citizen not to answer in what might be a possible self-incriminating way when questioned about something serious."

"Damn you mister!"

"Ah Lenny mate, you should have got here earlier."

"I would have but I bumped into your bleddy mate outside. He called me a 'local yokel'. I put the cockney bastard straight, Maccy, straight over the wall by the knackered gate."

"You should have shot him mucker."

"Sorry mate, I did consider it."

"Rio considered it too. Thank you for tidying up, Lenny."

"You're most welcome, Rio. Any time maid, just you yell!"

"I will, Lenny."

"Nice one, Lenny. Has he gone?"

"Naw, he's still snoozing behind the wall I reckon."

"Okay, I'll deal with it now mate. Jill, get me a pail of water love please!"

"Don't take the bleddy piss, Maccy. That idn't bleddy funny."

"Yes, it bleddy is maid."

"Fair enough, just the one time, Maccy, never again okay, or you'll end up like the poor pig!"

"Sure girl, I would have asked Jack but I didn't want him falling down again, after what happened last time. I would never hear the last of it." I am so good, I'm better than I ever realised!

"No, you ain't husband. Self-praise is no recommendation."

"We'll see about that later. You're the doctor yank."

"I was wondering when it might be my turn. It'll make a change Brit."

'No, it won't!'

"Who bleddy said that, Maccy, Maccy!"

"No idea Tex. It wasn't me. They do say it's always good to get a second opinion maid."

"Yes but only if you know where it's coming from and who's giving it!"

"I think I'd rather not know maid."

"Me neither Brit. It gives me the shivers all over."

"You don't usually complain love."

"You don't know that husband."

"I do now maid."

"That ain't exactly fair, Maccy Tamryn."

"Do you know something maid. I've spent half my working life not knowing or even finding out what some folks are called, even you at one time. Then you come along and with half a dozen or more."

"They ain't my fault Brit. I didn't choose them!"

"It wadn't a complaint maid."

"Right answer!"

"Was it?"

"Jesus Maccy, get a priest in here, get Michael and Reg in here, they can work together. It's getting darned scary now."

"That was me yank."

"You damned fool, have you been doing it all the time husband? I might need to shoot you!"

"Naw, I was just replying to you the one-time maid. Maybe I should get them both in if it's scaring you so much. It was definitely a man's voice I heard. Wait up!"

"It was a man, Maccy. What's up now husband?"

I don't reply. * Scratching my head with an absent mind, I walk over towards the old peak cap I placed on a nail some twenty years ago. The faded green, dusty garment from the days of steam still holds together surprisingly. I remember it so well the day of Granddad's funeral even though I was probably only seventeen and Dusty was just a year younger. Dusty and I found the old man halfway down the quarry, the ancient G W R cap was grasped tightly in his cold hand when we discovered his lifeless, stiffening body. Granddad's last journey was to the farm after he left The Maltsters. I replace the cap without brushing the dust off, why would I? there's no need to change anything. It cannot be anyone else but Granddad I decide as it was his wake at the time. The very man who became a father to Dusty and I as we were growing up without one. We are in his favourite pub, now I own it. The old chap never drank anywhere else apart from his own cider shed on a Sunday morning, where he did all the brewing. Even ma would never drink anywhere else than the Maltsters. It seems as if Granddad is happy with the way things have turned out. We never had much while growing up, we just had ourselves, it was all we needed. Now, Padraig is here, he isn't taking Granddad's place, he's just looking after it for him. I knew there was nothing to fear, the Maltsters has a warm feel, there's no chill inside these walls. To be sure it is he and he is here is a wonderful feeling. I must tell Dusty and ma.

"Don't worry yank, I know just who it is."

"You do?"

"Oh yes maid. Nothing to worry about. It's an old friend and he's staying, I doubt he would leave even if we asked him to. Michael and Reg wouldn't get anywhere with him anyway. I don't need nor want them interfering, there's no need. Everything is as it should be, Rio."

"I trust you honey. Is he friendly then?"

"No better friend could anyone want, believe me maid."

"Doesn't the cap need a clean up, Maccy."

"No no, I don't think it does. It's best left as it is. Take my word for it. Granddad won't thank you for it, on second thoughts he might?"

I'm certain I hear an audible sigh as we turn and walk away from the grubby headwear. It seems it's a perfect world right at this minute. What more could anyone want than to know their forbears are checking on them? I can't think of anything better! Despite Dusty's devil-may-care ways I know he will feel the same as I do.

'He will'!

Thank you Granddad. I did not reply to the sound in my ears as I'm certain I didn't need to. I know the old feller heard me! He can see and hear me but as I can't see him, there's no need. I believe we might not hear his voice again. I'm sure he will stay!

She waits at the door for me. "Did you hear that maid?"

"Nope honey, I never heard a darned thing! What did he say husband?"

"Nothing much maid, he didn't have to. Where were we?"

"On the way upstairs, Maccy."

From that day on I knew I had done right with The Mermaid and Lenny. My friend and his little family belong there in town as I and mine belong here overlooking it. Granddad hardly ever went to Padstow, not because he didn't like it, because he didn't need to go. I certainly take after him, and for another very good reason; I can't see Rock from here! I don't believe I will ever leave Little Petrock for somewhere else and it makes me appreciate what Rio went through to come all this way when and how she did. Not all life is a barrel of laughs, just a big part of it. The rest is something else altogether!

Authors note:

* When this occurred is in the The Mermaid and Bow by this author.

Chapter Twenty-three

And let us all Unite

And so being a landlord, a hotelier and a wanderer is in my blood, it was bound to happen. We do what we're supposed to do. There are no choices I believe. It's all set out. I have also always believed it. I have kept my thoughts to myself, or I'd be known as a weirdo wherever I went. I almost certainly am in any case, Lenny's sister, Alice thinks so. We cannot all be perfect. Life would be far too boring. Nobody can ever accuse me of being such. In any case, as I say we have no choice, none of us do. We play the cards we're dealt; with luck we play them well. If we don't, we can only blame ourselves.

I'm doing exactly what my great Grandfather did and almost by accident more or less. At least my ancestor did do it by accident. Henry Tamryn was playing Poker with some poor sod who didn't like to lose. Provoked, Henry shot the loser and suddenly became a saloonkeeper. It's not really the sort of thing you should be trying at home. In any case, you most likely don't have a saloonkeeper knocking about at home. Alright, the shooting of a landlord might not have been an accident, on the other hand it might have been. It is possible Henry might have been aiming to miss. We will never know, will we? At least I haven't accidentally shot anyone. I'm still reasonably young yet! I sincerely hope no-one points a gun at me and knows how to shoot it properly.
* My great aunt Renee did attempt to ventilate Dusty and I with a Winchester rifle when we first visited Hickok as teenagers, Renee's eyesight was crap thankfully.

Henry might never have had a restaurant – according to written accounts, he had the equivalent of an expensive soup kitchen, it cost a man his life anyway - I think we have a tad more to show for it than that. It's just my own opinion. Henry had emigrated to Kansas in the early eighteen seventies He set sail for Cork, Ireland first to inform his extended family, from there onward to America. Once there, Henry met David Evans who had been travelling on the same vessel though the two did not meet until disembarking. Both stole a ride on a cattle car and decided they would travel together, very soon they were disembarking. The pair did not have to walk far before reaching a rail-side hamlet with no name. The new friends played poker and by luck won the 'soup kitchen' by default when their opponent had lost all of his stake money and shortly after became very deceased.

The loser had returned angry enough to attempt to kill both men and even his own common law wife, the 'cook, - Henry had used the term loosely while making notes in his diary. The woman was at least cohabiting with the former owner. My Great Grandfather had to defend himself and his friend. Henry had no choice but to shoot the knife wielding, irate gambler. Any argument regarding the premises was at a sudden end. It is documented Henry had paid a sum of money over to the suddenly out-of-work saloonkeeper. He did not live long enough to make use of the gift. At least the sum had been more than enough to pay for his funeral the following day according to newspaper editor, George Benford.

Henry and Renee eventually married and lived happily for some years, he even became Mayor of the little prairie town that eventually became known as Hickok City until sadly dying in a fire while attempting to rescue others from a burning building. I know I can never live up to my ancestor's heroics, I will try extremely hard not to put myself in his position. One day Henry shot and killed a man, on another he did everything he possibly could to keep a man alive.

In my own case and much closer to home, Peter, a bloke who used to live in a skip might become a relative – it could be anything - of some sort. I picked him up on the road-side one dark night and now he could well become my cousin-in-law if there is such a thing, my beautiful but weird cousin would also become his step-daughter, I may become related to her twice over but her mother and I will only be connected once. If Lyndsey were to marry Dusty, he could possibly be arrested for something. I don't think it will happen; you never know with my brother. Even closer to home but back in time; my father married my mother almost twenty years after I had arrived, my brother put in an appearance a year later something he doesn't do often unless he's in trouble or skint. Only recently I called my dad, 'Dad' it was purely accidental. Personally, I feel there is so much in my blood and the possibility, probability for more, there will be hardly any space left for my own!

Never mind all that, what can I say about Jill and Jack that hasn't been related at least a million times before. They aren't over the hill and never will be as they keep falling down before they get to the top. I do have a problem with the original pair, how is it they get water from the top of a hill? Surely it would have been easier to wait at the bottom until it got there. The two are also surrogate parents to three Muscovy ducks who might believe they are cats; they seem to have had nine lives each so far. I am actually surprised there aren't more of them!

Now about, Lil the Tart who is the deceased mother of a daughter who is possibly following in her mother's footsteps in her selected vocation and for a while was encouraged by a vicar called Reg who has a brother who is a copper and is called Ronnie and they are both twins whichever way you look at it. Only the names and the coincidences of their birth warrant a cursory examination. The twins in no way whatsoever compare to their infamous namesakes. Reg the rural rector and Ron the rural regulator. When you put it like that, they do sound a tad dodgy. They are not. I'm sure the vicar isn't, the jury is still out on Ron!

My younger sibling, Dusty, I can't think of anything good to say about my brother other than he and Selina, who is a helicopter pilot in the Royal Air Force, could possibly join the 'mile high' club on their wedding day and live happily ever after under a canvas construction that doubles as an Identified but non Flying Object. There's no way they'll get it off the ground. Dusty, my one and only sibling, irascible, irritating, infantile, irredeemable and irrepressible to the female of the species. I like my brother, I just don't do what he is capable of doing and anyway I'm glad I only have the one, which is most likely what he says about me.

So, to Michael the man of the cloth. How the hell did that come about? One day he was a nasty little shit exactly like Lenny and I and sometime later he's officially preaching from the pulpit. It makes little sense. The three of us regularly played snooker in the chapel he now presides over. Michael would taunt the slightly tubby woman in the off license - to be fair most of us did as teenagers - he taunted Ron the copper. He once threw up during a driving lesson because he was still pissed from the night before. There was one time when Michael and I talked about stealing the lead off the church roof, we didn't do it as somebody had got there before us. Another time he stole the vicar's ladder, to be fair stealing the vicar's ladder has forever been a Padstow pastime, everyone does it except Reg, it being his ladder. Michael, or Methy Mick as we call him, has always been sex mad, mad because like his dad, he can't get any. At school he tried to sell any new kids to the school their free milk. It wasn't that long ago he stole a condom machine from one of the town's other pubs, he got it all the way home and found it was empty. You should have heard the language. He didn't need to have done it as the girl had some of her own, he told me afterwards. It was all pretty pointless as Mikey had pulled a groin muscle ripping the machine off the wall. Michael thinks ministering is looking after any female who comes within arm's length. My mate took up sign language and none of them were particularly pleasant. And then Mikey got a sign from the big feller upstairs and started wearing a dress to work. We found out why a little later, it was so he could be better prepared when a nice maid did take a fancy to him - there weren't that many - he didn't have to take so much off! Lenny and I have prayed many times for Michael, it has made little difference. He is still a randy reverend, a pervy preacher.

"Just think, Mikey, if you were to fall in love with a mermaid, you still would not be able to get your leg over, neither would she for obvious reasons!"

"That is not the slightest bit funny, Tamryn. You can go to hell."

"After you, Mikey, after you. Best of five frames?"

"Yeah but only if you bring the Scotch, you tight-fisted tosser."

"To borrow a well-worn phrase, Mikey, I hope your congregation shrinks!"

"And I hope yours falls off, Maccy. I'll see you at the chapel!"

"Bring glasses, Mike and winner takes the leftover Scotch!"

Michael is as good as his word "To absent friends, Maccy."

"Who is missing now?"

"Lenny of course."

A couple of days ago, Lenny told me he had to get home early, the bugger wanted the evening off.

"He most likely deserved it mate. Lenny is a grafter."

"I suppose, anyway I asked him why he wanted to get away early and he said he's on a promise. I said don't count your bleddy chickens, mucker. Guess what he said."

"Just bleddy tell me, Maccy!"

"I'm about too for Christ's sake, he said he doesn't have any."

"Right, sounds fair."

"So, I said; just point and count at where they might be if you did have a flock. The tosser did what I suggested, then he says; 'there's one of the buggers missing'!"

"I asked him if he knew which one it was?"

"Yeah, yeah. It's your bleddy break, Maccy."

"I broke last time you tosser. Shut your face, I'm trying to talk here. Nobody wants to know about your bleddy inferiority complex."

"That was over a year ago! I don't have an inferiority complex!"

"You bleddy should have. I thrashed you then and I will now. Start praying." Things did not go my way.

Where was I, Stan, my dog, an animal I always denied was mine, died and Lenny got a goat that lives with either of us and eats anything but meat which is probably okay. I am still the owner of a three-legged piece of meat that still lives and breathes, who could eat a whole lamb at one sitting anyway. I have a small lake full of eels which I had forgotten to jellify, there is still time to complete the operation, not on the eels, on the cheerful little lamb, I like to think of it as cheerful, it stops me feeling guilty for partially dismembering it. I should mention Farmer Bird here as he lives next door and does a brilliant imitation of a chicken without even knowing he is doing it. Bird spends most of his time cooped up at home apparently.

Now too Lenny, I'll keep it short as anything of interest has already been said about my lifelong friend. Who am I trying to kid? Lenny and I were educated in the school of hard knocks. What I mean is he and I, after school was out for the day, would engage in our daily competition of knocking on as many doors as we could before we reached home. The knocking was never difficult as most cottages around here didn't have gates. If they did, we would lean them against the front doors before knocking. No, the hard part was the not getting caught kind. Trust me, despite the speeds we may have achieved, we often did! There was hardly ever any punishment coming our way from ma. She would be more interested in finding out which of us had won each afternoon. As for our ma? Ma is the one constant in the lives of everyone of us.

Lenny Copestick fell in love with Lavinia, a nymphomaniac from The Isle of Dogs. The blissful couple live in a converted pigsty now which they occasionally share with a goat. If it wasn't a pigsty before it most likely is now! They have a daughter called Rio which is the same name as my wife who doesn't live in a pigsty. I met Rio by accident in Kansas, not Texas, which is where she comes from but Texas, which apparently is very dark at night as it only has the one star. It must be true as all Texans call it: 'The Lone Star State', it is the other side of a stream that belonged to me but doesn't now as it had to be sold as we couldn't bring it home to Little Petrock. It didn't matter as we already have 'Lost Souls Creek', our own stream in the village which has a bridge called the 'Bridge of Tears' crossing it and it stops cars from falling in the water and keeps lots of folks feet dry when they need to cross over it.

Lenny, Lavinia and the delightful baby Rio also live with and in, a Mermaid. The Mermaid and Bow used to be mine, now she isn't. Think about it, disappointing as it can be, there is only so much one can do with a mermaid.

If I have forgotten anything and I know I could not have, as I am sure I would remember. Unlike my Great Grandfather, I've always been crap at cards!

"You're not great at most things Limey!"

She does have an unfair streak and she is a mind-reader which isn't useful. I guess all Texan women are like it. There is one thing I do well but she's far too shy to mention it.

"No, I ain't damn you!"

Like I said!

Last but not least the newest addition, Lily. She has so far not spoken. She will very soon, she's only a couple of weeks old!

"Start the party, Dusty, you too Tex."

"I happen to think the party started the day I got here Brit."

"You're not getting the last word maid, not this time."

"Think again Brit."

"I'll start the party dad!"

"Fair enough, Maccy Junior. You have to start somewhere kid." My son is sixteen now, God help Little Petrock!

And now we might be on our last journey to Kansas and Hickok. So much had been going on; I did not think we would ever make the trip.

At the last moment I did the unthinkable; I asked Lenny to accompany us to the States. I had previously asked Lavinia, expecting her to say, 'no way!'. She actually said she could do with the rest. 'When are you leaving? Don't rush back.'

Unlikely as it might have been the flight was uneventful. As smooth as the proverbial, pretty much. I looked at the car hire attendant. We have met previously. This time there is no re-kindling of the animosity we had exchanged previously.

"Are you going back to Hickok, Mister Tamryn?"

"We are. I believe I told you I would return."

"You did sir. I well remember also. I have just the vehicle for you."

"Thank you." I received the keys for what seemed to be a brand-new pick-up, a friendly smile and what I believed to be a sincere wish for a safe journey. Just the red carpet seemed to be missing.

"What was all that about, husband?"

"Nothing much, wife."

"Hmm!"

We four arrived at Hickok before it got dark. It was silent and nothing moved. It is truly still a ghost town. We walked across the main street to the creek where we first met and the place where we first went to sleep under the stars together. Rio had disappeared before I had woken, and I thought I would never see her again.

And then they appeared through the heat-haze. A dozen Hell's Angels walk slowly towards us, recognition instant from both sides. It could not be better. All of them recognise Rio first and make a huge fuss over her. I remember she was once one of them. The leader realised then who I was.

"Maccy the Englishman, dammit, so you came back, buddy. Did you two just meet somehow?"

"No, Chuck, Rio is my wife, we have a child now. This is Lyndsey, she has been here before. Lenny here hasn't! Treat him gently buddy."

"Dammit, y'all did well. What are you doing here?"

"We didn't think you would still be here, Chuck."

"Hell yes, we never did leave. Nobody wanted to. There are others, they'll get back soon. Have you come to run us off, Brit?"

"I don't think so, yank. This is most likely our last visit. We came to deal with the old cemetery."

"It's all good, Brit, we kept it up for ya'll though we never expected to see ya agin."

"I appreciate it. Problem is the town is sold now, feller."

"We heard. We'll have to move on I guess."

"Why would you need to move on, Chuck?"

"There's nothing for us here now. If we don't go the new owners will get us moved off, I reckon."

"Rio, Lyndsey and I came here to check on the cemetery only. Seems to me with the land surrounding the cemetery there is enough for you guys to stay put. That whole area still belongs to us, just not the town. Rio can explain better."

"Rio?"

"I think what my husband means is; it's our gift to you providing you keep the graves clear and free of varmints and tumble-weeds. You'll have a lease, peppercorn rent. It's up to you guys."

"You're kidding right?"

"No, Chuck. My wife is not kidding, all we ask is you keep the gravesite up. We'll lease the land to you for as long as you want it. Build what you like!"

"Don't know about you, Maccy but I reckon a trip to the Circle K might be in order. Let's party!"

Chuck looked around at the smiling faces of the group. A lot of nodding is going on, there seemed to be a silent agreement to the stated terms. We leave the truck where it is and all four climb on the back of machines that will take us the Circle K drug-store. It's great to be surrounded by these bikers for the half hour it takes to get there.

The remainder of the Angels eventually arrived, and we partied and slept where we all laid as we did each evening throughout our short stay. Lyndsey and I had gone back to the newspaper office and taken away any remaining papers and records, we searched the Plainsman Hotel and did the same there, though there was little to discover. Renee hadn't been much of a writer nor hoarder. We had taken one last look at the cemetery just before we left and said a few words to those who can never leave, Hickok. I don't know why we took the papers, it seemed to be the right thing to do. They will soon turn to dust if we leave them. The Angels spoke more or less as one as we climbed into the pick-up.

"Anything else you need us to do here, Maccy."

I didn't have to think about it. "Just one small thing please guys. A creek needs a bridge. A bridge needs a name. How about 'The Bridge of Cheers?" I looked up and what did I see? Almost twenty hairy-arsed Hell's Angels blubbing like babies.

"What's up with you bunch?

So, 'Bridge of Tears' it is then!"

Just leave us one of each of your British coins, we'll build them in. Vaya Con Dios, amigos."

"Shall I give him a bleddy slap, Maccy?"

"What for, Lenny?"

"I think he swore at you, mucker."

"No idea, what did you say, Chuck?"

"Vaya Con Dios, my friend. It means ya'll 'Go with God'."

"See Lenny, now you don't have to fight."

"Bleddy 'ell, this place is bleddy boring."

"Lenny there are nearly twenty of them."

"It would be a fair fight, mucker, we have Rio and Lyndsey on our side!"

"Let's give it a miss mate, okay?"

"Okay!"

"Thank you, Maccy."

"What for?"

"The cemetery!"

"We might never see it again, husband."

"Who knows, wife? When we get back, we have one more task to fulfil, Rio."

"What would that be?"

"We're going to church; everyone is going to church." I had not forgotten what Reg had said to me just before we left, when a man of God is in trouble, what can you do? Return home and sort it out!

"Wosson, Maccy?"

"Michael, spread the word mate."

"Why do I have to do it?"

"Cos you're the bleddy expert word-spreader, mucker."

"What's the word?"

"Free wine and a biscuit in the church this Sunday."

"In the church, you're turning the bleddy church into a bleddy wine bar? That idn't on, Maccy, he won't be happy. We'll all be bleddy doomed!"

"Michael, you and I have drunk more than our fair share of Cider and Scotch in the bleddy chapel over the years. Just spread the word drekly mate. Bleddy hypocrite."

"Don't tell me how to do my job, Tamryn."

And so, it came to pass. Reg got the shock of his life when he came out of his little cubby hole on Sunday morning and saw there was not one empty pew on our first Sunday back from Kansas. We had stitched up the locals good and proper. We sang and partied until Reg ran out of cheap red wine from Barcelona which in fact is a miniature village just outside Looe. The collection plate overflowed due to selling biscuits at a pound a pop. Oh, come on, the bleddy wine was free, we didn't have the heart to charge for it. It would have been illegal anyway and there were half a dozen uniformed coppers involved in the impromptu sing song which followed. We did have to fetch more wine from the Doom Bar!

---

* This occurred in the Mermaid and Bow by this author.

Epilogue

Lenny never really wanted to be a landlord but in the end, my best friend was left with no choice. In all our days, never has Lenny needed to rely on me for anything, but I have had to rely on him many times. I doubt he even realised it, he still doesn't and never will, but it is a fact. There are very few Lenny's in the world. I have had the best there is. Yes, he has punched my lights out on more than one occasion – I see it as a compliment. Lenny doesn't see it as anything other than his duty.

We two are in the same boat now near enough. I do wonder if fatherhood has sunk in for him yet. Probably not, Lenny won't fully realise until it's Father's Day, I always forget!

"You can say that again, Brit!"

"Butt out yank, I don't bleddy need to! You're not supposed to be in this bit anyway." My wife does not like to be left out of anything.

Lyndsey, what can I say? The enigmatic Lyndsey is fast becoming the office manager from hell. I feel it won't be long before she takes the Maltster's over completely. From being a guest bridesmaid at my wedding, she is suddenly a self-appointed manageress!

Jill has virtually become owner of the kitchen, her partner Jack is in charge of anything that needs doing that no one else can do. Jack of all .... never mind!

Peter is mostly away with the fairies as is my brother Dusty, who has more experience. Lavinia, I don't really want to talk about in case I annoy her.

One strange thing about my misfits is it seems no one ever wants to leave and go to greener pastures. I can only think they don't have a clue where to find one!

Lastly, my friends who don't actually work for me. Twotrees, a let's say 'slightly flexible' copper, his twin brother Reg, a creepy vicar and Michael, a man of the cloth, who I went to school with. Michael is continuing his education, mostly in the bedroom of a boat on my small lake.

I personally think I have done much to help all who I have mentioned and those I have not. My obituary might possibly state 'Maccy Tamryn, always thinking of others'.

"Why, husband?"

Acknowledgments

My personal appreciation to all who have helped me in some way to produce Doom Bar Days and Nights. Firstly, Teresa's stickability. Mac' McCarthy who introduced me to Maccy Tamryn. Debbie and Ashley of 'The Old Millhouse', Tim for his superb artwork and Jacquie for her forbearance. Thank you, Charlotte, Jane and Dudley once again for your understanding. Thanks Chris, affable landlord of the Ring O' Bells, St Issey. Special thanks to Jay and everyone at The Maltsters Arms at Little Petherick. Lastly: Wikipedia.